FROM THE

DARKEST

HOURS

13 DARKLY TWISTED TALES

THE *FROM* SERIES VOLUME 11

by

Jeremy M. Wright

First paperback edition by Stone Gateway Publishing, August 2025

ISBN: 979-8-9999201-0-2

Printed in the United States of America.

For the Koenig family: Benji, Cheryl, Bob, Dan, Rick & Dave.

Some of my greatest childhood memories were spent with all of you!

Also by Jeremy M. Wright

<u>Fiction</u>

Chasing Daylight

Man of Exile

From Shadowed Places:
13 Darkly Twisted Tales Volume I

<u>Young Adult Fiction</u>

The Good Ship

Paper Moon Landing

"Beware the dark pool at the bottom of our hearts. In its icy, black depths dwell strange and twisted creatures it is best not to disturb."

Sue Grafton

CONTENTS

Here at the Fold

Sam watched the two punk kids in both mirrors strategically placed at the far back, near the coolers of soda and beer.

There were a few spots inside the convenient store that were a visual dead zone for the reflections or cameras. Sometimes the five finger discount hoodlums figured that out and took advantage. But these kids, well, by Sam's guess, they weren't the brightest crayons in the pack. They would buy something, he knew, but what they hid in pockets and up their jacket sleeves was way more than the single item they would purchase.

Sam knew a bad thing when he saw one. These kids fit the bill. Their jean jackets, and oh my God, he couldn't believe jean jackets were on their way back into fashion, were covered with black Sharpie writings, declaring the logos or names of their favorite heavy metal bands. It was the hair, too. Long, unkempt, and all out greasy from lack of washing. Kids these days don't give a lick about appearance and how the world perceives them. Instead, they lived by a code of self-centered worth and all-out not giving a crap about anything outside their tiny world. But that was what the world had transformed into, Sam figured.

The kid with eyes so dark brown they almost appeared black glanced over his shoulder. Sam watched the monitor so they wouldn't suspect he was eyeballing them over the rack of potato chips.

Sam looked at the clock behind him. It was noticeably darker, which meant it was almost 1:51 in the afternoon. Things would start happening soon after the moon moved across the path of the sun, creating that brief artificial sunset. But here, of all damn places, that darkness seemed to stretch on far longer than it was supposed to. But the long shadows weren't a priority for concern. It was what happened during the eclipse.

Sam punched numbers into the register. It was one of those old jobs, an antique, before everything went the way of bar codes. He never bothered to upgrade the thing after he bought the store and saw no reason to. It worked perfectly fine and had no need to take up space in a landfill just because it was old. Hell, he was old, but he wasn't about to give up the ghost just yet and fill an unnecessary space in a graveyard somewhere.

He watched the boys, entered more numbers, and waited. They spoke low, and he was sure they were about to bolt out the door.

The taller of the two moved over to the cherry-flavored crushed ice machine and began filling a large cup. The other boy hung out at the back of the aisle, failing to look Sam's way because he was the weaker one and the guilt of what he was doing would get to him if he made eye contact.

The moon dimmed the sun a bit more. He knew these kids wouldn't make it home before the light winked out. As much as he hated the idea, they'd have to stay here with him until it was all over.

"Hello, sir," the slushy kid said as he took a brain-freezing slurp from the straw and winced.

"Young man, didn't anyone tell you it was a bad day to go out? Didn't your parents warn you?"

He snorted. "Dad's probably three sheets to the wind by now at his favorite watering hole. Mom tunes into her soap opera shows, knitting and pretending there's nothing else in the world, especially me. So, no, I wasn't told not to go out. Why?"

The other boy joined his friend at the counter, placing a small beef jerky stick beside the slushy.

"Look outside. Tell me what's going on now."

Both boys looked, maybe searching for a cop who was about to make them empty their pockets and run them home to their parents, who wouldn't give two licks about their stealing.

The older boy shrugged, not understanding what he was supposed to see.

"It's cloudy. Or was there something else?" he asked as his black eyes studied Sam.

"No, not cloudy. A full solar eclipse is on the way. Then comes the fold."

The boys looked at each other, sure the old man had just dropped his last mental marble, and it rolled off into the drain and was gone forever.

The younger boy said, "Yeah. I remember my mom saying something about it. We're not supposed to look at it, though. Right?"

"That's right. It can do serious damage to your eyes unless you watch the event through a pair of special glasses. But it isn't the eclipse I'm talking about. It's the fold we need to worry about. And when I say *we,* I mean the three of us. Now, that'll be seventeen dollars and seventy-one cents," Sam said as he input the slushy and jerky prices into the register.

"You're insane. There's no way we're paying that for a drink and a small stick of jerky."

"Well, there's also the four candy bars, gum, additional jerky, plus tax. However, the four beers you've got wedged in those baggy pants aren't leaving the store. That's a no-go, boys."

"Wait, you're accusing us of stealing? We're up here to pay for our stuff, and you're trying to force us to pay more?" the older boy asked.

"Mister? What did you mean when you said that it's the fold we need to worry about?" the shy boy asked.

"Look. You can have the items, but you're paying for them, except the beers. And to you, young man, the fold is hard to explain, but you're going to see exactly what I mean real soon. I have to lock this place down. We've only got eight minutes," Sam told them as he came around the counter.

Moving to the front windows, Sam removed the flimsy paper solar glasses from his shirt pocket. The lenses had a deep tint that allowed nothing around to be seen except the sun. A fingernail sliver of light was still visible. Sam fished in his pocket, grabbed the ring of keys, and then removed his glasses. He selected the front door key, slid it into the lock, and sealed everyone inside.

"What do you think you're doing? We're still here."

"What are your names?" Sam asked.

"I'm Lewis and that's Nick," the timid one said.

"Seriously? You didn't have to say our names. I told you before to stop being dumb," Nick said.

"Look, fellas, I don't give a crap about your shoplifting. Not today, anyway. We've got bigger fish to fry, as they say. Things are about to get hectic around these parts because no one knows which way it's going to fold."

"This is kidnapping," Nick said.

"No. It isn't kidnapping, kid. Saving your life is what I'm doing. You can thank me later."

Lewis whispered something in Nick's ear. Sam was sure he heard the word "crazy", but that was all right. He knew they'd find out soon enough that crazy was just up around the bend when the sun winked out.

"Sir, I'm going to need you to unlock that door. You can't hold us here. If you want to call the cops because we five-fingered a few things, then that's fine. But you can't lock us in," Lewis spoke up.

Finally, growing some stones on you, huh, kid? Sam thought and looked outside again.

Even though the doors were closed and the air conditioner was silent on this early spring day, Sam could feel the temperature drop. The light got a little funny, too. It wasn't just that the sun was dimming at midday. It was also the waves of other lights, different colors moving into reality just as it had when he was a boy and witnessed the fold.

Sam saw Nick reach into his jean jacket pocket. He didn't pull his hand out again, but held it there, indecisive about his next action.

The kid has a blade on him. Well, he might need it, Sam thought as he stepped back from the front windows.

"Look, we don't want any trouble from you. And you sure as shit don't want any trouble from us. So here," Nick said and began unloading his pockets of the stolen items.

"I'm not your dad, kid, but watch your mouth in my store. There's no need for vulgarity and attitude. Just calm yourself."

Sam felt it then. The sun's absence. A solar eclipse isn't like many people believe. It doesn't turn into a full dark experience where everyone becomes engulfed in a cave-like darkness. There's plenty of light that gets around the moon's surface. But here in Youngstown, light came from other places, other times.

"I need to turn off the lights. We don't want to be a beacon to those around," Sam said as he started for the breaker box in the storeroom.

Nick's hand quickly went into the same pocket and just as quickly withdrew. It was a small pistol now gripped in his hand instead of another stolen candy bar.

A .38 Special. Probably a fake, a good fake, but not believable enough to keep me from flicking off the lights, Sam thought.

"I'm gonna need you to stay right there, sir. I want those doors unlocked."

"Well, which is it? Stay right here or unlock the doors? I'm going to ask you to keep that finger from going into action for the moment. You can shoot me in the back, but the light needs to be off right now. As soon as it's over, I'll happily turn the lights back on and open the door. I'll even let you keep all those items on the counter. No charge."

The gun came up as Sam passed the boy. If it were real, he didn't think a bullet would suddenly tear through his back. The kid was too nervous to take that drastic step.

Sam slid by the stacked cartons of soda and other goods standing by for when the shelves depleted their offerings. He opened the panel door and flicked off the main breaker, cloaking the entire store in darkness. He'd made sure earlier to remove the bulbs from the backup emergency lights over the stockroom door and over the bathroom doors.

It was getting light again, but it wasn't from the moon already circling away. It was an unnatural light. Even the boys noticed the difference. When Sam stepped from the stockroom, the kids had turned and studied the odd green and deep orange light moving through the windows like a reflection off water.

"What is that?" Lewis whispered.

"The fold. It's opening. It's why I locked you in."

"Sir, we'd really like to go home now," Nick said, but evident in his tone that he really didn't want to step out that door.

"Like I said before, I don't know which way it's going to fold."

"What does that mean? You keep saying the word 'fold' for some reason. What folds?" Nick asked.

"Pocket that gun first, and I'll tell you." After Nick shoved the small pistol back into his jean jacket pocket, Sam said, "Reality, time, or maybe even dimensions. I don't know. No one could ever explain it. I'm the only one old enough around these parts to remember the last one. I was all of eight years old when the eclipse last came through these parts. When I said that I don't know which way it'll fold, I meant that time or dimension will touch like the pages of a book. But there's no telling what's in one chapter from the next. Think of it like two galaxies passing through each other. There will be collisions between planets and stars, but eventually everything will keep on moving as it was before. I guess it's kind of like that," Sam said, but then realized the explanation was far beyond a couple of fifteen-year-olds.

Light fluctuated outside, like a fire in a hard wind. The merging of colors was like sun rays trying to break through a stubborn rainbow. Blues and yellows became greens. Reds and blues became purples.

"This is that ominous change of color I remember so well. It stuck in my mind like glue, even to this day," Sam whispered, more to himself than the boys who watched gap-mouthed.

Sam could see silhouettes in that mix of colors. Some were men, while with the others he couldn't tell. They could have been anything from anywhere.

The boys moved to the windows, watching that crazy shift of colors with unblinking stares.

"This is awesome. Do all eclipses look like this?" Nick asked.

Sam shook his head, knowing the kids hadn't listened to a damn word he said.

"It's best to stay away from the windows. They're thick and have a heavy layer of polyvinyl between the panes. They won't blow in if something rams them, but we still don't know what we're dealing with. So please come back here to where I am."

Neither boy moved until a dark shade shot across the lot between the gas pump islands. Both responded with an involuntary step back.

Though the eclipse dragged on longer here than anywhere else across the world, there was still plenty of visibility, especially with the lights from the fold. It was nowhere near the brightness of a full sun and left plenty of long shadows to conceal almost anything.

Something erupted outside. The windows vibrated viciously, which made both boys jump again. A fireball flash accompanied the sound. But that wasn't all. More flashes moved across the landscape, like fireflies in a mating frenzy.

Sam nodded, now understanding what stepped out of the fold.

"I wasn't expecting this. Youngstown is rich with history, but this, my God, I don't know if we can survive it."

"Sir, I—" Lewis began, but something with intense velocity cut him off by smashing into the front window. It came all the way through, leaving an inch-round hole punched through the panes. Needles of glass sprayed across the store. Instinctively, all three of them crouched. The object lost its power after it struck a metal bracket supporting a variety of chips, found the floor, and rolled against Sam's shoe. A metal ball shot from a musket.

"It's way worse than I thought," Sam said as he picked up the steel ball and rolled it between his fingers. It was so hot that he quickly dropped it.

Lewis reached for it.

"Don't. You'll burn your fingers."

"What is it?" Lewis asked.

Sam remembered he was dealing with a couple of teenagers who knew little of the real world outside of their game units and cell phones.

"It's a bullet from an old gun. We just folded with the Battle of Youngstown in 1863."

Both boys stared at Sam and then looked at the musket ball again. He could tell from their expressions that nothing was computing inside their heads.

"Huh?" Nick asked as more gunfire sounded.

Sam took a deep breath with a slow release.

"The Civil War, you guys. I know they don't teach history in school anymore, but you've had to have at least heard of it!"

"Sure," Lewis said. "The north and the south battle against slavery."

"Right. There was a lot more to it, but, yes, the fight between the north and south against slavery. And now we're stuck right in the middle of it."

Sam could tell the battle was moving closer. Silently, he cursed himself for not going with reason this time around. He could have closed the store and gotten far away from the eclipse's path until everything was over, when the chaos had dissipated.

Something screeched outside. It was fingernails on a chalkboard multiplied by ten. The sound caused them to clamp their hands over their ears instantly. It went on for a full minute. It wasn't one thing screeching, but many.

The gunfire accelerated. It had changed from a systematic repetition to a frantic need to kill enemies in close quarters.

"This isn't real. You're doing this somehow," Nick said while gripping the gun tighter.

Something slammed against the front door, followed by a scream of terror that Sam had never heard before in his life. It was the scream of a man desperately wanting to die just to escape the pain of death.

There was an eating sound. Noise of tearing, maybe clothes or even flesh, Sam figured. A gulping followed, and the unknown occurrence outside the doors continued for far longer than Sam wanted to hear.

Sam held his finger to his lips. Any movement inside the store would guarantee the end of all three of them. He thought he knew what the screeching had been, but he prayed it wasn't. If it were, that meant that there were several folds. One hell became two as multiple timelines stacked on each other.

Sam eased down, belly flat on the floor. With slow movements, he used his hands to pull himself closer to the doors. The low lighting provided little to see from this distance. He felt like an idiot in front of the boys as they no doubt wondered what the hell this seventy-year-old man was doing crawling around like a snake.

"Sir?" Lewis asked, but left it at that one word.

Two feet from the door, Sam stopped. Blood, or what appeared to be blood, splattered across both doors. It ran in rivulets like heavily applied wet paint down a wall. Through the gore, Sam could see something feeding. What it consumed was obvious enough. A small man, a union soldier, was giving up pounds of flesh to feed a monster.

What that monster was quickly became more evident as Sam's vision adjusted to the night. It was a creature that went extinct tens of millions of years ago. Sam pinched his eyes closed. He wished beyond all wishes that he had listened to his nagging mind about being a thousand miles from the eclipse this time around. But here he was in the thick of it, and it would probably kill him.

Sam pushed back slowly. He needed to stay with the boys, set deep in the store's shadows.

In a whisper, Sam said, "Avoid talking. Stay right where you are. Any movement inside, and they'll get curious. I think there are enough soldiers outside to keep them busy."

"Mister, I want out of here right now. I don't want to be a part of your stupid game!" Nick said as the pistol rose from his lap.

Sam clamped a hand over the boy's mouth. Nick instantly fought back, not with gunfire, but with swinging arms.

The side of the pistol clocked Sam across the side of the head, giving him a shower of stars in the blackness. He momentarily prayed he'd black out. Being unconscious would make things easier to get through the fold. If one of those big damn reptiles broke through the front door, he'd prefer to be mentally swimming in a dark abyss as they began devouring him. The bright lights in his vision receded. Sam removed his hand from the kid's mouth.

He whispered, "That was unnecessary, dammit. I'm trying to keep all of us from being shredded apart. You both need to understand the seriousness of the situation."

Sam felt where the pistol bludgeoned him. His fingers came away with a slick of blood.

"Give me the keys to the front door," Nick said and pressed the short barrel to Sam's left cheek.

Quickly reacting, Sam swatted the pistol away, pushed to his feet, and dragged the boy to the door. With his lips against the kid's ear, he hissed, "This is the situation. Look at it. Look really closely because your depleted brain cells of a mind need to understand. If you honestly want out of this door, then I'll open it for you. Maybe you'll get five steps or even twenty, but it will bring you down. There's more than just that one. Plenty more. You can't escape them all. So go back over there, sit the fuck down and keep your mouth shut."

Sam shoved the kid harder than he meant to. Nick pin-wheeled his arms, trying to keep upright, but lost the battle against gravity. His gun-free hand reached out for a hold, and he found one.

Sam saw it all in slow motion. It was like watching an eight-millimeter clip of a movie, but the projector was losing power, barely able to crank the reels. Frame by frame, Nick fell. His left hand seized a shelf with overly salted chips. The bracket the musket ball had partially torn through gave up its last bit of strength, and the shelf went down with Nick.

To Sam, the contents of that shelf hitting the floor were equivalent to Macy's Fourth of July celebration. Every wrapped treat was its own explosion. The metal shelf on tiles was the grand finale.

With disbelief, Lewis turned away from his friend on the floor and looked at Sam. His brows curled down with anger as he witnessed his friend being assaulted. Even though Sam's action was justified, he knew the boy was about to step into the realm of stupidity.

The kid went for it anyway. His eyes found the released pistol and snatched it. Bringing it up with a quaking grip, he pointed it at Sam's chest.

As Sam's mind ran through a thousand words to dis-arm this boy before he made a life-altering decision, an-other screech sounded. This one was right outside the door. It was the sound of a hunter in need of bringing down more prey.

When the thing rammed into the front door, Sam didn't have time to give Lewis advice about holding back his fire. It was the suddenness of the moment that made his finger yank the trigger.

The bullet went through the door glass just below the push handle. The report of the small revolver shocked Sam's ears into that annoying *eeeeee* sound. The sound of the creature outside the door, though, punched right through Sam's temporary deafness. It was a cry of pain and rage rolled into a single sound. It made a noise then, a call for help, Sam knew. He also thought about how accu-rate those Hollywood dinosaur movies were. It was like a large dog barking, but with an ailment of laryngitis, sound-ing more like a squawk.

The glass pushed in, causing a spiderweb of cracks around the bullet hole. Then a nail, rather, a talon, the size of a fillet knife, hooked through the hole and pulled the glass outward. The seals at all four edges began giving as the animal was determined to destroy whatever had in-jured it.

Sam slowly melted deeper into the shadows of the store.

Nick had curled into a ball, arms wrapped around his legs to somehow magically protect him from the evil com-ing through the door. Lewis aimed the pistol directly at the threat that tore the glass away.

It was an odd reversal of characters. Maybe having the gun gripped and in full control had been what made the switch happen, Sam figured.

Sam reached out and slowly pushed the kid's gun hand down.

He said, "All you'll do is piss it off more if you can't deliver a headshot."

But the moment didn't matter. Outside, muskets fired, people screamed, and creatures squawked in anger. Sam couldn't tell in the low light, but the beast at the door either collapsed or had turned to battle the soldiers. As it pulled away, the hooked talon took the window with it. The three of them were now vulnerable to whatever savage thing wanted to come through that opening.

Just as Sam began prying the gun from Lewis' hand, something did come through the windowless frame. Not a monster, but a man.

His boot caught on the bottom of the frame and sent him sprawling across the laminate flooring. The musket broke from his hold and disappeared down an aisle.

The creature, expired sixty-five million years ago in this timeline, charged inside. Sam was quick, because it meant certain death by mauling if he wasn't. The gun fired a single shot, and that shot found the reptile's large right eye. It exploded like a water balloon, spraying a viscous guck across Sam's face and in his mouth. He spat the vile fluid out, but kept his eyes on the creature sliding across the floor toward them. He was ready to pump more rounds into the thing, but it failed to move again.

The soldier, a young kid not much past his eighteenth birthday, kicked, trying to get his boots to bite into the flooring and push him away from the thing that tried to eat him.

"What is this? What is that? Where in the hell am I, mister?" the kid stammered with an exhausted breath.

The kid kicked his way to the farthest back shelf. His eyes moving in a rapid chaos of searching faces and his surroundings.

Like speaking softly to a scared puppy peeing on everything, Sam said, "Calm down. It's dead."

"Calm down? Calm down? There's got to be fifteen more of those things out there," the kid huffed.

"Then I recommend staying inside," Lewis said.

The young soldier looked Lewis over, specifically his clothes and shaggy hair. He said, "Kid, we've got a war to win. I don't have time for strange people, strange buildings or giant lizards."

On hands and knees, he shuffled down the aisle and retrieved his musket, leaped over the dead velociraptor and back out the shattered door.

"The fold has to close soon. Dear God, I hope it closes soon," Sam said, mostly to himself.

Nick began huffing, causing a wheezing inhale and exhale. He rocked back and forth with his arms hugging his knees.

Sam knew the kid was in the grip of either a panic attack or a mental breakdown. This fold of timelines was too much for him to comprehend, giving him a fractured mind. Sam only hoped the damage wasn't permanent.

"He shouldn't have done that. He's gonna die out there," Lewis said.

"Maybe. But he's a soldier who has a duty to perform. He needs to follow orders," Sam offered.

Something jetted past the pumps. It was quick, and experienced enough to stay in the shadows until the time came to spring claws and teeth on its prey.

Lewis offered a slight whimper. Nick remained oblivious of his surroundings.

An ooze leaked from the dead velociraptor's mouth. A clear liquid mixed with blood gave it a Pepto Bismol appearance.

Sam couldn't believe a single shot had put the creature down. Even a close-up headshot didn't seem like it was enough to bring down a hunter like this. He pressed the release and inspected the rounds. Two rounds used and four remained. A herd coming through would finish them. He couldn't fight off that kind of primal viciousness.

Sam looked at Lewis as he grabbed Nick's shoulder. He said, "Let's carefully and quietly back our way into the storeroom. The door is flimsy, but it'll conceal us until this event is over."

As if knowing what move they were about to make, another creature charged through the empty door frame, stepping right on top of its fallen brethren. Its large head lowered and sniffed. In a display Sam couldn't believe until he witnessed it, the thing rotated its head and placed its forehead against the other. Sam knew, sure as he knew anything in his life, that this creature was mourning the loss of its companion. Then its grief was over. Its eyes slowly rotated up to get a good, hard look at who had killed its mate.

Its breath sucked in long and deep. What came out was the most God-awful screech Sam had ever heard. That sound drove an icicle through his mind, heart, and down his spine to chill every little part of him. It was a sound of rage and sadness converging into a single bellow.

Sam's shot went high as he figured the thing was going to leap. Instead, it hunkered low in its charge. The bullet went through the glassless door into the multi-colored, unnatural twilight.

As a row of daggers went to clamp down on Sam's face, severing the life from the body, a can of beans cracked into the creature's head.

A menacing hiss rolled from its throat as it turned its attention to Nick. He'd broken from his hypnotic state, deciding he very much wanted to live. Lewis quickly joined, seizing any hard object to propel at the animal.

Sam appreciated the boys' effort. In staging a defense, they believed the animal would turn tail and run. While with most living animals today, this might be true, but a predator and efficient killer like this didn't back down from a fight, especially when it was a meal large enough to feed the pack.

Sam knew the animal was going to make a move for the kids. He snagged the scaly leg as it began moving. Sensing the hold, the animal kicked. The massive foot crushed Sam's chest, instantly splintering ribs and stealing his breath.

Even unable to pull in air, Sam steadied his aim. The bullet pierced the left hindquarter.

The animal was quick to react. But instead of turning on Sam, its jaws clamped on Nick's ankle and began dragging him toward the front and out the windowless door. Nick reached out blindly, searching for a hold on something that would keep him inside the store. He found Lewis' hand, but the creature easily dragged them both. Its tail slashed, catching the racks near the front door. Newspapers and packs of gum slingshot at Sam as he fired, ending with another miss.

It was the purple light Sam remembered from his boyhood. Two primary colors clashing into each other, the blues and reds heavily mingling, creating a violet shade one might see before or after a severe storm. It was the color that indicated the closing of the fold.

Sam knew he just needed to keep these damn kids alive a bit longer.

With his breath returning, pins of pain stabbed his entire torso as the expansion of his lungs drove those bastard shards into tender organs. Pushing up to a crawl position intensified every nerve ending, almost causing him to give up all rescue efforts.

The screams from both boys being dragged from the store brought his motivation back. Fighting the black out as he got to his feet, he felt the feed of adrenaline run an unstoppable locomotive through his veins. Sam roared like the primal animal he pursued.

Going through the door frame, he stumbled and went down, red-hot needles spiking his soft tissue again. But his hand was out, grasping, and clutched Lewis' outstretched reach.

It was impossible for the velociraptor to pull all three of them closer to the pack. Despite the effort, the animal released Nick's destroyed ankle and glared at Sam with fury that he had yet again interfered.

Sam shot the remaining round. The report wasn't nearly strong enough to shock his ears as it had in the confines of the store. The bullet disappeared into the rough texture of the animal's left side. It had been a pitiful shot, catching more skin than meat, but it deterred the animal, causing it to back up a little more. That was all it took.

The purple haze covering the earth then divided. The blues and reds of the atmosphere split. Yellows, oranges, and greens also made an appearance as the colors stacked on each other like a rainbow.

The velociraptor crouched. Even injured, it was prepared to annihilate all three of them.

As the thing sprang, those multi colors expanded as if taking a deep breath before its final task. Like God's universal hammer driving into them, the colors merged with an intensity only ever seen through Sam's eyes.

Sam welcomed the dimensional collapse. He expelled a held breath, reawakening the pain of his broken ribs, but he'd never been happier to be alive.

"It has closed. Thank God Almighty, the fold has closed," Sam told the boys.

A momentary quiet followed Sam's statement. Then the agony of Nick's ankle called out to him, breaking him from the fascination of time having stacked on itself. He didn't deliver it in a scream, but a moan, like he was trying to wake himself from a very realistic nightmare.

Sam pushed through his own pain to crawl forward. He inspected the boy's foot. He said, "Well, it sure got some teeth in you. But you're lucky. Wearing high-top sneakers and denim jeans spared your ankle a fate that could have been much worse. Lewis, run inside the store and grab some rags from behind the counter. Better call 911 while you're at it. I'm not sure how bad things are around here for other folks, but it might take them a bit to get here."

"Yes, sir," Lewis said, not hesitating to help his friend.

"You could look at this another way. It could be karma talking to you, boy. If you hadn't tried stealing from me, illegally carried a gun, and had followed my directions before everything got bad, maybe none of this would have happened."

Inside, Sam smiled. Regardless of the decisions made today, with the exception of Nick shooting through the door, the fold still would have happened. It just seemed like an opportune time to rattle some sense into a kid who was already starting down a bad path in life. Maybe the thought would stick with the boy, pushing him to make smarter decisions during his life. Sam knew he wouldn't be around to see the results, but he hoped the fold had scared the boys straight. If the fold was going to be good for anything, at least it could be good for that.

Lewis came jogging out of the store carrying several white rags. He said, "An ambulance is coming. They didn't say how long, though. She just said as soon as they could."

"That's fine. I'm in no hurry. There's not much they can do for broken ribs except to wrap up my chest good and tight. Besides, the next eclipse around here won't be until 2047. So, I'll be yellowed bones beneath the ground by then. Lewis, tie those rags around that bite good and tight. It isn't bleeding much now. An infection is going to be the least of your worries. Just think of the glory, though. You're the first person in history to be bitten by a dinosaur. Congratulations."

Nick smiled at that thought.

As Sam tried propping himself up, something dug into his elbow. He rolled his sight over to it. A .38 caliber bullet, slightly deformed at the tip, lay on the parking lot surface. This one had fallen free from its body when the fold closed. Inside the store, there would be two more bullets lying on the linoleum, one he'd punched into its hindquarter, and another he'd shot in the first velociraptor's eye socket.

Nothing stays when the fold is done. Except memories, I suppose. What is part of our world will remain. What is part of their world or time or whatever goes when they go. We clashed, and then we parted. The universe has a wicked sense of humor, I'd say, Sam thought.

He didn't even need to check, because he knew, he just knew that the musket ball inside the store was also gone. Because nothing ever remains after the fold has finished its sporting amusement.

Inheritance

"So, what's in the box?" Dillon Maylin asked the attorney across from him.

He'd decided four seconds after walking through the lawyer's door that he hated the man. Before the lawyer even attempted a smile or offered a handshake, he knew he hated him, simply because he was a lawyer. Worse than that, the man was his father's lawyer. Edgar Abrams was one of the Maylin Firearms Company lawyers and overseer of the Franklin Maylin estate.

Mr. Abrams held up a finger, indicating that the son of his employer was unimportant to the world of business. He finished writing on a form, closed the document in a manila envelope, and looked up.

"I'm unaware of the contents that your father left for you in his will. Honestly, I'm amazed he left you anything. As you know, your brother, Colin, will inherit the business and the estate in which your father resided until his death."

"Of course. Colin has always been our father's lap kitty. Besides, I told my father over nine years ago when I left the estate that I wanted nothing from him, except for him to rot in hell."

Mr. Abrams winced at the remark. His face twisted, battling between holding his tongue and cutting loose his thoughts on the matter.

"I'm sure that whatever it is, isn't much," the lawyer said.

Dillon looked at the small, two-foot cubed crate sitting on the lawyer's desk.

"Well, when I said I wanted nothing from him, that includes the items in that box. So, I'm going to leave it with you. You can toss it in the dumpster or set it on fire. I don't care."

"You've just signed for the item, so now it's yours to do with as you please. You can take it with you out the door and do those things you suggested. Perhaps there's clarification inside, a last attempt on your father's side to make amends."

Dillon snorted.

"My father never made amends with anyone. It wasn't in his character. A drunk, an abuser, a man who thrived on belittling his wife and children, and a man of great solitude when he wasn't being those other things is what he was. The last thing he could ever be was a father."

Mr. Abrams kept his composure despite the accusations against his employer.

Dillon waved his hands as if dismissing everything said.

"It matters not. This is a final gift. Your father deemed it to you in this legal document. So, please take that with you when you leave my office. Enjoy your remaining years, Mr. Maylin."

Silence filled the room as Dillon locked eyes with the snake of a lawyer. He debated leaving the crate on the desk and walking out, but figured the lawyer would just drop it on his doorstep later this evening.

Whatever it is, I swear to all that it will burn in the fire pit tonight, Dillon thought.

He slid the box off the desk and found it far lighter than he expected. He was sure there was packing foam inside, but unsure of anything else. It wouldn't surprise him when he later opened it to find nothing at all except packing material. It would be his father's last sick joke to give him what he asked for, nothing.

Dillon stepped from the office, offered no goodbye to the secretary, and headed for the elevator. As he moved from the fifth floor to the lobby, he rotated the box, looking for any labels to help him figure out its contents. The box gave up no secrets, as no writing or labels marked the crate. Though cheaply constructed, the box would still require a hammer and pry bar from the garage to open it.

Touching down at the lobby, the doors parted to a man he hadn't seen in nearly a decade.

The man began to step into the elevator until he noticed the individual before him. His thoughts were undoubtedly running full speed, trying to decipher why his brother was at this particular downtown building.

Dillon debated saying nothing. He could have passed his brother, and Colin would have let him go without a word of greetings.

"Hey," Dillon offered.

Colin's eyes switched to the empty elevator. Dillon figured that his brother wished to abandon the lobby as Dillon had abandoned the family years before. To Dillon's surprise, Colin lingered.

"How have you been?" he asked.

"Good. I suppose."

Colin glanced at the box and said, "So, what brings you here?"

"This box, I guess. I was called here by Mr. Abrams."

Colin's eyes narrowed. Displeased with an item being willed to his brother.

"What's in it?"

"I have no idea. I'm gonna have to smash it open. Maybe I'll just send it down to Dad by way of flames in the fire pit tonight. I haven't decided.

"It sounds like something you would do. You never had an appreciation for anything given to you."

"Well, it's been great catching up. Enjoy your fortune of death and destruction."

Dillon turned and headed for the entrance.

"How much do you want for it?"

Dillon turned.

"You want to buy this box from me without knowing what's in it?"

"That's right. I figured you wouldn't want it anyhow."

Colin removed his wallet from the inside suit pocket and opened it. Large-denomination bills packed the leather folds. Colin selected three bills and held them out.

"You are seriously offering me three hundred dollars for a mystery box?"

"Correct."

"It just eats you alive that he left me something, doesn't it?"

Colin pulled two more bills loose. Holding out five-hundred dollars.

"I think I'll keep it. It'll drive you bug-shit mad not knowing. That's worth far more to me than five hundred dollars."

Colin pocketed the money and said, "When you hit skid row, give me a call. Unlike Dad, I might find forgiveness in my heart and extend a helping hand."

He turned and stepped into the elevator. The doors closed, severing any last comeback Dillon could think up.

Dillon dropped ice in a glass and poured scotch over it. He settled into his suede chair and took a sip. He could feel it calling him from the kitchen table. That damn crate, begging to be opened, so his father could get the last laugh.

I'm the one laughing, old man. You're dead, and I'm alive. Your soul is corrupted and mine is clean.

Dillon never minded stepping away from the family business and fortune. It was blood money, built by a century of manufacturing weapons. Though he never preached against war and weapons of death, he just never could hold a gun and take the life of an animal as his father stood at his side, instructing him where to place his sights and to squeeze the trigger. Failing to take the shot, his father would go on a rant, calling him weak and pitiful, someone who would never amount to even a fraction of his brother's worth.

Open it, weakling. See what I've left for you. See how I've valued you as a person, as a so-called son. Open it. I will laugh in my grave!

Dillon could hear those words as if his father had actually spoken them. They were words he would have said if his body weren't deteriorating in an expensive box underground.

He knew he was going to look. The curiosity of the situation was too great to ignore. He couldn't even commit to destroying the box by fire before he knew what his inheritance was.

He finished his drink in a final long gulp and immediately poured another one for after the box was opened, because he was sure he'd need it.

The pry bar and hammer clanged together as he dropped them on the table beside the box. He turned the wooden cube, trying to find an edge he could work the pry bar into and begin the miserable task. Finally, a corner edge that wasn't as sealed as the rest accepted the tapered points of the pry bar. Dillon began delivering blows to the curved edge. Crackling wood sounds filled his house as he worked the bar up and down as if trying to jack up a car.

The nails and wood gave with a final, defiant lightning crack of resistance. The lid fell away in splintered pieces onto the table surface. White foam packing peanuts filled the box, and he was reluctant to stick his hand inside them to find what they concealed. As twisted as his father's humor had been, it could very well have been a dead animal, much like one he couldn't shoot as a boy. A parting gift from a man to a weakling.

Dillon's arm vanished to the elbow before he felt something. It certainly wasn't animal fur, but possibly wood. Seizing the edge, he pulled it from the box. Static cling held the foam to the object until he shook them loose. At first, Dillon thought it was a small picture. As he laid it on the table, he realized it was a framed dollar bill. Not any ordinary dollar bill, but the one that adorned the wall in his father's office. He hadn't seen it since he was a kid, after he had sneaked into the office when his father was using the bathroom. Dillon had received a hand across the rump for his disobedience, and that was the last time he'd seen inside that room.

The bill was a symbol, a status of where the Maylin family had started and where they had evolved in both wealth and ingenuity.

Now he needed that drink. The entire glass went down in one swallow.

"Why would you give me this?"

Dillon poured out the remaining foam peanuts, scattered them and then looked in the box. There was nothing else. Turning the frame over, he found an envelope taped to the back. Inside was a folded single page. He recognized his father's writing and nearly went to the shredder without reading it.

"Well, Dad, I guess I'll give you that last shot to tell me what a disappointment I am to you and the generations before. I can accept that, because you never did beat me down in spirit like you thought you could."

It read:

Dillon,

It seems reasonable for me to convey my final words to you through some damn letter instead of in person. We never saw eye to eye, did we? You took after your mother in character, as Colin took after me. He and I are very much alike, as we're strong in both mind and business sense. Though I loved your mother to the best my heart would allow, she was weak, just as you are weak. Can I really fault you for having no backbone? Yes, I can. I tried so many times to make you a man, to show you the world will chew you to pieces if I couldn't man you up. It became the single failure in my life. That probably makes you happy.

This is my one gift to you. It's the start of our legacy. It's the only thing you will inherit. It's your self-worth. A single dollar. This is the money my great-grandfather first made as he began manufacturing ammunition. That first dollar paved the way for billions more. All of which you will see none of it, except this bill. It was your choice to turn your back on being extraordinary. You deserve this bill, and all that's inherited with it.

You once told me to burn in hell. Well, I'm here, and I'll save you a seat. It'll be sooner than you think.

Franklin Maylin

Dillon leaned back in the chair, the wood creaking from the weight. It was no surprise his father would roast his son with his last words.

What an arrogant prick. The letter didn't close with "Your Father" or "Dad." It was the final stab in the back for him to write this letter before departing this world. Well, Franklin Maylin, your efforts were a waste of precious time.

Dillon grabbed the hammer and bludgeoned the frame and glass to death. Digging through the shattered glass, an edge ran down Dillon's finger, delivering a cut so sharp he barely noticed, until a thumbprint of blood marred the bill.

"Shit."

At the kitchen sink, Dillon ran cold water over it, and the bleeding slowed. He then wrapped several paper towels around his finger and returned to the table.

"I bet you're laughing in your grave now. Aren't you? Crazy old bastard. Sorry, President Washington, your time of hanging on a wall is all done now."

He crumpled the bill and letter together and went out the back door. Flipping the lid off the fire pit, the balled-up paper went in, followed by a dousing of lighter fluid and a match. Unlike gasoline, lighter fluid is a slow start. The exposed edges blackened at first but began flaming out. Dillon popped the fluid top again and fed a steady stream into the flames. He watched from a lounge chair until even the crumpled core had become black ash.

The urge for another drink made itself known. Even though two drinks had already caused him to wobble as he went inside, he thought one more would help put his mind into a deep sleep, a place far away from any thoughts of his father.

As he snagged the glass from the table and began turning toward the small bar, his eyes caught the impossible.

Lying under the wreckage of broken glass and wooden frame was a dollar bill.

Dillon stared at it for a long minute, not fully under-standing. He flicked the broken glass to the side and pulled the bill free. He didn't remember the serial numbers, but the year printed on the bill was 1919. It was the same year as the bill that had gone up in smoke.

"Bullshit," he said and flipped the bill over.

No blood from his cut thumb marked the currency.

Dillon dropped the bill and looked around. His ears peeled open for any sounds.

Someone is here, he thought.

Taking the hammer as a defensive weapon, he moved to the front door. He checked that it was still locked before heading to the living room. Room by room, he cleared the house, finding no intruders.

Looking at the bill, he said, "I don't know what you're all about, George. If someone's playing a prank on me, they'll get the blunt end of this hammer."

The bill's serial numbers were a bit blurred now by his intoxicated mind. Dillon had managed to memorize them because this bill had an appointment with the fire.

Taking his third scotch with him, Dillon dropped the bill on the smoldering paper already in the pit, but it needed a match to get going. At first, it refused to burn, until Dillon dumped the contents of his glass onto the dy-ing flame. A rush of fire almost took his eyebrows off. It took a hot bite out of his hand and scorched away the black hair from his knuckles and upper arm.

"Son of a bitch," he said and shook his hand. "Head on down to hell, George, and help my father reminisce about his participation in further corrupting society."

The bill didn't reappear under the broken glass again. Instead, it lay flat on the bathroom sink, with the tube of toothpaste covering George's entire head. He saw it after he grabbed the toothbrush from the glass holder and went to put a dollop of paste on the bristles.

Well, kiss my happy ass.

He lifted the bill and inspected the numbers. They were identical to the last bill he set to burn.

Someone is playing mind games at my father's last request.

Dillon went to the bedroom, retrieved a pen from the bedside table, and drew a five-pointed star above the serial numbers. Going back to the bathroom, he crumpled the bill, dropped it into the toilet and flushed. The paper shot down the pipework and was gone.

"All right. Let's see what you do now," he called out through the house.

Dad must have had dozens of those fake bills printed. His humor was always a hard twist to the side of the sadistic. But who the hell is playing this game?

The only place Dillon hadn't checked during his search was the attic. He knew there was no way someone could crawl noiselessly in and out of the two-foot access panel multiple times without him noticing.

Sliding into bed, the alcohol and stress of the day had hammered its toll. Despite the possibility of someone being in his home while he slept, it didn't stop him from quickly drifting off.

The gunshot woke him. It was one of those surreal moments when a dream and reality briefly merged when someone quickly transitioned between the two. He knew it was the dream that had awakened him, but that dream had a fierce grip of teeth on his mind, because the shot sounded very real. His ears were even ringing as he looked around the darkness of his bedroom.

"No! Daddy!"

Dillon's frozen state broke when he heard the little girl's voice. He fumbled, nearly knocking over the lamp before finding the switch.

There was a dead man lying against the wall beside his reading chair. A blonde girl, no more than seven years of age, kneeled beside him. She was crying, with her arms clasped around the man's neck. The hole in his chest had pumped out all the blood it was going to give. A man dressed in clothes from a different time stood a few feet back from the girl and the dead man. A large revolver was in his right hand, smoke leaking from the barrel. He stared at the girl and the lifeless body of her father.

"Now, here's what I'm thinking. Someday, after spending all that time in an orphanage, stewing about me getting even with your daddy, you might have developed a seething hatred for me. That hate is a hard thing to let go of. I know. Then there might come a time when you want to come looking for me so you can right what was wrong. Look at me, girl. This here is a square deal between me and your daddy." He said and then pointed the gun at the little girl.

"No. Just stop," Dillon said.

The man spun, as if not realizing he was in someone's bedroom, having just committed murder in front of a stranger.

The gun trained on Dillon. The heartless black eye of the barrel stared him down. His hands reacted, going up automatically, showing he held no weapons.

"What's this place? Who the hell are you?" The man's voice was gruff, tinged with damage from a lifetime of smoking.

"Just hold on. I'm unarmed. My name is Dillon Maylin. You're inside my home. You just murdered someone in my house."

"Maylin? You related to Edgar Maylin?"

"No. I mean, yes."

The little girl cried harder.

"Which is it? No, or yes?"

"Yes. He was my great-grandfather."

The man snorted.

"Great-grandfather. A man can't be a great-grandfather at thirty years of age. He's the man who owns the general store."

"Edgar has been dead for like seventy years, mister."

"My father used to say that if a man isn't right in the head, the best thing you can do for him is to end his suffering."

The hammer fell on one of the six chambers. Dillon felt his heart explode from the impact. As breath forced out of his body, he felt the impending evacuation of his bodily fluids begin pushing free.

The breath came back with welcomed relief. Dillon's panic subsided as the glow of the lamp showed no gunman, crying girl, or dead man on the floor. More importantly, there was no large-caliber hole in his chest.

Rotating on the bed, Dillon jabbed his feet into the bedside slippers and scrambled for the toilet before the dam broke and flooded his underwear with urine. Knowing the full body quake would cause the stream to go everywhere except where it was supposed to, he sat instead. As the pressure released, the nausea overcame him. He seized the trash can and held it to his face, and a vile mass ejected into the plastic container. When he figured he had finished subjecting himself to bodily evacuation, he collapsed onto the cool ceramic tile.

Dillon lay on the floor for countless minutes and listened. He waited for the clopping of boots across the hardwood floor of the bedroom. He waited for the click of the gun's cylinder to rotate another round. He waited for the phantom to end him.

None of that came about as Dillon pushed himself from the floor and used the wall to steady himself. He leaned over the sink, rinsed his mouth of the lingering bile and spat. Then a cool splash of water went onto his face.

As he started to turn, he noticed an odd feeling in his left slipper. Kicking it off, he stared at George, and George stared right back at him. Someone had placed the bill inside his slipper while he slept. With anger, he snatched the bill, seeing that the serial numbers remained the same, and even the blue-inked five-pointed star hovered above those numbers.

"Enough! This game is over! I don't care how much my father paid you, but if you don't get your ass out of my house in a minute flat, you can explain it to the police."

Dillon charged into the bedroom, ready for a fight. Even though his fighting skills were a fantasy, he knew his abundance of weight gave him an advantage.

The reminiscence of a horror dream hung in the air like a thick fog. It hadn't been a dream, though, and he was sure of that. It was an act, a dreadful play his father had orchestrated and paid for before his death. It was a simple punishment to drive his oldest son mad, possibly enough to push him toward suicide so he could take a seat at his father's side in hell.

No blood marked the floor or wall where the man had lain. No scent of expelled gunpowder hung in the air.

Dillon began believing that prior to his return home from the lawyer's office, some asshole had entered his home and spiked his liquor bottles with a hallucinogenic drug. As the thought rolled through his mind more and more, it began to explain so much. The belief that he'd destroyed the bill multiple times, and the ghosts in his bedroom, was due to an enhanced drug he'd unknowingly taken.

The bill went through the shredder. The liquor went down the drain, and the open contents in the refrigerator and cabinets went into the trash container out back. He was satisfied that he'd tackled the obstacle of being a deplorable sideshow freak for his father's team of miscreants. The show was over. Now was the time to move forward without the hovering cruelty of his family's name cursing the remainder of his life.

He thought he had beaten them.

The goddamn bill was under a refrigerator magnet when he went to retrieve the milk for a bowl of cereal. All he could do was stare at the damn thing. It taunted him. He was sure old George's faint smugness had transformed into a full-on grin now. His eyes even seemed a little more open, wider so he could take a good look at the man he tormented. He pulled it loose from the fridge, not noticing when the Winnie the Pooh magnet fell to the floor.

"I'm still feeling the effects of whatever crap they put in my drink," Dillon said, but his statement wasn't convincing.

He felt fine. As he had shaved this morning, he studied his reflection. By all accounts, except for the extra bodily bulk, he looked healthy. His eyes weren't bloodshot or watery from a bad trip. His pulse didn't race out of control. If anything, he felt average this morning.

Dillon thought he just might take the day off work. He had an overwhelming sense of having to visit his father's lawyer again today. He wanted, no, needed answers to this three-ring circus he experienced last night.

More importantly, he had an overwhelming sensation that he needed to take his gun, the one bestowed on him at the age of twelve by his father. Mr. Abrams had a deep commitment to preserving the Maylin legacy. Disclosing anything about ol' George's first introduction to the family might be one of those deep, dark family secrets that so few people know about. Mr. Abrams just might need some per-suasion by way of gunpoint to give up the family dirt that Dillon desperately needed before he went bug-shit crazy.

Dillon dove onto the lobby tile floor when the first gunshot went off. It was a wake-up call that his life was about to end, just like last night's event. Throwing his hands over his head, he peered beneath his elbow, trying to get an idea of where the shooter was. Rotating his body, all he could see were a dozen feet holding perfectly still. All the toes pointed in his direction. He began a low scramble to his right. Using only the edges of his sneakers on the tiles, he aimed for the cover of the secretary's desk.

Dillon felt the hot kiss of a bullet catch his rump during his maneuver. He offered the lobby area a growl of pain as panic grew more intense. He gave up the belly slide and moved up to hands and knees. That was when he noticed the attention was all on him.

Men in power suits and women in business skirts all watched him with just a little fear, but mostly amusement. They were all deciding what level of unstable this man was. Was he harmless to all others except himself? Or was he the dangerous kind that often made an appearance on the nightly news accompanied by a death toll?

Dillon looked around, ready to take cover again if he spotted the shooter. There was no shooter because no one else was panicking. All eyes locked on him and waited to see what he might do next.

An overweight security guard came running out of the back room. The brief jog had already winded him as he studied the lobby people and then Dillon, who was still down on all fours on the floor.

"Sir? What seems to be the problem?" the guard asked.

At first, Dillon thought the large man was responding to the loud reports that may have been gunshots. But now he understood the guard must have seen his bizarre behavior on the security monitors and come running to see what all the fuss was about.

With his hands on his hips, he said, "Are you, um, you know, having an episode or something?"

Dillon knew what that meant. The man was questioning whether Dillon was off his meds.

Dillon took slow, deep breaths to get his heart under control before he collapsed face first onto the tiles again. His mind raced, trying to find a reasonable answer for an unreasonable action.

A lie came out so easily. "Um, yeah. Damn. I'm sorry about all that. Yeah, I suppose you could say it was an episode. You see, I left the army a few years back. They sent me home a broken man suffering from PTSD. For a moment, I thought I heard shooting. I hit the deck in response. It's an automatic thing. I'm okay though. I believe the panic has run its course."

"Okay. Well, that's good to hear. I thought for a moment I was going to need local PD help," he said and held out his hand to help Dillon to his feet.

"Everything's okay now. I just have an appointment with my lawyer. Thanks for checking on me."

Dillon went to the elevator, pressed the fifth-floor button and convinced himself not to look back, because he knew the overweight security guard was still suspiciously watching him.

The elevator chimed its arrival, and Dillon stepped in. He honestly didn't even know if the lawyer was here, but he hoped he was. He didn't think he could handle another day dealing with the goddamn reappearing dollar bill and the phantom gunman shooting at him, making him look like an escaped mental patient.

Entering the outer office, he offered a quick glance at the secretary. Without slowing, he went to Mr. Abrams' office door.

"Wait. Can I help you?"

Dillon heard her get up and shuffle after him.

Mr. Abrams looked up, not at all surprised to see him here.

"Dillon, I don't have time for this. I have a meeting in ten minutes."

"Well, then I'll only take up nine of those minutes. We need to talk."

Mr. Abrams held up his hand to his secretary. "It's all right, Mrs. Blake. Give us nine minutes. If he hasn't walked past your desk heading for the elevator by then, call security."

Without a word, she closed the door.

Dillon reached around his back, making Mr. Abrams tense. He pulled out his wallet and removed the dollar bill that not even God could make disappear.

Before placing the bill on the lawyer's desk, he glanced at it. Ol' George had changed again. He looked more demented than before. His eyes were a little buggier, with the left one hitched upward as if pulled by a fishhook. His grin had morphed into a smile. His teeth were spaced wide and now pointed little bastards, like the mouth of a piranha.

Dillon tossed it across the desk as if George had snapped those teeth down on a finger.

With a smooth action, Mr. Abrams picked it up and turned it over.

"So that's where it went. It wasn't in the inventory of contents of your father's estate. I think I know why he gave it to you. It seems logical, actually."

"I'm listening. Explain this game being played on me."

Mr. Abrams' eyes narrowed as he switched from the bill to Dillon.

"Game?"

"Yeah. You know. The dollar bill that refuses to vanish from existence and the bearded man wearing century-old clothes shooting blanks at me. Did my father set this up before he died? Maybe it's sort of a last laugh from the grave."

Mr. Abrams smiled then. It was the kind of look Dillon wanted to wipe off the man's face by instantly sticking a gun against his eye socket.

"So, it's true then?"

"What's true? Explain."

"Your father once told me about the legacy behind this bill. Your great-grandfather began manufacturing ammunition under his own brand name and started selling it out of his general store. This dollar bill paid for the first box of ammo that went out the door. The man who bought it, Victor Henry, if I remember his name right, went to his previous employer's home that night and shot his ex-boss down. The story goes that Victor developed a thirst for killing after that. He ended up killing forty-three people with that box of fifty bullets. Law enforcement surrounded him, and he shot himself, becoming the forty-fourth person to be killed by that ammo. So, a nonsense curse was born to give this bill diabolical merit. I always considered it a fabricated story of a haunting, much like the Winchester Mansion. But you say you saw him? That he actually shot at you?"

"I did, and he did. He shot me dead center in the heart last night while I was lying in bed. So, you don't believe any of it?"

Mr. Abrams shrugged. "I investigated the matter long ago. My research revealed that there really was a Victor Henry in 1919, and yes, he really did murder forty-three people and then himself. Now, there's no way to find out if he really did use the first box of Maylin ammunition. The articles I found never mentioned the brand used. It was one of those details during a homicide investigation that didn't matter back in those days."

"So, it's no game? You're saying I'm really haunted by a serial killer?"

Mr. Abrams held up his hands and said, "That I couldn't say. Speculation has always been that when Victor Henry ate that last bullet, his soul got pulled into this dollar bill. Your father spoke of strange happenings occurring at the estate, but never dove into detail. I'm not one to believe in supernatural hauntings and such. Maybe the entire thing is your brother playing a practical joke, though I doubt it. He's got too much on his plate now that he's taken over the business."

Mrs. Blake popped her head into the office and said, "Do you still want me to call security?"

"No, that's all right. We're about done here." When the secretary closed the door, Mr. Abrams slid the bill across his desk and said, "Your father gifted the bill to you. Since you're a Maylin, that Victor Henry curse falls on your shoulders. If he shot you, as you've said, he obviously can't kill you. So, you might lose some sleep here and there, but you'll go on living. I trust these will be our last words together. Good day, Mr. Maylin."

Dillon took the bill with a shaking hand. He dropped it on the floor and briefly thought about leaving it and walking out. But he knew it would find him again. Maybe buried in the damn frozen lasagna he planned to eat to-night. Hell, for all he knew, the cursed thing might pop right out of his colon the next time he used the toilet.

As Dillon looked at the evil transformed features of the first president, he thought, *He didn't see it, did he? He would have said something about it. He would have asked if it was a joke dollar bill because the president looks like a raving psychopath.*

Dillon fell hard onto the sofa. The springs and other supports barked with protest.

Fishing in his front pocket, Dillon gripped the bill and pulled it out. He half expected to see George had morphed again, maybe now looking like a deranged clown, much like the one from that Stephen King book. But he hadn't changed, at least not yet.

Dillon wondered about the blood. He'd left a bloody fingerprint to the right of George's picture, but after that first burn out back and the bill's return, the blood was gone. The inked star remained, though.

Was that some sort of blood sacrifice? Had the blood stirred the soul within the bill, the demented soul of Victor Henry?

The floorboards creaked upstairs. Dillon quickly shot a look at the white ceiling. His breath held. A solid mass seemed to lodge in his throat as if his heart had jumped about six inches.

He began getting up from the sofa quietly, and the springs sounded their appreciation. Moving to the stair-case, he peered around the corner, finding no one on the stairs. Waiting for another noise, he began wondering if he'd had a psychotic break. It made sense. If someone hadn't drugged him, then it was something in his delicate mind that had snapped like an old rubber band. He couldn't understand why everything was coming apart now. The death of his father hadn't played a role in it since they despised each other. The face-to-face with his brother had been a bit stressful, but not enough to warrant a mental collapse.

Dillon started taking the stairs, one slow step after another. He moved up and then waited, listened, and then went again. He knew there would be no sneak attack on his part because he couldn't hide his advancements up to the second floor. Halfway up, he found an empty hall leading to three bedrooms and a bathroom. When he put his foot on the top step, a woman no more than twenty-three years old came out of the back bedroom in a full-on sprint. Her mouth was open wide, and a shriek came out that would have scared the bejesus out of a banshee. Then her head came apart in an almost high-dollar horror movie experience. Blood sprayed everywhere, including across Dillon's shirt and face. Her body crashed at his feet as all muscles gave out.

The gunman, Victor Henry, stood just outside the room, arm extended and smoke seeping from the barrel's end.

Dillon's hand gave out then as his grip on the railing abandoned its entire purpose. His knees began going limp, too. He didn't remember much after that, except a fall backwards as the stairs desperately tried to take his life.

When Dillon woke, everything hurt. He was confident that his back hadn't shattered from the fall, but that didn't rule out the possibility of fractured vertebrae. No gunman stared down at him. No spatter of blood marked his face or shirt. He used his hands to pull the rest of his body away from the steps, so he could lie flat and take a mental inventory of the severity of his injuries.

It didn't take long to figure out he was going to be a bruised purple mess for a while, but nothing seemed broken.

The couch had become his only place of rest for nearly a full day. Dillon hated hospitals, and he'd be damned to go only to be sent home with a few aspirins and a four-thousand-dollar medical bill.

Being incapacitated gave Dillon plenty of time to consider his next move. It was the lawyer's words that came calling back.

Your father gifted the bill to you. Since you're a Maylin, that Victor Henry curse falls on your shoulders.

"That's right, Mr. Abrams, but I'm not the only Maylin left."

When Dillon's body finally allowed mobility, he began cutting wood to replace the damaged side of the crate. It was an easy thing to duplicate, since it was plain pine and not some exotic wood.

The bill, with ol' George's scary as ever face staring at him, went into an old, battered frame Dillon found at a thrift store. He'd paid one dollar to display the dollar. It seemed a fitting price.

Dillon knew Colin would be at the office. He was the newly appointed big man in charge, and it was certain he'd be there displaying his position of power.

"Can you tell Colin that his brother is here to see him?" Dillon asked the secretary when he walked into the outer office of his family's empire.

Dillon didn't know her, and she didn't know him. Her suspicious eyes rolled over him before picking up the phone.

"Yes, Mr. Maylin, there's a gentleman here claiming to be your brother. He has a large box with him. Okay. Yes, sir." She hung up the phone and pressed the button to release the door's magnetic lock. "Go right in, Mr. Maylin."

"Dillon! Don't tell me you've already found skid row and need the help I offered?"

"You've always been a funny guy, Colin. I changed my mind about the deal the other day. I'm willing to let this crate go and whatever is in it. I've decided I don't want any part of it. So I'll sell it to you if the offer stands."

Dillon slid the box onto the oversized mahogany desk.

"Colin leaned back in his chair, staring thoughtfully at the crate.

"Well, that was an offer from two days ago. That five hundred is off the table."

"You're unbelievable. You've just inherited a multi-billion-dollar company and now you're trying to nickel and dime me to death on a deal? You're only in that chair because I let you have it. I stepped away, paving the way for you to take it all."

"You mean that you cowered from your responsibilities? That's what you did. Being the oldest, you were the so-called heir to this throne, but you couldn't rise to the challenge."

"It wasn't cowering. I just never wanted to be a part of manufacturing death."

"Well, I suppose we have different perspectives on that topic. So, I'll give you the three hundred I originally offered."

Dillon would have given the damn thing away, but he didn't want to seem eager to snatch the money and run.

"Fine. I really don't give a shit one way or another."

Colin pulled his brown leather billfold from his inside suit pocket and tossed three bills across the desk.

"If you don't mind, I need you to write a receipt that I sold you my inheritance. For tax reasons, of course."

"Certainly," Colin said and pulled a paper tablet to him, sporting the company logo on the header. As he wrote, he said, "It's not too late, Dillon. You could still come on board here."

"And work with you all day? No thanks."

"No, definitely not. We have a new opening in the custodial department," he said and smiled as he scribbled a receipt and signed it. He tore it loose and slid the paper next to the money.

"Like I said, you've always been a funny guy. Enjoy your mystery box. I'm sure it's a laugh riot, just like Dad wanted."

Dillon couldn't help grinning as he passed the secretary and stepped into the elevator. He finally felt free. It had only been two days, but those days had been a maddening hell.

To celebrate, Dillon made a double pour of scotch. Sitting at the kitchen table, he really wondered if it was a curse. Would Colin suffer at the hands of a man who died over a century ago? Would he see a victim's head come apart as they ran toward him? Maybe as they looked to him for help, pleading for the living to do something, because even in death, they couldn't seem to get away from the madman.

A floorboard creaked a few feet behind him.

Dillon set his drink down, took a hard breath as he looked up. He didn't want to look back, because only dread was found back there.

Instead, he looked down to grab his drink again. That's when he saw it. Through the bottom of the glass and the amber alcohol, the picture was magnified.

Ol' George had come back the instant he'd looked away. With the magnification of the glass, it almost looked like the long-ago dead man was crawling out of his frame, because now his hands were visible. His curly hair was beyond wild, sticking out in tufts every which way. That disturbing smile with all those pointed razor teeth had grown wider, impossibly wide. His fingers had transformed into claws, pulling him through the portrait's frame. He looked more and more like that child gobbling, sewer clown from the Stephen King novel. This time the bloody thumbprint had returned next to the ex-president. It pushed itself from where it had absorbed into the bill days before. Now it fought its way back to the surface, wet and fresh, as if two days of being exposed to the air hadn't happened at all. It was a statement. An exclamation saying, hey, buddy, we belong together now. We even made a blood oath on the deal. You're not getting rid of me so easily. We've got a lot of delicious memories to make.

A pistol cocked behind him.

Dillon clamped his eyes shut and waited to be shot.

Again.

Roadside Crosses

"My psychiatrist said I need to do this. She claims it's a method of self-healing or some such bullshit. I'm not really sure I believe all that, but I'm willing to try," the man said and gestured like a wheel turning, a way of moving on.

"Excuse me?" Mason Billows asked around a mouthful of egg and sausage biscuit.

He looked across the park bench at the lean stranger who settled down at the other end. He figured the man was one of those people often roaming the park, ranting to themselves about government conspiracies while rummaging through trash containers.

"You must have me confused with someone else," Mason said.

Someone who might give a shit, Mason thought.

"I've selected you. Most people these days turn a blind eye to the troubles of the world, especially when it's right in their face. They fear that getting involved takes up too much of their precious time. People don't realize how the opportunity to right the unjust actions in the world is within their reach. Everyone can do something. Are you one of the many who will walk away when you can stop it? I'll leave it up to you to decide," the man said.

He placed a folded piece of paper on the bench and slid it between them.

Mason looked at the paper and then at the man and back to the paper.

"What's that for?"

"It's a way to stop it. It's not exactly what my psychiatrist had in mind, but it's what I came up with."

The man stood then. With no more words to share, he strolled down the park path, watching a man play catch with his golden retriever.

He looked like a man now unburdened of all his worries, leaving them upon another man to endure.

Mason stared at the paper after the park woods consumed the man. The wind fluttered the paper's edge, and Mason seized it before it took flight. He pressed the remains of the biscuit into his mouth and wiped greasy fingers on his jacket. With both hands, he unfolded the paper, and instantly prepared to release it if he saw something he didn't like.

Mason's eyebrows scrunched in. Written on a single line was a series of numbers. He turned the page over to find it blank.

"What the hell am I supposed to do with this?" he asked the nearly empty park.

It didn't take Mason long to figure it out. In fact, after he left the park, he had jammed the paper in his pocket and forgotten about it until arriving home from work and emptying all his pockets onto the entryway table.

After picking up the paper and unfolding it, the numbers were obvious. GPS coordinates. He had never looked up locations before, but had seen countless television shows and movies where such numbers led detectives to some sort of clue.

After a quick app download, he entered the numbers. The app indicator showed a rural road twenty-five miles southwest of Atlanta.

"Why the hell are you giving me a location way out there?" Mason asked his empty house.

Even though his mind pushed for understanding and an almost need to drive to the location, he dropped the slip of paper into the waste bin.

After an hour, Mason leaned back in his office chair, causing half a dozen vertebrae to crackle. The monitor had numbed his eyes and mind. He needed something else to focus on. He needed to step away from his home office for a while and get some air.

He opened his phone and the GPS app. The coordinates were still there, and a blue button declaring directions was just a tap away.

"This is probably a bad idea, but for the love of mercy, I need to get out of here for a while."

Mason rolled up the garage, slid into the sedan, and reversed into the street. As always, traffic was a shit-show. Half of all drivers fell into the mind-set of self-centered assholes whose daily errands superseded traffic red lights and common courtesy among other drivers. Mason kept his irritation pinned down. He knew that letting those assholes push him into anger meant they won the road battle.

Hitting the suburbs brought with it a decrease in traffic and stress. Vehicles soon became scarce as Mason slid onto country roads. He periodically checked the guide to see how close he was to his destination.

When his cell chirped, announcing his arrival, he pulled onto the grassy shoulder, shifted into park, and cut the motor.

In the near silence, other than the ticking of an engine cooling, Mason saw and heard nothing. No dogs barked. No music came from a nearby house. Nothing.

He pulled the lever, opened the door, and stepped out. The peacefulness of the landscape instantly embraced him. He had always dreamed of country living and the desire to step away from the madness of city life. Such aspirations weren't within reach at this time until the corporate ladder offered the next rung for him to step up and grab a more impressive salary.

He leaned against the front fender and studied the surrounding area. Tree branches bent slightly with the breeze, and blades of grass followed suit.

Mason couldn't figure out his purpose here. It didn't take much thought before he realized the park stranger had sent him on a wild-goose chase. He'd fallen victim to another man's cruel prank.

Moving to the driver's door, he paused when he saw something. A roadside cross.

He, of course, knew the heartfelt gesture the cross represented. A loved one had lost their life on this road by one tragedy or another.

Mason went down the gradual slope of the ditch. Stopping beside the cross, he studied each side. Neither side held any writings to indicate who had lost their life along this road. It was a simple wooden cross painted white.

What struck Mason as odd was that someone had disturbed the dirt in front of the cross. Not just disturbed, but completely dug up and replaced. It was soft under his fingers.

His heart did a chaotic gallop as he looked over the area. It was just large enough to conceal a full-sized person.

Using his cupped hands as makeshift shovels, Mason pulled dirt toward him, casting it between his legs in a frantic search to find what he hoped wasn't really there.

"Please don't be here. Please don't be here," Mason said with each heft of removed dirt.

As he began believing this really was a sick joke played by a deranged man, his fingers scraped against something. He instantly drew back, as if stung by a scorpion.

There was a shape just under that final layer of dirt, and it was very much the shape of a face. Despite this, he clung to the belief that it was a cruel prank, that a real human was not buried there, but instead a department store mannequin.

With delicate fingers, he swiped away the remaining dirt.

It was a man. Human in all aspects of the word. Falling back into a sitting position, Mason felt defeated that he had somehow not acted fast enough to save this man's life. As his initial lack of involvement went, he couldn't shake the feeling this person's death was a single step in a marathon race.

Mason saw the edge of something poking out from between the man's lips. He began reaching for it, then pulled his hand back. He knew that handling anything at a crime scene was a felony, possibly giving him the chance to enjoy the amenities of state prison life.

Mason pinched it and pulled it free before overthinking the situation he'd placed himself in. The paper was folded three times. Keeping his fingers along the very edge, he unfolded it.

You must hurry. I don't believe I can hold it off much longer. Darkness draws near, and the beast inside is awakening. You have to stop me. Please.

Written below was another set of coordinates.

"This is goddamn insane."

Mason dug into his front pocket and pulled out his cell. After pressing 911, he stopped before connecting the call.

They'll blame me. They'll believe I'm the one who killed the man and placed him in a shallow grave, even if I'm the one who brought them to the site. They'll accuse and interrogate until they're blue in the face. Despite what I protest, they'll hold me because I'm their only suspect. He'll kill again soon. Or he already has.

Mason opened the GPS location app and punched in the numbers. The location was six miles away, leading him farther from the city and immediate help if needed. He briefly thought of shooting off a quick call to tell the police he'd found a body, but he had no knowledge of how to make his phone number invisible to any kind of caller ID. There was no way to make an anonymous phone call at this time. As the note said, he had to hurry. He was in a time crunch now.

Mason saw the roadside cross from a hundred yards away, painted bright white like the other one. What was most noticeable was that someone had already filled the grave.

He looked at the dashboard clock. 6:47. Dusk was beating away the sunlight, showing a promise of full dark coming soon.

Mason didn't fully understand what the man meant by, the darkness was coming, and the beast coming with it. But he thought he knew. It was a time warning. When dark fell, the man would unleash the insanity and kill again.

The man in the first grave had been dead at least a full day. Maybe two. It was only guesswork because he was far from the expertise of a medical examiner.

Mason's car came to a sliding stop along the ditch. With tentative steps, he approached another shallow grave.

Looking down at both ends of the road, he saw no cars approaching.

He let his knees buckle, dropping into a crouched position on top of the grave. This time his digging was less frantic, and more meticulous, as if unearthing dinosaur bones.

It was a woman this time. He found her curly auburn hair before he brushed the dirt from her face. She had been beautiful just before a man with death on his mind had found her.

Mason wondered if the man and woman were married. He knew it didn't matter.

It was there, just as the other one had been. Slightly protruding from her lips was a folded paper, and he damn well knew what was on it. A plead for him to stop the madness and the coordinates to another grave.

"I can't do anything for you right now. I'm so sorry," he told the woman who was now somewhere else in the universe, far beyond his voice.

Mason pushed himself up. Leaving the woman behind, he typed in the new coordinates and fell into the driver's seat. Kicking the engine to life, he peeled off the gravel shoulder towards his next destination.

"What am I going to find when I get there? Huh? Another body in a grave if the light is completely gone? Or you standing there with another victim if I arrive on time? You sick son of a bitch!"

Mason had no answers and really no solution. He just had to get there before dark. His foot went down harder on the accelerator, the sedan ate up the road the best it could with its economy engine.

He looked at his phone mounted on the dash. The blue dot of his vehicle seemed too far away from the red dot of his destination. Mile by mile, the darkness was more pronounced.

When the blue dot covered the red dot, Mason slammed the vehicle into park and quickly pushed himself out of the vehicle. Through the trees, he couldn't detect even a faint glow of the sun. He moved to the right side of the road, the same place the other graves had been. He turned the flashlight on his cell. The light gave him visibility at his feet as he moved down the slight embankment, but not much beyond that.

"I'm here. I'm here. Let me help you. We can figure this out without more people dying. Please."

Mason made a slow circle, trying to find the victim or the predator in the roadside shadows.

Mason's knees buckled as the exhaustion finally took hold. The horror of the evening had just been too much to endure. Still shining the light around, he found no white cross, and no freshly dug grave. What he saw in the white light was a pair of footprints in the dirt. Footprints facing him. Someone had been standing there moments before his arrival, waiting.

An engine came to life just down the block. Headlights came to life, too.

Mason squinted and held his hand up to help shield the blinding lights.

He could hear the roar of a motivated vehicle barreling down on him. As the vehicle came toward the shoulder and down the embankment, he knew who was behind the wheel.

Mason had been too goddamn late. The man had waited in this spot until full dark, but Mason failed in the task of stopping him.

He couldn't get his tired legs to get him up as the truck hit the bottom of the ditch.

He knew, oh God, how he knew, before the sun rose there would be a white roadside cross right here beside another shallow grave. And during the morning hours, the stranger would find another poor soul to play a demented game.

Such Games We'll Play

The box was sitting at the end of the driveway. Lucy almost ran the damn thing over as she turned off the gravel road and onto the concrete. Her eyes were gazing across the long front yard, anticipating changing out of her work clothes and tackling some stress-relieving gardening.

She caught sight of it as the tires hit the driveway.

Instantly stomping the brakes, Lucy reversed so she could get a good look at what was left in the way. It wasn't a delivery-type box that some carrier was too lazy to walk the distance to the front door. It was about the size of a jewelry box. Small enough that it nearly got crushed.

Lucy shifted into park and stepped out. She couldn't get herself to pick it up right away. The situation was far too bizarre to just accept it and retrieve the box without a second thought.

Stepping up to it, Lucy saw it was wooden, meticulously made. The box itself was light colored, maybe birch, but the design had another aspect to it. It was wrapped with dark wooden bands on all four sides and topped with a wooden bow. A completely wrapped wooden present, bow and all.

Lucy nudged it with her left foot, sliding it several inches, and was not really sure if it would do something unexpected like explode or have a snake spring from it. It did nothing at all except beckon to be picked up. She gave in then, deciding it was a simple prank, probably by Trevor, attempting to freak her out over nothing at all. It was lighter than she had expected. An artisan had intricately carved a bow on top, made from a single piece of wood.

The dark wood of the bow and bands was where all the weight was. Likely made of mahogany, she figured.

"Beautiful," she said, and she turned it over, inspecting all sides.

She found no seams, nor a way to open the lid easily and see what hid inside.

Lucy heard the gravel of the road popping under tires as one of only a few neighbors had also come home from work. She recognized the red car as it came to a stop behind her.

The window went down, and Megan Jefferson from two houses up poked her head out.

"Everything all right, Lucy? Are you broken down or something?"

Lucy went to the open window and said, "No, I suppose everything is fine. I came home and found this sitting at the end of the drive. I nearly ran it over."

Megan held out her hand, and Lucy placed the box in it.

"Crazy," she said as she inspected the box with wonder. "It's pretty. Does it open?"

"Not that I can tell."

"So, do you figure someone left it there, or it fell off the back of a trailer or out the back of the garbage truck?"

"Trash pickup isn't until tomorrow, so I don't think it's that. I think someone placed it there. It was in the middle of the driveway and sitting upright."

"So weird and completely creepy. I'd toss it in the trash if I were you. Or maybe bludgeon it with a hammer to see what's inside. If there is anything inside." Megan shook it, and hearing nothing moving, she handed it back to Lucy.

"I'm not sure what I'll do with it. I don't think I'll destroy it, though."

"Anyway, if you're intending to go into the city this weekend, just let me know. We'll make a day of it."

"Sounds good. I'll see you later," Lucy said and slid back into her car.

She placed the box on the passenger seat and rolled up the long driveway. She couldn't help glancing at it, as if a jack-in-the-box clown would suddenly spring out.

After dinner, Lucy went down the hall to head upstairs to shower when she saw the box on the entry room table where she'd left it. It took only a second for her to notice something different. A small panel had slid out of place. One of the side pieces between the dark colored wooden bands had moved itself out of position. Bending low, Lucy inspected the piece. Now more than ever, she didn't want to touch the thing. The object had gone from slightly weird to creepy bizarre in no time.

She took a picture of the box and sent it to Trevor.

He called a minute later, and said, "What's with the picture?"

"Did you leave this in my driveway?"

"No. Seriously? Why would I leave something in your driveway?"

"I don't know. I thought it might be a stupid prank or something. Men do stupid shit like this all the time."

"They do? How many people have left wooden boxes in your driveway?"

"You know what I meant. I couldn't figure out how to open it earlier. Then it started opening itself."

"What do you mean it's opening itself?"

"One of the side panels slid out of place when I was in the other room."

"Maybe it's loose."

"It slid out sideways. Gravity can't pull things side-ways. Can it?"

"Is that a serious question?"

"Nevermind."

"So, do you see anything else that might move?"

"What do you mean?"

"Like a puzzle box. One thing slides out of the way, allowing something else to move."

"I haven't touched it since it moved itself. Anyway, I've got to shower. I'm dirty from the garden."

"Do you want some shower company? I could get to those hard-to-reach places."

"Wow. Right from the creepy box and into full pervert mode. That's got to be record time for you."

"I've never had a creepy box conversation before. Be-sides, my full pervert mode is always at front and center."

"Well, that's true. I'll talk to you tomorrow."

Lucy disconnected. With cautious hands, she picked up the box. She tried moving one of the adjoining pieces like Trevor said, but couldn't even get them to wiggle.

Going upstairs, Lucy decided on a long bath instead of a shower. She figured she could study the mystery box while the lavender and warm water eased muscles.

"What are you?" she asked the box while sliding deep into the bubbles and felt every part of her body relish the sensation.

Her fingers poked and prodded edges, corners, and the flat sides, resulting in no movement. As she reached out to place it on the small table beside the tub, her palm nudged the bow. It rotated slightly. Quickly pulling it back to her, she finished the rotation of the bow a full ninety degrees. Another panel popped open on the opposite side of the first. Just as Trevor had said, the thing was a puzzle box.

But who and why would someone leave it in her driveway? What could possibly be the grand plan?

The next trigger was behind the now exposed area of the previous move. She pressed the inside panel and was rewarded with a *click*.

As if on some sort of hidden springs, the four wood bands previously strapped across each side lifted upward slowly. Next, the top released slightly, enough so that she could work a fingernail into the gap. She hadn't even been able to see a seam earlier, but now she couldn't believe she had missed it. The lid didn't give up the fight easily. It resisted as if a vacuum seal kept the lid pulled in tight.

When the lid finally gave, something dark, about the size of a mouse, sprang out. Her reaction was instantaneous. At about the same time the thing hit the water with a *plop*, Lucy had flung the box, and heaved her body from the slickness of the tub's porcelain surface. Her feet couldn't find immediate purchase, and her body went down hard into the water. Her left knee cracked against the bottom of the tub, shooting a lightning bolt of pain through her entire leg. Gallons of water sloshed over the tub's rim and onto the tile floor. Lucy followed the wave of water, landing with a breath-stealing impact. Her legs piston against the slick tiles, trying to push herself away from whatever had gone into the tub with her.

Lucy pulled the bath towel from the rack. Covering herself up, she leaned against the wall, watching with dreaded anticipation that something would jettison from the water, and slither across the tile toward her.

As the moment failed to get more chaotic, her heart slightly calmed.

It's just a mouse, Lucy. Just a stupid mouse. A mouse that somehow survived, who knows how long, in a sealed box without air. Go look in the tub. You'll see the damn rodent swimming in the bubbles, trying to figure a way out before it drowns.

She did look then. With cautious movements, she lifted herself from the floor. She leaned forward with ready muscles, having every intention of bolting through the door if she saw something unnatural poke out of the water. It was impossible to see anything in the mountains of bubbles. She knew she needed to yank the drain plug, releasing all the water so she could capture the thing and get it out of the house before it got somewhere inside where she couldn't get to.

The submerged chain to the drain stopper made her uncomfortable about putting her hand into the water to retrieve it.

Lucy grabbed the toilet brush from its holder. Working the brush around the beaded chain, she had enough grip, and the plug came free of the drain. Something slashed across the surface, knowing its watery domain was quickly reducing. The bubbles had finally given up. As the water was several inches from being completely gone, she tried to see what it was.

It held no certain shape, because its body constantly shifted from long to short, and wide to thin. To Lucy, it almost looked like a spilled cup of oil that refused to even moderately disperse in the water.

It hit the shallow end, where the tub swooped up into a backrest. A tail, looking very much like the flat tail of an eel, formed. Even with the new appendage, the thing could go no further with the thrusts. It swiveled and followed the water until the drain drank it in.

"Oh, thank Christ," Lucy said and exhaled pent-up stress.

To make sure the thing couldn't work its way back up the pipe, she ran scalding water for ten minutes, making sure the thing was forced through the pipework and pushed farther from her home. Then Lucy worked the drain plug back in, praying she'd never see it again.

Lucy knew she needed to eat something, but her nerves were still a wreck. Instead, she popped the cork of a bottle of red wine. The puzzle box sat next to the half-empty bottle of alcohol. She continued to study it even though the nasty secret was revealed. She needed answers about where it came from and why. The inside held no explanation. There wasn't even any residue from whatever that unholy thing was.

Lucy flipped through the neglected stack of mail. It was the same weekly crap, except three letters from the same address were something new. She worked a finger under the flap and ripped the envelope open.

Feeling stuck? I pay top dollar for houses in your community! Call for a fast turnaround and get yourself out from under a suffocating mortgage. You sign and I hand over cash. $$$

The second and third envelopes had much of the same, only worded differently to help build the enthusiasm of potential sellers.

"Wow. A persistent prick, aren't ya?"

Most of the junk mail found its way to the trash, and the bills and magazines were dropped on her desk for later attention.

It was the groan inside the walls that woke her. Lying in the dark, Lucy stared at the ceiling, trying to determine if the sound was one from a now fleeting dream, or actually something in her house.

The noise came again. It was the sound of indigestion rumbling through the guts of a giant. Only the giant was her home.

Lucy sat up. Flicking the bedside lamp on, she listened for more sounds. The groan came from the wall behind her bed. She knew that within the walls were the water and drainage lines for the upstairs bathroom.

Her thoughts went to the black slug the size of her fist. The terror of that goddamn thing hadn't left her thoughts all day, not even in dreams. Such a thing existing made her believe that she'd imagined the entire ordeal. A sleep-deprived and overworked mind could play such games with someone's mental stability. No, she knew it wasn't possible for her to hallucinate such a vivid time frame of her evening. Even Megan had handled the box, shaken it even, and questioned Lucy about it.

She knew the box was on the dining room table, open and empty.

The master suite bathroom gurgled. Lucy instantly turned her sight to the left. A night-light glowed above the sink. She was sure a horror movie moment was about to reveal itself. Something dark and sinister rising from the sink basin. Reaching to destroy the nightlight, it would then finish transforming under the cover of darkness.

Lucy cursed herself for letting her imagination run wild.

The lamp beside her could only push light so far. Working her way out of the sheets, she slid her feet into the slippers at the foot of the bed. Reaching through the door, Lucy flicked the light switch, chasing away all the shadows. The sink held no surprises other than droplets of water still clinging to the porcelain.

The sound of a watery belch came from behind her. Brown liquid spewed from the tub drain in a small geyser.

Something moved within that dark liquid, but what it was Lucy couldn't tell. It went back down, and the nasty water went with it. The pipework began to groan again. Something bubbled in the toilet.

Lucy used her slipper to push up the lid. She fully expected an octopus-like monster to come shooting out, tentacles spread and attaching to her face and then sucking the life from her body.

Bubbles pushed out from the air trap below the tank. Black muck instantly followed, looking very much like the thing from the box. It moved in swirls around the bowl and then began pushing out from the water, reaching for the toilet rim.

Lucy screamed then. A scream louder than she'd ever managed before. The thing reacted, pulling back in what almost appeared as fright. She gripped the lid and slammed it shut, nearly fracturing the porcelain bowl. She heard it swimming around. With dread realization, Lucy noticed the gap between the seat and the rim. The thing wasn't solid, but more like jelly, and she knew it could easily squeeze through that space.

Lucy slammed her palm on the lid, and with her other hand stabbed the flush handle and held it down. The water gurgled as the tank dropped its supply into the bowl. As the waterline hissed to a stop, Lucy listened for movement. Little by little, she lifted the lid. Her nerve-racked mind was convinced that she was about to die, that the thing would spring out, attach to her head, and suck her brain right out of her skull. She almost convinced herself to flee through the front door.

The goddamn thing was gone, flushed away with all the water. But she knew it hadn't gone far. After all, she thought the hot water rushing down the tub drain had pushed it all the way to the main sewer lines on the street. It had gone then, but not far.

She knew the universe was laughing at her now, because the intense pressure on her bladder made itself known.

Lucy knew there was no way whatsoever she was going to plant her ass on a toilet seat where some alien-like creature had just been swimming laps in the bowl. She couldn't even convince herself to step into the tub and let her urine trickle down the drain. She didn't know what the creature was, what it wanted, or how dangerous it might be.

Hurriedly, she went out the back door, making sure none of the neighbors' lights were on, and squatted against the fence.

When the relief was done, Lucy went back inside. She listened to the house, and more importantly, to the pipes within the house, but all had thankfully gone quiet. Despite the midnight terror, Lucy quickly fell off into unsettled dreams.

The plumber stared at her stupidly, trying to grasp what the woman rattled out.

"No, ma'am, I've never heard of a black slug living in someone's drainage lines. You said someone gave this thing to you in a box? That it got down the drain and has been tormenting you since?"

The man struggled to hold back a smile, but couldn't stop his eyes from the action.

"I know you think I'm crazy, but this thing won't go away. I don't know who gave it to me or why."

"Well, I ran a scope down every drain I can access. Other than a mild buildup, which is typical of a house this age, it isn't a concern. I didn't see anything living or even dead in there."

"So, it's gone?"

"Well, whatever it is you say you saw, I never caught it on camera. So, it must be gone."

Lucy knew how much the man was laughing on the inside. She knew full well he'd be sharing this encounter with all his plumber buddies, laughing it up about the lady on Hilltop Street and her devil black sewer slug.

"Well, okay then. Should anything else pop up, just give me a call."

Lucy thanked him and saw him out the door.

Lucy heard the toilet gurgle at two in the morning. Her arm snaked out from the blanket, gripped the lamp switch, and brought light to the room. Half-heartedly, she propped her head up and looked at the bathroom. Water flowed from the seat gaps, sloshing onto the floor, making its way from tile to bedroom carpet.

Lucy peeled off the covers. Quickly, she snapped the bathroom light on and seized the bath towels, dropping them at the base of the toilet.

She knew it could be a mistake, but she hit the lever. Instead of more water flooding out, it forced the bowl water back down the line.

"Go away. Please. Just leave me the hell alone." Lucy whispered and placed her forehead on the lid.

It didn't go away. In fact, the thing started speaking to her.

Two nights later, as Lucy washed the dinner dishes, a sound came from the kitchen sink drain. She didn't notice it at first over the running water. When she turned off the faucet, the chirping sound was far more noticeable, echoing through the pipes.

She leaned over the sink and peered into the dark drain. It sounded very much like a baby bird hungrily calling after its mother.

"You have got to be shitting me," Lucy called back at it.

An entire bottle of foaming drain cleaner went in. Lucy prayed the chemical reaction would either kill the thing or force it to flee from her house.

Sitting at the dining room table, Lucy sorted through the stack of mail. There were four more letters from some real estate agency willing to wheel and deal her out of a home.

It wasn't the sound of gushing water or the sound of chirping pipes. What woke Lucy was the sensation of a wet tongue slicking its way across her right cheek.

She catapulted from the bed, tangled in the sheets, as she tried blindly running across the room. Ignoring the wrap of blankets embracing her legs, Lucy's focus was on slapping her palm across her face, trying to dislodge whatever the hell was crawling on her. Her body went over like a felled tree. Going down, the left side of her upper ribcage was sucker-punched by the edge of the vanity against the wall.

Her hand came across it then, and instantly she knew what the hell had attached itself to her. The ungodly black goo had found its way from one of the drains, slimed its way across her bedroom, and worked its way up the bed and onto her face.

It came off her skin with a sucker-pop sound and sailed across the span of the bedroom. Rolling across the carpet like black jelly, it righted itself, as if there was a right side of it, and quickly began slinking back to the bathroom.

Lucy knew it aimed for the safety of a drain where she was unable to capture it. Quickly, she kicked loose the blankets tethered around her legs and scrambled on hands and knees after it. She seized a slipper from the foot of the bed and pushed herself harder as the thing found the tile of the bathroom.

Lucy reached all the way out and brought the rubber sole of the slipper down on the mass. Either from surprise or pain, it chirped.

It almost broke Lucy's heart to hear it, but the part of her, completely fed up with the harassment this thing caused, knew it needed to be destroyed.

It exploded out from beneath the sole. But like the tendrils of some alien race resistant to giving up life, those broken globs stretched out and then pulled itself back together.

It clambered up the side of the tub, suckered appendages forming, pulling it faster, determined to find safe harbor.

Lucy reached with her bare hand, longing to snag the thing before it found freedom. It shot like a rubber band from the tub's edge to the drain. Then it was gone, but not without offering a defiant whistle-chirp at its departure.

Sleep had become impossible. Even normal home activities after work became a state of constant paranoia that at any second, a large black slug would be flying through the air right at her.

She looked for it in every glass when she went to get water. She looked for it in the pot when she began making dinner. She even looked for it in her shoes before heading out for a drive because her nerves needed a break from the insanity. In the bathroom mirror, she saw a face hardly recognizable. Her bronze complexion had gone pallid. Her eyes were sunken and bagged skin now beneath them. The stress had taken a toll on her hair, too. It began falling out, as she'd noticed more collecting in the hairbrush.

With frustration, Lucy wiped away the tears. Anger broke loose then as she swiped her arm across the dining room table. Her dinner plate and pile of unsorted mail went against the wall and to the floor.

The thing whistled-chirped from the kitchen drain, almost like a taunt.

"Shut up! Shut up!" Lucy screamed until her voice went hoarse.

With a wet rag, she began mopping up the spilled remains of her dinner, now on the floor.

It was there. It called to her with simple words. They were words of sincerity and comfort. Words to carry her away from this madness.

Feeling stuck? I offer an easy way out! Lightning-fast service that can break you away from the burden of your home. I can close the sale in just two weeks! Extremely fair prices offered. Call the number below and break free from your restraints.

Lucy began giggling then. A maddening laugh because a perfect answer gave her exactly what she needed.

She stood, leaned over the sink and continued the laugh, letting the thing know that it had tried its best, but she couldn't be beaten. There's always a way out of every situation.

"I told you this one was a perfect deal! Look at those ten-foot ceilings. The woodwork is incredibly impressive.

So ornate. So far, I've only seen a few details that need changing. Basically, my out-of-pocket expenses will probably be the lowest I've ever had. With the sale price plus closing costs, I'll profit at least one-hundred thousand on a quick turnaround."

"Very impressive. She was an eager seller."

Wyatt Stevens looked at his new protégé and smiled.

"Well, there are always methods to get uninterested people to suddenly find a desire to sell."

Wyatt went to the kitchen sink. Placing his briefcase on the counter, he flipped the latches open and removed a wooden box. After a series of sliding panels, he removed the lid and set it down.

"A puzzle box? What for?"

Wyatt smiled as he removed a small, sealed bag from his suit pocket. The kid watched him shake a few tiny flowers from the bag into his palm. Next, he lowered his hand to the bottom of the sink and waited.

"Back in 2017, I had checked off one of the items on my bucket list. I'd always wanted to tour the Amazon River and experience the wonder of raw nature. It was absolutely the greatest experience of my life."

The kid heard something whistling and chirping in the drain.

"The guide I'd hired had gotten us a bit lost. There's so many off-shoots from the main part of the river that even guides can get lost from time to time. Well, it was our third morning on the river when we woke up with stuff crawling all over us."

Something black, long and thin, stretched out from the edge of the drain. To the kid, it looked like a thick black hair that suddenly formed an eyeball at its end.

Cautiously, the rest of the mass worked itself over the edge. The kid watched it sit there, as if contemplating whether he were a threat.

"At first, we thought they were leeches. They must have squirmed up the side of the boat while we slept. But when we went to pull them off, well, they didn't come off so easily. They stretched like, oh, I don't know, like tar, I guess. We all went into a panic, trying to tear them off. I got a few of them detached and realized they weren't feeding on us at all. I later discovered that they're cold-blooded creatures. All they wanted was our body heat during the night. Kind of like a Texan finding a rattlesnake curled up with him in his bedroll. Of course, these creatures present no harm at all. I just couldn't help myself. I had to bring one home with me."

The kid watched the black slime begin moving toward Wyatt's hand, and the flowers he held.

"These flowers are also from the Amazon. I import them to feed my little friend. It's one of the few things they eat."

As the kid watched the slug-thing worm onto Wyatt's hand, he asked, "So, how does something like that scare someone so much? I mean, the previous owner walked away so quickly she left a lot of money on the table. She could have gotten far more for the house from someone else before handing it over to you."

"That's the beauty of it. People fear what they don't understand. My little friend here is an unknown factor in life. They don't know what it is, and they don't want to. They just want it to go away. But when my friend gets settled in a new place, he just doesn't want to leave."

"I don't get how that drives them out."

"He's a water fanatic. He moves through the pipes with a ruckus you wouldn't believe. It's hard to understand how something so small makes such a big noise. I think it's like a form of playing. I don't know for sure."

Wyatt tried working the thing from his palm by using his thumb to push it back into its box. It resisted, clearly enjoying the warmth of Wyatt's hand. But the box contained a small heap of edible flowers, which was enough to persuade the thing to go back into confinement.

The kid said, "It's a heck of a way to make a living."

Wyatt worked the lid back on the box, then slid the panels back in place until it was an ordinary-looking birch box with a wooden bow.

"There we go. Well, now, there's a property I've had my eye on that's about a half mile from here. Let me show you how this game begins."

Orphan Kind

It was the thump-slide coming from down the hall that made the headmaster, Henry Tillman, roll his eyes.

"Let me assure you that Melody is a very sweet girl. She's very bright as well. She's a bit melodramatic at times, but we believe it's only an attention-seeking method. We honestly think you'll find an attachment with her right away."

The Fredricks turned toward the door, more expecting a mountain of a child by the sound of the ruckus she made.

Thump-slide. Thump-slide.

When the girl stepped in the doorway, the Fredricks shifted their sights down. She wasn't a large girl at all, but barely reached four feet tall. Their smiles immediately formed as the girl watched the new couple, perhaps anticipating what kind of people they were underneath.

"Hello there," she told them in a sweet voice that instantly snagged the heartstrings of any person longing to bring a child into their home.

Melody started forward, maneuvering her braced leg off to the side and then swinging it forward until it clunked against the hardwood floor, followed by the sound of her suitcase dragging behind her.

"I know what you're thinking. A crippled girl like this has no place in the modern world. What good would a girl like this serve in an ordinary family setting? It seems like a disabled child would be more of a hindrance than a benefit in any capacity. I'm unwanted, unloved, and unfixable.

There's no reason to feel bad about it. Things are just what they are. No one is to blame. So, thank you very much for coming. It was a pleasure to meet you."

With that, they watched the girl turn and thump-slide her way out the door and back down the hallway.

"Oh my God," Susan Fredricks said. "I absolutely love her!"

"I was thinking the exact same thing," Charles Fredricks said and took his wife's hand as they both stared at the empty doorway.

"That's wonderful! As I've said, she's a sweet girl who desperately needs a loving family," Mr. Tillman said as he gathered the adoption papers.

"May we ask what happened to her? Why does she need a leg brace?" Mrs. Fredricks asked.

"Unfortunately, Melody was involved in a severe car accident two years ago. Both her parents died as a result. The accident crushed Melody's leg, and it never healed properly. You should also know that there was some head trauma. Now please don't misunderstand. Melody has no mental deficiencies due to the accident. The only physical difficulty is with her leg. I'd say, all-in-all, Melody came out of that terrible ordeal with a special gift. You'll see."

Mrs. Fredricks said, "Your bedroom is right upstairs, directly above our room here on the ground floor. It's certainly large enough to accommodate any interests you might pick up. I'd be happy to take you to the bookstore if you like to read. Or I know this lovely antique shop in town that I'm sure could have a dollhouse, if you'd like something like that. We're very flexible with whatever you may like."

"Um, that's really kind of you, but I don't need anything. You've already opened your home to me, and that's more than I deserve, Mrs. Fredricks."

"Please, call me Susan. And that isn't true. You deserve so much more. You're a bright, beautiful soul who deserves everything you get."

"That's kind of you to say. I'll try to think like that."

Mr. Fredricks said, "Well, we'll let you get settled in your room and let you know when dinner is ready. Susan is cooking a nice pot roast. So, I hope you're hungry."

"I am, Mr. Fredricks."

"Charles."

"Of course. Charles."

"I can get that bag for you."

"No, please. I can manage. I would love for you to treat me as you would any other child. I may have special needs, but I can take care of most anything. That includes chores. I'd like to help out around here as much as I can."

"Well, okay then. I'm sure we could find certain tasks for you to tackle each week," Charles said.

Upstairs, Melody placed her suitcase on the bed and gazed around the room. She thought that they had done well with trying to style the room just as they figured a little girl would adore. But there was something else about it. It had the subtle appearance that the room style often changed. She couldn't put her finger on it, but it seemed as if the Fredricks could easily switch out furniture to accommodate a boy or a girl.

She moved her belongings to the floor and lay on the bed. She admired the comfort it offered and knew how quickly it could put her to sleep.

Lying on her stomach, Melody could see between the slats of the headboard. Someone had carved something in the wall. She slid off the bed, grabbed the top arch of the footboard and pulled. The bed was heavy as she jolted forward and back, trying to force the legs to slide across the carpet.

Melody went to the exposed wall.

Travis was here.

Gina was here.

Oliver was also here.

It's not safe.

You should run.

Melody traced her finger along each groove of every letter. She thought it was sweet that others had found a way to deliver a word of warning. But she didn't need it. She knew she was safe enough. It was impossible for these people to harm her.

"So, may I ask why you decided to adopt?" Melody stabbed a cut of pot roast and slipped it into her mouth.

"Well, Charles and I wanted children, but were never fortunate enough to receive one. We know how many wonderful children there are in the world who need a good home. We decided to open our doors to someone like you."

"I'm the first child you've adopted?"

"Of course. You haven't run into any other children around, have you? Why do you ask?" Susan asked.

"In my room, children have carved their names on the wall. Travis, Gina, and Oliver. They said they've been here."

Charles said, "Really? Written on the wall? I'm not sure how we missed that when we moved in."

"It must be from the children of the previous owners. We've only lived here going on six months," Susan said.

Melody watched them closely and said, "No, Charles, not written, but carved into the wall. You can be honest. If you have adopted before and it just didn't work out and you had to return them, I won't be offended. Sometimes things don't work out. Children can often be disappointments."

The couple smiled at their new daughter, offering kind eyes.

Susan said, "No, we would never return a child. I believe something like that would certainly crush a child's spirit."

"Oh. Okay. So, you've never returned a child. What about burying them in the backyard?"

Susan's fork fell to her plate, causing mashed potatoes to spatter across the table linen.

"I'm only kidding," Melody said, and offered the laugh of an innocent girl who knew no secrets.

After a moment, the Fredricks also laughed, but reserved.

"Whew! For a second there, I thought you knew our darkest secret!" Charles said as he continued laughing.

"I joke around a lot. I meant no harm by it."

Susan touched Melody's forearm and said, "You're safe here."

The carving on the wall said otherwise. *It's not safe.*

"Of course. You're very nice people. Your home is very lovely as well," Melody said as she finished her plate.

Susan said, "I hope you saved room for cherry pie."

A crash downstairs made Melody shoot up in bed. She instantly recognized the sound of breaking glass.

Maneuvering out of bed, Melody didn't bother putting on her leg brace, but instead went right for the bedroom door. Opening it slowly, Melody peered into the dark hallway and watched the descending stairs to the main floor. She half expected to see either one of the Fredricks come upstairs, or perhaps an intruder.

She understood that since the country had recently muscled its way out of the Great Depression, people still took to breaking and entering wealthy neighborhoods, stealing valuables to compensate for years of unemployment.

The top step creaked under Melody's weight. She heard nothing and continued down. Using the banister for support, she reached the bottom step. Under the soft glow of the lamp left on in the living room, she could see something broken lying on the floor in front of the hearth. Moving into the room, she saw that it had been a ceramic statue of some kind.

Crouching low, the best her damaged leg would allow, she grasped the largest piece and moved it closer to her eyes. It was the face of a child with red lips, cheeks lightly brushed pink, and a smile frozen in laughter. On the floor were porcelain painted balloons. Melody looked at the figurine collection sitting on the mantel. It was a park scene with children playing, a carousel, and an ice cream truck. Also, small wooden benches and trees in various shades of fall colors covered the area.

"What have you done?"

Melody whirled around so quickly that her left leg failed to compensate for the sudden action, and her strong right leg couldn't support her wobble. Her knee buckled, and the rest of her body followed down to the wooden floor.

Susan stood in the doorway, hand over mouth, and eyes staring at the destroyed figurine.

"Why? Why would you do such a horrible thing?" she asked. She then crouched beside the shattered pieces.

Susan gently collected the largest pieces, including the one from Melody's hand. She looked over the remains as if disbelieving something so precious could be broken. Perhaps believing the vision was nothing more than a vicious nightmare.

"I was asleep, and I heard something—"

Susan's hand shot out like a whip, catching Melody's cheek, and just as quickly returned to the porcelain fragments.

"My mother gave me this when I was no more than your age. You have no right to destroy my things. Do you believe that it's all right to ruin other people's valuables because you have nothing of your own?"

"No, ma'am. I didn't break it. I found it on the floor."

"Oh, sure! Sure! I suppose it just jumped right off the mantel all by itself! Or maybe there was an earthquake that didn't disturb anything else in the entire house except for this one thing. Is that what happened?"

"No, ma'am. I swear that I was in my room when it broke."

Charles came up behind his wife and gently gripped her arms, easily lifting her to her feet.

He said, "Accidents happen. Let's not do anything regrettable, Susan. It's late. I want you to go back to bed, and I'll clean this up. Tomorrow we might be able to mend this with a little glue and patience."

After Charles had moved his wife back to the bedroom, he returned to where Melody was using her hand to brush the pieces into a pile.

"I didn't break this. Please believe me."

"I do. It's possible Susan broke it by accident. She has issues at night. Sometimes she sleepwalks and bumps into things. She also has what the doctors have called 'night terrors.' I'll clean this up. You should get back to bed."

Susan lay in bed, her body rigid and unable to move. Her eyes moved as far down in their sockets as possible, trying to get a glimpse of whatever had entered the room. No words were able to form, only low vibrating breathing coming from her as the anxiety of the moment fully gripped. Something black shifted beside the door. It nearly blended with the other shadows, but the green eyes gave it away.

The paralysis was more powerful than any of the previous ones. She couldn't turn her head even slightly to see Charles sleeping beside her. The night terror only allowed the movement of her eyes.

It stepped to the left of the door and melted into the wall like a liquid. Moving in slow waves, the thing defied gravity, drifting up the wall to the ceiling. It didn't stop there. Blackness slid across the white ceiling, and the shadow stopped above her.

Susan's chest rose and fell in panic as the voice inside tried to scream her mind awake.

It separated from the plaster of the ceiling, pushing down toward her as a human-like shape formed. The brightness of the eyes intensified as it studied her.

Its mouth finished forming and opened, showing hundreds of teeth like tiny nails.

Susan's eyes watered as the lids failed to close.

Its body stretched until it was nose to nose with her. Its breath was pungent in her face. Its fingers were very much like talons as the left hand reached for her. All fingers closed, except one, and that single nail raked across Susan's cheek, drawing blood.

Melody heard Susan deliver a shrill scream that vibrated throughout the house.

She smiled to herself, knowing the game had begun.

The following evening, Melody watched Susan's shaking hand attempt to deliver spaghetti to her mouth. Half of the noodles shook loose before the fork slid across her lips.

"Susan, what happened to your face?" Melody asked.

Susan's left hand fingered the long scab across her cheek.

Dabbing her mouth with a cloth napkin, Susan said, "I'm not sure. I might have accidentally scratched myself during the night."

"Charles said that you suffer from something called night terrors."

Susan looked from Melody to Charles and back. She said, "That's right. It's something of a complete paralysis when I can't move at all. Sometimes I see things that aren't there."

"It sounds awful."

"That must have been when I scratched myself."

"But how can you scratch yourself if you couldn't move?"

Susan narrowed her eyes in thought.

"Huh. I'm not sure. Maybe I did it after the paralysis ended."

Melody focused on Susan's blue eyes. She could feel the sensation creeping across her brain. Images from photographs she'd been shown by the orphanage's headmaster. Images of innocent children now lost but far from forgotten. She projected those images from her mind to Susan's. Only she put her own fun spin on things.

Susan's fork fell to her plate with a startled clatter, much like the night before. Her sight was transfixed by the children sitting at her dinner table. Children who have defied the impossible by simply being here.

"Oliver?" Susan said so low that her husband barely heard her.

Charles turned to his right, half expecting to see the ghost of a child. Melody's powers failed at projecting visions to multiple people, so Charles saw nothing more than an empty chair.

"What?" he asked his wife.

Susan ignored the question. Instead, she asked a question of her own.

"Are you here to forgive me?"

Oliver shook his head.

"I don't want you here. I banish you from this house!" she screamed the last part and slammed her fists down on the table to emphasize her demand.

Charles seized her wrist, trying to calm her irrational state.

"Stop this. You're frightening Melody."

Another girl, Melody's age, stepped from the kitchen, gently took a roll from the center plate and held it out to Susan.

"Gina?"

Melody shifted her eyes to the far end of the table, where a second boy stood. His grin was impossibly wide as he studied the woman who had once taken on the responsibility of being a mother to three children in desperate need of a home.

The boy named Travis placed his hands on the table. With ease of strength, he raised his body onto the table, placing his sneakers onto the linen. In a crouched position, the boy quickly maneuvered toward the woman in an awkward scramble.

Susan's reaction was immediate. She slapped at Gina's offered roll, finding nothing but air, and then she pitched backward in the chair. Her breath punched out of her as the chair's back collided against the floor.

"For Christ's sake, Susan! What is it?" Charles asked, and he moved to help her up.

"It can't be! You were all disappointments! You can't be here!" Susan screamed as she fought Charles' hands on her.

She kicked at the chair, pushing herself toward the kitchen door. Her legs maneuvered around, getting her turned over. Now on hands and knees, she shuffled toward the back of the house.

Melody laughed at the absurd behavior of a woman desperately trying to escape her own mind. She calmly stood from the table and followed the frantic woman and her confused husband out the back door.

A hard rain had started an hour before the events of dinner took a wicked turn. The downpour didn't faze Susan as she battered the door latch until it gave up and spilled her from the house and onto the rear deck. Looking over her shoulder, three children slowly paced behind her, eyes never drifting from the woman who had wanted to show love, but could only display a dissatisfaction with everything ever offered to her.

In her mind, Melody made all three of them smile, a viciousness about to show discipline to an extreme degree.

"Susan, just stop! You're going to hurt yourself!" Charles called after her as he tried to keep up with her manic shuffle from the house.

Susan began screaming then, words a jumbled mess that Melody couldn't understand. She knew it didn't matter. They were foreign words of fear that only Susan could comprehend.

"You're gonna burn in hell! You're gonna burn in hell!" Melody made the children chant in a playground taunt.

The neighbors' backyard lights began flicking on one by one, each curious about the ruckus next door. With an umbrella opening overhead, an elderly woman stepped onto her porch. "Charles? What on earth is happening over there?"

"I'm very sorry for the disturbance, Mrs. Wilson. Susan seems to be having some sort of episode."

"She'll catch her death in this rain," the old woman said.

"I killed you ungrateful bastards! You can't be here. It isn't possible!" Susan screamed and then toppled down the half-dozen steps onto the saturated lawn. Her body hit with a hard splash.

Melody thought the impact stole her breath, because Susan's mouth worked open and closed, with no words spilling out.

"What did she say? Did she just say she killed someone?" Mrs. Wilson asked as her hand moved to her mouth.

"It's only an episode. She's not even aware of what she's saying," Charles called to the neighbor, but the woman had already disappeared inside.

Melody stood on the threshold, staying out of the rain. Her mental projections have never been this clear before. She even projected rain soaking Susan's hallucination, adding authenticity, further fracturing the woman's mind.

"Burn in hell. Burn in hell," the children continued.

Lifting herself up, Susan made a mad dash for the corner of the property. Collapsing to her knees, her hooked fingers became shovels. Her arms became the driving force to peel the mud from the yard. Charles grabbed for her, trying to stop the insanity.

Her hand came around, balled into a tight fist that brutally hammered Charles' left temple.

Melody watched him spin from the unexpected assault. His knees went weak as unconsciousness washed over him. With a wet slap, Charles sprawled across the yard and lay still.

Susan continued to dig, heaving out handfuls of mud between her legs like an animal.

A face appeared in the shallow grave, and the rain began washing it clean.

"He's here! Oliver is right here! I told you he can't be real!" Susan called out to her unconscious husband.

She looked up, studying the faces of the three children standing before her. Oliver smiled, one of relief, and he faded away in the rain.

She slid to her left, and with wet hair hanging in her face, she began desperately digging again.

"Burn in hell. Burn in hell," the chant continued, although now a slight whisper.

Another face found the storm-cloaked evening. Travis also smiled and disappeared from Susan's mind.

Flashlight beams moved across the side yard. Melody turned her focus and saw two patrolmen come around the house. They paused when the lights found the unconscious man and a woman down on her knees moving earth with her hands.

"Ma'am? I'm going to need you to stop what you're doing," one patrolman said, but his voice was weak in the downpour.

With their hands moving to the pistols at their sides, both uniformed men cautiously approached Susan. When they saw two faces buried in the mud, the pistols came out of their holsters.

"Ma'am, stop moving!"

Susan's fingers peeled away the mud from Gina's face. In turn, Melody released the image of the ten-year-old girl from Susan's mind.

Susan began laughing then, as the haunting vision of three live children left her sight, and only the dead ones remained.

"Sweet Lord in Heaven," one patrolman said.

Melody sat on the living room sofa, trying to give a performance of shock to all the uniformed faces coming and going from the house.

"Sweety, can I get you anything to drink?" one asked.

"No, sir. I'm fine. Are those the other children, Travis, Gina, and Oliver? They wrote their names on my bedroom wall. They said it wasn't safe here."

A woman with graying hair came through the front door. She immediately fixed focus on Melody. She crouched and seized Melody's hand.

"My name is Patricia Mathers. I work for child services and welfare. As I understand it, Mr. and Mrs. Fredricks adopted you just yesterday."

"Yes, ma'am."

"It's okay to be completely honest now. Have either one of them harmed you since bringing you to their home?"

"Um, Mrs. Fredricks got mad and slapped me when one of her porcelain figurines fell off the mantle and broke. But I didn't even touch it. I swear it. I was in bed when I heard it break. I came down and found it in pieces on the ground, but—but she thought—"

Melody accelerated her performance as the tears began flowing. She dropped her head into her hands and rocked back and forth as the sobs intensified.

"Honey, you've done nothing wrong at all. These were apparently very bad people with a very dark secret. I don't even know how they could have adopted three other children who have gone missing, and no one bothered noticing."

"Mrs. Mathers? I think I can shine a light on that. There's a bunch of paperwork I found in the desk drawer. They have papers from three other orphanages across the state. The documents show separate names they've gone under to adopt. Quite a terrible racket they had going on. Adopt kids just to kill them," the officer said, and then quickly looked at Melody, offering a silent apology for his bluntness.

A man in a business suit walked out of the kitchen and said, "Well, I asked Mr. Fredricks lots of questions. Before claiming he wanted a lawyer, he was adamant that he had no idea his wife had actually murdered those children. He said after they adopted, he came home from work each time to find that his wife claimed to have returned the children to their orphanage because they weren't a right fit for this home."

"This should prove otherwise," the patrolman said and handed the stack of papers to the detective.

After a quick read through, the detective smiled and said, "Well, yes. This is a perfect nail in his coffin. His statement completely falls apart with this proof."

A husky voice came from the front door, making them all turn.

"My name is Mr. Tillman. I'm the headmaster of Saint Cecilia's. I recently approved Melody's adoption by Mr. and Mrs. Fredricks. I'm appalled to learn that someone found children's bodies here."

The detective stepped forward and shook Mr. Tillman's hand.

"Unfortunately, that is true."

"I just can't believe it. They appeared to be very honest and caring people."

"You shouldn't blame yourself. They were great deceivers. But they're all finished now before they can harm another child."

"Do you have any more questions for Melody, or can I take her back to the home?"

"Um, well, she's been through a lot. So, it's all right with me if she leaves. I'll come by if I have anymore questions."

"Thank you. Melody? Would you come with me?"

Sliding into the passenger seat, Melody looked at Mr. Tillman.

After starting the engine, he turned and smiled. "That's got to be a record for you. In just one day, you broke them down and even got Mrs. Fredricks to reveal where the bodies were buried. The world is a far better place with those two people spending the rest of their lives behind bars."

"I suppose so. Ever since the accident that damaged my brain, I've gotten better at controlling the images I project onto someone else. I can picture them more vividly now. Mrs. Fredricks really believed those children were there, or, at least, in some sort of ghost form."

"You're building your skills. I believe you'll be able to do incredible things as time goes on. Maybe something even more than you can do now. It's a tragedy about what happened to you, and the loss of your parents, but I believe

in good reasons for certain things happening to the innocent. The Fredricks are the third couple you've exposed.
Their depravity was far greater than that of the previous
ones. That's a hell of an accomplishment. I have to ask you
something, and you can say no, of course, but I received a
phone call earlier today. The headmaster of the Bella Rose
Home for Girls called. He's in desperate need of your gift.
They're having a similar situation with missing orphans in
Boston. You would only have to go for a little while, and
then you could come back here. Is that something that
might interest you?"

"You know that I don't like hearing about missing orphans. Of course I'll help. Besides, it sounds like fun. I've
never been to Boston."

In Suspension

I'd become obsessed. My desire to right a wrong consumed me. The need to exact long overdue justice became my new lifestyle. My presence in Griffin Walker's life was that of a shadow. A shadow kept at a safe distance, anyhow.

I feel no need to go into extreme detail about why I wanted Griffin Walker dead. Actually, the want was long over. Now it was a need to see it through, because of my failing health, and the dread that he could continue to live long after I give up the ghost.

There's not even any reason to tell you my name. By the end of this, I'll be dead, and if God is gracious, Mr. Walker will have joined me on our trek straight into the roaring inferno of Hell.

I've never had confirmation from any sort of doctor that I am, in fact, dying. But I believe it's one of those rare occasions when a person senses it coming. It was a long way off months ago, but I feel it creeping ever so closely now, looming, if I dare say. My obsession was likely the driving force behind my physical decline. It ate at me like a cancer undetectable by any modern medical machine. A psychiatrist would perhaps title it a corruption of an overly focused mind. It was an obsession, plain and simple. Only this obsession was of the physical and mental killing kind.

Griffin Walker killed my wife. Not personally, of course. A man of such wealth and stature in society never dirtied his own hands with such a task. Nor would he risk a life of incarceration by doing the deed himself. His simple order handed down to either one of his bodyguards or a hired hitman was all it took to seal the deal, and seal my wife's coffin, as it were.

I fucked up. My sole attempt to end his miserable life went horribly wrong. It was an attempt brought on by the controlling rage of a grief-stricken mind. There had been no planning, only a need to see his last breath slip from his body in a gurgle of red bubbles. Going at him head-on resulted in Griffin leaving the encounter unscathed. I barely evaded arrest, getting away through the downtown alleys along with his bodyguard's bullet in my right thigh.

I removed the slug myself and used a medical-grade staple gun to close the wound.

During my downtime during the healing process, I formulated plans. Most of them were pathetic, anger-induced visions involving high explosives, or an army of hired guns to help me complete my revenge. I have no knowledge of how to obtain explosives or hire men willing to see my mission through. Something like that would take money and connections. I have neither.

I was an insurance salesman before stress and anxiety debilitated my life. Now I'm nothing. A degenerate living on tax dollars because I'm a broken man.

There's one thing that pushes me from the bedsheets each morning. One question. How can I kill Griffin Walker?

The man lives in the penthouse of the G.L. Stevens high-rise in downtown Chicago. The building is near fortress stature. With highly sophisticated security cameras, access cards to enter through nearly every door inside the building, and guards who monitor the lobby and make routine rounds throughout each floor, making for a nearly impractical intrusion.

I've determined the only way I can get to Griffin is to hit him where he lives. A home breach can catch him off guard. Though it's still unclear to me whether his hired muscle stands beside the penthouse elevator doors, or if they're welcome inside his home during the time they're not guarding him on the street.

As a simple plan began forming, it morphed with serious complications because of the unknown factors involved. I still had no working knowledge of the inside of that building, other than the basics of security. Aside from preposterous scenarios derived from an overabundance of watching action movies, I found my mind melting from the strain. I approached the realization that there was no method I could come up with to fulfill my revenge. My ideas were a farce because I lacked the intellect and skill set to formulate any half-assed plan.

The idea eventually came. It was so stupidly apparent that I'd overlooked the obvious. I was sitting at the kitchen table clipping coupons to lower costs and increase product purchases for my money's worth to get me through the next two weeks.

What came to me was that I needed a job. My hyperactive nerves, a result of a mental breakdown, forced me to leave my insurance job four months ago. My formerly pleasant customer service skills experienced a sharp decline. As my agitation levels rose, the complaints began pouring in. That was when my boss decided I needed a permanent vacation from the company. The severance package was demeaning, especially since the cause of my breakdown was the death of my wife. Basic sympathy has little place in the workforce. Corporations have a single goal to make money and keep the shareholders happy. Personal tragedy is a blemish on the big picture, so they send in the fixer to restore the otherwise majestic portrait. And the conversation with the fixer had landed me in the unemployment line. My situation got fixed through the corporate method.

I had timed the encounter perfectly. After watching the building for upwards of three days, I knew when the shift change was. I caught one of the security guards walking out the front door at the end of his shift. I quickly questioned whether the building might be hiring new guards. He told me that a new position was being posted, and I should inquire about possible employment at the hiring agency. He gave me the name of the agency, and I thanked him.

I went to the other side of the downtown area to get an application turned in right away. I had no idea of my chances based on other possible applicants and that my previous work history held no similar position.

Luck was in my favor. Two days later, the service called me in for an interview. I felt like I'd flown through the one-on-one meeting with flying colors because I told him exactly what he wanted to hear. Two days after that, I was called again and told to report to a medical facility on the west side of town for a drug screening. I didn't even take aspirin after removing a bullet from my leg, so the drug report wouldn't hold alarming issues.

After that, things began rolling faster. An orientation lasting two weeks took place at a facility three blocks from my new job. It's a place where prospective new hires are trained for security guard positions.

I did well. The driving force in my mind was to start the new job and learn all the unanswered questions about the building so that the formulation of a plan could begin.

I started growing a beard when the idea for the job first found its way into my thoughts. Griffin Walker knows my face, because I had tried to kill him seven months before. Whether he made the connection that the woman who was going to testify against him was my wife didn't concern me. After the attempted murder, the authorities never infiltrated my home, or slammed me to the ground, clicked on cuffs and arrested me. I had expected all that. Walker must have simply not placed my face in relation to the woman he ordered to be killed. Perhaps he figured I was another deranged, drug-degraded individual the city notoriously churns out. The beard growth was for identity concealment in case we came face-to-face in a chance encounter.

I learned early on that the likelihood of seeing Griffin Walker was a far stretch. He never wandered around the building. A ride from the penthouse to the parking structure is the only way he moves through the building. There was a slim possibility of a meeting if my job requirements included routine checks of the parking area or manning the security booth at the garage entrance.

The job itself was mundane. With a security team to protect the wealthy and their abundance of senseless overpriced art, seemed a pointless mission for the blue-collar man to work up any concern over. But it was a job, it paid decently enough, and it would get me to the endgame.

"When you were a kid, did you think your life would turn out much different?" Stanley Bates asked me from behind the wall of screens watching every corridor throughout the building.

"Young people never suspect they'll be widowed at the age of thirty-seven."

The words came out before I could hold my tongue or formulate a satisfying lie.

Stanley leaned to his left enough to see me around the monitors and arched an eyebrow.

"You're widowed? I'm sorry. I didn't know."

I was sitting at the desk at the end of the room, going through a standard operating procedures manual to enhance my knowledge of my job requirements.

"Life has a funny way of kicking you in the head when you're not paying attention."

"I'm sure," Stanley said. "How are you coping?"

"In suspension."

"In suspension?" he asked.

I don't know where it came from. It was all that popped into my mind. I couldn't very well tell him that I was coping by planning a strategic revenge scheme that involved getting a security job at the building where I planned to destroy the life of the man who killed my wife.

"Well, a traumatic life event can throw one into a state of limbo, or suspension, as I like to call it. It's a place of disbelief that your life has taken such a dramatic turn. While in suspension, you either accept life's curveball and transcend through the best you can, or you allow it to corrupt your soul, and you never leave limbo until the day you die."

"That's fucking grim, man. So, you're still there, in suspension?"

"Yes," I admitted. "I'm trying to push through, but it's so goddamn hard. But I believe a breakthrough is right around the corner."

Actually, the breakthrough is forty-eight floors up, I thought.

"That's good to hear. I'm pulling for you. It can't be any way to live. Grief sours the heart and mind."

"That it does."

I hadn't yet decided how I was going to kill Griffin Walker. At first, I simply wanted him to stop breathing instantly. I didn't care how it had come about. Now, part of me desired to see the process become a long and painful one. The idea of seeing the consequences of his actions come alive in his eyes as he fully realized the certainty of his death might bring me a certain peace. I didn't think it would, but there's always a chance.

I was partway through a bottle of Irish whiskey, trying to think beyond the haze of alcohol as my eyes fought against the night. The TV was on, but I had no idea what program was playing. Before the first glass, I had been wildly imagining Walker's death. Scenarios of blood, screams, and begging filled my thoughts. But I knew I didn't want that. I've never been a violent person before Amy died. I didn't think even now I could journey down that dark road. The thought of honoring her good name with extreme bloodshed was no way to go. If there is an afterlife, how could I explain it to her?

Don't get me wrong, Walker will die by my hand. It's unavoidable at this time. I just can't convince myself to do it by way of sinister actions, perhaps viciously disconnecting his body parts and such before his heart gave out from lack of blood supply. I'm not mentally built like that.

I can build the terror, though. That action would give me a far more enjoyable conclusion.

The night won. My eyelids lost the match, and my mind slipped to a restless place of hate and anger. The clock rounded to three in the morning when my eyes shot open. An acidic river flowed up my chest. I had only a moment to get myself upright and to the bathroom or trash container before the rush came out. Thankfully, the lid was already up as the evening's alcohol consumption rejected the contents of my stomach. There wasn't much, as I had eaten very little after my work shift. After the event was done, I relaxed my body onto the tile. There's something to be said about a bathroom's tile flooring. It's a strange phenomenon how cool tiles can aid someone's body wrecked with sickness. I let it work its miracle over me as my stomach eased, and my mind began to clear.

My life in suspension, I thought as my mind pushed for more sleep.

In suspension, two words that repeated with a maddening determination, as I wanted nothing more than to check out for the rest of the night.

Then I had it. A perfect vision of Griffin Walker dangling from a wire high above the street below. The terror-stricken look on his face played through my mind, causing goosebumps to ripple down my arms.

The dread of knowing about death approaching can sometimes be more terrifying than the final deed itself.

My life is in suspension. So why not his life as well?

My thoughts gained rapid momentum over the following weeks. A plan of vengeance was finally coming together, especially now that I had moved to the overnight shift. I needed a bit of material, but as if God's hand had something to do with it, I didn't know. I readily found the material on the thirty-second floor, currently under a stalled construction overhaul. Permit issues and lack of funding left the floor in a ghost-like state. I hadn't seen a single construction worker since my employment began. The contractor had delivered the building material to the work area, but now it sat unused on the floor until the financial issues were resolved.

During shift rounds, I'd stopped on that floor numerous times. I needed several heavy gage steel square tubing. They were there, just as fate intended.

The night shift crew consisted of two men. Because most of the building was office space and the top ten floors were residential, only a small security force was necessary.

Doug Moore was a middle-aged introvert. His preference was the night shift, which offered a limited opportunity for interaction between office workers or residents. In the several shifts I worked with him, I hardly saw him at all. It was possible he often found a nice place to hide and slept through the shift. It became a perfect time to begin my project.

I left the security room and took the freight elevator to the thirty-second floor. The square tubing was nearly too long to fit on the elevator. I had to angle one end into a high corner so the doors would close. The elevator, of course, didn't go to the roof. So, I had to carry the steel up two flights. As long as I didn't drop one and make a huge racket, no one would be aware of my presence at two in the morning.

I swiped the key card, unlocking the roof door. It was the north face of the building I needed to set up my device.

The task took three more trips before I had all the necessary tools. After that, I returned to the security station. Doug was not in the room or anywhere on the monitors. His work-shift hiding place was phenomenal, and it worked to my advantage.

I returned to the roof and got to work. The lack of light was a hindrance to my efforts, but it wasn't like I could blaze up work lights on the roof in the middle of the night.

I didn't think that welding steel beams together would alert anyone within the neighboring buildings. It was as bright as a small sun, but gave off very little noise. I'm a novice welder, but I know the fundamentals. Each weld was spotty and a far cry from even being mediocre, but I was confident that they would hold weight.

I turned on my phone light and inspected my final work. I think God had smiled down on me then.

I released an exhausted breath and began gathering tools to return them back to the thirty-second floor.

I couldn't finalize my plan tonight. Now, at nearly five in the morning, some residents would begin their day. Also, secretaries would begin their morning paperwork and organize business practices at the various companies throughout the building.

Death had to hold off one more day. Besides, I knew I needed a bit more prep time. I was walking blindly into the situation of the penthouse entry. There was no way to research much. All I could do was wing it with the unknown factors of how to obtain entry and what to do about the one or two bodyguards.

I couldn't kill them. I knew that for sure. Bodyguards are just hired men there to protect the cash giver. Although one had drilled a bullet in my thigh months back, but it was exactly what he'd been paid to do. I didn't fault them for that, and I certainly couldn't kill for it.

I went to a sporting goods store right after clocking out. I chose the largest container of bear spray offered, as well as a bundle of high-strength rope. After that, I went to a hardware store. I bought a full-face respirator. I didn't believe it would completely cancel out the fiery punch of the bear spray, but having a covered face to keep any spray out of my eyes and filters to reduce most of it from reaching my lungs was a beneficial purchase.

Returning home, I put the items into my work pack, which always holds my lunch.

I tried to sleep, but my mind refused to settle. I was finally going to get my long overdue vengeance or die trying. I also worried that someone had gone to the roof, seen my construction, contacted the property owner, and had it removed. And again, my restless mind focused on getting through those penthouse doors.

Sleep eventually came, though a twisted nightmare journey through dark passages of the mind is the only place my dreams took me.

The TV was on, but I heard none of it as I ate lunch and later dinner. My thoughts traveled at light speed as different scenarios of the coming night played a wicked dance of possibilities. I hated being unprepared. I suppose if I had more patience, I could further research the penthouse layout by somehow gathering the building's construction plans. That took knowledge of how to accomplish such a feat. I'm not a smart man. Besides, my patience was all drawn out. I needed to end this before my mind fractured, and a final mental breakdown put me into some sort of asylum where Walker would be forever out of reach.

An hour before leaving my apartment for the final time, I wrote it all down. Everything. A confession and a reason why life had pushed me toward such a brutal end. I ranted about the injustice of the world. I complained about how good-natured people are often victims of the wealthy and powerful. My confession may fall on deaf ears, but I'll never be around to witness it.

"What's for lunch today?" Doug asked as we clocked in for the night shift.

"I'm going all out tonight. I broke open a fresh pack of bologna with lettuce and mustard."

It was a lie. I had no final meal plans. I suppose I should have indulged like they do with death row inmates before that final walk to the electric chair or lethal injection room. I kind of figured a stomach filled with one last tasteful desire would amount to me throwing up, shitting myself, or both, as jittery nerves racked my body. I needed full control of myself tonight, so the luxury of my last meal went unfulfilled.

It didn't take long before Doug did his vanishing act. I took the opportunity to go to the roof and make sure my work from the previous night remained. It did. After that, the night became a nerve-racking wait until an hour late enough that I knew Walker would be in bed.

The body and mind can only tolerate so much. Everything began shutting down. I felt my head bobbing as I watched the monitors. It was the movement on one of the screens that ran off my tiredness.

I recognized the guy. It was one of Walker's bodyguards. He'd stepped off the lobby elevator and made a beeline for the front doors. From there, he used his access card to unlock the doors. On the outside cameras, he stepped onto the street as a black sedan rolled up. The man walked around to the passenger side, got in, and the vehicle disappeared down the city block.

I didn't have a clue what to make of this, but it could only be a good sign. Now there was possibly only a single guard instead of two. Of course, I couldn't even be sure Walker had two guards today, or just one. I wouldn't know until I got up there.

The building's security team has a key to gain access to the penthouse floor in case of emergencies. I dropped my backpack in the elevator and opened it. The respirator went securely over my face, and I tightened the straps. I stood and slid the key into the slot next to the penthouse button. Turning it, the penthouse button lit up. I jabbed it, and the elevator doors closed. As I rose toward the forty-eighth floor, my heart ramped up as adrenaline surged through it. Nausea hit me, but I was glad my stomach was empty. I pulled the canister of bear spray from the pack, slid my finger under the spring-loaded safety tab and waited.

His expression was blank at first, maybe figuring the second guard had returned. When he saw the mask, the panic alarm in his mind went off. His hand instantly went to the holster at his waist. Before he even got fingers on it, the first-round blast of spray hit him directly in the mouth and eyes. His body reacted in a fit as his hands swiped at the orange liquid. His mouth coughed and spewed capsicum and saliva as his body reacted to the attack. Even while fighting through the struggle to breathe and see, the guard slid his hand back to the gun. I hit him with another blast and then stepped forward. My leg went up and out like I'd seen it done a million times in martial arts movies. There was far more behind it than I'd planned to deliver. The impact caught him directly in the chest, driving him back against the wall. The second impact drove the fight from his body as muscles gave out and unconsciousness consumed him. I worked quickly as I pulled lengths from the roll of duct tape, fixing his hands behind his back and ankles together. I hated to do it, but a rag went into his mouth and a circle of tape around his head to secure it. I worried that the pepper spray would cause inflammation in his sinuses and air wouldn't get through his nose. With his mouth gagged, he could suffocate. I watched him for a minute. A stream of snot slicked out his nose, and air pulled inside.

"I'm sorry about that, but I can't have you screaming your head off when you come around."

I looked at the door. There was a keycard reader. I rummaged through the man's pockets, praying to find an access card. His inside jacket pocket gave me what I needed.

I also confiscated his gun and a pocketknife. I dropped them in the bag and went to the penthouse doors.

Swiping the card, the reader beeped, followed by the sound of the double doors unlocking. My movement inside was painstakingly slow. I couldn't be sure if Walker had heard the fight outside. There was a chance he was making his way to the door, or even on the phone with the police.

A quiet, dark apartment was all that greeted me. The place was massive, with over seven thousand square feet of space for one man to call home. Wall-hung art, statues on pillars, expensive throw rugs, and such were in abundance. Walker was a man who flaunted his wealth, using it to show the world his power. His life of corruption and manipulation funded all his overpriced art purchases.

I moved across each room in the dim glow of night-lights. Turning from the kitchen, I made my way to where the bedrooms should be. There were five bedrooms. Four rooms were empty with beds still made, but the fifth, with the door slightly open, showed a figure under the sheets.

I had him. I finally had the bastard who ordered my wife to be murdered. My hand went back to the bag, finding the spray and an eagerness to empty the remaining contents into his face.

That moment mirrored a movie scene where overwhelming disbelief greets the intruder. I ripped back the black silk sheets, my finger beginning to press the button on the spray, when I faced nothing more than a row of pillows.

Walker wasn't there.

"I've been waiting for this," someone said behind me.

There was a pop, followed by a bolt of lightning surging through my body, causing all muscles to go taut. Even my index finger strained, causing a blast of pepper spray to jet from the canister.

My body crumbled just as the lightning gave up its torture. Although the spray hadn't been a direct hit, the sting was enough to persuade the man behind me to cease his assault.

I saw him then as I fell. Griffin Walker had known of my upcoming attack. As he backed away from the burning cloud, I saw the Taser in his hand and the trail of wires leading to my backside. I had little time to react. I reached for the wires and yanked the barbed prongs free of my skin. I quickly rotated again to face him.

The canister rose and delivered what remained. I released it when the nozzle sputtered. Getting to my feet wasn't easy, as every muscle protested. I knew I had seconds before Walker began a second attack. I was all over him like a deranged ape.

The gun in my bag was too easy. I needed to inflict pain, as the loss of my wife had devastated every aspect of my life. My arms became a blur of righteous anger as my fists slammed into every part of his face. His nose, cheekbone, and eye sockets gave under the force.

The events since stepping off the elevator had sapped my energy. Each strike became pathetic.

He saw an opportunity. He clawed at the respirator, managing to break the seal, causing the burn of sprayed chemicals to work inside my lungs. I rolled off him, turning toward the bedroom door, and then I released my held breath.

Walker turned over as overproduced saliva, snot, and tears expelled the foreign matter from his body. He coughed hard into the carpet and then groaned like an animal unfairly tortured by a sadistic owner.

Pushing to my feet, a downward force bludgeon me back down. Walker had managed to fight through painful blindness, retrieved my dropped pack, and began a defensive attack. The roll of duct tape and the bodyguard's gun inside the bag crushed muscle and bones as he pinwheeled it across me.

I shot my right leg out, working it like a piston against his ankles. One joint either rolled or broke as Walker plunged back down with a yelp.

I grabbed the dropped bag and scurried for the bedroom door. I wasn't planning on fleeing, but I needed a moment out of his reach to get my bearings. The ill effects of the Taser caused an extreme weakness in my arms and legs.

Outside the bedroom, I reached inside the pack. My fingers felt the barrel of the gun, and I pulled it out. As I rotated it in my hand, a thousand splinters blew apart from the door. An arrow of wood impaled the outer corner of my left eye.

I screamed in pain. Walker screamed back in victory.

I raised the gun, fingered the safety off, and shot through the bedroom wall. My feet kicked at the floor, pushing me farther out of shotgun range. When my back collided with the sofa, I spun onto my hands and knees and scampered for cover.

Walker fell as he came out of the bedroom, narrowly saving his brain from being splattered by the round I'd just sent his way.

My eye watered and bled, and I knew I couldn't fight with only one good eye. I reached up and gently touched the area. The splinter was large enough that I could get a thumb and forefinger on the tail end of it. I pulled without hesitation. The viscous goo pushing out from that wound helped the splinter to come free. I threw it off to the side, and with fury, fired twice more at where Walker had been. He wasn't there to catch a bullet.

Blurriness impaired my left eyesight, but I could still make out objects, especially moving ones. I tried to slow my panicked breathing, hoping that hearing Walker's movement through the area might give away his location. It did. His struggle to fight off the pepper spray continued as he wheezed for breath somewhere in the massive kitchen.

I quickly poked my head over the counter. Buckshot instantly annihilated the toaster, but thankfully left my head unscathed. Keeping my head low, my gun hand came up, momentarily resting on the marble counter before my finger twitched the trigger twice. A storm of curse words echoed across the penthouse, followed by a shotgun blast that was nowhere near me. It had instead blown out an overhead kitchen light and drywall.

Walker groaned, and I thought I recognized the sound. It was one of pain and defeat. I believed my hysterical firing had actually hit him, causing his finger to pull the trigger inadvertently and blow the ceiling apart.

I rose slowly. My body was ready to retreat if the shotgun swung my way. In the darkness, I didn't see it in time, but it didn't matter, anyhow. The eye of the shotgun barrel stared into my very soul and then clicked.

My wince was automatic, but so was my acknowledgment that the chamber was empty.

Walker had slumped on the floor, with his upper body leaning against the base cabinets. His grip gave out, and the shotgun dropped to the tiled floor.

"I knew you'd come. Eventually. A man bent on vengeance can never let go. I have known it ever since I found out you began working here. It was far too coincidental that you just happened to get a job at the building in which I live. You tried to kill me once before. It didn't work out well for you. When I saw you weeks ago, I knew this moment was coming."

"So, you know who I am?"

"I do."

"And you know what I'm going to do?"

"I know what you want to do. But a man like you, well, I firmly believe you don't have the stones to go through with it. I could. To me, killing comes naturally. I watched you through the elevator entryway camera. You couldn't even kill William."

"He never wronged me. But you, well, you went all the way to the top of my shit list in rapid fashion."

Clutching the bullet wound in his stomach, he still managed to laugh.

"I gave the order to William to execute your wife. How does that sink in?"

"That might change things a bit."

Walker winced as the pain of a gut shot racked his body.

"I'm gonna die on this fucking floor."

"Well, it's a nice floor. Probably worth more than my entire house. But no, this is not where you die."

With that, I stepped forward and smashed the side of the gun into his temple, just short of caving in his skull.

I think it was the wind that woke Walker.

The roof of a forty-eight story building catches quite the wind gusts, especially when one is dangling over the side of it.

The cable secured his right foot, and his left leg began a rapid, panicked kicking as vertigo overcame him.

"Jesus Christ! You've lost your goddamn mind! Get me off here!"

"Do you really want me to get you off there?" I asked while leaning against the roof's edge wall. "All right then."

I kneeled, retrieved the bolt cutters and stepped up to the hangman's stand I'd created the night before. I pulled the cutter's handles apart, slid the cutting edge over the cable fastened to the bracket base, and began closing them.

"Wait! Just wait a damn second. I didn't mean to get me down like that!"

Walker looked down at his impending doom. When he did, he ceased his thrashing. The dawn's first light revealed chaos far below. I watched him narrow his eyes, desperately trying to understand the scene he had suspended above.

I pulled the cutters away from the cable and went back to the wall. Leaning forward, I looked over and saw a crowd gathering. They weren't necessarily moving in to watch the man floating over the side of the building, but studying and filming the corpse on the sidewalk.

"You son of a bitch," Walker hissed.

"That one is all on you. If you hadn't told me that he was my wife's killer, he'd still be bound up next to the elevator. Instead, well, splat."

Daylight had come enough that the people below now saw Walker and his predicament. Their attention from the duct-taped man below moved to the man who was going to share the same fate.

"Please. My fucking foot. I can't feel it. It's goddamn coming off."

"If you can't feel it, how do you know it's coming off? So, I'm curious. Why exactly did you send off one of your bodyguards? If you knew I was coming for you, why wouldn't you want a greater defense?"

"I wanted to face you. I figured you'd be too chicken shit to attempt anything with two guards here. I told him to leave through the front so you would see. The idea behind the Taser was to incapacitate you. I'd planned to bind and torture you until your body gave out. I needed to teach you a lesson. You're a pathetic twerp who was likely walked all over during your life. I'm a man who takes what I want, because that's what real men do."

"Interesting. And how is that working out so far for you tonight?"

I was ready, because I knew it would happen at any moment. The metal roof door banged open, and three men joined us. One was Doug. The other was Stanley, who must have just arrived for the day shift, and a city patrolman. I had already moved back into position. The cutting blades gently pinched the wire.

At that moment, I don't think any of them could form a logical question to ask me. Dumbfounded, they intently watched, just as the crowd below did.

"What is this?" the patrolman asked. He didn't give me a chance to respond. "Sir, I'm going to need you to stop what you're doing."

"I'm not really doing anything."

His hand was on the butt of his sidearm, but kept it holstered for the moment.

"Why are you detaining that man?"

Detaining? I thought and chuckled.

"I'm really not. He's free to go anytime."

"You need to let him down."

"I've discussed it with him. He doesn't want down."

"You know what I mean."

Doug stepped forward, showing his hands that he had no ill intent other than to talk.

He said, "It's all right. We're listening. Why have you done this to Mr. Walker?"

I looked over my shoulder and said, "That's a question for him. Well, how about it, Griffin? It's confession time. These men want to know. We're all eagerly waiting to hear."

Blood had found its way through his bandage that I'd secured to his stomach while he was unconscious. Now, a small stream rolled down his neck. Bandaging his gunshot stomach was never about saving his life, but delaying death a little.

"I'm getting bored with waiting," I finally told him, as his mind was no doubt working out conclusions for all possible scenarios.

"Okay. But you have to swear it on your wife's name that you'll let me go. If I tell them, you'll let me go."

"On my wife's good name, I swear I'll let you go. But they are the witnesses to your murderous confession."

"Fine. That's fine. Christ," he said. He'd probably figured his team of lawyers would get the confession thrown out by deeming his statement was a false one used to remove himself from peril.

I saw the uniform patrolman had removed the strap from his gun. His hand rested on it.

I shook my head. "You won't make it. Even if you do, my grip on the handle will come down, and I'll still cut the line. Just relax. This is nearly over."

Walker said, "I killed his wife! Okay? I mean, I had his wife killed to keep my ass out of prison. She was going to testify against me. I was looking at twenty years if they found me guilty. That man down there did the action for me."

Upside down, Walker furiously pointed to the splattered corpse far below.

"So, in short, you ended an innocent life so your pathetic criminal ass could stay out of prison?" I asked.

"Yes! Yes! That's what you wanted to hear, right?"

"I only wanted the truth, and that's what you gave me. Stanley, remember what I said about living a life in suspension? Well, I've pushed through. I've transcended to wherever the next stage takes me."

Before anyone could offer another word, the cutting edges of the bolt cutters came together. With a vicious metallic *ting* and a whip-like scraping, the cable pulled free from the bracket I'd constructed. Walker instantly disappeared from our view, but his voice found us just fine. It was nothing important, because he had nothing left to confess. A fury of screams and curse words was all that reached us.

The three men stared at me, mouths gaped, knowing there was nothing left to do to save the man's life.

They hadn't seen it before because my body had blocked their view. Now the uncoiling blue rope got their attention.

I stepped onto the ledge and said, "I let him go. You can't call me a liar about that. This was never going to end any other way for both of us."

I saw the rope had nearly gone its full length, so I stepped off the side. I didn't want the rope tied to my ankle to rip it from the socket as Walker's body pulled me free from the roof. I needed no more pain in this life. I desired only unfiltered joy.

I saw Walker's face a second before he hit. It was exactly what I'd worked so hard to achieve. His face consumed by pure dread, and then undeniable death.

I followed, because this world has no place for broken men.

Keepsake

"I've got the most wonderful idea. This will be so much fun. You'll see. We're married now, but we still have so much to learn as our years together go on."

Trent watched Cathy jitter with excitement at what she was about to propose. He couldn't help but smile. Her eagerness to please him was absolutely adorable. Trent had won the state lucky lotto when it came to finding the perfect single woman in all of Minnesota. Between her beauty, kindness, and income, he felt very much like all numbers had been called on his ticket.

"Okay. I'll say you have my interest. What's on your mind?"

A busboy bumped their table, rattling empty plates and wine glasses. He offered an apology and disappeared through the kitchen swing door.

"How about we keep one thing, one secret to ourselves? And then after I don't know, a year, we'll show or tell the other what it is."

Trent said, "Well, I'll admit that's a very bizarre way to start a marriage. But it might be a little fun keeping just one secret. So, are we just not going to tell the other, or are we going to place an item or a confession note in, oh, I don't know, a locked box or something?"

"That's a great idea. I have some old wooden boxes in the garage. We could use them. We'll put a small padlock on there and, after a year has gone by, we'll open the boxes together. It'll be so much fun. Kind of like a time capsule."

"Exactly what kind of secret are we talking about?"

"Oh, I don't know. Something you didn't feel comfortable enough to tell me at the beginning of our marriage. When we've settled into each other's ways, we'll open the other's box and talk about what's inside. It'll be our final moment of fully understanding each other. A moment to begin absolute trust from that point on," Cathy said and reached across the table to take Trent's hand.

Trent's eyes roamed to the restaurant's ceiling as his mind cycled through a life before Cathy. The days of a single man making trial-and-error paths through life.

"Okay. Why not?"

Cathy had retrieved the boxes from the garage shelf, cleared assorted junk from them, and brought them inside. When Trent came home from work the following day, they were on the coffee table. One of the boxes was already sealed shut. The other had its lid flipped open, empty space waiting to conceal his secret for a full year.

"I've already put mine inside the box," Cathy said.

Trent looked at the closed box and the new clasp and padlock fixed to the front.

"Well, you certainly didn't waste any time."

"Go ahead. Get yours done and then we'll place them in the closet."

Trent watched her as she watched him.

"Well, since it's supposed to remain a secret, I might need a bit of privacy."

"Oh. Okay. Sorry. I'll leave you the room."

"There's no need. I plan to do it in the garage." Trent picked up the small crate and disappeared through the garage door.

Sitting on the bench stool, Trent heard the shuffle of feet just beyond the door. They stopped, and he knew

Cathy was on the other side, ear pressed to the wood, intently listening for any telltale signs of what he might be placing inside his mystery box. He smiled. She was entirely too cute in that way of hers. She had come up with the idea, and already she'd become impatient. Her desire to know so quickly consumed her thoughts. He laughed a little, unaware of how she could make it through an entire year of not knowing.

Trent heard her footsteps quicken to the kitchen counter as he pushed the garage door open and stepped inside.

"There we go. It's all done. Now, if you'd just hand me the keys," he said and held out his hand.

"Oh. Of course." She fished in her pocket and pulled out a key, placing it in his open palm.

"And the other one?" he asked with a slight grin at her antics. "New locks always come with two keys."

"Oh, do they?" Her hand slipped into the same pocket and retrieved the second key. "I suppose I didn't realize."

He laughed this time and said, "You're a crazy girl sometimes."

Stepping into the guest bedroom, Trent said, "Where should we put them?"

"The closet is fine. There's space on the top shelf."

Trent had completely forgotten about the boxes for weeks, but while vacuuming all the carpet in the house, he noticed the boxes on the shelf. Unlike Cathy, his desire to know wasn't extreme, but he was slightly curious.

Trent clicked the vacuum into the upright position and turned it off. He hesitated as he reached for them. Just like Cathy, his curiosity was building. He knew he wouldn't be able to look inside without breaking the lock or clasp. But just maybe if he shook it a bit, the movement inside might give him a more educated guess as to what it could be.

Both boxes came down, and he placed them on the bed. He knew Cathy's box was at the bottom. He moved his box to the side, and he picked up the other, instantly realizing how light it was. At first, he thought it was empty, but when he shook it like a child holding a Christmas present, something shifted inside. It wasn't the movement of something hard, but it bounced softly against the sides.

"Hey, where's the key to the shed's lock? I was going to move some of my things out of the storage locker so they could be at the house. I can't find the key anywhere."

"I have no idea. That lock was there when I bought the place just before we met. I never bothered having someone cut it off. So, I just always kept the mower and such in the garage."

"Well, maybe the previous owners left a bunch of stuff in there. If they didn't find the key before leaving, they could have said screw it and abandoned those items. I'll borrow some bolt cutters from Zack."

"I'm honestly not worried about it."

"It's a large shed. That's unused space we could put all the lawn equipment in and free up some garage area."

Against Cathy's request to leave the shed alone, Trent was able to borrow bolt cutters from the neighbor. It made no sense to have an additional building on the property and keep it unused. He wanted the garage area for parking cars, especially when it stormed. He certainly didn't want to bark his shins against clutter just trying to get in and out of his vehicle.

The lock was relatively new. It was a big bastard that required all of his upper muscles to go into overtime working the bolt cutters to clip through the steel. When the lock clasp gave, Trent ripped it from the latch, and in frustration, threw it towards the back of the property into the tangle of vines and saplings growing along the fence. Next, he flung open the door in a swelling rage to find the shed completely bare.

"Sure, makes sense to keep a big-ass lock concealing nothing," he nearly shouted.

He tried to calm himself as he stepped inside. The deed was done, and now he had access to the empty space.

The interior was perfectly adequate for most items in the garage, including the shelves overloaded with rarely used stuff like camping chairs and tents. He pictured where he could set up the shelves and a suspended lumber rack for future wood projects.

Trent stepped back, and the floor groaned. Looking down, he saw a keyhole where there shouldn't be a keyhole. Kneeling down, he swiped his fingers across the inset lock plate, knocking the dust free. It was an old key latch, like one he figured he'd find in a preserved Victorian home. The latch accepted a double-sided skeleton key to trigger tumblers on both sides of the lock. There wasn't a lot to locks such as this, he knew. Typically, there was one or two tumblers to push out of the way to unlock them. They weren't like modern locks, where half a dozen tumblers needed to be set at the right height to turn the bolt.

Retrieving his phone, Trent turned on the flashlight. It was nearly impossible to see inside the black hole. Even placing the top of his phone under his chin so he could get an unobstructed point of view into the darkness did no good.

Trent heard a car door close out front. Cathy was home from work. He thought about holding back the information of a strange door at the bottom of the shed. The need to find out why someone kept a secret beneath the shed was too great to ignore, and he didn't want to share it with

Cathy until he knew for sure what was under there. It could very well have just covered a shallow hole where some kid had once hidden his treasures, valuable only to him.

"I saw you through the kitchen window. I see you have got it open. I guess it does offer up some space for odds and ends."

Trent slid his foot over the keyhole and crossed his arms as if he'd been studying the interior.

"It does. I was just standing here trying to figure out what I was going to put in here and how to place everything."

"Well, just don't clutter it. Leave room so we can walk around and get to what we need to get to." She kissed his cheek and headed for the back door.

The damn thing was unpickable. He'd started with a bulky nail file, but quickly gave it up in favor of one of Cathy's bobby pins. Even though movies portray the hairpin as the ultimate method to pick any lock, it failed this time. He switched to a heavy gage wire that got knotted up in the lock and was a bastard to get back out.

A thought occurred to him. Retrieving a shovel from the garage, Trent went to the back of the shed so that Cathy couldn't see him from any of the house windows. He began digging at a shallow angle, determined to uncover whatever the hell was under there.

After digging nearly six feet in, the shovel struck rock. As he cleared more of the hole away, he used his cell flashlight and realized it wasn't a rock, but poured concrete.

It's some sort of goddamn bunker, Trent thought.

There was no use in working with the shovel anymore. He knew he'd need a goddamn jackhammer to break his way through. Even if he managed to pry open the door inside the shed, there was no telling if another door, this one sealing the underground concrete structure, wasn't waiting below the wooden hatch door.

Scoop by scoop, he began hefting dirt back into the hole. Using the handle as a tamping tool, he was able to repack all the earth dug out.

Words started to tumble out at the dinner table. He began telling Cathy all about it when he suddenly stopped himself.

"You found what?"

Trent wondered about the glamorous possibilities that lay inside that bunker. It could be a haven of his and his alone if he just kept his mouth shut about it. And more than that, what if a previous owner had forgotten something valuable locked away inside it? Or maybe the previous owner died, and the beneficiaries of his estate had no knowledge of what lay buried in the backyard.

"Um, my bowling trophies in the garage. I found them in a box. I thought I lost them during the move," Trent said.

"Oh. Well, that's good to hear. Are they going into your office?"

"Possibly. I'm not sure. I'm just happy I found them."

"Did you get enough to eat? There's plenty of mashed potatoes left."

"I did." A thought jumped into Trent's mind. He asked, "When did you buy this house? Do you know who you bought it from?"

"I told you I bought it about a year before we met. Oh, Smith or Schmitt or something like that. Why do you ask?"

"No real reason. I just thought it was weird how they kept the shed locked with nothing in it."

"Well, after cleaning it out, they might have relocked it out of habit. Or they didn't want the neighbor kids playing around in there while the place sat vacant. They probably meant to leave me a key, but then forgot. What's the big deal?"

"It's not a big deal. I was just curious."

There was another point of curiosity that picked its way across Trent's mind over the next week.

What the hell is in Cathy's confession box?

He couldn't imagine what kind of secret she could be keeping from the world. She was sweet, honest, and one of the most trustworthy people he'd ever met. He knew that what was in her box matched his own. Her bizarre request to conceal a confessed secret in a box for a full year left him stumped. Trent racked his mind and came up with nothing. He had shared all of his life's hopes, dreams, and regrets with Cathy before they walked down the church aisle.

As Trent stood in the spare bedroom with the closet open, he tried to find every excuse possible to walk away from the box of mystery. But he couldn't acknowledge a single reason that would help him give up the wonder. He'd decided that if Cathy found out, she'd just laugh it off as if he were a kid unable to wait for Christmas morning presents melee.

Pulling the box from the upper shelf, Trent set it on the bed. He knew the basics of picking a lock. Television had shown that he'd need two wires to work a lock open. He would use one wire as a tension and the other to work the tumblers into position until everything fell into place. The lock Cathy used on the boxes was as simple as they got.

After retrieving two small paper clips from his desk, Trent formed a teardrop shape on the end to use as his tension lever. The other he straightened, but then used his thumbnail to pry small humps along it to give it ridges like a key.

The attempt was a success, though took far longer in time and aggravation than he expected. The lock jumped in his grip. He rotated the shackle free from the latch and flipped open the box. A neatly wrapped cloth was inside. Picking it up, he felt something small wrapped within. Shaking the object loose, he let it fall into his palm. It was a bronze, double-sided key. The type of key that would fit perfectly in an old fashion lock, just like the one he'd tried to outsmart in the shed.

"You've got to be shitting me," Trent said as he rotated the key to study each side.

Engraved on one side, between the decorative doves on a loop and the shaft, was the number 1313.

"Why did you have it this entire time? Why did you lie about never being in the shed?"

Before, he had been sure Cathy knew nothing of the hidden door inside the shed. She had claimed the previous owner had left the shed locked. But if that were true, then why would she place a key for the lock inside her box if she had no idea what the key opened?

It was a mystery box that opened a mystery box. Now he could finally know what lay through the hatch door and beneath the shed.

Trent looked at his watch. Cathy wouldn't be home from work for nearly an hour. He figured it gave him ample time to investigate.

Trent left the box open and on the bed as he went out the back door. The key slid in and rotated with no resistance. He hefted the door all the way up until it stayed in place. Another door lay below, only this one built of heavy gage metal and a modern electronic keypad lock.

The key in his hand opened two doors, he knew, as he looked at the engraved numbers. He punched in 1313, and the lock confirmed the code with a beep and a green light. The sound of disengaging deadbolts followed.

Automatic lights flickered on below. Although a flood of light instantly chased away the darkness within the earth, Trent felt ice roll down his spine from the oddness of the underground space.

"Hello?"

He knew how ignorant it was to call out. There was no possible way someone was hiding below.

The spiral staircase dropped a dozen feet to a concrete floor.

"Unreal," Trent said, and his echo bounced back at him.

Placing his right foot on the first step, Trent felt the surreal moment of walking into another world, like stepping through a wardrobe into Narnia.

The rotation of steps landed him in a perplexing room. Poured concrete walls and floors made the underground dwelling highly durable, resistant to water leakage and foundation cracking. He did a slow turn in the white-painted room, studying the area that held only thirteen small dressers with five drawers each. Sitting on top of those dressers were random items. A pair of glasses, a tie, a golf glove, a Harry Potter book, and dozens of other odd belongings.

Opening a drawer revealed a thick gray sweater and black leather driving gloves. Opening the drawer below it, he found framed pictures, some with a man by himself, and some with Cathy. Some photos were slightly intimate as someone snapped a picture of the couple kissing or warmly embracing. Each drawer of every dresser held the remnants of a past life with other men. Thirteen men, to be exact.

Trent picked up a pair of eyeglasses, extra thick for a man blind to the world without them.

The voice behind him caused him to whirl around.

"Those belonged to Calvin. I used to mess with him in the mornings and take his glasses off the nightstand. He'd wander around the bedroom and bathroom, bumping into shit trying to find his glasses. It was hilarious fun."

Cathy was sitting on a step near the top of the staircase. Her face pressed between the metal spindles.

"You scared the shit out of me. What is all this? Who built this room?"

"Keepsakes from thirteen husbands. Thirteen men who all failed at a single task. Don't open the box for a full year. It's such a simple request. And every goddamn one of them couldn't resist. Just like you, I discovered them down here snooping. Oh, I've broken the rules too. But they're my enforced rules, so I'm entitled."

Cathy tossed a pressed flower that landed at Trent's feet.

"What kind of crap is that for a secret? A flower? Does it represent anything special?"

"Just my love for you. That's the single rose I gave you on our first date. On our second date, I found it in your trash. So I pressed it and saved it. I apparently have no astonishing secrets like you, so that was all I could think to place in the box. So many of those men's personal items are here. So, where are they? What happened after they disappointed you?"

Cathy rolled her eyes. "Do you know the story of Blue-beard?"

"Only vaguely."

"It's a well-known tale from the 1600s. Of course, there are several versions of Bluebeard's exploits. But basically, a wealthy nobleman has taken a young bride. He offers her all her heart's desires. One day he must leave on business and entrust her with the keys to his kingdom. He has but one rule. The chamber in the basement is a forbidden place to travel. Of course, after he departs, she can't help herself. She simply must know the secret. She goes through the chamber door to find the bloodied bodies of his previous wives. All of whom were disappointments because they broke the only rule. For me, it was thirteen husbands, followed by thirteen deaths. Thirteen-thirteen. The code to the door."

Cathy stood and removed a remote from her pocket. The click of a button activated the steel door. It closed with a soft seal, as would a coffin lid, followed by the sound of engaging deadbolts.

"Of course, unlike Bluebeard, I have no enthusiasm to keep around corpses, only the items they cherished most."

Cathy took the spiral steps with satisfying relish as her eyes never left him. Her sight took in his terror, especially when her favorite knife came out and settled into a very familiar grip.

Nothing Is Normal
in the Drift

Roger Klavan saw the kid on the roadside. He sat on a green duffel bag along the edge of the shoulder. The kid was young, not even in his twenties yet, Roger bet. With worn-out blue jeans, a black leather jacket, and slicked-back black hair, Roger knew why the passing cars were reluctant to pick the kid up and give him relief from the June sun. A cigarette dangled from his mouth as he used a fingernail to clean out dirt from another fingernail.

His thumb did a half-hearted raise as he heard Roger's car approach. His head lifted slightly as the car slowed, and the anticipation of a ride made itself known.

He didn't immediately get up when the Cadillac wagon stopped. Roger could read the arrogance in his features through the cloud of smoke. He leaned across the seat to see the kid better before all-out offering a ride.

"It's got to be Hell's temperature with that leather jacket on."

"A bit," the kid said, offering no more.

"Where are you heading?"

"South is all. As far as you can take me."

"All right. Toss the bag in the cargo area," Roger said and hitched his thumb at the back of the station wagon.

The kid still didn't make a move to stand. He asked, "You're not a fruitcake or something?"

"A fruitcake?"

"Like you're planning on driving me out to the woods to have your way with me or something like that? I don't go for that shit."

"Not at all. That's not my way in life."

"How about trying to hurt me? If you even think it, it'll turn out really bad for you."

Roger was sure that a kid like this held a switchblade in his hip pocket. A kid on the road needed to protect himself in any way possible.

"It's not my style. Do you want a ride or not? I'm wasting gas here."

Roger let his foot off the brake a bit, letting the car begin to roll, indicating to the kid that the window of opportunity was about to peel away.

The kid finally stood, grabbed the duffle bag by a strap and carried it around the back. He opened the rear door and placed his belongings next to Roger's cargo.

The kid moved with self-importance, as if the only design of the world was that everyone needed to wait for his next move or word. The door opened, and the kid slid inside. He inhaled a final pull from the cigarette before flicking it into the tangle of roadside weeds.

"I'm Roger," he said and held out his hand.

The kid took it and delivered a knuckle-grinding squeeze before releasing it. It was a powerful moment for him, letting Roger know he wasn't about to take shit from this old man.

"Your parents gave you a name. So, what is it?"

The kid looked out the windshield and said, "Charlie."

Horseshit. This kid is no Charlie. A Frank, or Johnny, or even a Victor, but sure as shit not Charlie.

"That'll have to do, I suppose."

"Well, it's all you're gonna get. Like it or not."

Roger shifted into park and turned to the kid.

"Listen, Charlie, you need this ride far more than I need a mouthy, arrogant kid in my passenger seat. Respect goes hand in hand. So, you can drop the tough guy act, or you can take to your heels and hope for another ride that might tolerate your attitude."

Roger watched the kid, anticipating Charlie's mouth was about to get him ejected from the vehicle.

The kid looked out the side window, mentally reliving the swelter of the sun. His ego instantly dropped several notches.

"I'm sorry, sir. You're right. I appreciate the ride. Life is tough on the road. I was just showing that I wouldn't put up with anything."

"Good. Now that we've got that all cleared up, I bet you could use a bite to eat. It's my treat."

"That's very thoughtful of you, sir. Thank you."

Roger turned up the volume of the radio as Elvis' latest hit found the airway.

"I saw the King in concert last year. It would have been a terrific show if it weren't for all those damn screaming girls. I could barely hear the music coming out of the speakers. Every time he started swinging his hips around, the girls screamed even higher. I'm amazed I didn't start bleeding from the ears," Roger said.

Charlie laughed and said, "Yes, sir. He's a certified magnet for the ladies. So, are you a Bible salesman or something? I mean, it's none of my business, but I was just curious about all the boxes in the back."

"No, Charlie, not a Bible salesman. It is a supply and demand business that I run. I peddle goods that make people feel good. It obliterates worry and stress for a short while."

Charlie watched the older man, anticipating what exactly his supply could be.

"Is it like cocaine or something?"

"Far more enjoyable than that white powder that's going around."

Roger veered off the highway and into the parking lot of Blanche's Dine-In Dine-Out Restaurant.

"I'll explain inside." Roger said as the car came to a stop.

"Anywhere you like, gents," the waitress called out as the blast of air-conditioning greeted them.

Roger slid into a booth near the front windows. Charlie sat across from him as he took in the layout of the restaurant and its patrons.

"Decent place. The waitress is a little hot number, too," Charlie said as he watched the young blonde sashay toward their table.

As if by magic or sleight of hand, a small clear glass bottle was sitting in the center of the table. Roger held a single finger on the metal lid. His attention was directly on the kid, and paid no attention to the young woman headed their way.

"The experience is pure enlightenment. It's a space somewhere between heaven and temporary bliss. You'll find you have more energy, your mental awareness will be firing on all cylinders, and the sex drive, oh my God, the sex drive is a complete mind-blowing sensation."

Roger smiled inside, knowing his line of pure crap had grabbed the girl's immediate attention the second she was within earshot.

"Hey, guys. Do you need a minute with the menu, or do you know what you want?" Her eyes slipped to the glass bottle and the white pills inside.

Roger knew he had her then.

"We'll both have a burger with American cheese, house fries, and a root beer." Roger looked at her name tag and said, "Thank you, Helena. What a pretty name."

"Well, I appreciate that, sir. I'll get your order in." She turned to go, then instantly turned back. "If you don't mind my asking, what's that?" she asked while using her pencil to point at the jar.

"I suspect you overheard me. It's everything I said and more. Is it something that may interest you?"

The girl looked awkwardly at the men and then over her shoulder to see if the cook was listening.

"I mean, yeah, it sounds like a blast. How much for one?"

Roger leaned back, considering a reasonable payment.

"I'll tell you what. I'll exchange you one if you cover the meal."

The kid watched the interaction between his new road partner and the waitress. He realized they were about to get a free meal for the price of a pill that could very well have been aspirin, as far as he knew.

Roger opened the jar and shook one loose onto the table, fully aware of the young woman's decision.

"This better be everything you say it is."

"And more. I recommend holding off until after work. Preferably when you're home alone."

"Oh, I've got two roommates."

"Very well. That should be an interesting night for all of you. Now how about those burgers?"

Charlie couldn't refuse a soft bed for the night. After a late dinner at the burger joint, Roger suggested grabbing a hot shower and bed before tearing out of town in the early hours. As it turned out, they received a free room for the price of one pill. A courtesy deal that Roger had struck with the owner.

Charlie was sure the old man was going to put some perverted moves on him behind the motel's closed doors. But when it came down to it, he never did. He really just desired a shower and a bed. That was okay with Charlie, because the bed was a slice of heaven compared to his bed-roll in an empty field.

Lying in bed under the soft red glow of the neon lights bleeding through the curtains, Charlie thought again about the damn pills. The way Roger had smoothly conned the girl into a swap, a single pill for a free meal. He wasn't so sure of Roger's claim.

Although Charlie had asked him if the stuff was an LSD trip-out-of-your-mind drug experience, Roger denied that it was any such thing. It was an experiment of an en-lightened mind to open up the world to surroundings you never knew were there before. It makes you see the real world without the filters of the mind that obscure both the terror and the bliss that's always right in front of you.

Charlie figured that Roger's spiel was nothing more than a salesman's bullshit pitch to build hype about a prod-uct that was a long stretch from the facts. Still, the idea of escaping the turmoil of life for a short while called to him, and he was beginning to listen.

As Roger lightly snored in the adjacent single bed, Charlie silently slipped from the sheets. The neon glow helped him find the car keys on the nightstand and made it easy to maneuver to the door. The hinges offered no complaints as he rotated the door open and stepped out-side.

The motel's parking lot offered an eerie welcoming as the quiet made Charlie believe that he and Roger were the last inhabitants on the planet.

Charlie slipped the key into the rear door lock and popped it open. There were maybe fifteen boxes filled with glass bottles, all holding Roger's secret stash of mystery pills. What he found in the first box wasn't pills at all, but newspaper articles. Charlie slid into the backseat, and under the dim glow of the dome light, he flipped through each article. Every single one of them read of mayhem and murder. Charlie was beginning to understand his travel mate seemed to have a strange fascination with the morbid side of life.

Charlie removed a bottle from one of the boxes. He studied the pills inside. They really did look like aspirin, but knew by the way Roger spoke of them, they were nothing generic.

Charlie shook the jar, spilling two pills into his palm, and tucked them in his hip pocket. He wanted to place one on his tongue now and let it seep into his system, but sleep had been pulling at him. He knew he needed at least a few hours of rest before Roger wanted to hit the road.

"Did you sleep well?" Roger asked as they left the hotel room and rounded the vehicle to the rear.

"Like the dead. I haven't slept that well in nearly two weeks. Thank you for sharing the room. I could have slept in the car just fine."

"Think nothing of it. Are you a sleepwalker?"

"No, why?"

"I heard you went out late last night."

Charlie's face flushed a bit as his mind desperately searched for an excuse.

"I needed a smoke, is all. I didn't want to do it in the room. I figured it would bother you."

Roger's look was inexpressive as he turned to Charlie. His eyes weren't necessarily hard, but inquisitive. It was a look stating disbelief without saying it outright.

"I could show you the ropes of this business. I think we'd work well together. It's all a matter of trust."

Charlie couldn't stop his eyes from going to the ground, a tell he knew Roger would instantly pick up.

"Yes, sir. Trust is an important thing."

"That's good to hear."

Roger closed the back door and headed for the driver's seat. Charlie's fingers probed his hip pocket. Deep down, he found the white pills. Pinching them between his forefinger and thumb, he brought them out. With a smooth movement, they slipped inside his mouth. His tongue immediately told his mind to spit the bitter pills out, but Roger was suspiciously watching him over the roof of the vehicle. Charlie smiled and worked the dry pills down his throat. Without water, they got stuck midway. His throat piston, trying to force them down or out. Just as he figured he was going to retch them up, the muscles of his esophagus finally banished them to his stomach.

"Everything all right?" Roger asked as they dropped into the front seats.

"Um, yeah. Just a bit of heartburn is all. That burger didn't sit well last night. It might have had too much fat in it. Too much fat always gives me heartburn. I'll be fine."

"Things like that affect us old guys. A young man like you shouldn't be afflicted with such a malady.

"My father had it. He passed it on to me. No big deal. Life goes on until it doesn't," Charlie said and looked out his window as they pulled away from the motel and headed to unknown parts of the world.

"Life goes on until it doesn't. I like that saying. It's truer than people realize. Take today, for example. Well, today could very well be the last day you or I ever saw. One second we're here, and the next second we're not. You never know when your number gets called. I suppose only some sort of supreme being knows what comes next," Roger said and cracked the knuckles of his left hand, and then his right.

"I suppose so."

Charlie felt a warmth flood through him, as if he'd just thrown back a couple of shots of southern whisky. His face flushed, and a shallow tremble rippled through his extremities. His hands shook, and he clasped them in his lap so Roger couldn't see the new development of his passenger's physical being.

Holy shit, this is some fast-acting stuff. Definitely not aspirin.

"Have you ever been to Texas before?"

Charlie's heart began a rhythmic gallop, so much so that he could feel his pulse hammering in various parts of his body.

I shouldn't have taken both. A dumbshit idea. He's gonna know. He's gonna know I got into his stash.

Charlie switched his sight from Roger to the road before them. The color of the day was morphing. A heavy shade of orange had dropped on the landscape, as if the beginning of dusk had instantly followed dawn. He narrowed his eyes, trying to determine if something unnatural tinged the sun's beams or if the drug was affecting his vision.

Roger said, "People live in a fantasy world. If they only knew of the terror that surrounded them on a daily basis would shock most of them into an immediate death."

Elvis' latest hit fell off the airwaves, followed by a local news report.

Gatlin police were called to a residence in the late-night hours by a neighbor claiming to hear screams for help next door. As the police attempted to get the attention of the homeowner, a young woman exited through another door, running at the police with hedge trimmers. Trying everything possible, the officers were unable to calm the woman down and get her to release the weapon. The police shot Helena Daniels to death as the officers defended their lives. The story grows even more bizarre as additional police arrive and find a gruesome scene inside. Ms. Daniels' roommates were cut to pieces with the same hedge trimmers she attempted to injure the officers with.

Charlie knew the name Helena. And Helena had two roommates. And Helena took a single pill from the man in the seat next to him.

Charlie's eyes made a slow, mechanical rotation across the orange scenery until they locked on Roger. He was leaning forward with eagerness as the news report rolled out, as if his ears couldn't wait for further details of carnage. Both hands gripped the top of the steering wheel, flexing slowly with an almost orgasmic longing. His wide eyes switched to Charlie. They were no longer the eyes of a man, but something inside straining to get out. Just like the scenery outside, the blue of his irises and the black of his pupils instantly changed. The irises were now a deep yellow of a dying sun, and the pupils, stretched to double points like the eyes of a venomous snake, was the color of Hell's oldest raging fire. And Charlie saw Hell in those eyes, because Roger was something old, ancient, maybe, Charlie figured.

Roger's fingers elongated, stretching into pointed appendages, and from each end a yellowed talon pressed out of the skin folds like cat claws. Roger watched the road again. He was speaking, but Charlie heard nothing said.

His sight now fixed on the man's mouth, where a hundred needle teeth moved up and down with the movement of his jaw. His lips faded all color until only black remained.

Charlie clamped his eyes shut, visually banishing the godforsaken demon next to him.

You're losing it! Breathe! Just breathe!

"I can see it in your face. I've seen it countless times before. You're sliding deep into the drift now. Soon there will be no going back. Once you've drifted, it closes behind you. It's a sealed door after that."

Charlie heard him but understood none of it.

With his eyes still pinched shut, Charlie asked, "What does 'in the drift' mean?"

"As I've said, your world is a fantasy. A make-believe realm of the human condition. Time and circumstances have settled blinders over your eyes. Ever since then, some deity has proclaimed that we can't touch you or make known that we're here. But I found a way. A simple pill that strips the blindfold from your mind. Once you slip back into the drift of reality, when you fully understand real life, then there's nothing that can stop us."

Charlie let his left eye creep open, but his right one instantly shot open when he saw that Roger wasn't Roger anymore. He had nearly doubled in size. The thing hunched over the wheel with its face almost touching the windshield as the car's space couldn't accommodate the massive thing. The seat springs and supporting brackets groaned in protest, as the thing's weight greatly exceeded the recommended limit. His skin had changed, too. The pallid complexion of an older man had gone scarlet, very much the tone of some demon right out of Hell.

"Once, somewhere outside of Albuquerque, I picked up a kid not much older than you. He'd also stolen a pill from my supplies. As soon as he fell into the drift, he dug his own eyes right out of his head. So gross. Please don't do that. The blood gets everywhere, and it's a real bastard to get off upholstery," the red giant said in a voice that was still very much like Roger's voice.

Charlie screamed then. The scream came from deep down inside, possibly torn loose from his soul, if that were possible. He felt his vocal cords give, and a pitiful moan followed.

Roger turned to watch him as he still maneuvered the vehicle down the highway. The left side of his face hitched up in a grin as he studied his passenger's manic mental collapse. Then the Roger-thing also screamed. Not a scream of terror, but one of mocking joy as he knew Charlie could now see all of him, as he is, as he always was, a larger-than-life monster only ever mimicked before in silver screen horror flicks.

Small horns corkscrewed from the Roger-thing's hairline. As he turned from the road to look at Charlie again, the pointed tip snagged the vehicle's headliner and peeled the fabric back.

Charlie spasmodically bounced forward and back in his seat as the grip of unprecedented fear took hold. His right hand fumbled for the door handle, but his broken nerves couldn't seize it in the first three attempts. Then, his fingers curled around the metal lever and began to pull.

"Wait. You're gonna kill yourself falling from the—" Roger began, but the kid had already thrown himself from the vehicle.

Charlie tipped back out the open door, letting his spine punch the pavement at fifty miles an hour. His head reacted to the impact by snapping back, bludgeoning his skull against the unforgiving concrete. Then the momentum of forward movement rolled his body off the road and onto the grass of the shoulder.

Charlie heard nothing as the surge of adrenaline coursed through his entire body like a lightning bolt. Unaware of the road rash and three broken fingers, Charlie was on his feet, running behind the station wagon. His arms frantically waved back and forth, trying to slow traffic coming from the opposite direction, desperate for someone to drive him away from the madness.

When Charlie looked over his shoulder, some kind of giant lizard was scampering across the road behind him. It was the size of a monitor lizard, but grossly deformed, as its eyes hovered above its head on small, fleshy pillars. It had white tufts of hair in small patches across its body and wrinkled gray skin where no hair grew. It moved across the road on six legs instead of four, chasing after Charlie with a desire to play, and not maim.

Charlie spun forward, and as he did, his body moved in front of the ice cream truck. No one heard the impact over Charlie's scream tearing through decimated vocal cords.

The ice cream truck's brakes locked, causing a howl and bark of rubber as the vehicle instantly struggled to obey the command.

Roger braked too. Shifting into park, he worked his massive body out of the station wagon. Lumbering toward the accident fifty yards back, he could see there was no chance the young man had survived the impact. In fact, it looked to him that the boy had also been pulled under the tires, causing bodily damage that no skilled surgeon could mend if the boy still breathed.

A man twenty years Roger's junior shot out the driver's door and went to the front of the vehicle. Staring at the gore covering his grill, he finally broke the spell and kneeled, searching the undercarriage of his cool treats vehicle. When he leaned back up, Roger saw him wobble, as the sight of unintentional carnage was too much for him to bear.

Roger was there to catch the man as dizziness and a near faint overcame him.

"Whoa! I got you, fella!"

Roger used his muscle mass to hold the man while gently lowering him to the pavement.

"That's a lot to take in. Just sit here and catch your breath."

"That kid came out of nowhere. I couldn't even get on the brake before—before—before we hit."

"Sure, buddy. Don't you worry. I saw the entire thing in the rearview mirror. You're right. He came out of no-where. He did for sure. Nothing could have been done."

"He must have been running from that white dog. Must have thought it was trying to bite him or something."

Roger whistled, and the animal that looked very much like a six-legged, wingless dragon waddled over. The animal showed no signs of viciousness, only curiosity.

The highway travelers all came to a standstill, looking at the two men petting a white dog, but the men's eyes transfixed on the ice cream truck and the body tightly rolled underneath.

No one saw the reasoning behind Charlie's mad dash from the area, because none of those people were in the drift.

The county police and an ambulance showed up soon after. Roger had consoled the driver as much as possible, but the torment inside the man's heart was fierce. Roger knew of one way the man could slip out of the realm of grief.

Police took the driver's statements and witness reports. Roger, standing two feet taller than the cop's six-foot frame, offered his recount of the incident. No panic ensued over the creature that looked very much like a devil because, again, no one had the luxury of seeing reality until they slid into the drift.

As Roger watched the medical team try to remove the mangled remains of the boy from beneath the truck, an idea came to him.

"It sure is getting to be a scorcher. I'm standing here and I can't help but see the decals of all those cool treats on the side of your truck. Say, when this is all said and done, how about we make a sort of trade?"

SOUL SURVIVOR

Randall Iverson felt a lump in his throat. It was the terrifying sensation of a man knowing he was about to die, and helpless at preventing it.

The mountainous man, who worked for Mr. Ansaldo, escorted him with a firm grip on his upper arm. Randall didn't know his name, but knew if he tried to run, the man would twist him in half before he got three feet.

Mr. Ansaldo knows I stole from him. He's going to beat it out of me. He's going to have this giant break my fingers, and when I confess, he's going to put a bullet through my head. Why the hell did I think I could get away with it?

"Randall!" Walter Ansaldo called out after the big man pushed him through the office door. "Victor, please be careful. Mr. Iverson is my guest this evening."

"Sorry, Mr. Ansaldo. I don't always know my own strength."

"Perfectly all right! It's okay. You can leave us now. We'll be fine. I will let you know if I need anything."

The big man nodded, headed out the door, leaving the two to get acquainted.

Randall nervously rubbed his hands together, unsure of what to say. He thought about blurting it out, a quick confession followed by a desperate plea for forgiveness.

"Please, Randall, have a seat," he said and motioned to the single chair opposite the large mahogany desk.

"Thank you, sir."

Mr. Ansaldo waved his hand. "Please call me Walter. I don't know if you know this, but you and I are very much alike. In more ways than you've ever realized."

"Oh? I didn't know that."

"Of course you didn't. There's probably not much about me that you would know," Walter said. He removed a cigar from the humidor, clipped the end, and slowly lit it with a match. "I started out with nothing. My mother worked two jobs just to keep us off the streets. My youth was a time of self-motivation. I wanted money. I wanted power. I always felt I deserved it because I was a young punk who could move the world if I just had the opportunity to do so. I was willing to trample anyone to get what I wanted."

"You certainly achieved all that, Walter."

"I did. Far more than anyone knows. Money, power, control of all the state's politicians, and the dirt on all those around here who have any social leverage. I'm the guy behind the curtain controlling the puppet strings."

"I'm envious of all that you have," Randall said and looked at the floor, trying to understand where the conversation was rounding toward.

"Is that right? Envious of me. That must be the reason you stole from me to begin creating your own empire. Is that it?"

Randall felt the blood rush from his face. It was such a quick action that he was sure he was going to black out.

"Sir, I can explain. If you could just give me one chance to make things right."

"Of course! Of course! That's why you're here! If anything, I'm well known for giving second chances." Walter leaned back and watched Randall through a cloud of smoke. He pointed with the cigar and asked, "What do you think of that chair you're sitting in?"

Randall, instantly confused, looked down. There was nothing special about the chair, really. He knew it was nicer than anything in his apartment, but not by much.

"Ah, it's very lovely, sir."

"Walter."

"Sorry. Walter."

"That chair is significant. What I mean is that chair has killed sixty-one condemned men."

Randall's eyes went wide as his mind desperately tried to find a way out of the situation that was going to end with him in a pine box.

"Oh, relax. I don't mean I killed sixty-one people who sat in that chair. I meant the chair itself. You see that chair is quite a relic. I purchased it four years ago. The Louisiana State Prison board got tired of pumping money into updates at one of their prisons outside of Baton Rouge. So, they allocated funds to build a new prison and abandoned the old one. Well, they auctioned off what they could to help pay for the new facility. But that thing right there wasn't for sale. In fact, it was on the short list of things to be decommissioned by way of fire in the prison yard."

Randall looked at the chair again, completely unsure of Walter's direction with this conversation.

"I'm afraid I'm not following."

"Sixty-one people have died by way of electrocution in that chair. Ol' Sparky is what inmates across the country used to call those execution devices. Anyway, I got some inside information about their scheduling to burn it. So, I offered quite a sum to the demolition crew to get me that chair before it became cinders.

He's got a twisted perversion for the macabre. One man who can own nearly anything on the planet, and he wanted a chair of death, Randall thought.

"It is—ah—very nice."

Walter slammed his fist down on the desk, rattling all the glass trinkets.

Jeremy M. Wright

"It's not nice, Randall! It's sick as fuck that I had an overwhelming desire to own that chair. But there's a very important reason for it. Sure, it isn't the chair's fault sixty-one people cooked in it. It's just a stupid instrument designed to kill." Walter took a pull on his cigar and watched through the expelled cloud at Randall's expression. "Relax. I'm just trying to make my point. Forgive me if I get a bit wound up. Sixty of the men I couldn't care less about. They were all scum who got the ending they deserved, followed by an eternity of roasting in hell. But the last one, the one who sizzled like a sausage the final time that big switch got flipped, well, he's the real reason I needed that chair."

Randall quickly stood, not in a desperate attempt to flee, but because the idea he was sitting where sixty-one men had evacuated bladders and bowels for the last time caused an acidic flow to shoot up his throat.

The gun came out lightning quick, like a Wild West gunslinger. The silver barrel stared down at Randall, daring him to move again.

"Sit your ass back down," Walter said with a smooth command.

Randal did. He hit the chair without realizing he'd moved.

"Sir—ah—Walter, I mean, I admit that I did steal from you, and I'm willing to pay it all back, plus interest. It's just that my daughter is sick and needs a—"

"What she needs is no concern of mine. When you steal from an employer, you fracture the trust. Once you do that, there's no way to mend that bond. So, as I was saying, the last man to cook in that chair is the importance of why I needed to own it. My life as a youth was a hard road. I grew up in the slums of New Orleans. Many nights I went without supper because my father spent it on

141

alcohol. He was an intolerable man to live with. His name was Walter Jonathan Ansaldo Senior. Listen closely now. I'm going to give you the facts."

Randall felt nausea overwhelm him then. It felt like an unexplainable weirdness course across him, rather, a sensation of something beginning to creep through him, just under the skin.

"Long before they decommissioned that execution device, there had been rumors dating back decades about that chair being haunted. Prison guards were sure that a little of the evil inside each man somehow seeped into the chair at the moment of execution. So, it stands to reason that sixty-one men left a piece of their soul inside that chair. Again, sixty of the men are not my concern. It's the last man who sat there that piques my interest. My father. The man who, in a drunken rage, brutally beat my mother to death with a wrench. The same man who threw my little brother into a wall and then through a window, causing him to fall three stories to his death. I wasn't home at the time. I had been out with my friends, causing teenage mayhem. Otherwise, I would have been victim number three. He sat on death row for nearly twenty-three years before they finally flipped the switch and juiced him to hell."

"Sir, with all due respect, what does your previous family life have anything to do with me?"

"Everything, Randall! Everything! You see, today is the five-year anniversary of his death. When an anniversary date comes around for all those sixty-one men, they get a chance to escape."

Whatever Randall felt suddenly intensified. There was an unexpected inability to move. The effort of just trying to lift his arms from the armrests was impossible. He felt the nausea turn to sheer confusion, as if his thoughts were no longer his. His mind pulled back as his mental control was taking a backseat to a more powerful entity.

"There it is. I can see it in your eyes. My old man is surfacing. From what I understand, you'll still be fully aware of what's going on, and feel every bit of pain I decide to administer. This will be the third time I've met my father face to face since his execution. It will also be the third time I've killed him and sent his soul back into that chair until next year, when we play this game all over again." Walter leaned forward and licked his lips as if savoring the remains of an exquisite meal. "I know you can hear me, Pops. I can see that darkness working its way out of the chair and into the body I provided for you."

Randall tried to speak, tried to deny this was really happening. His thoughts were still there, sort of, but the voice had left his control. He sensed his head and heart saturating with hate, consumed by it, really. With a terrifying thought, he suspected this must be what Bruce Banner felt when the Hulk seized the reins and unleashed a fury of destruction.

Walter Ansaldo Junior opened a desk drawer and removed a device that confused his father. As he pulled the bands over his head, securing the goggles, and pressed a switch on the side.

"Night vision goggles. I've changed the game since last time. I get to watch you struggle. I get to watch you bleed."

With that, Walter slammed his hand down on the silver button on his desk. The overhead lights blackened, leaving both men in a sinister game of death.

"Survive one hour and I'll let you stay in that body. Over one hour and your damned soul goes back to the chair."

"You ungrateful son of a bitch. I'm going to dig your eyes out with my thumbs, then crush your skull with my hands," Randall heard himself say.

"There's nothing intimidating about that body. You'd be lucky if you could crush a bird with those hands," Walter said.

"A chickenshit is what you are. You put me in a weak body because you can't fight a real man. You never could. The only way you ever won anything in life was by cheating."

Walter instantly moved as the green night vision showed his father sprang from the chair, lunging forward onto the desk, and reaching out. The body was young, so it was quick and flexible. He knew that factored into his one-hour timeline. This time, his father might very well survive. But he had plans for all of that.

Walter silently went to a switch on the wall and flicked it. The sound of gears activated, followed by the groaning slide of walls. Walter watched as the plain walls disappeared and behind them remained walls consisting of razor blades and nails, with all points aimed at drawing blood.

His father walked slowly, testing each step before committing. His hands waved about, searching for a grip on his son. Two feet from the wall, his left hand quickly drew back after being bitten by sharpened steel.

"Sonofabitch. I wish you had been home the day I threw your brother out the window. You would have gone right after him," he said and wiped a smear of blood across his shirt.

"How does it feel to be hunted?" Walter whispered, and then quickly moved back out of reach.

The old man angrily thrust toward his voice, his desperate hands needing to break bones. Walter shoved, driving his father toward a wall of pain. His old man blindly tripped over his own feet before being planted into razors.

"Having fun yet?" Walter asked.

He looked at the bloody handprints being left on the concrete and smiled.

Walter looked at his watch. Fifteen minutes and his old man had barely offered blood. Quietly, he went to the desk, pressed another button that dimly lit an exit sign. Next, he opened a desk drawer and retrieved the cattle prod. The first shock was at the base of his father's spine, activating a symphony of nerves.

"Time to move on. I'm bored with this room. Go to the exit," he said and shocked him three more times to get him moving.

"I swear I'm going to end you," his old man said.

This isn't fair! Get the hell out of my body! It isn't my fault. I didn't kill anyone. Give me my body back! Randall thought.

Talking to him in the darkness was a voice, deep, calculating, but oddly calm despite the torture game being played.

You'd better listen to me, kid. With or without your help, I'm getting through this. I refuse to be condemned to that chair for another year. If we can work together, we'll live. In order to put me back in that chair, he has to kill you. You have a daughter and a wife. I can read your mind. I know how important they are to you. Work with me, and you'll see them again.

Randall knew the old man was right. He would die.

What do I have to do?

I don't have full control of your body. It's like trying to work the limbs of a two-year-old. We have to concentrate together just to operate like you normally would.

The cattle prod offered another nerve jolt, blinding Randall's thoughts in a white light.

Left, right, left, right, the voice commanded.

Randall obeyed. He needed to see his family again. To hold his daughter at least one more time was enough motivation to listen to the voice of a murderer.

He looked up, seeing the soft glow of an exit sign. Crawling, he reached out for the wall, expecting to receive razor cuts, but found a door instead. It swung easily under his hand. Together they pushed through, feeling the ground transition from concrete to cold steel. His hands detected dead space on both sides. He heard the door spring shut behind him and the deadbolts engage.

The world of darkness fled as lights nearly as blinding as the sun triggered on overhead. Randall felt the old man lose himself as the abrupt change was just as jarring to him. He sensed a buckling of their grip on the steel girder below. His disorientation was so severe that Randall felt his head dipping into the empty space on the right.

The old man caught them enough, giving Randall a moment to get his bearings.

Below them was nearly a forty-foot drop into a motionless fan.

"Ooo. That was a close one! I haven't even started things yet," Walter said from an elevated lookout.

Randall looked up, seeing the slit along the metal wall and Walter's beady eyes watching through it. The room was cylindrical, with metal beams meeting at a center point like a giant wagon wheel.

Two things happened at once. The beam contraption Randall balanced on began a slow spin, and the fan below did the same.

"Do you see the door? It will open and close at set intervals. The longer you take to get through it, the faster the fan and platform speed up. Take too long and there's no way you can hold on! Then for you it's the shit hitting the fan!" Walter cackled then, a shrill laugh triggered by his own pathetic joke.

"You're such an asshole!" Randall yelled, realizing his thoughts could control his voice.

Randall thought, *Okay, so we're copilots. We both have some control over my body. Well then, we work together, and we can beat him.*

Now you're talking, came the reply.

The metal door Walter claimed to be an exit, opened for no more than three seconds before offering a defying slam.

Randall shuffled on hands and knees across the girder to the center. There was a less chance of becoming dizzy and falling from here. He also knew it was an advantage to see the door and calculate the timing from when it opened and closed. He would be able to tell which girder he had to be on to be the closest to the door.

Then the wagon wheel and fan kicked up another gear and threw off his entire calculations. There was no way to measure his timing from any girder to the door the exact moment it opened.

He's not playing fair. He stacked the odds against us. All we can do is work our way to one end and pray the door opens right when we need it to, Randall thought.

So we do that, the old man replied.

Randall shimmied down the girder in the direction he was already facing, so he wouldn't have to turn and risk falling into the spinning blades. The increased speed of the fan grabbed at his body and clothes, trying to unbalance him and push him from the beam and into certain death.

Randall was halfway down the beam when the door opened. His rotation was nearly perfect to catch it if he'd been closer, but the distance was too great, and he'd fall to a gruesome death if he'd attempted to leap it.

"Keep your eyes on the target! Part of me wants to fall so I can see what the fan does to your body, but I also want you to make it to the next stage! Oh! It's all so very exciting!" Walter screamed through the slit wall.

If we fall into the fan, I hope it sprays blood in his eyes and mouth, Randall told the old man.

The old man offered a bellowing, raspy laugh.

Everything geared up again, and Randall pulled himself tighter to the girder. The centrifugal force of the wheel pushed him closer to the steel wall against any possible resistance his hands would allow.

The door rotated open again, but at the same time came a different sound. Randall looked over his shoulder, seeing what looked like a bowling ball fixed to a chain strike at the center of the wheel. It instantly began retracting into the ceiling thirty feet above. The door slammed shut, followed by another bowling ball colliding with the wheel in front of him. Randall quickly pulled back to avoid the thing knocking his head off. Shrapnel of the material blew apart, digging into his face like slivers of glass.

A fury of curses vibrated through Randall's head as both men found choice words to title the man cowering behind a layer of steel.

Randall caught a glimpse of the door opening, followed by the sound of a chain as another ball dropped.

Move! The old man commanded, and Randall followed the order. He fully expected the ball to shatter his spine mid-leap, causing him to become a pureed mess in the blades below. He hit the open door with enough velocity to drive him halfway through. His ribs had taken a mule kick from the threshold. His lack of grip on the inside door frame caused his legs to be battered against the tremendous speed of the rotating wheel. He hitched his lower body back and forth, creating enough push to work himself through the door.

Randall clawed at the floor, desperately trying to pull himself out of the way. Then the door triggered, catching the metal edge on his left shin, hammering the bone before shoving it out of the way and locking shut again.

"Son of a bitch!" Randall yelled and cradled the injury.

The pain rumbled through the nerves of his leg, bringing undeniable surrender to his mind. But there was no surrender in Walter's game. There was only death.

Push through it. Think of your little girl. Think about how much you want to see her again, the old man said.

I don't need a fucking pep talk from a murderer! You killed your own wife and son! Your goddamn words mean nothing to me!

Yes, I've done terrible things in my life. That place of isolation, concrete and steel, made me see every fault I ever had. I killed them out of fear for my own life. This is no time to get into it, but I'd taken some bad drugs. It made me see the faces of monsters and not my own wife and child. Forget about that now. Get your ass up!

Randall felt the old man's efforts to control his body, and he joined in. Together they stood in yet another pitch-black room, but that uncertainty didn't last. Lights around the room began rapidly blinking with a strobe light effect, causing a nauseating illusion of things moving at clipped speeds.

The fucking floor is moving, the old man thought. Randall could sense downright dread in that statement.

Everything just seems like it's moving or moving differently than it's supposed to. It's what the light does, Randall told him.

Look, dumbass!

Randall tried to focus even with the mind-spinning blink of the lights. The old man was right. The floor was a mass of snakes. Long and short ropes of slithering bodies moved across the room. All of them were looking for the same thing Randall needed: a way out.

Over a loudspeaker, Walter's voice reverberated through the room.

"I remembered a trauma you suffered when I was a kid. It was a summer day after school was out, and you took us to the park. It was one of the few nice things you ever did for us. Anyway, lying in the grass, a garner snake slithered under your bare legs. I'll never forget the terror on your face that a harmless garner snake created. You've always had a fear of snakes, haven't you? So here I've offered a variety. There are a few poisonous ones, so do be careful. One of them is not like the others. Only there will you find your escape!"

What does that mean? One snake is different? Randall thought.

He could sense the panic building within himself, but knew it was the old man's phobia overcoming him.

Relax. No sudden moves. Don't kick them or step on them. Slow and unthreatening steps and they'll have no reason to bite. We have to figure out what he meant. Work with me. We have to walk through the room if you want out of here.

Randall sensed the panic subsiding as the old man tried to pin down one of his worst fears come to life.

In unison, they slid each foot through the tangles of snakes. Each movement was delicate and unthreatening. Randall knew he had to get them to move so they could determine which one was unlike the others. When the first snake tried slithering up his pant leg, the old man went into a frenzy. His left leg came up and violently shook, trying to work it out before it got to his crotch. It was long, but not aggressive, and easily came back out.

The flashing lights were making Randall's head throb. It also made it extremely difficult to tell one cluster of snakes from another. Finding one particular snake in a room of hundreds proved nearly impossible.

Randall bent over and pulled each sock over the cuff of his pants, keeping any additional slithering investigators out of his private business.

In the far corner, a lone snake lay motionless. Whether sleeping or dead, Randall couldn't tell.

Over there, he told the old man.

Moving along its side, Randall watched it, waiting for a strike. He didn't know the names of most snakes, but this one he did. It was a coral snake. Red, yellow, and black bands covered its skin. This snake was one of the poisonous ones Walter had warned him about. Randall nudged it with his shoe and quickly pulled back, expecting the thing to take a bite in protest. It didn't move. He did it again, only this time stepping on it to get some sort of reaction. His shoe caused it to roll belly up.

It's dead, the old man said.

Not dead. It's fake.

Randall crouched and picked it up. A rubber snake mixed in with hundreds of very real snakes. He turned it over while working his squeezing fingers along its body. When he got to the head, he felt something hard. Inside its mouth was the key to his freedom. As Randall turned his eyes to find the door, the light quit flashing. The darkness enhanced his hearing. All the bodies moving along the floor and the defensive hissing at each other heightened considerably.

Keeping his soles flat on the ground, Randall pushed bodies out of the way. One snake didn't like being bullied, and it struck. He felt the snag of fangs on denim at his upper calf, but was almost certain no fang broke skin.

Reaching the door, Randall ran his hands over the steel. There was no doorknob, only a key slot into a deadbolt.

When the door rotated open, Randall found himself in Walter's office again. Only this time, the walls of broken razor blades remained.

The door behind the large desk opened. Walter stepped through while smoothly raising his arm. A small arrow from a handheld crossbow was released.

Randall had no time to react, resulting in the arrow driving into the meat of his right thigh. The pain was not as severe as he expected as the denim pants slowed its speed. The game of death he'd been forcibly playing was the focus of his anger now. He moved forward on a damaged leg. Walter was cocking the string back, trying to load another arrow before he got there. Randall leaped over the desk, scrambling with a rage as his last mental thread was near breaking. The hook of his fingers grabbed Walter's shirt as his body slid off the desk. The fat man came down on top of him as he hit the floor. Now, having the disadvantage of the man's full weight on him, he did the only thing he could think of doing. Randall grabbed Walter's crotch and squeezed with what little energy he had left.

The fat man howled and bucked, trying to work his weight into a standing position. Randall let him go, taking the opportunity to slide back along the floor.

Walter followed him, drawing back his enormous leg, and then delivering a brutal kick to the ribs. Randall gripped the end of the crossbow arrow, sliding it free from the muscle of his thigh. When Walter kicked again, Randall drove the point into the man's shin, feeling it skid off bone before plunging deep into nerves, tendons and muscles.

Now! We take him now! The old man hollered.

The arrow was reluctant to let go, but as Randall twisted, it came free and he immediately reinserted into the big man's right side, punching into the liver. Then with a fury he repeated the action, brutally destroying important organs with manic glee.

Despite his nearly depleted strength, Randall grabbed Walter's suit jacket and spun the man, resulting in him collapsing into the chair that had eaten the souls of sixty-one men.

Walter expelled a hard breath, splattering the surface of his desk with red. He was trying to speak, trying to complete one final insult before the light dimmed from his eyes and blinked away forever.

"Thank you, son. You've given me the greatest gift anyone ever could. You gave me a second life, and a business of power to do what I wish. With this young body there will be so many decades to build this into an empire."

The large man who had led Randall into the office opened the main door, stupidly stared at the situation that had gone so far off plan.

"Kill him! For God's sake, kill him!" Walter demanded.

"No, no, no. I played your game and won. There's no one left here to die except you."

The giant at the door looked at his boss, knowing the man was about to expire. He then looked at Randall and said, "I'll leave you to finish business, sir. Anything you need, please don't hesitate to ask."

"And just like that, I'm accepted as your replacement," the old man said and snapped his fingers.

Randall moved around the massive desk and took a seat in the oversized chair that was more of a throne than anything.

Walter's hands were slick with blood as he desperately tried to hold the flow of life inside as long as possible. He knew he was epically losing the battle.

"But will it last? Do you know how many people tried to overthrow me? There's always a bigger dog who wants it all," Walter said.

"Very true in this disrespectful and vicious world. No one has any loyalty anymore. But I'll knock them down one by one when they come calling. Until then, I sure will enjoy playing games with my son. I suppose I'll see you again this time next year."

Unable to do anything but search for another breath, Walter barely realized what his father was saying. He tried to roll his bulk off the chair, desperate to keep the godforsaken chair from devouring a part of his soul. He couldn't. No matter how much the will was there, he'd tapped out on every bit of strength he once had.

As the old man watched his son die in the same chair that had stolen his life years before, he thought of the possibilities this new life could bring.

He said to Randall, "It's you and me now, kid. Together we're unstoppable, as we proved here today. With your wife and daughter at your side, we'll be royalty in a land of cretins. They're safe around me. I swear it. This is a new life for both of us. Family is everything. Except for him. We've got time, you know? We have a full year to decide just what kind of delicious game we want to play."

Randall knew the old man was right. He wasn't capable of running an operation as complex as this by himself. He needed a man with a hard, deceitful heart to make it all happen. One body and two minds were pure power no other man could match.

He looked at the pathetic ruin that was Walter Ansaldo Junior and smiled as his mind created elaborate rooms of death beyond any level of mayhem the world has ever seen.

Strange Behavior

Caleb was humming again. Millie smiled at her son's nonchalant perspective on life. Boys at the age of four have no worries about any aspect of life other than sugar-based snacks and cartoons. That outlook was ideal, and people should cherish it, because adult life eventually drains it from everyone.

The spring breeze rolled through the open windows, bringing with it the aroma of lavender and honeysuckle.

It was a safe neighborhood, Millie knew, but that didn't stop her from going to the front windows every so often to make sure Caleb hadn't ventured out of the yard. He was in the driveway as usual, selecting another chalk from the bucket of assorted colors. A four-year-old's artistic touch frequently adorned the driveway. She could see a bright yellow sun sporting a smile and a birthday hat. A boy riding a bike off a ramp. Also, a horse prancing through a meadow. At least, that's what she thought they were.

She moved into the living room, sprayed down the coffee table with cleaner and wiped away the fingerprints and cup rings.

After making her way through the living room with cleaning supplies, Millie became instantly aware that she hadn't heard Caleb hum in quite some time. She quickly went to the front door, dreading she'd find an empty spot where a small boy should be. But he was there, standing instead of sitting. A red chalk was in his right hand, which Millie thought it was odd because Caleb was left-handed.

He wasn't looking at his artwork but instead, staring off into the meadow across the way.

"Honey, why don't you come in now?"

He didn't move or respond in any such way.

"Caleb. You've been out here for a while. Come get something to drink."

Millie received the same ignored response.

She went down the front steps and placed her hand on his shoulder. Her touch triggered no reaction. She followed his sight, finding absolutely nothing that would captivate the short attention span of a young boy.

Then Millie saw what he had drawn. But it couldn't be by his hand. It was impossible. The chalk drawing was made up of half a dozen colors and took up an entire square of the driveway. Not only that, but as Millie's eyes rolled over the work, she noticed how the details were far beyond the skill set of a four-year-old. In fact, it was so well done, Millie decided only someone entering creative arts college could harness the keen vision and artistic hand to pull off the chalk drawing.

The drawing showed a white airplane destroyed by the impact against the earth. A blaze of red, orange, and yellow chalk flames rolled out from that carnage. The drawing also gruesomely detailed mangled bodies outside the wreckage.

"Caleb, who drew this? Who was here?" Millie began shaking him then, trying to snap the boy out of his comatose state.

Then he did. His eyes faded back from a hypnotic state, and he smiled at her.

"Mommy!" he said and wrapped his arms around her.

"Caleb, was someone else here with you? Can you tell me who drew that?"

Caleb looked at the chalk drawing and smiled again.

"Airplane!"

"That's right. Who drew the airplane?"

Caleb shrugged and asked, "Can I have a snack?"

"Yes, but first tell me who was here."

Caleb shrugged again, unsure of what she was asking.

She looked at it again. It was a horrible nightmare vision no four-year-old could ever conceive. Then she noticed something she hadn't seen at first. Above the disaster scene in white chalk, he had written: 27.

When Mike got home, Millie instantly grabbed his arm and pulled him into the dining room.

"Did you see it?" she whispered.

"See what? He whispered back and grinned.

"On the driveway. The chalk drawing Caleb did."

"No, what is it today? Let me guess, it's a boy hanging onto a bunch of balloons floating through the sky. It's dark outside. I didn't notice anything when I pulled into the garage. Why does it matter?"

Before leading Mike outside, Millie confirmed that Caleb remained in front of the TV. She had turned on the driveway lights and nervously crossed her arms as she looked down.

Mike followed her gaze. Then he said, "Shut the hell up. Caleb didn't draw this! Did you hire someone so you could pull one over on me?"

Millie removed her phone from her pocket, opened an app, and played the home security video at three times the speed. She rotated the screen so Mike could watch the video of Caleb drawing the plane crash across the driveway. He moved with such focus, knowing the exact details that needed to be defined on the drawing.

Mike looked away from the screen, studied the driveway, and then looked at Millie.

"That's impossible. He's only four!"

Millie slowed the speed to normal and turned it to Mike again. She had stepped outside, spoken to Caleb, touched his shoulders, and still the boy stared off into the distance.

"He was completely catatonic. He had no idea I was there. Then he snapped out of it as if nothing had happened. But look at that drawing. It's completely sinister. Even if he had a genius gift for creating art, what would possess him to draw this? Someone doesn't go from a sun wearing a birthday hat to a plane crash with bloody bodies all over the ground."

"What do you suppose twenty-seven means? Or the one?"

"The one?"

Mike pointed to the area just below the plane wing. Millie hadn't noticed it before. Clearly it wasn't just a random line, as it had a horizontal line connecting below and the swoop at the top of the line.

"I didn't even see that before."

"I don't understand it. I also don't want it left here," Mike said. He went to the coiled hose, turned on the water and began washing the chalk colors away.

"I've tried and got nowhere. When you're finished, try talking to him. See if he remembers any of it," Millie said.

Millie took the bacon off the burner and placed it on a plate. Caleb was bouncing in place next to the counter while targeting his eyes on the first piece he was going to snag.

"Go ahead," she said, and he instantly snatched the bacon.

When Mike walked into the kitchen, the small counter TV switched to the local news.

"Late last night just outside of Liston, a plane crash claimed twenty-seven lives. The flight bound for San Francisco began experiencing engine trouble nearly half an hour after takeoff. The pilot requested an emergency landing. That was the last the control tower heard from the crew. To make the story even more astounding, rescuers discovered a sole survivor among the wreckage. The man was injured, but alive. Paramedics transported Edgar Stevens to the Hopewell Hospital. He is in stable condition."

The news switched to the morning forecast.

Millie and Mike looked at each other and then at Caleb. He was drizzling syrup across his stack of pancakes.

"I have no words," Mike said.

Caleb snorted and said, "Daddy forgot words."

After Caleb went to his room to play, Mike said, "Do you think there's any way we could get him to write down lottery numbers?"

"Be serious."

"I'm totally serious!"

"What do we do?" Millie asked.

"I'm sure it's a coincidence."

"Sure. I could see how you'd get to that conclusion. A drawing of a plane crash. Twenty-seven dead people and one survivor only a few hours later. Just a big old coincidence."

"How would it be possible for him to know that?"

"Maybe he's—a—what's it called? Oh, precognitive. People born with foresight into events that haven't happened yet."

"I don't believe any crap like that."

"Then explain it."

"I can't."

"As you saw on the video, he was in a trance of some sort. Regardless, he predicted what was going to happen."

"So, what do we do? We can't tell anyone. They'll call us liars and attention seekers. They'll say we changed the time on the security footage. Do you really want to go through that? Or put Caleb through it? He doesn't even remember doing it. Maybe it's just a one-time thing."

"But why would he get a vision? How is a four-year-old supposed to change the outcome? We couldn't even take it seriously until we saw the news."

"We let it go," Mike said.

"What if it happens again?"

"Then we deal with it. If it's something we can change, we'll see what we can do."

Caleb had become a carefree boy again. Nearly three weeks had passed without an incident.

When Millie called Caleb in for lunch, she saw an image that wedged an iceberg into her heart. As he ran past her to ravage his sandwich, Millie saw what he'd been working on. Filling the same driveway square that previously held the plane wreckage scene showed a large building. Millie stepped outside to get a better look. There was a plus symbol at the top of the arch.

Not a cross, she knew, but the symbol for first aid. A hospital. Lying near the entrance was a body, a nurse, judging by the uniform. A red pool surrounded her body.

Written in perfect grammar and penmanship below the chalk scene were the words:

If she couldn't love him, no one would ever love her again.

"Sweet Jesus," Millie whispered.

She instantly took a picture and sent it to Mike. When he called two minutes later, she answered.

"I had hoped that we were done with this," Mike said. His deflated voice sounded like that of a man approaching a mental breakdown.

"We can't ignore this."

"I agree. It looks like a nurse at a hospital in the drawing."

"So what do I do?"

Mike was silent for a minute, then said, "Anyone we call is going to think we're crazy, but we have to do something. You start by calling the local hospitals. Talk to the head administrator. Explain Caleb's visions. They will think you're bonkers, but you need to try to get them to listen. Just tell them to be extra alert today. I'm guessing it'll be today. The other event happened a few hours later."

"Okay. What are you going to do?"

"I know a few people to call. They have connections with the police department. Maybe they can do extra patrols around the hospitals tonight."

"Okay. I'll get to it. I love you."

"Love you, too," Mike said and hung up.

Millie didn't feel like she was making headway with anyone who answered the phone. She knew it was at least putting a bug in someone's ear, and that kind of manic phone call often got repeated to coworkers. Most of them wouldn't take it seriously, but it was there in the forefront of their minds when they left the hospital at the end of the shift. Aside from phone calls, there wasn't much else to do.

When Mike got home, he asked, "Have you spoken to Caleb about it?"

"No, and I wasn't going to show him what he had drawn. I'm sure, like before, he wouldn't remember. Besides, he doesn't need that image in his head."

"I agree. Well, I spoke with a couple of people. They got the word out. Likely, they'll have patrolmen making frequent rounds at the three hospitals in the area. Besides that, there isn't anything else to do without more information."

The evening news came on as Mike and Millie were clearing off the dinner table. It wasn't a story of a nurse surviving an attack as they had anticipated. Instead, it was additional information about the plane crash weeks before.

"In a bizarre twist to a story we brought you back in April, the FAA and state inspectors have released additional information on the plane crash just outside of Liston. As we reported before, twenty-seven people, including the pilot, perished in the crash. One man survived after being thrown from the wreckage. The man wasn't wearing a seatbelt, raising questions about why. The FAA has also released the flight deck recording. On the recording, Edgar Stevens, the sole survivor, ordered the pilot to tell ground control about possible engine failure. Then, the recording captured the pilot telling Mr. Stevens that he had obeyed the order and to put down the knife. Then we hear what can only be determined to be the sound of the pilot, Mitch Henderson, being repeatedly stabbed to death. When authorities reached the crash site and found Edgar Stevens still alive, paramedics immediately rushed him to Hopewell Hospital. He was discharged three weeks after his hospitalization. Authorities are now seeking him for further questioning."

"He killed the pilot? Why would someone do that?" Millie asked.

"Do you think it's the same man who will try to kill the nurse?"

"I do now. Can you call your friend and get the police over to Hopewell Hospital?"

Mike was instantly on the phone, calling his connection.

"Taylor, it's Mike. Millie and I now believe the plane crash survivor taken to Hopewell Hospital will kill a nurse there. Would it be possible for you to call the police chief and let him—"

Millie watched as Mike's expression fell flat. Although she could hear Taylor speaking, she couldn't make out what was being said.

"Oh, my God. Did they catch him?" After a pause, Mike said, "Okay, sure. Please keep me informed."

Millie watched Mike hang up and instantly take a seat.

"What is it?"

"They found the nurse dead in the parking lot, lying between two cars."

"Oh, Lord. All we tried to do, and it didn't change anything!"

"I don't think we can. I think these visions are definite outcomes."

"That doesn't make any sense. If something is, I don't know how to put it, speaking through Caleb, then what's the point if all our efforts always get us nowhere?"

Mike shook his head. "I have no answers to that. And what do we do if he has more? Do we ignore them? Do we erase them as quickly as possible and continue on with our lives?"

"There's more to it. There has to be. I can't believe for a second that we're just going along for the ride and watching that man continue to murder good people."

"Mommy, look at all the people!" Caleb said as he tugged on Millie's shirt.

"Hmm?" Millie said as she sat at the dining room table. Her thoughts were miles away from this house and the lunch she was supposed to be preparing for Caleb.

"Lots of them!"

"What are you talking about, honey?"

"Come look!"

Millie got up and followed Caleb to the front windows. There, she found a crowd gathering in her front yard. At first, she thought the neighbors were having members showing up for a party. Then she saw local news decals printed on the sides of vans and cars.

"What the hell?"

Caleb looked up at her.

"Sorry. Bad word."

Before she could even think about what to do next, the doorbell rang. The door glass was frosted, but she could make out a large group on the porch.

She didn't like this. Whatever it was, it seemed like an invasion of privacy.

She opened the door only slightly, keeping her foot wedged behind it in case someone tried to barge inside. She also kept Caleb behind her and out of view.

"Yes?"

One man with a bellowing voice trumped all others as he said, "Mrs. Miller, I'm Carl Malone with Channel Nine. We've been told that your son had several visions. One vision of the plane crash and one about last night's murder at Hopewell Hospital. Can you please give us more information about this?"

"Where is your son? May we speak with him?" another asked.

"Has he had any visions today?" A brunette in a blue pantsuit asked.

"Is your son psychically connected to a serial killer?" A blonde wearing a yellow dress demanded.

"What?" Millie asked. "Are you insane? Get off my property!"

"Young man, are you the one having the visions? If so, what's going to happen next?"

Millie realized Caleb had pushed his way to her side and now watched the hovering crowd yelling out questions.

"Don't even think you're going to question my son. He's four years old. You people need to get your facts straight before intruding on people's lives. Now get off my property before I call the police and file harassment charges on all of you!" Millie pushed Caleb back and slammed the door.

Millie's heart sledgehammered against her ribs. She didn't want to call the cops and possibly make matters worse. So she called Mike and rattled everything out.

"Are they still at the door?"

Millie looked and said, "No. They've moved back to the street and sidewalk."

"That's public property, so we can't do anything about it. If they get on the lawn, then call the cops. I think after a while, they'll realize you're not coming out. They'll get bored and leave."

"They scared the hell out of me with all those questions."

"Someone leaked to the press about us calling around, warning that a nurse was going to be killed. Just stay inside and away from the windows. I'm going to duck out of work early."

"Good. The sooner you get home, the better."

Mike had to bully his car through the horde of reporters blocking the street. They rapped on the glass and called out questions. When he stepped out of the car, several of them walked right into the garage, pressed microphones and cameras in his face, and bombarded him with questions.

"Get your ass out of my garage! I'm going to have the police here in two minutes if you don't step off my property."

Mike began shoving them out. When he was certain they'd all cleared the door, he jabbed the button and closed the garage.

Walking inside, he said, "A bunch of damn vultures."

"I took the phone off the hook. It was nonstop ringing. Luckily, they don't have our cell numbers."

"Well, let's just put them out of our minds. As it gets dark, they'll head on out."

Mike went around the house, securing the windows and doors, and also pulled the shades that Millie hadn't done earlier.

When they put away dinner leftovers and cleaned the table and dishes, Millie peeked out the front. Most of the crews had left except for two, who seemed ready to pack up. There was also a man across the street watching. She didn't recognize him but figured he was a neighbor walking the block, trying to understand why news crews were at this particular house.

Millie and Mike settled down for a movie after Caleb went to bed. It was a spy thriller that Millie didn't enjoy much, causing her mind to wander to problems within her own reality.

Mike was shaking her. She shot up, expecting a level of chaos.

"Relax. You just drifted off. Let's go to bed."

Mike helped her off the couch. She used the bathroom and brushed her teeth. When she checked on Caleb before putting herself to bed, she found him awake. He was sitting in the dark at the plastic arts and crafts table they'd bought for him. His back was to her, and the unexpected sight rippled a cold shiver across her spine and down her arms.

"Caleb? What are you doing out of bed?"

He didn't answer or even twitch at the sound of her voice. She knew instantly what this was. Slowly, she stepped behind him and peered over his shoulder at the drawing.

Millie's eyes widened, and her hand went to her mouth as a single word escaped.

"No."

Caleb was still in his far-off place when Millie pulled the sheet from beneath his hand. She had only to study it for a few seconds to fully understand what Caleb had drawn.

When Millie hit the hallway, the light blinked away. She ran into the master bedroom's door frame, situated herself, and then retrieved her cell from the nightstand. Turning on the cell's flashlight, she found Mike had already checked out for the night. She frantically patted his chest and then lightly slapped his face before he finally came around.

"What's wrong?"

Millie thrust the drawing at Mike. She moved the flashlight so he could see the disturbing artwork their son had produced.

"What's with the flashlight?"

"The power just went out."

"From a storm or something?"

"Mike, look at the goddamn paper! We're in serious trouble. I'm going to get Caleb."

Mike did look at the paper then. Millie's voice triggered the alarm in his mind that something was seriously going south in a hurry.

Caleb had sketched another work of art that was far more dreadful than the previous two. This artwork was close to home in every sense of the word.

There were only two colors. The black silhouette of a man stood before a red door. The numbers above the door: 157. And to finish off the terror, a hatchet was in his right hand.

Our house! He's coming here! Mike thought and then shot out from the sheets.

Mike grabbed his own phone from the table and unlocked it. He dialed 911 and hit the green call button. Millie came into the room with Caleb wrapped in her arms.

Mike leaned to look at his son. The kid was out of it, catatonic like before.

"Is he okay?"

"I don't know. He still hasn't come out of it."

Mike pulled the phone from his ear and looked at the screen. The call never went through. He did it again, but faced the same result.

"What is it?" Millie asked.

"The call won't go through."

Mike saw the NO SERVICE message at the top of the screen. He turned Millie's phone on and saw the same thing.

Millie asked, "What does that mean? How do we not have service? That never happens."

Mike was silent for a long moment, thoughts running a race of terror.

"They make a device that can jam signals, like phones, from sending or receiving. If this guy is here, then he doesn't want us calling for help. He killed the power, and now our chance to call out."

Millie's voice dropped to a panicked whisper. "You're saying he's here? He's in the house?"

"I don't think so. He would have already come at us by now."

"So, we get out of here, and run to a neighbor for help."

"He might be ready for that. Forget the neighbors. We get the fuck out of dodge. Quietly, we get to the garage. We get into the car, and I'll back us out of here like a lightning bolt. When we get down the street, we should be out of range of the jammer and able to call the cops. Stay right behind me and be quiet."

The stairs creaked a bit as his foot hit the third step from the top. He winced and waited. He heard nothing from downstairs.

The garage door rotated on silent hinges. Mike turned the cell light back on because no windows offered moonlight for guidance through the tangle of junk.

They stopped when they saw the car's hood open.

"What the hell?" Mike asked and moved closer. "Oh, Christ. He is here somewhere. He cut the battery cables."

"Pull the rope and manually open the garage door. We can run from here."

Mike did. When he hefted the door, it only rolled up an inch before meeting resistance. Moving the light around, he saw that the man had secured padlocks through holes in both tracks, preventing the rollers from going any further.

"Shit," he whispered. "I don't have anything here to cut those."

"We have to go out one of the doors. Please. We have to go now," Millie said, nerves causing a full-body shake.

When they slipped out of the garage, someone began speaking in an absurdly calm and slow voice.

"It seemed rather unfair to me that the three of you nearly wrecked my plans to show Nurse Jenna how much I'd fallen in love with her during my hospital stay. You had tried, but my success was your failure."

The man's voice came from nearly all parts of the house, as if he were everywhere.

Millie began to open her mouth, but Mike clamped a hand over it.

In her ear, he whispered, "No talking."

Mike nudged Millie toward the front door, but the voice was there.

"I see you. There's nowhere to hide. There's no escape. I am an inevitable doom. Not even a plane crash could kill me. I wanted it to end. That's why I killed the pilot during the flight. But a higher power wanted me to survive, to continue doing all the awful things I've done."

The voice was next to the door. Quickly, Mike grabbed Millie's shirt, pulling her away from the door, backing them into the kitchen. He knew he needed a weapon. The block of assorted knives was there on the counter, but missing the key components to help save their lives. The man had hidden all of them.

"I believe there's a connection. It seems like the universe has driven the two of us together in some phenomenal way. Caleb and I are becoming one. So, I need him as much as he needs me. I have to take him from you. But don't worry, I'll spare you from your lingering grief by dispatching both of you tonight."

Millie squeezed Caleb tighter. Mike, as quietly as possible, rummaged through the drawers, trying to find any sort of utensil to use as a weapon. The best that his searching fingers revealed was a meat tenderizer. With good weight and pointed nubs, he knew it could do serious damage if he managed a direct hit.

Making their way to the back door, the voice came again.

"I think it's divine intervention that has brought this about. God wants Caleb and me to be together. I'll teach him well in the years to come. I'll teach him everything I know about taking lives."

Mike saw it then. It wasn't a man at all standing by the back door, speaking the tongues of a lunatic. It was a handheld radio. Mike pointed it out to Millie, and they both understood. The man wasn't everywhere, but his voice was. Mike didn't know how many radios he'd set up throughout the house, but he felt severe anger at the deception.

Mike swung the meat tenderizer and destroyed the radio. Pieces shot across the living room. He grabbed the handle of the sliding door, unlocked it, and yanked it to the side. As he seized Millie's arm to push her through the threshold, a hatchet came from the darkness of the backyard. Mike felt the edge bite his forehead, but he'd managed to avoid a death blow thanks to reflexes. The metal buried deep into the doorjamb, digging through the metal flashing and then into the wood.

Mike's mind screamed for an action of defense. So he obeyed. He pinwheeled his arm around, driving the tenderizer with as much force as his terrified body could create. The kitchen utensil did exactly what it was designed to do. The dozen pointed tips chewed into the meat of the man's hand as he tried to wrench the hatchet free. Mike saw skin and flesh tear loose from the hand, creating rivulets of red that immediately offered blood flow.

The man offered only a grunt of pain. He retaliated by ramming his foot into Mike's stomach, reeling him back into the house. The blow had instantly stolen Mike's breath, but he kept himself from realizing the pain because he needed to live for Millie, and especially Caleb.

As the hatchet came free, Mike slid the door shut and flicked the lock. He knew the man could easily swing the blade into the glass and shatter the entire pane, but that would raise the alarm and drive neighbors out of their houses. Help would come then. Mike knew the man wanted extreme privacy during his reign of butchery. He kept Millie and Caleb behind him as he backed away from the door, pushing them toward the stairs.

"That was very unpleasant, Mike. The news reporters made you out to be a nice, hardworking man. But you're not nice at all. I'm going to hurt you really bad for that." The voice came from two or three radios on the main floor.

"We've got to go up," Mike said over his shoulder.

Millie backed up each step, all the while expecting to see the man suddenly appear at the staircase landing, and then charge at them. Her body slid across the wall and found the first door opening. Caleb's room. She quickly set him down and went to the door to help Mike move the dresser in front of it.

"It's a hollow door. It can't withstand a hatchet," Mike whispered. "The dresser will help, but he's going to get in here."

A soft knock at the door, followed by a whistle.

"Knock, knock. Let me in."

The doorknob rotated, and he began pushing the door open. They threw their weight against it, desperately trying to save Caleb from being raised by a psychopath.

"Millie. Mike. Listen to me now. I'll make it as painless as possible. I've been doing this for so very long that

I know how to make it last or make it quick. You have a choice."

Millie heard Caleb doing something behind them. Looking over her shoulder, she saw his hypnotic state had continued. He had returned to his craft table, coloring again.

"Hold one second," she said.

Before Mike could protest, Millie moved off. She gripped the unfinished work from Caleb's control and looked it over. It was a partially drawn bed with hidden weapons beneath. She ran over to Mike and thrust it at him.

Mike understood and ran to the bed, ripped the mattress away from the box spring, and revealed what Caleb had done. The intruder hadn't hidden the entire set of kitchen knives from the block. Caleb had subconsciously taken them sometime during the evening.

Mike seized a long, serrated blade and a carving knife. Millie took the next two longest ones left. Waiting for the man to try the door again, they watched their son frantically work the crayons across another sheet of paper. Neither of them could force out final words of love to him, because in doing so, they knew they'd never survive the night.

"I see you!"

The voice roared behind them. Millie screamed and whirled. Her hands went into panic mode as the blade edges swiped at empty air. She saw the radio sitting on Caleb's nightstand. The madman had already been in Caleb's room tonight.

It was too late. Without both of them holding the dresser in place, Mike was no match for the intruder. A hard shove against the door forced Mike off balance. Taking the opportunity, the man pushed through the gap, already swinging the hatchet. It sank deep into Mike's left collarbone.

Mike screamed. Millie screamed. Even Caleb screamed as the trance finally broke.

Millie came forward. Her right hand drove the blade as deep as it would go into the man's guts, and then she twisted it. An explosion of red coated her hand. Then she pushed the other blade in. Despite Mike's horrific wound, he thrust his uninjured arm up, sliding the carving knife with ease into the man's lower jaw and pushed until bone stopped the blade.

The intruder released his grip on the hatchet, leaving it embedded in Mike's body. Millie, with both hands still holding the blade handles, pushed.

The intruder rocked back, and then forward, his muscles still undecided about which way he would fall. He reached out for Millie as his legs gave out first. She quickly pulled back, letting his hand catch nothing.

After the man fell hard on his backside, Mike said, "Finish him. It's like we always say about the movies we're watching. They think the bad guy is dead until he rises to kill one more person. Make sure. For all of us, make sure that fucker is dead."

Millie didn't hesitate. She gathered the remaining knives from where Caleb had stashed them. She sat on the man's stomach, pinning his arms down with her knees. With an untapped anger that one man had permanently wrecked their sense of security in the world, Millie hammered each knife down until every blade from the butcher's block had found a new home.

When the bloody deed was done, Millie searched his overcoat. Within the outer pocket was the device preventing them from reaching out for help. She figured he must have turned it off every time he used the two-way radio to taunt them. Millie smashed it over and over into the man's face until the plastic shell shattered to pieces and the electronics spilled out.

Caleb was curled in his father's good arm. His face pressed deep into Mike's shirt.

Millie gathered clothes that had spilled from the drawers of Caleb's toppled dresser and pressed them firmly around the hatchet blade. Using her free hand, Millie unlocked her cell and called for help.

"911. What's your emergency?"

"An intruder injured my husband. Please send an ambulance."

After receiving the address, the operator asked, "Where is the intruder now?"

"Dead. He's dead."

"Okay. So, you were able to kill this person?"

"We did. We did it together. His killing spree is over, all thanks to my son."

"Excuse me?"

"Just send a damn ambulance. I'll tell the police everything."

Mike's blood loss had been significant. Millie had tried to stifle the flow, but his complexion had gone pallid by the time the police and ambulance arrived.

Millie knew Mike had fought hard against the ominous black cloak pushing through his vision. He was a man who very much wanted to live. He wanted to grow old with her. He wanted to see his son grow up and begin a wonderful family of his own.

But Millie knew the truth. When she picked up Caleb, holding him tightly in her arms, she had seen it. Caleb's final sketch that sat on his craft table, declaring what was hopefully his last vision, but undoubtedly the most painful one of all.

A drawing in black crayon. A woman and a young boy stood before a headstone, which read:

Michael Fredrick Miller. August 3rd, 1984-May 5th, 2025. Devoted husband, father, and a hero.

The 442 Special

The tinkle of the bell above the door sounded as Ash Locklund stepped inside the shop. The blast of air conditioning was heaven sent as he left the humid July on the other side of the threshold.

Ash was a man who got noticed. At nearly six and a half feet tall and a solid 250 pounds, he was difficult to blend into any crowd, especially with a shock of Scottish red hair and beard. It was also unfortunate, given that his occupation typically needed anonymity. People tend to recall a man of such size after the crime has happened.

The door swung shut, offering another tinkle of the bell.

"I'd like the 442 special," Ash said.

"Have a seat. I'm about wrapped up with this guy."

Ash settled his bulk into a chair far too small for him and waited.

The man in the tattoo artist's chair was built by gym muscles, not muscles designed by a life of hard work. Sporting dozens of tattoos, even several across his shaved scalp, he had an intimidation most men would avoid. No one wanted an unnecessary trip to the ER just to prove alpha status. And the man with a newly inked busty blond on his forearm dropped his eyes when Ash looked at him.

Ash knew that it was not only his size that intimidated the man, but his request for a 442 special. A request like that meant the man about to receive the special ink was not a man to grapple with.

Ash leaned back, closed his eyes and quickly felt himself pulled into sleep. Only ten minutes had ticked along before he felt Cavanaugh tap his leg.

"Come on back. What's it gonna be this time?"

Ash said, "I need to look in the book really quick. The husband said he wants it done peacefully."

"Got it. Take all the time you need. I don't have any other appointments today. You want a beer or two? You're gonna need it to drown out the pain."

Ash didn't have to eliminate the pain because life contains pain, and pain can be regulated in most cases. Beer did sound good, though.

Cracking the cap on the first one, he took a slug and opened the book. The artwork was categorized by intensity. What he needed was low on the pain scale for his client's target. The front of the book offered tattoos of varying degrees to effortlessly and quietly dispatch someone.

"There's a couple of quick on-set poisons in there that work well, from what I'm told. The mark goes fairly silent from what some say," Cavanaugh said.

"Yeah. I was thinking that, too." Ash pointed to a small tattoo of a glass vial with a cork stopper. A label wrapped the bottle, with no words, just a skull and crossbones. "Let's do this one as long as it's fast-acting."

Cavanaugh leaned to the left to see the image. "It is. It's the quickest one I've got."

"Good. Let's get started."

Ash downed the rest of the Bolivian beer and opened a second one as he slid into the reclined leather chair.

Cavanaugh stepped to the wall-mounted safe, spun the combination and rotated the door open. With both hands, he removed the beautifully grained snakewood box and placed it on the table. He slid the bronze latch, flipped open the lid, and revealed glass bottles of ink. Black, blue, and red were the only colors available for special tattoos.

"All right. Let's get rolling," Cavanaugh said.

Although ordinary tattoos usually require an artistic touch, a 442 special didn't need such intricate details. But that requirement didn't stop Cavanaugh from delivering perfection.

He had completed the poison bottle in black, with the exception of the skull and crossbones done in red. The ink moved inside the bottle as he tilted his forearm back and forth. Slow and majestic motions moved in a way that transfixed those with curious eyes.

"Beautiful," Ash commented.

"Thank you. You know the score. Five grand for the work."

Ash removed an envelope from his front pocket and handed it over.

"Until next time," Ash said. Shook the artist's hand and exited the shop at 442 Majestic Street.

Ash could have done the job nearly anywhere, but again, he needed anonymity. He wouldn't be a hard man to find if the police put a BOLO out on him. If ever he was marked by any authority, his career as a handler would be over.

Some call it wet work or being a cleaner. He preferred the term handler because he took care of problems. He handled things. The rich always wade waist-deep in problems, so business was good.

It was by stupid luck Ash overheard two men at a bar three years before. Even in whispers, they couldn't hide their conversation from him. Ash had the ability to read lips. His mother had lost her ability to speak due to throat cancer and had been too stubborn to learn the new skill of sign language. So, he learned to read her lips. It was a talent that came in handy on certain occasions. From across the bar, Ash intercepted their private conversation.

They were talking about a tattoo parlor on the west side. 442 Majestic Street. Something called the 442 special. An ordinary tattoo brought to life by a bottle once used to capture a witch's final breath. At least that's the tale, one man said.

Ash laughed into his beer, causing the mouthful to return to the mug.

The man looked at him. Ash stared at his phone as if an amusing video had caused his laughter.

"You can do things with those tattoos, depending on the kind you get. Tattoos that could injure people, even kill if you wanted to go so far," the man said.

Drunkenly, the idea festered in Ash's mind as he stumbled back to his apartment. Being a two-count felon held the impossibility of being hired by a legit business. And oh, how he had tried to turn over that metaphorical leaf and start fresh. Society was a crippling bitch, though. Society never lets someone's mistakes fade from view and rarely offers second chances. So, income came in small doses by way of carpentry work, back-breaking labor that had a quick tendency to destroy joints, making a young man appear elderly by way of slow, shuffling movements.

He despised the life given. Something needed to change, and he needed it now.

The following night, both men were at the bar again. He moved across the room toward them. They almost appeared ready to bolt through the door as they watched the hulking figure move at them in the low light. He held up his hands to settle nerves before they ran and he missed the chance to find out more about the 442 special.

It was an astonishing revelation, a life-altering conversation. The mystic ink called to him, and a few days later, he answered.

And now his services were available, and the money rolled in. Ash took the initiative to handle problems, and his payment compensation unburdened any inflictions of his heart or mind that may be troubled with his new profession.

Ash watched through the diner window. His mark was inside the salon across the street. Ash tasted nothing as he chewed and swallowed a grip of fries. His focus was absolute, even when the waitress came by to check on him. His lack of acknowledgment offered her an eerie feeling, enough that she dropped the bill on the table and didn't return.

Learning the habits of a marked person was always good business sense. Such a routine can accommodate a time and place when the deed needed to be done. Just as he knew that she would be across the street Tuesday afternoon for a manicure. People become predictable when you start paying attention.

Tonight, Willow Delmont would meet up with her lover for a throw of passion before returning home to await her husband's arrival from his business trip.

Ash watched as she pushed out the front door and rounded the white Lexus to the driver's side. She walked with false importance, as if the world should stop and admire her. She'd come up from nothing. The only thing attributed to her success was her runway model appearance, which was enough to land her a wealthy husband. Ash knew the frequent business trips Mr. Delmont made caused the fracturing of the marriage. She had grown lonely, needing the touch of a man to feel whole again. Mr. Delmont had told Ash he could forgive his wife's affair, but she refused couples therapy and any kind of reconciliation. She was gearing up to demand a divorce and half of all his assets.

Mr. Delmont had said, "She deserves nothing. She was trash when I found her, and she's trash now. I'll be damned if I'm going to let her walk away with half of everything I built. No court should allow such deceit, but they will. They'll give her what she wants. She's entitled because she was married for ten years to a man who was married to his work. That's what they'll say. So, I need this done. I need it done while I'm out of town, making for a solid alibi. The prosecution will pit everything they have against me, but airport surveillance and conference surveillance and more will shatter all their nails as they try to drive them into my coffin. Without proof that I hired an expert, their case will crumble. So, I'm hiring you to handle the matter. I'm told you're very good at what you do."

That conversation had occurred three days before. As Mr. Delmont had inquired about the level of professionalism, Ash assured the man that he would handle the issue accordingly.

Ash also assured him that there would be no court battle. The woman would check out, and there would be no evidence of foul play. He also replied that the less the man knew about the ordeal, the better for everyone. Ash laid out the basic result. The woman would get her ticket punched long before her husband arrived home from his business trip. After being dropped off by the Uber, he needed to go inside, find his wife, and immediately call the police. Don't delay. Don't stop and celebrate with a drink. Contact the authorities immediately.

Mr. Delmont assured Ash he would play the grieving husband with Academy Award finesse.

Ash didn't need to follow. He knew where she was going. He would arrive when their passion was at its highest, making them unaware of his outside activity.

The bus stop was a mile out from where Willow was likely engaged in a bottle of wine with her lover before the dial turned up and the clothes came off. He had time to spare.

His walk was leisurely. His cowboy boots clacked on the neighborhood sidewalk. Several residents were outside enjoying the day either mowing lawns, washing cars, or playing with young ones. Even with Ash smiling at those he passed didn't deter them from remaining cautious. A stranger, a mountain of a man, in this neighborhood wasn't welcome like any other. However, no one would dare to ask him about his business in these parts.

Luke Stevens' house was at the far end of Deerwood Street, tucked deep in the woods. Under the cover of trees, Ash was able to avoid security cameras at several corners of the house.

Willow Delmont's Lexus SUV was unlocked, making his job of getting inside much easier.

She was singing. He didn't know the song. It was some R&B station. If it wasn't classic rock, he was at a loss to know who the artist was. With the singing and the gentle motion of the vehicle, the twenty-minute drive nearly lulled him into a comfortable sleep. He was calm, and it needed to stay that way.

When the vehicle rolled into the garage, her phone rang through the Bluetooth speakers.

She groaned before answering.

"Yeah?"

"Hey. I was thinking when I get back tonight, we could go out to eat. We haven't had a date night in a long while."

"I suppose."

"Great. I'll book a table at that Italian restaurant on Highland Street."

"Fine."

"I love you. See you tonight."

"Okay."

The line went dead. Ash smiled at the lack of *I love you, too* response.

"Fucking dickhead," she said and then popped the door and got out.

When he heard the inside garage door close, he sat up in the cargo area. There was a maroon BMW next to him. He pulled the lever and raised the rear door and slid out.

There was no more purpose in hiding. He was here to do a job, and she was going to face it in all its terror just before her light blinked out for good.

Willow was standing at the kitchen sink, washing her hands, when he stepped through the door. She heard the soft squeak of a hinge and turned.

"Don't make it tough on yourself. Let this moment be less painful than it needs to be," Ash said as he closed the gap between them.

Her mind broke through the shock of a giant inside her home and charging toward her. She reached for the pot on the stove. Ash instantly pulled it from her grip before she could rear her arm back. His right hand clamped over her mouth as his body pinned her against the counter. He forced her head back and down as his arm rotated up. The shifted angle caused the poison bottle to move along his forearm, across his wrist, toward his thumb. With his left hand, Ash pressed his forefinger to the cork stopper and pulled his finger away from the bottle. The cork, pinched under his control, popped free from the bottle. Blue ink rippled from the bottle, moving like a small stream within the layers of skin, hitting the web of flesh between his thumb and forefinger and vanishing. The liquid transferred from his body to hers as the blue ink marked her lips like a moving drawing of a comic strip. Then, it was gone. Forced through the part of her lips and doing its odd piece of magic.

Willow's eyes went wide, searching Ash's face for reason or logic to this attack. Then her body began hitching as the poison didn't attack her entire nervous system but instead worked its way only to her brain. With the sorcery of a witch's dying breath, the ink communicated the idea of death by lethal poison. The human mind, arguably one of the most incredible creations on the planet, is sometimes its own worst enemy. If the ink infused with a witch's final breath told Willow's mind that she was dying by a toxic substance, her body would act accordingly. It's what made the 442 special oddly unique. Willow's life would slip away, and not even the world's best medical examiner could explain the reason for her death.

When her fight was over, Ash stepped back and let her fall. It was a slow crumple as muscles not completely dead to the world resisted the collapse. By the time her body did a full sprawl across the hardwood, the life-force had vacated the shell. The job was done.

Ash looked at the back of his hand. The bottle and cork had faded out of existence just as the other devices of murder once marking his skin had done. Evidence of a mystical killing tattoo altogether disappeared from the universe.

Ash exited through the garage side window, one of only two areas that didn't have camera coverage. Ash had instructed Mr. Delmont to lock the window while he waited for the police. Even an unlocked window can be a suspicious thing to authorities looking for any signs of foul play.

The courier service arrived two days later. He answered the door to find the same delivery person from the last three jobs standing at his door. He signed for the parcel, sat on the couch, and opened the box. Inside were fifty thousand in cash. He had paid five thousand out of pocket for the tattoo, leaving him forty-five thousand for a few days' work. Not a bad gig. High risk meant high reward.

Ash was six beers down when the nightly news came on. His eyes were heavy, and the alcoholic stupor almost allowed his mind to check out for the night. But it was a name said during the report that brought him back to reality.

The reporter explained that two days after Calvin Delmont found his wife collapsed on the kitchen floor when returning from a business trip, he also died under curious circumstances. A maid who does the weekly cleaning found Mr. Delmont in a recliner. She first thought the man was sleeping, but he was cold, unnaturally cold to the touch when she tried waking him. The CDC had locked down the property and was monitoring neighbors for any abnormal health issues. There was no need for public alarm, only concern, as the authorities had no answers as to how Mr. and Mrs. Delmont died. Details would continue as soon as the medical examiner's office released more information.

"Well, holy shit," Ash said.

He hadn't minded Mr. Delmont at all. He'd been a trustworthy employer who had given him the necessary information to see the job through. He had even promptly paid the fee. Ash had actually hoped the man would spread the word about the services he offered. A businessman with sizable wealth and connections could have given Ash an unending supply of jobs until he'd decided he just didn't want to do it anymore. He was sure a beach in an unfamiliar part of the world was in the books for a retirement plan, but now it was going to take a bit longer to get there.

Another job made itself available three days later. Ash was eager to dive into a new mission, but his excitement showed. His quick contact with the employer, and his immediate requests for information, scared the person off because the employer ignored his texts and calls. Two days later, things changed. The potential employer reconnected and began hashing out details of who the mark was and how things needed to proceed.

The situation gave Ash pause. The employer refused to meet in person. Even grabbing a cup of coffee was out of the question. The anonymity was most important, and Ash understood that. There were many law enforcement operations situating an officer with the false qualifications of a man who took care of certain problems for a fee. But the reverse was also true. It could always be a law enforcement agent looking to hire someone to solve a problem illegally, setting a trap for an instant arrest.

Ash hated the idea of not meeting with an employer for the sole purpose of giving him a chance to read the man. The flow of speech and body language would instantly tell him if the job was a police set-up or a legit hiring. He'd grown up knowing the bullshit of others, and he could read a lie as if it were written on a page.

The text had stated that the client preferred the mark to suffer extreme pain. Ash knew no law enforcement division would request that, even with it being a farce of an operation.

During the course of two days, the information rolled in. The next target was a man, the CEO of a financial investment company. Ash suspected his new employer was either another within the company eager to move the man out of the way so he could take the top seat, or it was a client financially destroyed by a con job of an investment group. He didn't care. The agreed price was seventy-five thousand. It was an excellent addition to his retirement beach fund.

The guy's name was Clive Fitzpatrick, a British prick who had moved to the States four years ago to set up a U.S. branch of his financial institution.

Ash hated the British and their over-inflated self-worth. He thought that maybe this time he might actually enjoy the kill. His research revealed Fitzpatrick claimed the position of royal ass to his employees. Though none of them would file a harassment against him and risk losing their employment positions. It didn't stop them from ranting about him across various social platforms.

It started to sound like Mr. Fitzpatrick deserved a painful removal from the planet. His employees would be thankful because there was nothing worse in the world than having an ungrateful, shitty boss. Such situations made life intolerable when there was no need for it. The world was better off with such men blinked away from existence.

Ash moved his large frame through the door of 442 Majestic Street.

Cavanaugh was sitting at his desk reading a magazine about the fine art of skin ink. He peered over the edge at Ash.

"Another special?"

"Yes, sir. But there's no hurry if you're taking a break."

"No worries. I get a break only when clients aren't here. Come to the back. Want a drink?"

"I do."

Cavanaugh poured Ash a double shot of whiskey and set it beside the book of unusual tattoos as Ash flipped through the album.

"What are you thinking about on this one?"

"The client wants it done painfully. What the client wants is what the client gets. Whatever gets me paid." Ash tapped one drawing. He said, "This must be it. I can't even imagine the agony of burning alive."

Cavanaugh looked. Ash pointed to a red can of gasoline.

"That'll do it. Painful for sure."

Ash grabbed the glass and downed more than half with a single swallow. Settling into the chair, he laid his right arm on the rest and waited for Cavanaugh to begin work.

Ash's head tipped to the left as the muscles in his neck fought no resistance to the movement. In fact, the muscles throughout his body didn't react to any demand. The only thing he could seem to control was his eyes. With his head tilted to the left, he rotated his eyes to the right.

Cavanaugh sat beside him, smiling.

"Welcome back. It looked like a nice nap. A chemically induced nap, anyway. We've got some business to conduct. I was okay with all this assassin shit by way of tattoo death until just a few weeks ago. I mean, hell, I'm the one who started it all. I found that bottle at an online auction of strange artifacts. Honestly, I thought it was total bullshit how the bottle supposedly captured the final breath of a dying witch from the seventeenth century. I just figured it would be a fun conversation piece to keep around. Weird shit started happening, though. I could tell it wasn't an empty jar. Something was inside the damn thing. It moved around inside like a mist stirred by a breeze. There were times I'd stared into that glass and could swear something stared right back at me. It's kind of like looking at a cloud and seeing a face in it."

Cavanaugh took the three bottles of ink and placed them back in their box.

Ash was trying to talk, but the only things he could rely on were his eyes. They switched focus around the room from Cavanaugh to the ink bottles, and then to the safe in which he returned them.

"Oh, sorry. I forgot to tell you. I spiked your drink with a simple cocktail. Then, while you were out, I injected you with a special neurotoxin blend. You won't be able to move, but you will feel everything."

Ash desperately wanted to ask questions, but his mouth wouldn't work.

"Yes. I can see by the confused look in your eyes that something is very off and you'd like to know why. So, I'll tell you. Willow was my sister. Had I known her husband wanted her dead, things would be different. She would be alive, and you wouldn't be lying in this chair about to suffer unimaginable pain before your light blinks out for good. I've been hard at work while you've been dreaming. I hope they were pleasant dreams, because it'll be the very last bit of good in your life. I'll let you see what I've done."

Cavanaugh lifted Ash's head and wedged a folded towel under it, giving him a view of the tattoos covering his chest.

"I briefly thought about doing you quickly. Instead, I wanted you to learn all about the career you practice so diligently."

Cavanaugh placed his finger at the bottom of the tattoo, below Ash's right pectoral muscle, and swiped. The small pile of tattoos that looked like pebbles shifted across his skin. What came spilling out of that disturbed nest were ants, each about half an inch in length. With an agitation to seek and destroy whatever had ruined their mound, a dozen agitated ants spread out. The stingers went into action, pumping phantom venom into Ash's torso. He could only grunt in retaliation to each sting.

"These are called bullet ants. They're native to South America. Of course, as you know, these ants are only ink, but the sensation of each sting is very real in your mind. You really do believe all these suckers are stabbing the hell out of you. The witch's breath is telling your mind that it's so. It's quite fascinating how well it all works."

Cavanaugh watched the black ants work their magic pain across Ash's body. With his eyes fixed, his mouth slightly gaped, looking like a child seeing something nearly impossible to be true.

Ash's hissing broke the spell. Cavanaugh leaned back and smiled. He swiped his hand across the area again, brushing the grains of dirt and a dozen ants off to the side. The ink faded into nonexistence, as if never having marked the skin.

"Well, that was fun. It was a lot of work putting those little buggers all bunched up and then tattooing an ink mound on top. But now I'm beginning to see the value of entertainment in it. You should be happy, though. My brother-in-law got it much worse than you. I spent nearly two full days inking things across his body and then putting them into action. Did he tell you why he wanted her dead? Of course you can't answer, but I'm sure he didn't. There was probably no call for the why of the job. Money really was the only issue, I'm sure. Do you care to guess what might be hiding behind door number two? No? Let's see!"

Cavanaugh again swiped across the ink resembling another mound. This time, only two agitated things moved out of the rubble.

"These are called bark scorpions. They are the most venomous scorpions in North America," Cavanaugh said and then flicked one to make it go to work.

The tail shot forward and down, driving the bulbous end with the stinger into Ash's flesh. Its body jittered as it forced the surplus of venom from one body to another.

Cavanaugh hooked a finger under the waistband of Ash's boxers. The second scorpion quickly investigated the shadowed domain. Cavanaugh released the band with a snap. A second later, Ash offered a whining moan as the scorpion delivered its release of venom into tender parts.

Cavanaugh groaned as well and said, "I can't even imagine. Ouch to the tenth degree! But you're a big, strong man. You can take it, right?"

Cavanagh lifted the waistband again, and the scorpion wandered out. Quickly, his hand wiped across Ash's skin, striking the scorpions away from the universe.

Intensely angry welts appeared across Ash's stomach and torso. His body's reaction to stings, so convincing of the imagination that they became real. Tears seeped from the corner of Ash's eyes as the burn of the venom punctured just as deep in his mind as it was in his body.

"They say, 'Reap what you sow'. I honestly planned on spending days having fun with you, but that would be a major waste of ink and time. In the end, you'll be dead anyway. So why bother?"

Ash began to feel things. First, it was a hard tingle in his legs, followed by soft movements of his tongue. Muscles were reawakening. His body, far more robust than most, was quickly metabolizing the drug Cavanaugh had injected into him.

Cavanaugh removed the hand towel from Ash's stomach, revealing the tattoo beneath. The man had used a lot of red ink for this particular work of art.

It was a gas can, a fraction of its normal size. It was the old metal kind, usually found affixed to the tailgate of a utility vehicle.

"No," was all Ash could get his throat to croak.

"I'm not going to lie. I think this will hurt a lot."

Ash could sense his hands slowly opening and closing. Muscles were fading from their chemical dream state, returning to his control.

"I certainly don't envy you," Cavanaugh said and placed his forefinger on the latch that would pop the top and release the flood of gasoline.

"Wait," Ash managed to say.

Ash's strength was far from full power, but the fist had enough on it to drive Cavanaugh back, moving his fingers away from the can's lid. His legs limply rotated off the table, nearly pulling the rest of him off in total collapse. The muscles held him, though, giving him the chance to stagger toward the back door. He knew if he got away, he could later return when his mobility was at top power, then he could exact justice against Cavanaugh's depraved sense of evening the score.

But that plan went out the window, as he couldn't get his body to stay on a straight path. As if pulled by an invisible rope, Ash veered harshly to the left. Attempting an immediate stop did little good, either. His upper body kept going as his lower half lost momentum. The result was a hard belly collapse onto the glass table in front of the sofa. Under Ash's bulk, the glass instantly gave up resistance.

As Ash sank through the splintering jagged edges, the wood frame gave out, too. The impact drove glass shards deep, punching through skin and parting flesh. Ash gasped for breath, and as he did, he took in the hard odor of gasoline. Rolling onto his back, he surveyed the damage, but already knew the results.

Two pieces of glass the size of paring knives had sliced through the red ink. What seeped from that can was black ink, sputtering out with the assistance of a phantom air pressure within the container.

The ink gas rolled over the swollen, damaged areas caused by the scorpions and bullet ants. The pain drove deep to his core, igniting nerve pain that spread like wildfire throughout his body.

He sucked in a breath and hissed a release. As he did, his mind desperately clung to any idea out of the situation.

Cavanaugh kneeled next to him. He held up his right hand with all fingers curled into the palm except the thumb. He showed Ash what was inked across the skin of the inside pad of his thumb.

A strike-anywhere match.

"Again, I don't envy you right now."

The nail of his middle finger pressed to the match head and flicked across the inked skin.

A red-ink flame came to life as if it had been a real fire.

Cavanaugh reached out gently, as if to help his fallen friend.

Something Is About to Happen on Platform Four

My arrival in the new town started out with far more blood than I would have appreciated. Not the part about being a butcher's assistant, but the event that came later as the sky pulled away the sun. I'd gotten used to the ways of being an assistant in various towns I'd stopped off in.

"Two pounds of the chopped lamb for Mrs. Gilly," Mr. McComb called out.

"Right away, sir," I called back. I fetched the meat and wrapped it in white paper and tape and brought it to the front.

After Mrs. Gilly left the store, Mr. McComb watched out the front windows. His eyes stared out toward nothing as his mind wrestled with a deep thought.

"It was a hell of a bad idea to move to this town, young man."

"Sir?"

"We're on the cycle event for tonight. Things are about to get extreme."

"I'm not following."

I thought maybe Mr. McComb was talking about a bicycle rally of some local tradition. I had no idea about this town called Milford. I'd only met my landlord and Mr. McComb when I instantly got out to job hunt. A town of less than fifteen hundred didn't offer much by way of employment, so I had to lock something down fast to get some money rolling in. Luckily, the town butcher shop needed an extra hand, and with my previous experience in that area, the job was mine if I wanted it.

"I figured someone would have told you by now. A train is coming in tonight," Mr. McComb said, as if that explained everything.

"I wasn't aware a rail system ran through this way."

"It doesn't. Not for a long time now."

"So, there's a train coming to town, but there are no rails?"

"Right. You'll see. Whether you like it or not, you'll see."

The doorbell tinkled, and an elderly man shuffled in. He said, "Hello, Myron. How about fixing up an eight-pack of ground chuck patties for me?"

"My new young fella would be happy to get that."

I was already in the cooler, counting out eight patties before Mr. McComb finished his sentence.

Though the hum of the cooler motors was loud, I could still overhear the two men conversing.

"Got yourself all situated for a lock-in tonight?" Mr. McComb asked.

"Of course. I've been riding this rodeo since before you stepped foot on the earth. As soon as I get home with this order, I'll lock everything down until dawn."

"Good to hear."

I went up front and handed the order to Mr. McComb, who rang up the purchase.

I went to the front windows and watched the old guy get into an equally old truck and roll down the road.

"You know I'm new to this town. I just wandered in on Tuesday. But yet you talk to me like I'm supposed to get the gist of what's happening. A part of me thinks this is some sort of established play you've concocted to have a little fun with the new kid in town. If I'm perfectly honest, I don't like mind games at all."

Mr. McComb approached the front windows, placed his hands on his hips and glared outside, pensive.

"I know you're new. Hell, the entire town knows when fresh blood steps foot in this place that's a couple miles east of Nowhere, USA. I never meant to be vague." He pointed down the block. "Do you see that old wood sided building at the far end? The one with the near collapsed roof?"

"I do."

"That building is the old train depot. The last time any real train pulled into that station was nineteen-twenty-eight."

"Real train?"

"I'll get to that. Anyway, a mob of justice waited at that station on platform four. Word had it that the Carthill gang was on that train coming from Tucson. Sources claim they'd just robbed three banks. They were notorious bank robbers in the early twenties. Anyway, this town was a thriving one back then, and the Carthill group were looking to retire and settle down with their families. They chose this place. The band of lawmen waited. When the group stepped off onto platform four, there was some resistance. Some fought the law. Some even drew guns. No one was harmed. At least not right then."

I looked down the block at the retired and crumbling station. I was sure this was a farce. As I thought before, Mr. McComb was having a little fun at my expense.

"So what happened to those men?"

"They hanged every one of those men in Old West style. No right to a fair trial. No judge or jury. The next morning, all fourteen men hung by their necks at the gallows. Not a single man had hung there since the late eighteen hundreds. Fourteen of them dangled all at once. I could never have imagined being hanged. If your neck doesn't snap on the drop, then you kick and groan, expelling every last bit of air, hoping to suck in one last breath, desperate for another moment of life, even though that moment was gonna be more pain," Mr. McComb shook, as if a cold breeze had found him.

"So, they let the women and children go?"

"They did. But then things got bad. The wives were able to prove that none of their husbands were associated with the Carthill gang. In fact, one of them was a doctor, one was a dentist, a barber, and so on. None of those men was a lawbreaker. Each one was an upstanding American. Someone fed the sheriff some seriously bad intel. It's said the Carthill gang actually headed up north to the Rockies. Fourteen innocent men hung because the sheriff and all he appointed took justice in their own hands. Fear gripped the townspeople before the train even arrived. They didn't want any savage bank robbers anywhere near here. They were the first ones to call for blood. The sheriff had heard enough of it and acted without just cause. With only a little time, those men could have proven their identities. But the law gave them no time."

"So, this is a true story?"

"It is. All the townspeople will verify that for you. We've all seen the train roll up, the doors open, and the evil spill out. There's no joke about it, and there's no escaping it."

I slapped Mr. McComb on the shoulder and said, "A hell of a story, sir."

"The story isn't over. If you're looking to survive the night, you need to understand all of it."

I went around the counter, turned on the sink and washed my hands.

"Okay. You said the words 'real train.' What did that mean?"

"Well, the sheriff, the whole town, for that matter, knew they were in serious shit. They'd executed fourteen innocent men. So, the members of the town council eventually convinced the governor and the railway company that they no longer desired a rail system to stop off in this nowhere place. They said they were tired of the riffraff funneling into town and never leaving. So, they were able to end transportation to our town. But the following year, train number forty-nine rolled into the station and mayhem disembarked. When I said a real train hadn't stopped here since the twenties, I meant it. But after that year, the train always arrived. A ghost train, some townsfolk call it. After the first killing ended, the entire town took it upon themselves to remove ten miles of rails. It did no good. It comes like clockwork."

I grinned. The man had a prime imagination.

"You should write a screenplay and sell it to a studio. Maybe there's a movie there, maybe not. But it would interest quite a few filmmakers."

Mr. McComb slowly shook his head.

"I know how it all sounds. Just do me a favor and stay inside tonight from dusk till dawn. This is the anniversary of those fourteen deaths. From the place you're renting, you'll be able to see the old train station. You'll see a train pull up even though there are no tracks there anymore. You'll see the doors open, but not what exits that train. Stay inside. They can't get in. Ghosts, or whatever they are, can't get inside. If you step out, they'll slip inside you and make you do unthinkable things. I don't know how else to put it. You should head home. I'm closing early today. Be here at eight in the morning. If you've listened at all to what I've said, you'll be okay. Take a couple of burger patties and have a nice meal, watch some TV and go to bed early. Before you know it, it'll be morning, and the madness will be over. One other thing. If you hear someone screaming for help, don't be that guy who goes out to help. You'll want to. Hell, we all want to. But no good will come of it."

I wrapped a couple of patties and planned to turn them into meatballs and spaghetti.

"Thank you. I'll do as you said, and I'll see you in the morning."

As I headed through the back to the rear door, I heard Mr. McComb talk to himself.

"He doesn't believe a bit of what I said, and that scares me more than that damn train."

I'd stopped at the store. Spaghetti, sauce, and beer went into my cart, and little else. My budget was very limited. The beer was a treat I offered myself every so often. What's the point of living if you can't indulge?

The place I rented was a duplex. The guy on the other side of our adjoining wall, Jack, was quiet enough. No loud dogs or blaring music to grind my teeth in frustration. We'd briefly conversed when I was unloading my essentials from the car. I haven't seen him since.

The spaghetti came together nicely. The perfectly mixed meat and fat required only a sprinkle of salt and pepper.

I did as Mr. McComb suggested. I ate, had a few drinks and watched TV. The sunlight had faded from the sky just after eight. The heavy pull of sleep set its hooks into me until the train whistle shattered the quiet night.

It's one of those moments when your brain is in that fascinating place in-between sleep and reality that your unconscious mind picks up a noise that could be delivered from either realm. Mr. McComb's story had played across my thoughts all evening. That's why I was sure the haunting howl of a steam whistle was born from a dream.

I pushed up from the reclined chair and staggered to the front room. A headlight, extraordinarily bright, cut through the darkness of the town's east end. The same place that held a dilapidated train station.

"You have got to be shitting me."

I watched the train slow on tracks that supposedly no longer existed. The squeal of metal on metal sounded as the brakes activated.

"Nice one, Mr. McComb, but I don't think ghost trains make sounds. Then again, this is my first ghost train," I said to myself.

The distance from my place is a bit closer than from the butcher's shop. Also, I received a side view of the train versus more of an angled view from the shop. Needless to say, the arrival held a sinister sensation in my nerves, built on a story someone created for a mind game.

Smoke plumed from the stack as the engine passed the far end of the station. With additional metal grinding, the train finally came to rest.

I don't know why, but my heart ramped up pace, a mule kicking against my ribs. I honestly expected the doors to slide open and the zombified remains of fourteen long-dead men to come stumbling out. Their strange goal was to annihilate the inhabitants of this small town as a means of some long overdue justice.

The doors did open then. Some inaudible signal must have triggered the passengers to open the doors of the first two cars simultaneously. More metal-on-metal scraping as century-old casters ran across the weather-rusted door tracks. The passenger cars had no lights shining inside, and from what I could see, there was no movement.

Nothing stepped out, not even a train conductor to set out a small wooden platform beneath the elevated metal steps for men and women to disembark.

This is ridiculous. I've got to get a better view.

I opened the front door, despite Mr. McComb's warnings to stay inside. My hand reached for the screen door latch when a voice pushed me back.

"Don't even think about it."

Jack was across the way. Our front doors faced each other. He was also standing behind the screen, reluctant to go out.

"Please don't tell me you're dishing out this ghost train nonsense, too."

"So, you know the story? Well, I'm glad someone imparted knowledge to you about the ramifications of stepping into the darkness."

"I mean, I was told a story, but to be honest, I believed none of it."

"They can't come inside because they were never invited. But if you're outside, then that's public space. They can take you and use you like a vessel to get to the rest of us."

"A vessel?"

"Yes. Take over your body. Only then are they allowed to come inside. We can't stop them then. And every year, every goddamn year, it's some dipshit like you who steps out, giving them exactly what they want, and then the bloodshed begins. I've lost family members and close friends because of naïve newcomers like you. So, you will keep your ass inside all night."

"Jack, there's no reason to get angry. I'm just not a believer in ghost stories."

"Believe it, or don't believe it. I don't give a shit either way. But you will stay inside. You'll need to close the main door, too. A screen isn't enough protection. Do you have your cell?"

I pulled it from my front pocket.

Jack rattled off his number, and I put it into my phone.

"Any questions, you call me. Don't be stupid. There's nothing outside worth dying for. Call if you need to."

He closed the door then, and I heard at least three locks engage. The window curtain pulled aside, and Jack soundlessly watched me. His look was downright bizarre. I briefly wondered what he might do if I went through the screen door and stepped onto the porch. I sincerely didn't want to find out. This town was beginning to show its teeth to anyone who went against the grain and defied its ways.

I stepped back, offered a wave, and closed the main door. Then I twisted the latch of the single deadbolt. I stepped away from the door, so my silhouette let him know I was returning to the living room. I waited a minute, then went to the door and looked out the window. His curtain had dropped back in place.

I went back to the front. I expected to discover that I had missed a lot during my conversation with my neighbor. The street, yards, and train station were still devoid of people. There was something though. A small change to the night that most people wouldn't have observed. I saw it only because my mind desperately wanted to see something, anything, to give this folktale life.

It was the night itself. When an artist paints on a canvas, there's depth, delivered by subtle changes in color and curves. The night near the station had this, as a blackness near absolute moved in a lesser shade of shadows.

I called Jack.

"This better be good," he said as I heard the volume mute on his TV.

"It's Kyle from next door."

"I figured. Let me guess, you've already discovered five-hundred questions you want to ask."

"Not that many, but a few."

He sighed, declaring he would give in a little.

"Ask away."

"I see movement, a darkness where there shouldn't be darkness, impenetrable by the streetlights. Is this all real? Did a nonexistent train really arrive here with fourteen ghost men ready and willing to spread the blood of the townspeople?"

"You're part right. Not just the men who hanged, but all of them. The women and children, too. All of them."

"Because they lost their husbands and fathers?"

"Because they died, too. The women and children were all massacred. All those people came to this town, and not one of them ever left."

I stared at the wall, trying to comprehend the reasoning behind the slaughter of women and children.

"I don't understand."

"The sheriff and all those lawmen were facing their own execution for killing fourteen innocent men. So, to keep the families from screaming to high heaven and getting the attention of the government and other law enforcement, the sheriff decided they all needed to disappear. The lawmen took the rest of the family members out to the woods, and those people stopped existing."

The complete annihilation of fourteen families. I couldn't believe what Jack was saying.

"If you believe all of this town is cursed, then leave," I said.

"Cursed is damn right. Our ancestors screwed over all future generations. All the townspeople are unable to leave, ever. I've never stepped foot outside the town's line. People like you, out-of-town delivery people like the mail trucks, semi drivers and such, can leave anytime you like without repercussions. But me, well, my life will start and end in this place."

"No one has ever tried to leave?"

"In the early years, there were quite a few. None came back. Though some said they'd send help back to town. No help ever came. We all believe they dropped dead or worse when they hit the town limits. I'm not sure what help they could have sent our way. I mean, how do you expel a fucking curse from an entire town?"

The response to Jack's question came in the form of a screech originating several houses down the block. I got up and went to the window. Then I heard the voice of a child calling for help.

Knowing my intention before I did, Jack said, "Don't even think about it. Someone stepped into the night, and now one of those spirits or whatever took control."

"It sounds like a kid who needs help."

"That's what they want you to believe. They'll play on your humanity. The only person that'll need help out there is gonna be you if you walk out that door. Look, I'm gonna go. Just do what you're told. Stay inside. Go to sleep. By morning, all will be right again. Then, unlike the rest of us, you can bail out of here and find a normal town to live in."

The line went dead then.

I pocketed my cell and watched the night. Someone darted across the street in a run that I caught from my peripheral vision. When I centered my sights on the street, nothing was there except moving shadows.

Another scream broke the stillness of the night. So close that the windowpane in front of me vibrated loosely in the frame.

"Someone help me! Please."

Jeremy M. Wright

The call was pitiful, almost seeming a desire to die instead of actually receiving help. It was a kid's voice. I was sure. Had a kid escaped a house against the parents' demands just to challenge the passengers of the ghost train because they had disbelief in the tale? I didn't believe the story. Not even now, as I had witnessed an actual train settled before a retired station. I won't deny that there was a little validity to what I've heard, but it was barely there.

Someone needed help. I'm no hero, but I'm no coward either. If I could help, then I would.

I opened the main door, and the squawk of hinges triggered a response from whoever was outside. I held my ground at the screen door, though.

"Is someone there? I'm hurt."

The screen opened noiselessly, but I let it fall shut with a clack. The summer breeze had a cold bite to it that one would only expect in early spring or late fall. Going down the porch steps, I scanned my front lawn and all the surrounding lawns I could see under the glow of the outside neighborhood lights. Everyone sensible was safely inside.

If I accepted everything I've been told, then it meant that at least twenty-eight souls of husbands and wives now roamed the streets of town, looking for a body to slip into, to control. But again, there were also an unknown number of murdered children. So there was no telling how many damned spirits wandered this forsaken town.

Something hissed at me. An absurdly long exhale of breath funneled through tongue and teeth the way a cat might do. I spun to my left, expecting to see a large tiger prepared to pounce. But in the shifting shadows of an elm was a little girl no more than eight years old. Her yellow dress with red flowers fluttered in the night breeze. Her blonde pigtails hung motionless as she watched me watch her.

207

"You shouldn't be outside. It's late," I said.

As the wind pushed a tree branch aside, allowing the outside house lights to reach further, I realized they weren't red flowers at all adorning her dress, but splotches of what I could only guess to be blood. She fidgeted with something in her hands, the way a child might do when feeling nervous in front of a stranger.

"Can I take you back to your home?"

It was one of the dumbest things I think I've ever said. The girl confirmed that when she brought a kitchen knife to her face and licked the blade's flat steel edge. The blood came off, and perched on the end of her tongue until she pulled it back in and swallowed.

"Oh, you stupid sonofabitch!" Jack yelled at me through the front window. "If they take control of you and you try getting in my house, I'm gonna shoot you in the fucking face!"

As if Jack's statement were a trigger, the girl went into motion. She was small, but quick. Thankfully, I'd expected action the second I saw the blood-covered knife. Both my legs moved before her first step went down.

I ran because it was all I could think of doing. It was absurd even to think of fighting an eight-year-old girl. Even with my life on the line, I don't think I could have harmed her. Especially now that I understood she had no control over what her body did.

I couldn't get back to my house because she had been closer to the door. I figured a blade would spill my guts across the lawn before I could make it safely inside.

She screamed. It was a high-pitched, ear-bleeding scream only a girl under the age of ten could muster. I thought she had fallen and injured herself. With a glance back, I saw her falling behind. The scream was born out of frustration that my gain on her was mounting. Her small legs couldn't match my stride.

I weaved between houses, cut across to a parallel street and tried circling back.

That little shit must have been a mind reader, as she knew my only haven was my house because no other resident would dare to open the door for me. She had cut between two houses before I did. Lurking in the heavy shadows of someone's backyard, I felt the blade draw through my forearm. The blade's sharpness slightly delayed the pain, but the pressure revealed that something in the night had bitten me. My reaction had caused me to spin away, resulting in losing my bearings and tangling my feet in a mess of children's bikes and toys lying across the lawn. I hit with teeth-clacking velocity against the hard earth. The collision hadn't stolen my breath, so I sucked in air and then winced when my left side jolted a lightning peel of pain.

She came at me again while delivering that ear-exploding shriek. I take back what I said before. I wanted to hurt her. I needed to hurt her because I wanted to live.

When she was two feet away, I kicked out, driving the entire sole of my foot into her midsection. I held back a lot of the strength, sparing the girl a destroyed sternum. I didn't want the poor kid dead or maimed. I just wanted her off me.

All the breath rushed from her lungs, making the sound of a dying duck. I scurried on hands and knees and ripped the blade from her grip and then pitched it into the night.

"It hurts. It hurts so badly. Why did you hurt me, sir?"

They'll play on your humanity, Jack had warned.

I thought about his statement too late. The girl instantly had a fistful of my hair as her baby teeth clacked together, trying to gnaw my face off.

"You stupid little shit! Get your ass off me!"

I painfully gripped her hands and pulled them away, knowing clumps of my hair were still in her fists. Being so small, she was easy to spin around, though she fought like a deranged monkey. I avoided teeth as I got the crook of my elbow under her chin. I applied pressure and quickly increased it as her tiny fingernails raked canyons across my arm.

"Go to sleep. Go to sleep," I hissed in her ear.

She did. Her arms went limp, and the rest of her body followed. I didn't drop her, but set her down gently. Ghost or not, it was susceptible to the human condition if it wanted to overtake a body.

My plan was an ignorant one. Since I didn't understand any of the complexities of a possession, I ignored one fundamental law. A ghost, demon, or whatever, can exit the body just as easily as slipping inside someone. And now it wanted me.

Even in the darkness of the backyard, I could see that deeper shade of black begin spilling out of that little girl. If that thing got inside me, there was a good chance Jack was going to shoot me in the fucking face.

I spun and ran.

"I'm not even a member of this town! I just got here!" I tried reasoning with the moving shadow at my back.

It didn't care. It had one night to kill, and it wanted to seize it.

Dodging back toward the street, I saw my house two doors down, the door still wide open. I was going to make it.

Then another roaming black shadow appeared across the street. And another. I was sure the adrenaline surge was going to explode my heart before I made the door. I was a running back in high school, so I had speed, but I've never run a race against a spirit before.

I took the stairs three at a time. I had no time to bother with the screen door as I felt an icy cloak hovering, ready to abduct my body.

I dove. My fists were in front of me like Superman in flight. I went through the screen, steel strands of woven wire adding signature cuts to my already mangled arms. I hit the hardwood floor, rolled to the side, and kicked the main door shut. One of them had been right there on the top step. The answer to its cruelty was a wall-shaking door slam in its face.

I released the muscles in my neck, and my head bounced off the floor. I released a relieving breath and tried to calm my heart and nerves.

After a while, I forced myself up and tended to my injuries. I always travel with a small first-aid kit. I coated everything with iodine. I couldn't do stitches, which the blade cut desperately needed, but I had super glue. Once I got the blood to stop flowing enough, I squirted glue into it and pinched the gash shut. It stung like a bastard. After a moment, I let go, and it remained closed.

I pulled a beer out of the fridge. As I turned to collapse in the recliner, I saw someone watching me through the front window. The spirit had possessed the little girl again. She was smiling.

I gave her the finger and took a long swallow of the cold beer. Then I turned my attention away.

I only hoped that when this night ended, the little girl would somehow still be alive, but from what I understand about this cursed day, it wasn't likely.

During the night, I heard screams. I heard a car crash blocks away. And I heard two gunshots.

Minutes of sleep were few and far between during the longest night of my life. I eventually pushed out of the chair and made an omelet. I expect any meal after a near-death experience never tasted so grand.

With a full belly, sleep pulled at me until a rock came through the window. I shook free of the chair and hit the floor, making my damaged arms scream in protest. Crawling through the upper window of the front door was the little blonde girl who hated my existence for some damn reason.

The disorientation of sleep hadn't shaken free yet. I was confused about how this little shit was allowed to enter my home. Mr. McComb and Jack both said I was safe inside, that they couldn't come in. But then I remembered what Jack had said earlier. If one of them took possession of me, he'd kill me if I entered his home. In ghost form, they couldn't get in. But in human body form they could.

She wiggled and pulled her body through the small opening. The knife she had used earlier to likely kill her parents and carve my arm open was in her right hand. She had found where I had tossed it. I had to take her down before she got inside.

As I reached out, the knife went into a slashing motion, trying to ward off my defense. I barely avoided losing a couple of fingers. I reacted after her downswing and seized the back of her hand. I squeezed, giving no pleasure in her pain, only desperate to stop the situation. I ground her small knuckles together until the knife dropped tip first into the hardwood. It stuck and vibrated.

I yanked her through the rest of the way, knowing bits of remaining glass in the frame were slicing and dicing her lower half. I didn't care. I'd had enough of this shit tonight. I dumped her onto the floor and rotated her hands behind her back. She kept trying to bite any part of me to get free. I dragged her toward the kitchen. I knew I had a partial roll of duct tape. The miracle product was good for a million uses, including binding possessed children. I used my teeth to start it, then did four passes on her wrists and the same on her ankles. After that, I picked her up and roughly tossed her into the chair.

Her behavior flipped so quickly. She offered a look of sorrow, drawing her mouth and eyes down, a force of tears and small hitches in her breathing through the sobs.

"I'm not falling for it. Sit there and shut up, or duct tape goes over your mouth, too."

Then, in a moment of pure dread pushed through me. I called Jack again.

"What?" he yelled into the phone.

"One quick question. Can the spirit move at will from person to person? I mean, if I happened to have a possessed person in my custody, can that spirit just leap into me at will?"

"You can't be that stupid! You seriously have one in your house?"

"I do. It's the same girl as earlier. She broke in. She's fixated on killing me for some goddamn reason."

The girl laughed. Apparently, my statement was amusing.

"To my knowledge, they can only exit when the person is dead or unconscious, like when they no longer have control. Also at sunrise, just before the train leaves."

"Okay. That makes sense," I said. But it didn't. None of this made any sense.

As he had done to me earlier, I hung up on Jack. My nerves settled a little, as I could be sure that the black cloud of a spirit wouldn't drift out and take control of me.

"To his knowledge, it isn't possible. But can you rely on the word of a moron who has never left this town?" The girl asked.

I sat on the stool at the counter and watched her.

"Yeah. He's lived it every year. He's one of the experts as far as I'm concerned." I looked at my watch and said, "Besides, sunrise is less than an hour away. Then you get to go back to whatever hell you spend the rest of the year in."

"Sure, sure. You've been up all night. You should lie down and get some rest."

I pulled a strip of duct tape loose and slapped it over her mouth. I had no interest in what she had to say. She began bucking so much that I also had to tape her to the chair to keep her from falling on the floor.

I'm not a monster. I tended to her glass cuts with iodine. A scared little girl will be left behind when this asshole ghost abandons the body. She was likely now an orphan. I feared all the blood spotting her yellow dress had come from her parents.

She watched me with contempt. Her hard eyes were those of a killer whose only desire was to see my blood pooled across the hardwood floor before night's end.

The stench of something burning outside rolled through the broken glass. At the front window, I saw flames engulfing a house down the block. The structure would be left to burn until sunlight broke the horizon and the horror train pulled away from the station. By then, the house had no chance of being salvaged. Blocks away, a blood-curdling scream tore loose.

I looked at the girl. Her eyes crinkled in a way that told me a smile formed behind the duct tape.

"I've only been here two days. My ancestors had nothing to do with the deaths of those families all those years ago. No one here did. Those townspeople are long dead. You're no better than the lawmen who murdered all of you. You're ending innocent lives."

She mumbled something.

"I don't care what you're saying. There's no reasoning behind this madness."

I looked over my shoulder. An orange and yellow horizon was announcing itself. Daybreak had finally begun. Birds took up a call to welcome it.

"That's your cue. Time to get your ass out of Dodge."

She mumbled again. I gripped the tape and pulled it down.

"We'll be back this time next year. So, stick around and we'll play again then."

"Not a goddamn thing could keep me in this place."

Out the window, a horde of black shadows moved across the landscape, being pulled back to a phantom train.

"Well, goodbye then. It's been swell," I said.

There was obvious resistance as the spirit fought the pull. It wanted to say something more, one last stab to the jugular to build the fear that I would never escape the nightmare. It looked like a soul leaving a body, though I suppose that's exactly what it was. One soul left, and one remained. It went through the shattered window and drifted with the morning breeze. After a while, I could no longer see any blackness moving across the street.

All at once, the doors of the boxcars closed as abruptly as they had opened. A plume of white smoke erupted from the stack as the wheels began their motion. It soon took the curve of the tracks aimed toward the sunrise. Then it was gone like a fleeting, dreadful dream.

Behind me, the girl started crying. I had no idea if she was aware of what she'd been forced to do, but I pitied her mental torment from this point on.

I had no soothing words for her. I didn't even want to cut her loose, because then I'd have to explain the horrifying events of the night.

I travel lightly. It took only three trips to relocate my possessions to my car. She watched me with steady streams running from her eyes. I tried not to look at her, but I'm only human after all.

"I'm sorry. I really am. I wish you only the best possible future you can have in this place."

Then I walked out, leaving the door open. I walked across the small yard and pounded on Jack's door. He answered hesitantly. One eye was closed, as the other was barely cracked open to the morning sun.

"You survived," was all he offered.

"I did. So did the girl. After I'm gone, do me a favor and cut her loose."

I offered no further explanation. I slid into the driver's seat and kicked the motor to life.

I drove to Mr. McComb's house. I surveyed the damage the town had sustained. It was obvious that not only had a little girl been used to destroy this cursed town, but several other people had also tempted fate and stepped into the darkness last night.

"You survived," he said as he answered the door.

It must have been a common statement to say to someone the morning after the nightmare.

"I did. The thing is, I don't think I'm gonna stick around these parts. I feel the highway calling my name."

He looked over my doctored arms, but didn't ask for a story.

"I can't blame you. I would have been long gone if I had the luxury of doing so."

"I wish I would have listened to you with a little more belief. Anyway, is there a chance you can pay me for my first and last day of work?"

He leaned back and retrieved his wallet from the front table. He counted out six twenty-dollar bills, folded them, and passed them over.

"That's more than I earned."

"You deserve it. Take care and take flight out of here."

"Take care of yourself," I said and shook his hand.

The northbound road out of town eventually connected to the highway. At this early hour, the road was deserted.

I saw the town limits sign ahead. Then, one last thought intruded. I looked in the top pocket of my plaid shirt. Six bills nestled there. I slipped my thumb and forefinger inside and pinched the bills. Before I realized what I was doing, my arm rotated out the window and my fingers parted. The money sailed off, staying behind where it belonged.

Before the night began, I didn't believe in curses. I'd been ignorantly wrong. I didn't want any reminders or to take any part of the town with me. So, my earnings had to stay.

I had enough money to get me wherever I decided to land. I was going to make a clean start, leaving those horrible memories far behind.

The little girl had said we would play another day. I only prayed she was wrong. If I played again, I'm certain the madness would fracture my mind long before the rising terror stopped my heart.

Last Girl Found

Kelly Ray's feet were bleeding again. Over the previous two days they had clotted, mildly scabbed over by way of dirt and other forest debris, and then a fallen branch or rock broke them open again. The pain had at least toned down from its earth-shaking roar to a nearly inaudible growl.

A brook ahead made itself known by the sound of flowing water over rocks. It was a frequent water source during her trek through these unknown woods. She couldn't figure out if it was the same brook or if this land had many coursing through it.

Kelly's knees easily gave in to the buckle as she collapsed along the edge, dipped her cupped, torn hands into the cool water and drank. There was a slight metallic taste to the water, tinged with something not meant to be consumed, but she didn't have a choice. Drink or death. Food had become a rarity. Even though some bushes held a surplus of berries, she chose to leave alone what she couldn't identify. It was best to have an empty stomach instead of suffering from severe abdominal pain and diarrhea, and that would only trigger dehydration.

The nausea hit Kelly again. Her body violently rejected the water, splashing across the dead leaves. She fell onto her back. A branch bit through her T-shirt, jabbing at the skin, but she didn't care. Nothing mattered anymore, she decided. She would die out here, and that was that.

A hard pull dragged her toward unconsciousness. She wanted to let go. She needed to slip away from this madness of reality for a while. She knew if she gave in, the remaining daylight would be wasted. There was nothing she could do in the dark except wait for dawn. Kelly pushed herself up and crawled back to the stream. She took the water in slowly this time, giving her body time to process so there wouldn't be another rejection. Half an hour ticked by before she finally pushed herself from the ground and stood. Her entire body protested. Muscles threatened to go slack, and joints promised a total collapse. The thought of death drifted away, replaced by an eagerness to live. She needed to see her sister, Jasmine, and her parents, too.

"Fuck this. I'm gonna walk the fuck out of here, and I'm gonna destroy those assholes who took me," she promised the empty woods.

It was a hollow vow, because it had no teeth, she knew. The men who snatched her were rich and powerful. They had claimed as much. One of them, she was certain, was in law enforcement. The burlap sack they had placed over her head was not a tightly woven material, and glimpses of the world around her became visible at times. Snippets of faces, the room in which they held her, and even the light winking off a law enforcement badge of some sort. Then came the sounds of a belt loosening and clothing dropping to the floor.

If by happenstance she crossed paths with someone, she couldn't trust anyone out here. Even if by some miracle of luck she found a highway, there wasn't a single driver who might stop to offer help that could be considered believable with their genuine kindness. She could very well be delivering herself right back into the hands of the men she spent over a month trying to escape.

Something stabbed the bottom of Kelly's left foot. A sharp breath filled her lungs, and her teeth went into a grinding action. Within a minute, the pain of that injury slid into the realm of numbness with its other war battle-fatigued brethren.

The August day, at least she figured it must be August, offered plenty of daylight to travel. She had made a choice the first day in the wild. The sun needs to stay at her back during the early hours, and she will chase the sun in the evening hours. Out here, it was the only method she knew to keep from traveling in constant circles.

Something darted through the brush to her left, and Kelly instantly froze. The undergrowth was thick in that direction, blocking all views of what the animal could have been. It was no doubt larger than a squirrel or a rabbit as it made a ruckus shooting through the dead leaves. She only prayed it was a deer and not something like a bear. She knew she had no chance against such an animal. A minute passed, and she heard the noise stop, and then continue again as it headed away. She waited a bit longer, hoping the thing would direct its escape to any area of the forest other than westward.

As the sun ran its slow summer horizon retreat, Kelly felt thankful that soon she could unburden her tired body for the night. Sleep would be a fleeting thing during those dark hours, but at least her muscles would receive a welcome relief.

Building a fire wasn't within the realm of possibilities. Kelly had no idea how to start one without using matches. She knew it was possible, but the plans behind it were far beyond her skill set. She used her fingers as rakes and worked the fallen leaves into a large pile beside a fallen tree. The tree would be the perfect place to keep her back against during the night. Any kind of predators had no chance of hitting her from behind and overcoming her sleeping body before she had a chance to defend herself. With no fire to keep animals at bay, this was the next best thing to survive the night in unfamiliar woods. She broke off a thick branch from the fallen tree. It would make a nice club with good reach to fend off any black bears who may catch her scent and come to investigate.

Wedged against the log, she pulled in handfuls of leaves until her bed for the night consumed her. With only her face visible, she watched the nighttime forest come to life with nocturnal creatures. An owl somewhere in the treetops made a call, and then, with nearly silent stealth, it took flight, diving toward the forest floor. In the moonlight that broke through the cover of trees, Kelly watched the owl swoop, snatch something small in its claws, and then disappear again. A long while later, as her eyes started to give up the fight, a fox scampered out from cover. Only a dozen yards away, it took small steps while sniffing the ground like a bloodhound. A gorgeous white stripe shot a diagonal lightning bolt over its right eye and across its muzzle.

Beautiful, Kelly thought.

The fox was either on the trail of something or it had caught the scent of a human. It darted through the under-growth, and just like that, gone from her life.

Sleep came, if one could call it sleep. A restless wave of a dream morphing into the deepest terror of a night-mare. Not a nightmare of fantastical impossibility, but one very real. It was a dream of real life, and the tragic turn it made.

"Come on, Kelly! Show us your goods!" Skylar called out from the water and offered a whistle that broke into a spit-filled exhale.

The other three girls had already peeled away clothing down to their bare cheeks and ran for the cool lake water, losing the fight when their calf muscles submerged, causing all of them to pitch forward in a hard splash.

A Three Stooges moment, Kelly thought.

Kelly scanned left and right down the small beach, and then a long study of the surrounding woods.

"This is so stupid," Kelly told her friends as they began a splash fight.

"Kelly! Kelly! Kelly!" Their choir urged.

"Lord save me," she responded as she pulled off her shirt.

The woo-hoos and whistles continued until all her clothing had dropped to the sand. She held her arms out as a *what do you think* gesture and received applause for the show.

Being that they shared gym class, followed by showers, Kelly felt no embarrassment as they had seen each other nude dozens of times. But coming out to this secluded lake for a girls' day out to go wild and skinny dip had become an absurd idea. Plenty of people knew about this location, and every so often classmates scheduled a plan to drive twenty-five miles here to drink, party and swim.

July's sun had only warmed the surface of the lake. As she sank waist deep, the water temperature offered an invigorating relief from the heat. Her body adjusted quickly, giving her immediate appreciation of how good of an idea this had been. Diving under, Kelly swam away from the girls and popped up thirty yards away. She rolled onto her back, letting the sun warm her breasts as she made a slow backstroke toward the center of the lake.

"I'm not coming out there to save you if you start to drown," Tilly called out.

Without slowing, Kelly said, "I'm a two-time state champion at the backstroke. I think I'll be okay."

"Yeah, but how come you never did it while showing the crowd your boobs?"

Kelly didn't bother answering, and for some reason the girls laughed at her silence.

Kelly chuckled at their immaturity. She loved them like sisters. Although they shared many dramatic ordeals over the years, they had built a lifelong, unbreakable bond.

Ceasing her swim, Kelly bobbed in the water and watched her friends. Two of them were hooking Kara's feet and trying to catapult her from the lake and into the air. The effort ended with Kara just getting her butt out of the water and collapsing back down onto the other two. They came up choking on water and laughing.

Something crunched a branch in the forest behind Kelly. It was a firecracker shot that echoed across the narrow valley. She looked over her shoulder as she maneuvered her body to face that side of the lake. The other girls apparently hadn't heard, as their playing continued. Although Kelly's vision was perfect, the distance was far, and the thickness of the woods could have even concealed an elephant standing just within the tree line.

The sudden sense of vulnerability overwhelmed her. Four girls rounding the bend into their twenties, completely nude in a lake, had the makings of a sub-par horror film opening. Keeping in mind that they had piled all their clothes, phones, and vehicle keys on the shore added to her anxiety, causing a rippling chill to move through her body on the hot afternoon.

Swimming back to the beach, she made sure to keep her body beneath the water. If there was a watcher in the woods, she didn't want to give them anymore of a show than she already had.

Kelly knew she was going to sound panicky and over-reacting when she reached the others and told them her suspicions. She decided she didn't care. There was an uncomfortable sensation that wasn't letting go. She wouldn't let herself relax until they redressed, got back to the car and moved down the highway for home.

"Hey. Um, hey. I think it's about time to head out."

The three girls turned to watch her, forming their own reasoning for Kelly's suddenness to book it out of here and end the fun.

"Seriously? We've only been here for twenty minutes. I didn't drive all this way just to turn around and go back home," Tilly said.

"Yeah. We brought drinks and snacks. This was gonna be at least a half-day thing, Kelly," Kara added.

"I know. I'm sorry. Something is moving through the woods over there. I just got a little freaked out. But I want to go. We can do this somewhere else. Maybe at my house or something."

"It's the woods, Kelly. It's most likely a deer. Just chill a bit and you'll feel fine," Skylar insisted.

It was another crack on Kelly's right that made all of them flinch. Kara offered a startled cry that ran across the water like the call of a loon.

"Um," Tilly began, but was unable to finish.

"Just a deer," Skylar said again.

"It can't be. There's no way it got all the way from over there to over here so quickly," Kelly said.

"That is weird. What are the odds there could be two deer in the woods?" Skylar said and laughed at her own joke.

No one else laughed, especially when a third snap of a branch sounded, now behind them.

"Let me guess, what are the odds of three deer walking through the woods?" Kelly said and started swimming for shore. "I'm at least going to get dressed. I'm going to feel really dumb standing here naked if a bunch of people start turning up."

Tilly said, "No one would be coming from those directions. There's nothing out that way. I've Google mapped this place before. There are no houses for miles."

"She's right. Let's get dressed. What we don't need is a couple of perverted hillbillies spying on us and getting bad ideas," Skylar said, as she swam behind Kelly.

Doing the best they could to conceal body parts, they made the trip from water to their towels and clothes. The girls were pulling on shoes when a fourth branch breaking pulled their attention to the north.

"Yep. Like I said. This is so stupid," Kelly said.

"Where the fuck is my cell phone?" Skylar asked as she searched her pockets.

"Fuck your cell phone. Where are the goddamn car keys?" Tilly asked and went into panic mode as her hands became a blur, searching through the remaining pile of belongings.

"Does anyone have their phone?" Kelly asked, but already knew the answer by the terror-stricken expression they all shared.

"This isn't possible. Wouldn't we have seen someone going through our stuff?" Kara asked.

"Not with everything piled up close to these trees. We were all distracted. We need to go," Kelly said and stood.

"So much for the deer theory," Skylar said.

"Oh, my God. Now I feel stupid. I told Trevor that we were coming out to the lake. He wanted to come and bring a few friends. I told him no because it was going to be a girls' party. And he's like, oh a girl party drinking and getting all lesbo on each other kind of thing?" Tilly said.

Kara said, "Well, nice going. Like I really wanted a couple of horny boys watching me from the trees."

Kelly looked around and said, "That doesn't make any sense. If it were them, then we would have seen another car parked at the gate."

"Not if they got here after us," Tilly shot back.

"Even if they did get here after us, they couldn't have gotten halfway around the lake, especially without us hearing them. Also, why would they walk all that way?" Kelly said and moved to the edge of the trees.

"Okay, Trevor, you fuckface! Real funny! Get out here and give us our stuff back!" Tilly yelled into the woods.

No reply came as the girls watched for signs of life.

"Okay, so now I'm freaking out. Let's just do what Kelly said and leave," Kara said.

"Leave how?" Tilly asked. "They have the keys."

"We'll walk to the car and wait for someone to come by. Or if it is Trevor and his friends, they'll eventually find us waiting at the car. They won't pull this bullshit very long," Skylar said.

"Yeah, not if he ever wants to get laid again," Tilly shouted.

Kelly began walking down the road without further debate. She wanted to move away from the lake and the woods. She needed to be in a place where civilization existed. Even if it was only a highway rarely traveled.

Every minute, Kelly made them stop and listen. She had to know if people moved along the woods with them. When she was sure no one was following, she started again.

A wolf was on the path in front of them. It stood over six feet tall, and a body of predatory muscles was ready for a hunt.

Tilly grabbed Kelly's arm and squeezed the life out of it.

"That can't be Trevor. He's way too big," Tilly said and took a step back.

The wolf cocked his head, perhaps anticipating the four of them gearing up to run.

"We're done with the games, asshole. Give us our stuff back and we're out of here," Kelly demanded and stepped forward.

The man in the rubber mask slowly shook his head and then began walking toward them.

Wolves hunt in packs, Kelly thought.

Something moved on her left. Another man, similarly dressed, stepped out from behind a tree. He made a simple toss, and what landed at their feet made this situation very real. None of them spoke, just stared at hope broken to pieces. Four cell phones lay destroyed almost beyond recognition.

"Okay, so we fight. Use anything you can get your hands on to defend yourself. Get to the highway," Kelly told them and then turned to the men. "Okay. Well, are we gonna get this party started or what? You're about to realize what a dipshit mistake you and your boyfriend just made."

The two wolves turned their heads in a mechanical motion. Before Kelly even looked, she knew she had made an error by anticipating it was one man, and then mistakenly guessing it could be no more than two men. When she turned to follow their line of sight, a massively built third man stepped into view.

With two of them, we had a slim chance. But not with three of them. Three of them are too strong.

Kelly moved with a quick rotation. Her body going low, snatching a fist-sized rock beside the path. As she spun, her eyes were already looking ahead. The closest target was the third wolf, the most physically intimidating one, and Kelly had deadlocked her aim. Before the man had a chance to react, the rock raced the distance, finding perfect contact. Even with the added layer of the mask, the velocity of the rock with the added mass was too great to do anything other than cause severe head trauma.

His head did a hard snap back, followed by his body. It was exactly what Kelly wanted. It was as if she'd just fell a tree. The rigid shaft of his massive body went over with no resistance as gravity took hold.

And now back to two of them, she thought and looked for something else to throw.

Wordlessly, the other men moved forward, either in rage or perhaps fright that they would be the next target to fall.

Panic became the action of the moment. Kara thrust her leg up in an awkward motion of defense, which landed a hard blow to the second wolf's groin. He grunted, but didn't collapse. Her fight was far from over. She kicked at his grasping hands, causing several bones in his fingers to break.

The shot to the crotch hadn't caused an outburst, but broken fingers certainly did. He pulled his hand back, staring at the unnatural twisted directions of his middle and ring fingers.

"Fucking bitch!" he screamed and used his uninjured hand to deliver a blow to Kara's left eye socket.

Much like the third wolf, her head did a vicious snap back, connecting brutally with the hard walking path.

The man was in motion to drive a head-splitting kick when Skylar was quickly all over his back like a monkey throwing a tantrum. She sank teeth and claws into any bare skin she could find. The top portion of the mask, where his right ear was, came away with a rubber band snap, followed by a fast flow of blood running down his neck. As he screamed, he also pitched his upper body forward, propelling Skylar over him and onto Kara. Both girls cried out from the collision.

As Kelly swung a thick branch collected from the forest ground, hoping to hell she could home run the first wolf's head, she saw the third wolf sit up. He tried to move into quick action to help his friends seize control of the situation, but his body faltered as he tried getting up. Kelly was sure it would only take a minute for him to gather himself, and then it was game over for the four of them.

The distraction of the third wolf trying to get his feet under him caused Kelly's aim to veer. The branch missed the first wolf's head, and the velocity unbalanced her body. She spun, feet tangled, and crashed her backside onto the path. The wolf instantly reached for her. As his hand went to seize her throat, she lunged forward. Kelly's hands gripped his hand, and her teeth went into action. They clamped onto the web of flesh between his thumb and forefinger. Under the pressure and the working of her jaw, scissoring the teeth back and forth, the skin and muscle gave way, resulting in a mess of blood gushing into her mouth.

The wolf pulled his hand back, breaking the lingering strands of tendons. His destroyed hand disappeared into the other as he cradled it. His scream was the high-pitched misery of a man, and not that of a wolf.

Kelly spat the severed flesh at him.

Tilly was in attack mode, trying to fend off the second wolf so the other girls could get themselves up. That was when the third wolf finally pushed himself from the ground and began coming at them.

Kelly looked at her friends and shouted, "Run, god-dammit!"

———— · · ✄ · · ————

Something bulldozed through a mass of limbs, making a hellacious noise. Kelly shot out of the bed of leaves. The expectation of finding herself at the feet of three wolves brought on a full-body kick of anxiety. With her airway closing, then the increasing hammer of her heart and nerves dancing on a razor's edge of intensity made every-thing shake with a surge of adrenaline. She was sure she was about to die because her body wouldn't allow a gulp of air.

Backpedaling on hands and feet, Kelly rammed hard against the log that had been her shelter. Though uninten-tional, the impact jarred her body into taking a needed breath.

The rapid switch of Kelly's eyes revealed no immedi-ate threat. The ease of stressed muscles came, and she clamped her eyes shut and focused on slow breathing. The calm came quickly because the nightmare fled. Whether the noise that had propelled her so viciously from sleep was either of dreams or real life in these woods, she didn't know. All she knew for sure was that she was safe. If being lost and alone in the woods might ever be considered safe.

The first touch of dawn found the horizon to begin Kelly's third day of traveling through these godless woods. And so she walked on.

When the sun found its zenith, Kelly realized maybe the woods weren't so godless after all. What she found, she was sure, was the same point at which the terror began.

Once a quarry, now ten years flooded to become a secluded lake, lay before her. She walked to the cliff's edge, which, she recalled, was the same place the second noise had come from when they were nude and oblivious to any danger.

"Well, fuck me," Kelly said to no one.

Unfortunately, she didn't find any people playing in the shallows or on the beach. The place was devoid of life. What she would have given to find a family spending some outdoor quality time. She could let herself trust a man and a woman with children just long enough to drive her the hell out of here.

Even with careful movements, the sharp nub of a branch sank wooden teeth into the tortured pad of her foot. The warm, slick gush instantly let her know blood was running away from her again. None of this jumped into her mind, because now she was on familiar ground, and her survival chances had just increased twenty-fold.

Though the joy was there, the fear was right behind it. This place had at least once become a hunting ground for three wolves. It could still be. Kelly had no idea if the three packed up camp and moved direction for a new territory to play their game. The house they kept her in could very well have been one they found while prowling these woods. So, the loss of moving their operation was minimal. But if the property was owned by one of them, she couldn't be sure they'd give it up so easily.

They likely anticipated that she had died out here while desperately trying to find civilization and authorities who could help her exact justice. Men often share the belief that women have little inner strength, that they can't push their mind and body beyond all limits. And for this reason, she was sure they weren't looking for her anymore.

A bloody footprint marked a log as Kelly stepped free from the forest and into the partial clearing of the shoreline. It was the last blood offering she was willing to contribute to these endless, godforsaken woods. But now those red prints would only follow her down the gravel path to the highway, and to freedom.

Every second of the slow trek down the path, she was ready to duck for cover with even the slightest noise of a car or people roaming the area. The same caution applied when she reached the end of the path that ran onto the highway.

No cars came as Kelly looked left and right, trying to decide her best options for finding help. Southbound was a series of question marks. She'd never traveled that portion of the state. So, the only reasonable answer was to walk in the direction of Lander's Grove. The population was less than three thousand, but it could easily become a sanctuary until the police and her father arrived.

Kelly turned north and began the long walk. She could only guess from what she remembered over a month ago, but the town was nearly ten miles from the quarry.

With numb feet, she moved step-by-step, mile by mile, toward sanity.

Welcome to Lander's Grove!
A way station before the Gates of Heaven!

Kelly passed the town's sign with only a slight glance. It could be heaven, but it could also be hell. The jury was still out.

Kelly felt the townspeople watch her with eyes of bewilderment, maybe even a bit of fear. A man riding a mower absently braked as he studied her painful hobble down Cormac Street. There was no offer of assistance, only a questioning stare wondering why she had walked into their quiet town and what mayhem she might have brought with her.

A woman walking her dog gave the same reaction. As Kelly passed her, the woman's eyes shifted down to her bloodied feet.

As Kelly veered to the right, no one offered a single word of concern or help. An old town diner was ahead. The establishment had probably been here since its first residents settled. She grabbed the handle with a dirty and blood-caked hand and pulled it open.

Stepping inside to join the evening diners, Kelly felt as if someone had pressed a universal pause button. None of the patrons moved or spoke for a long time. Then, with neck-swivel action, their heads did a slow rotation in an almost choreographed appearance. This was a horror movie moment if ever there was one. It was a room of subservient puppets, all controlled by a single master. They fixed their gaze on her as if knowing exactly who she was and why she was here.

Then the awkward moment flittered away as Kelly's mind let the conspiracy theories fade. These were simply average people eating a very average dinner and offering an average stare for an unaverage situation.

With a hop-slide, favoring her severely damaged left foot, Kelly made her way to the counter and the single vacant barstool.

The waitress held a hand towel to her mouth in either shock or disgust as her eyes roamed over Kelly's destroyed figure.

"Young lady, is everything all right?" She managed to ask through the fabric.

Kelly sat down hard on the barstool as her muscles gave out. She surveyed the establishment and its people.

She turned to the waitress and said, "I don't know about you, but I sure could use the fucking strongest cup of coffee you've got."

————— · · ✕ · · —————

Kelly grabbed her purse and keys from the kitchen counter and yelled, "Cassie, you're making us late!"

Thumping down the steps with both feet together, Cassie wore her pink Dora the Explorer backpack and pink shoes that flashed lights with every step.

Kelly studied her daughter's frazzled blond hair and the jacket she wore inside out.

"Looking as lovely as ever, my precious one."

Kelly took her daughter's hand, set the security alarm, and went out the front door. After fastening Cassie in her car seat, she started the SUV and headed for Twin Pines Daycare.

Traffic during drop-off was always a nightmare, especially since the building bordered Lake Ridge Middle School.

Running Cassie up to the front where Mrs. Sandell waited, Kelly asked, "Who loves you the most in the entire universe?"

Cassie's eyes sparkled, and her cheeks pushed up as a smile formed.

"Mommy does! Mommy does!" she said as she bounced.

Kelly kissed Cassie's forehead and said, "Forever and ever. I'll see you later. Have a fun day."

Kelly wished Mrs. Sandell a great day and went back to the car. From the driver's seat, she watched Cassie converse with Mrs. Sandell in that adorable child-like way. She was, no doubt, explaining the wild adventure she had while traveling to school as she soared through the heavens on her winged horse.

It's incredible the turn of events that life hands someone at their most soul-crushing moment. A charismatic, sweet child, like Cassie, fathered by one of the most despicable, vicious people on the planet, didn't make any sense. When Kelly had first learned of her pregnancy, a desire, even a need, to have the child aborted came as the only option. With guidance and sympathy from family and friends, Kelly decided in the end that the child need not suffer the consequences of its father's actions. She would turn a horrific event into a lifelong reward. She was to have the child and decided there would never be any regrets about it. To this day, there haven't been.

Kelly shifted the car into drive and headed for class.

The plaza lot was full, but Kelly managed to grab a spot as someone backed out. She was a few minutes late, and the instructor was already addressing his taekwondo class.

The workout was far superior to any gym membership could offer. Every muscle in her body received ample exercise, with the added building of strength and stamina for any dire situation from this day on. She decided long ago that she would never become anyone's prey again.

Kelly spent ten minutes after class winding down and chatting with other students before needing to go home and shower before work.

Although Quintela's restaurant wasn't her place, she felt as if it were. With the menu created to suit her tailored palate, the place became a success. Businessmen and women from the neighboring downtown buildings made this restaurant one of their preferred lunch spots. Able to accommodate sixty diners, the place was a hopping madhouse during the lunch hour.

Kelly and the other staff always began prepping the most popular meals beforehand to get the food out of the kitchen soon after the wait staff brought the orders. It was certain that the business patrons had little patience for long waits. These were men and women who often wanted a fast, satisfying meal and a quick return to the office. This also made for a quick rotation of customers, allowing the restaurant to thrive.

At 12:30, one of the waiters, Simon, came through the kitchen, telling Kelly that one of the customers had requested a word with her.

"What's it about? I'm very busy."

"Well, he's been going on and on about the Parmesan chicken. He probably wants to praise you," Simon said, and winked.

Giving in, Kelly washed her hands and dried them with paper towels, and headed for the kitchen swing doors.

"Which table?"

"Table twelve."

Two men occupied the table. Both men wore suits, were clean-shaven, had their hair meticulously combed to the right, and even kept their fingernails well maintained. They carried an essence of importance. Men who could make or break any financial business with a single phone call.

The younger of the two turned and watched as Kelly walked toward them. His eyes roamed across every part of her, and a slight smile began.

She made her best effort to prevent an eye roll. Men frequently offered languishing stares with desires of perverted fantasies that traveled through their thoughts when they studied her.

The man was handsome in an almost romance book cover design, the shirtless stud type, minus the abundance of all the rippling muscles. So, Kelly's smile came much easier than if he'd been a balding, porky man with dominance needs.

"Hello, gentlemen. What can I do for you?"

"So, you're the head chef?" Without waiting for a response, he continued. "Very impressive for such a young woman. I've been told that you're the creativity behind the menu. Is that right?"

Kelly smiled. "All of us contribute input on each dish and what it needs to make it even better, but more importantly, what it needs to make it our own."

"Very modest. I like that. What do you think, Michael? How was the meal?"

The man to Kelly's right offered a small grunt as he finished the last bite. He retrieved his cloth napkin and wiped his mouth and hands.

Without looking up, he said, "Mmm, yes. Exquisite flavor. Thank you."

If a meteorite traveled from space, cut through the atmosphere, shot through the restaurant's roof and slammed into Kelly's chest, it might have delivered the same sensation as the man's words.

During and after the terror of her abduction in those woods, panic attacks became a frequent malady. They would typically hit at the most inconvenient times. Often,

Kelly was sure those moments were much like what death may feel like. The suddenness of being unable to breathe, a heartbeat drastically out of rhythm, spiral vision, and a rushing full-body shake becomes a trickster that leaves one very much alive and completely embarrassed when in the company of others.

This time, though, Kelly felt the trigger being pulled. The opportunity to crush it back from severe needed to be an immediate reaction. Identifying what is instantly happening can break the fierceness that the attack could bring. Though her experiences are never completely controlled, she successfully reduced things to a moderate roar. Breathing became a key factor. Slow and deep breaths through her nose and an even release through her mouth enhanced her body to a calmer state. Trying to focus on the younger man talking wasn't easy, but Kelly was sure she'd hidden her attack well. Neither man showed any alarm that something was wrong.

"So, I'll cut to the point. I'm investing in a restaurant two blocks from here that will be opening next month. We have an incredible staff lined up, but I'd really like to add someone of your caliber. The pay is excellent, with room to negotiate, top benefits, and five weeks of vacation, too."

Mmm, yes. Exquisite flavor. Thank you.

For fuck's sake, how many times had she heard those exact words, spoken with satisfied relish? The man's voice was one of three that often haunted her sleep, driving her from bed, gasping for breath on the floor.

Smiling, the man leaned back and said, "You'll pretty much run the show. Does any of that sound appealing?"

Despite the unlikelihood of the other man's exact words being heard during her lifetime, the astronomical moment could still be a possibility. There was only one way for her to confirm his identity as the first wolf who had appeared on the path in front of them. The mother-fucker who tipped the first domino.

"That's a very generous offer," Kelly said, surprised at how well composed she kept. Even her voice didn't waver. "But I'm sorry to decline the offer. I've very much made this place a home away from home. I would hate to leave it."

The man nodded, but didn't relent.

"I could also offer a flexible schedule for times when family matters may come up. We all know how that can throw a crimp in your day when you have work matters that need tending to."

Kelly leaned a bit forward. The man on her right was only half visible to her searching eyes.

"Again, I really do appreciate the offer. As I've said, it's kind of my family here, so I'm going to have to de-cline."

She saw it then, and the sight caused a slow surge of bile up her esophagus. Managing to swallow it back down, Kelly turned away.

"But should you ever change your mind, just give me a call. The offer will stand. Here's my card."

The man produced a business card as if it were the fi-nale of his magic trick.

Kelly turned, desperately trying not to snatch it ab-ruptly, but failing.

She stormed through the kitchen door. In a mad scram-ble, her focus never left the bathroom door past the stoves. She kicked the door shut and barely got her head over the bowl before the rush came. The acidic flood rolled out like the revolt of an inhaled, scorching flame that her body quickly needed to expel. When she was sure her body had rejected all the contents of her stomach, she slid onto the cool bathroom tile.

Hard, violent images sucker-punched her mind. The man reached out to seize her throat. The only thing she had left in her weakened arsenal was her teeth. They went into action like the vice grip of a pit bull as soon as they found purchase on something. What her teeth sank into was the soft web of skin, muscle, and tendons between his thumb and forefinger. She had worked those teeth with the determination that he would never use that hand again.

The man at the table was missing that section of his right hand.

When Kelly left the bathroom, several of the staff watched her with concern. She knew what she must look like, because she had felt a cold sweat covering her face as if a fever had just broken. There was no doubt her skin was paper white.

Emma came over with a glass of water. She said, "What's going on? Did you just get sick?"

Kelly accepted the glass, gulped down several mouthfuls, and swished around the last bit to remove the acid from her mouth before swallowing.

"Thank you. Yeah. I don't know where it came from. It just hit me suddenly."

Kelly continued her slow breathing. The water had helped, but the nausea was unrelenting.

"I think you ought to go home. We've got everything covered. We've got plenty of prepped food to get us through the rest of rush hour. Seriously. Head home."

Kelly gave in. Although she had no intention of going home. Going outside to grab some fresh air helped even more. By the time she exited the rear entrance and walked down the alley toward the street, she almost felt like herself after any previous panic episodes.

Scanning the sidewalks on both sides of the street, Kelly searched for a place with a good view of the restaurant's front entrance. Camden's Travel Agency had a bench seat in front of their windows. With the lunchtime foot traffic, Kelly figured she'd go unnoticed when the two men left the restaurant.

Crossing the street, Kelly removed her white chef's jacket to better blend in with the people.

Settling onto the bench, paying no mind to all those who passed in front of her, Kelly's focus was unwavering. She knew it wouldn't be long before the men left the restaurant. Then again, she thought about how long she had spent in the bathroom and the possibility they had left during that brief period.

As she began getting up to see if they were still inside, the two businessmen stepped through the front door. They conversed out front before parting ways. Only one of them she desired to follow.

Although he must have been twenty years her senior, he held an eye-catching appeal. She could imagine women often turned for a second glance. He offered the world the appearance of a handsome and successful man, but only to her was where a deviant monster lay beneath.

The fact that he could easily seduce countless women across the city was a psychological perplexity as to why he drew himself into the recess of a dark heart. Instead of courting women through ethical channels, he chose to don the mask of an alpha predator and take women by brutal force.

It was a game to him. A hunt. A challenge to drive horrific fear from any woman he pursued. But he wasn't alone in his sadistic quest. There were two others.

Kelly's thoughts began cycling through the tumblers of a lock placed deep in her mind. Through the door was a place she never knew. It was a primal place of rage and vengeance. It was in the realm of desperate measures to correct the unjust violations in her life.

As the man walked away from her down the sidewalk of 5th Avenue, Kelly cut a path through traffic and followed. Making sure to stay far enough back to avoid detection, she also kept behind a middle-aged couple, just in case he glanced back. He never did.

A block ahead, the man maneuvered between parked cars, circling around to the driver's side of a black Mercedes. With a quick disappearance inside, the brake lights came on and the engine kicked over. Kelly started to run. She rammed between the couple, offering a passing apology, and tried to catch up. Her only goal was to at least get the man's license plate number. If an SUV changing lanes hadn't caused the man to halt his merge into traffic, Kelly would have been too far behind to see the plate.

It wasn't the type of license plate she would need to write down before forgetting. It was a vanity plate. A single word reading: PRONTO.

As that word imprinted within her mind, she quickly became aware the wolf might suddenly glance into one of his mirrors, discovering the chef from the restaurant was tailing him. The sight of her would send up immediate red flags, especially for a man with a heart full of secrets and much to lose.

He didn't notice her. His own self-importance got in the way of paying attention to others, even though a simple glance would have spared him much future pain.

———— · · ✕ · · ————

Not even five years' time and a traumatic event could have fractured the bonds Kelly, Tilly, Kara, and Skylar held. Though life in adulthood is frequently a three-ring circus, they managed to make time for each other.

Though Kelly could honestly say that the bond between her and Tilly was the strongest. Kelly suspected why. Tilly blamed herself for what happened to them, in particular, the terror Kelly endured. It was Tilly's idea to go to the lake. Tilly boasted about it on social media. She had also been the one to drive them into nowhere. These three things, in Tilly's mind, were the simple factors that nearly got them all killed, and one of them to suffer at the hands of endless nightmares.

Kelly never blamed her for any of those unfortunate events. No victim is ever to be blamed for the vicious actions of men.

Sitting in Skylar's living room, each of them sipped their glasses of Merlot on their "Thursday night unwind", as Kara liked to call it.

Tilly was talking about her fiancé, Jared, and his roaming eyes over the waitress during their last date night.

Kara said, "You can't corral the horn-dog in men! It's in their DNA code to search for attractive women to mate with."

"Well, he doesn't have to be so damn obvious about it. He doesn't glance, but he studies as if he's about to begin painting a portrait."

"Yeah, probably a nude portrait," Skylar said, and the three of them laughed.

Kelly didn't feel like laughing. In fact, the discussion of sex-driven men blew a dark cloud through her thoughts.

The others realized Kelly's withdrawal from the topic, and their laughter tapered off. They looked at each other, unclear about how they could smooth the discussion over to something else.

"Relax, girls. I'm fine. In fact, I'm more than fine. I'm actually glad we're together tonight, because I need all of your help. I need it now more than ever."

Kelly shifted her curled legs from the couch to the floor and set her wineglass on the coffee table. She stared at her hands, trying to decide where to start.

Tilly said, "Kelly, you know you can confide in us. No matter what's bothering you, we're all sisters here."

Kelly offered a slow nod and said, "I know. I am going to confide in you. I'm also going to ask, maybe even demand, your help with something."

The change in conversation to a subject of seriousness held the other three on the threshold of not wanting to know and the impossibility of never finding out what Kelly was about to unload. But as Tilly had stated, it wasn't a friendship, it was a sisterhood.

Kelly lifted her eyes and watched each of them for a long moment before speaking.

"I found one of the wolves. There's no question it's him. He's missing the part of his hand I chewed away."

With their hands covering their mouths in disbelief, they waited for Kelly to continue the story of locating one of the men.

"He came into the restaurant with another man on Tuesday. The other man called me out of the kitchen to offer a chef position at a restaurant he's opening. The other man only said a few words, but they were words that drove me into the back to throw up. They're the same words I told you about. The man offering the job asked him what he thought of the meal, and he said, 'Mmm, yes. Exquisite flavor. Thank you.' Those were the words that sonofabitch said to me after every time he violated me."

The statement pushed the other's eyes to the floor. There was much about the abduction Kelly never talked about. They knew only about the basement confinement and the sexual assaults that took place there. The girls never asked her for specific details, and Kelly never offered. It was a way of washing those dreadful images from her mind, they figured, but never knowing her horror tale often consumed their thoughts.

"My God," Tilly said. "Two days ago, and you never called me about it? I'm a police officer. I could have taken action!"

Kelly held up her hands. "What action, Tilly? A man in a restaurant who is missing a chunk of his hand is not definitive case-closed proof."

Skylar asked, "So, what did you do?"

"Like I said, I ran and threw up every bit in my stomach, and then some. Then I told the staff I was going home sick. Instead, I waited outside."

"Did you confront him?" Kara asked.

"No, he didn't recognize me at the restaurant, either. It's probably because I had a damn sack over my head most of the time they held me. But I did get his license plate number when he left the restaurant."

"Well, we all kept your return home quiet. There were only a selected few who knew you walked out of those woods just in case they came looking for you. Even changing your last name should have kept them from suspecting that you survived," Skylar said.

"I'm not worried about that. I always believed they anticipated that I died in the woods. I changed my name as an added precaution."

"Christ. I can't believe this. There was not a goddamn lead all this time, and now you're the one who breaks the case open. So, what's the next move?" Tilly asked as she leaned forward, absently grabbing her glass of wine and finishing it off.

"A dish best served cold," Kelly said.

Kara and Skylar had no idea what she was talking about. But Tilly, now thriving in a law enforcement position, thirsted for good mystery novels, especially their plot twists.

"Revenge?" Tilly asked. "You're seriously thinking you can get revenge on this man?"

Kelly shook her head and finished off her own wine before grabbing the bottle from the table and refilling her glass.

"Not just him. All three of them."

They looked at one another, thinking the very same thing, but it was Skylar who asked it.

"So, you know who the other two are as well?"

"Not a clue. I'm gonna ask the wolf nicely who his associates are."

Kara leaned back on the sofa and said, "This is insane. You can't honestly be serious about thinking you can take these men on. Right? Going to the authorities is your only option. Help them build a case. With warrants, they can churn up every part of his life. His personal and financial life will expose something by way of proof!"

Kelly released a huge sigh of irritation.

"What fucking judge is going to sign off on any kind of warrant to search his home, business or financials? I don't know who this man is yet, but I can truthfully say he isn't a stupid man. Who knows how long these guys have been doing this to women? Who even knows how many women they've done it to since I escaped? It's been five goddamn years. Men with a sadistic drive like those three don't just quit when they have this kind of power over people."

"Jesus, Kelly, you're talking fucking bonkers right now. We'll find a legal way to destroy them. You can't do some John Wick action saying, hey you killed my dog and stole my ride, so I'm gonna stab your dick with a fucking pencil. You need to be smart about this," Skylar blurted.

"That's exactly what I'm planning on doing. I'm going to be crazy smart, because there's no way the big, bad wolf is going to win over on this Red Riding Hood again. I need your help, though. Each of you has something that can contribute to my cause. So, will you help me?"

If David Copperfield had just vanished before them, it would have yielded the same expression. Gap-mouthed, the three girls looked from Kelly to each other. Kelly anticipated one direction but prepared herself for the other. No matter which way their decision swayed, she was ready to go into action, even alone if need be.

"Okay, I can't speak for the others, but I'm willing to listen to your request," Tilly said.

Kelly knew Tilly would be the one most open to the concept of revenge.

"I've thought that maybe it's best if I tell you individually. That way, you're all in the dark about the others' involvement just in case this thing goes badly. All in all, I'll take complete blame if it goes sideways."

"Fuck that," Skylar said. "We're in it together or not at all. That is, unless you expect me to kill someone."

The three of them laughed briefly until they saw Kelly found no humor in it.

Kelly leaned forward and said, "You don't have to worry about that. I'll do all the killing."

After Tilly determined the seriousness of Kelly's statement, she put her head in her hands. She said, "Oh, my God, Kelly. I can't hear this. Jesus. I'm a fucking police officer! I can't hear about one of my best friends planning on murdering three people. You've lost it. We will get them. All three of them. But I can't hear about a murder plan."

Kelly momentarily thought about leaving and going head-on against the savages by herself. But she knew it would make things far more difficult.

"Kelly, we understand the trauma you went through, but killing those pigs isn't the closure you need," Skylar said.

"I'm really tired of people telling me what I need. I can decide for myself what I need. What I need is your help. What I need is to wipe these fucking low-life people off the planet. Do you remember the scene in *The Silence of the Lambs* when the senator's daughter is in the well and sees the bloody claw marks on the wall and the broken fingernail? I saw evidence just like that. I knew I wasn't the first, and I was sure as hell not going to be the last. What I also need is justice for all those girls before and after me who didn't get away. I need to be their voice because those girls are gone. Their family and friends never got to know what happened to them. They're just gone and now forgotten by local law enforcement, just another file tucked away in a cabinet in some room no one ever goes into except to add another lost girl file. I will tell you the most important thing of all. What I need is to make sure this never happens to another girl."

Kelly stood, grabbing hold of the bottom of her sweater, and pulled it over her head.

In perfect synchronization, the girls drew a breath, and their hands instinctively moved to their open mouths.

What they stared at were dozens of dental scars, vicious bites delivered by an abuser. Now five years old, but still showing no signs of fading with time. Those horrific reminders of the event were permanently etched on Kelly's body and mind.

"No," Tilly said in a whisper. And then she went to Kelly, tears a steady flow as she wrapped her arms around her friend.

The other two joined, and after long minutes of endless tears and soft sobs passed, the group parted, all studying the most horrific secret their friend had hidden away.

Kelly pulled the sweater back on, embarrassed by the attention of the scars. She sat and finished off her third glass of wine.

Tilly said, "I knew it was something, but I didn't want to pry. I knew there was a reason you always wore long sleeves and why you never went swimming with us again, not even here at Skylar's pool. I just thought it was maybe a feeling of vulnerability because it happened at the lake. I really didn't think it was something like that."

Wiping away the remainder of tears, Kara leaned forward and said, "Yep, fuck it. Whatever you need. I'm in."

The game, and yes, Kelly began to think of it much like a game, began to gain major traction when all three girls agreed to her request for help. It was an upfront promise before Kelly even revealed the beginning stages of her plan. She knew more than anything they came on board because they knew Kelly would attack this idea whether they were in or out. More than that, the three girls felt a certain gratitude that Kelly had fought the wolves so they could get free. But Kelly also knew it was mostly their guilt about getting away. They had suffered merely minutes during the encounter. Kelly had endured over five weeks of an event that would have crushed most people past their mental breaking point.

Tilly had come through on her part in a quick fashion. A simple DMV search of the vanity plate PRONTO gave her the name Michael Winters. Tilly printed out a copy of the man's license and showed it to Kelly. Now they had a name, an address and a face to direct their hatred toward.

On the following Thursday girls' night, Kelly slid a roughly drawn sketch across the coffee table to Kara. The three girls leaned forward, with their elbows perched on their knees as they studied it. With almost comical synchronicity, they looked up in puzzlement.

Still my three stooges, Kelly thought, but held back the laughter.

"What am I looking at?" Kara asked.

"I need you to build that. You're the engineer."

"Studying to be an engineer. But I am amazing at creating brilliant things," Kara corrected. "It looks like a kind of noose."

"Sort of. It's possible to use it for that purpose. I'm more interested in making it an interrogation device. I can't overpower Michael Winters, so I need an advantage. I have to make sure he doesn't get the best of me. I need full control the entire time I'm in his presence. Even with my taekwondo training, he could still manage to overcome me. With that mechanism, I can literally squeeze the information out of him about who the other wolves are. He won't tell me until he's at the doormat of death's chambers."

"Wow," Kara said and clicked her tongue in thought. "Okay. I've got a few ideas."

"It needs to be remote-controlled tightening and loosening actions. I also need you to create some sort of locking gear pins to make sure that if he gets his fingers behind it, he can't pull it loose. Again, I need full control."

Tilly looked at the drawing and then at Kelly.

She said, "You're going to get yourself killed. How the hell are you supposed to get that around his throat? You can't do it when he's sleeping. You'll have to do it when he's awake. That gives him time to fight back before you can even activate the thing and get it snug around his neck. Every nanosecond gives him the opportunity to seize the advantage."

Kara said, "Um, well, not if I create an activation pin. At the top of the gearbox, which will be at the back of his neck, I could make something like a grenade pin you pull the second the device is in place. It would be under spring tension. Releasing the pin would pull it taut, maybe even torqued down a bit more to keep his attention on what's choking him and not on you."

"Do you see? This is why I brought the idea to you."

Kelly leaned back into the couch's cushions and swallowed a mouthful of wine. The plan was coming together, one small piece at a time.

Skylar asked, "You still haven't told me what I'm supposed to do. Tilly found his identity and address. Kara is going to build that thing. So, what's my part?"

"You're a realtor. So, real estate. I need you to do a wide search around the lake where they attacked us. They held me captive in a house or cabin somewhere out there in the woods. If you can, I need you to find out what individuals or corporations own the properties across those hills and valleys. One or all of those men own that property."

"You're going to kill them. Aren't you?" Tilly asked.

Kelly could sense the gears cranking in Tilly's mind, the gears known as law and order. To a mild degree, Tilly had suffered the terror of those men, but her experience was a fleeting one. Now five years down the road, she had cycled through police department training and graduated to be an officer of the law. Her training had morphed her perception into someone expected to follow regulations in all situations. Kelly knew that Tilly, at least on the inside, demanded justice in the proper way. But now that Tilly had seen a small piece of the physical abuse Kelly suffered, she was keeping her opinion in a locked box.

Kelly pulled in a deep breath and said, "I honestly can't answer that, because I don't know. How can I let them live after what they've done? Like I said, the girls before me need this as much as the girls after me, and the girls who have yet to cross their path. Who can say how many women they've abducted, assaulted, and murdered during this spree of violence? They're three serial rapists and killers."

Skylar said, "You're right. Though I don't believe in murder, the world would be a better place with those three removed from existence. Let me investigate the property owners. It'll take a few days to get what I need."

Tilly said, "Promise me one thing. If we find irrefutable proof that these men have done all the horrible things we believe they've done, we'll take the approach of justice the legal way. Isn't it better that they rot away in prison for decades, knowing they can never experience the hunger and satisfaction of hurting a girl ever again? Isn't that more punishment than death?"

As Kelly locked eyes with Tilly, her mind ran to that place of possibility. Was there justice when three men got to live and left to reminisce for the remainder of their years on the torture of countless young women? Three men would find international notoriety. Three men left relishing their high praise from those who long to brave such accomplishments but who are too physically and mentally weak to see it through. Book deals. Television interviews. Countless articles and even television series desiring to recount their exploits. Blogs and vlogs being added during the building of a million sadistic fucks fanbase. All of this would continue until the world found a new obsession, a new bloodlust.

"I promise," Kelly said, even though in her heart she knew it was a promise impossible to keep.

———— · · ✄ · · ————

Michael Winters jabbed a thumb at the OFF switch of the treadmill. He toweled off the sweat from his forehead and hair as he came to a stop. Taking a long pull of electrolyte-infused power drink from the sports bottle, he eyed the patrons across the gym. Many of the women were challenging the treadmills and other lightweight workout machines to tone muscle rather than to build. The men were at the rear doing the opposite by tackling the equipment designed to enhance bulk by pushing the limits of weight capacity.

Michael watched the men straining to achieve several repetitions of bench pressing 250 pounds. *All brawn and no brains*, he thought. *What's really the point, gentlemen? Do you figure at some point in your life a semi-truck will roll on top of you and you'll finally have that challenge to lift it off yourself before it destroys bone and suffocates you to death?*

Michael laughed to himself and then rolled his eyes over to the women. Several of them had been watching him watch the men. They probably figured that's where his desires fell.

Several of the women didn't break eye contact. Even the soft curl of a smile formed as they held a momentary connection. He could have all of them if he wanted. With chiseled features of a comic book superhero, and the success of a young Warren Buffett, there were few women across the country who would refuse his advances. Though most people at any gym are ritualistic about attending for health benefits, a secondary benefit is watching the eye-candy of the other attendees. Michael knew this well. Over the months, both male and female had tried to score more of his personal information with lively conversations. Their advances didn't hold his interest. There was only one he thirsted for, and, as usual, she was right on time.

Stepping through the front door was a raven-haired beauty. She was perfect in every sense of the word. Her body was slim, but admirably curved in all the right spots. It wasn't only her body he thrived for, but her mind as well. Pushing through her third year of law school, Reyna Mathers was working her way up to becoming something of a force to be reckoned with.

Michael had yet to speak with her. He had no such intention of doing so either, at least not in public. Not before he takes her. What he didn't need was for her to go missing, and the nosy gym members mentioning to the inquiring detectives how a flirty middle-aged man was frequently at her side the moment she stepped inside. After a quick chat with the gym manager, the police would have video footage and his name to go with it.

Rule #1: Never abduct someone you know.

Rule #2: Control is the key to every situation.

Cassie was passed out with half of her face lying across the plate of macaroni and cheese. Of course, Kelly felt the parental need to record the moment for hopefully an embarrassing viewing to a future potential boyfriend.

"Peanut?" Kelly said as she lightly shook Cassie. "Time for bed, Peanut."

She gently pulled Cassie back from the remains of her dinner and began mopping her face with a damp towel. One curl of macaroni stuck to her bottom lip to which she unconsciously pulled into her mouth. A final dinner morsel going down the hatch.

After settling Cassie in her bed, Kelly went downstairs to the dining room. She poured a glass of Merlot and opened her laptop. Her search into Michael Winters had deepened over the weeks. She was so unenlightened by the search results that she began questioning her accuracy in having the right man.

Any wrongdoing Michael Winters committed remained hidden deep, so much so that she couldn't even find anything across the dark web. His social media accounts showed no anger, hate, or racist comments or videos. His Facebook friends numbered nearly a thousand. Tilly had run a criminal background check, finding no prior convictions or even a traffic violation on his driving record.

Kelly gulped wine and fell back in her chair. She knew that no one could be this much of a saint. There had to be some way to find his closet of skeletons. The answer came to her with little effort. She needed to become his shadow until he removed the face the public knew and bared his true nature. She had to be there when he turned sinister. Only then could she believe this was really Satan's minion in disguise.

"I'll have to follow him. I'll have to see where he leads next," she told herself.

The chirp of the phone made her jump. Looking at the caller ID, she began to relax.

"Christ, you just made me jump out of my skin."

Kara said, "All I did was call. Were you awake?"

"Yes, doing research online. What's up?"

"Good. Can I come over?"

"I suppose so. My brain won't shut down. So, there's no way I'll be sleeping much tonight."

Kara lived six blocks away. It took her only five minutes before she walked through the front door. Carrying a shoebox, she walked towards Kelly, who sat at the dining room table. She was about to ask for a glass of wine but saw Kelly had already poured her one.

"I love it when you bring me shoes," Kelly said.

"Custom made, baby. Though this one might be a little snug."

Kara set down the box and flipped off the lid.

Inside was a one-of-a-kind device. Conceived in Kelly's mind and brought to life by Kara's hands.

Kelly's eyes rolled over it with lavish awe. She figured it would be a device with rugged metal edges and mediocre welds. Kara's excellent machining skills transfixed Kelly's attention.

"Now, as you can see, all the important stuff is closed up inside the casing on the backside, but I assure you it's built by a genius."

"If you do say so yourself."

"Exactly. I've made it extremely simple to operate. Hang on," Kara said and went to the living room. She selected one of the smaller round pillows from the sofa and came back. "Let's pretend this is the asshole. All you have to do is loop it over his head. When it's in the position you want it, you press the red metal button on top, which will activate the tension spring."

Kara hit the button, and instantly the slack in the heavy-gauge braided wire coiled into the device. The fabric of the pillow wrinkled as the cotton inside gave under the pressure.

Retrieving the handheld controller from the shoebox, Kara rotated it around so Kelly could see.

"Very simple. Two buttons. The green T button is for tighten and the red L button is for loosen."

Kara pressed the T. With a slow rotation of gears, the line began disappearing inside.

"Okay. Okay. Let's not kill my pillow."

"Oh, sorry," Kara said and pressed the L before the wire started cutting through fabric.

"How strong is this thing? I mean, if I got carried away, would it completely decapitate him?"

"Probably not. The motor is from a screw gun. There would be too much skin, muscle, and bone to go through. Although it would for sure crush his trachea and suffocate him."

Kelly immediately took a seat. Her head swooned as everything about this plan was becoming very real. She was running into the territory of no return. With her wonderful gift, Cassie, coming out of an ungodly terrifying ordeal, she was now risking far too much. As she had told her girls, she needed to do this for those who forever went missing before and after her.

"You look unsure," Kara said.

"No. I understand how your device works."

"I wasn't talking about that. You look torn between going down two very different roads."

"Right. One goes to salvation and the other to damnation. Then again, it might very well be the same road."

"You know you can count on the three of us. We're here for you. Even if it's an action of breaking the law, we'll do it, especially if it helps you find peace."

"I know. And that's why I love you all so much. I have to do a bit of surveillance before I take that first major step. So, I still have time to change my mind. I don't think I will, but it's nice to know I still have the option."

Michael Winters finally exited the Sonic Boom Gym. During the last forty-five minutes of being parked in the lot, Kelly saw nothing except extremely fit men and women enter and exit. She figured it was one of those arrogant asshole gyms where men were yelling at each other, "Just one more! You can do one more!" followed by a triumphant growling yell from both individuals as one more was achieved.

Michael slowly paced himself as he headed for his car. He eyed the young ladies in spandex as they passed him.

Is he on the prowl? Is it the only reason he's here? Kelly wondered.

Michael Winters didn't drive off. He sat in his car, and through the dark tinted driver's window, he watched the gym entrance. This is how they sat for nearly an hour. Kelly watched the wolf, and the wolf watched for prey.

Several times he scanned the parking lot, maybe getting the overwhelming sensation that someone was also watching him.

Kelly had sunk so low that she could barely see over the steering wheel. Her cell popped up every so often to record, though she hadn't captured anything of interest so far.

When a raven-haired woman, twenty-three by Kelly's guess, left the gym, she knew this was the girl the wolf had pre-selected. He straightened up in his seat, and his neck craned with piqued interest. Then his cell found focus on the woman as Kelly's cell found focus on both of them.

With all the attractive women who had already left since he slid inside his car, Kelly knew this was the next prize he was going to snatch.

The appeal was certainly there. The woman was gorgeous, in the realm of supermodel status. Her skin was bronze, and going with the natural black hair and facial features made Kelly believe that her ancestors were from somewhere in South America.

Kelly didn't believe he was brazen enough to grab the girl here and now. With possible cameras and bystanders witnessing the event, it would make for a very stupid move. She knew the man wasn't stupid. He hasn't played this game for so many years without getting caught by pure chance. He's clever and patient. He'll strike when the moment is at its best.

The woman went to a white Lexus, and seconds later, she headed for the lot exit. The wolf was instantly creeping behind, being cautious enough to stay several car lengths back to avoid detection. Kelly did the same.

As the three cars drove down the freeway, Kelly's mind wandered. *Who's the real wolf now, Michael? You never realized another player had joined the game. Here I am! All without your permission. I'm stalking the stalker, and I'm going to end your reign of suffering.*

The woman made several stops. The first was at a coffee drive-thru, followed by an upper-class boutique. As the three vehicles made their way to the Windsor gated community, Kelly realized there was no longer a steady flow of traffic to hide in. She dropped back even more, nearly two blocks until she could just see the tail end of the wolf's car turning ahead.

And then they vanished.

Michael had spotted the blue Acura nearly fifteen minutes before. Panic is something he never did, but rather the unexpected picking up a tail brought a new interest to the game. He knew it couldn't be an undercover cop. He was far too careful to attract the attention of the authorities. Besides, he fully knew that his money and influence could easily block any prosecution, especially when he never left evidence behind. He always made sure of that.

When Reyna Mathers entered through the gate to her subdivision, Michael punched the gas and took the immediate next two lefts and then paused. He waited for the Acura to go by one block over. When it did, he crept around the corner, slowly making his way back to Blake Street.

The person was driving slowly. Brake lights flashed every so often. Now he wondered if he was just being paranoid. He had never needed to worry before, since the game had started nearly ten years ago. The authorities have likely connected many of the missing girls, but not all of them. If the FBI had known the actual number of the forever missing, they would have devoted more resources to capturing the wolf pack.

The three girls who had gotten away five years before had led the sheriff's department close to the wolves' den. Too goddamn close. But because the Virginia woods were so hilly and thick, they never found the cabin or the girl. Well, she had gotten away, hadn't she? But not until long after we had used her and were nearly ready to depart her from this world and eagerly move on to the next candidate. It doesn't matter. The woods had taken care of the chore we had failed to do. She became just another statistic as the authorities gave up the hunt, leaving her body to feed the opportunistic scavengers and insects. There's nothing but bones left of that little bitch who mutilated my hand.

Michael's distracted reminiscing put him too close to the car. He was certain the person was watching him in the rearview mirror.

———• • •)(• • •———

"Shit, shit, shit," Kelly whispered as she glanced in the rearview mirror. A black Mercedes turned the corner and came up behind her.

She tried to calm her galloping heart by telling herself that this is a rich subdivision and black Mercedes are as common as having a groundskeeper. The psychological manipulation did no good. She was sure the wolf had now slipped up behind her.

She felt it coming. The panic attack was rearing its ugly head. The sensation almost always started in her hands. First came numbness, followed by slight shaking. If she didn't get control of it, it would escalate to a full-blown attack.

"It starts in the mind and ends in the mind. Open the box, gather all the worries. Close the box and lock it. The box goes over the side of the boat. It's sinking now to impossible depths."

This was a ritualistic method to quench the attack before it took full control. Life's traumas have a funny way of disrupting someone's mental state long after the suffering has ended. But Kelly had learned to adapt. More than that, she'd retaken control in most circumstances by repeating those words, and by visualizing what she said. It starts and ends in the mind. That statement was truer than most people realized.

The vehicle was purposely staying back. Kelly could tell it wasn't a housewife running an errand. It was the wolf.

Her mind jumped into hyperactive mode as she forgot about the panic and focused on her next move. The only thing that made the most sense was to act like she belonged here. By making the wolf believe she either lived around here or was visiting someone, she would crush his paranoia about being followed.

She couldn't park in someone's driveway and wait for him to move along. He would undoubtedly wait as well, only to see if she went inside.

The idea came when she saw a man down the street washing his car in the driveway. She decided she wasn't going to be a resident, but a visitor.

She parked in front of the house. With a glance in the mirror, she watched the wolf maneuver to the curb. The man washing his sports car offered several curious glances as she stepped from her car.

Walking up the drive, Kelly did a quick survey of the property.

"Oh, you're right, Edward. Your home is absolutely beautiful! I'm Victoria Evans with Coast-to-Coast Realty," Kelly said and hugged the man.

She had made certain that her head blocked the man's perplexed expression, so the wolf wouldn't realize this was nothing more than a farce. More importantly, she didn't want the wolf to see her face. If he recognized her from the restaurant, he would instantly know she was on to his demented game.

Even being confused didn't stop the man from hugging back. A young, pretty girl had that effect on most men.

"I'm sorry, but I'm not Edward. You've got the wrong house. We're not selling our home. At least not anytime soon. What address are you looking for?"

"It is quite stunning. What sort of upgrades have you done since you bought it?"

"Uh, Ms. Evans, you really do have the wrong address."

Come on, come on, you snake. Just leave already.

Kelly then heard the crackle of small pebbles under tires as the Mercedes pulled away from the curb. She made sure to keep her back to the street, not even giving him a glance at her side view. The car slowed a bit as he approached, and then a strong hum as he headed down the street.

A mountain of bricks lifted off Kelly all at once. Out of the corner of her eye, she saw the rear of his car disappear down the hill. Then she noticed the stranger was staring, gap-mouthed, waiting for his statement to trigger acknowledgment in her mind.

Looking at her cell, Kelly frowned and said, "Oh my gosh. I feel so dumb right now. I am on the wrong street. Right number but wrong street. I'm so sorry to bother you, sir."

He laughed, unaware of how desperate her situation was.

"Not a problem at all. Have a great day, Ms. Evans."

Sliding into her car, Kelly released a heavy breath, and with it, expelled the minutes of tension.

He's gone. The wolf is gone. Relax. Deep breaths. Calm nerves. Go get Cassie and go home. Love on her. Make this day end with something good.

Although Kelly had yet to prove it, she fully knew the cabin was in this thicket of thousands of acres of trees. She knew because she had escaped from it.

Skylar had come through on her end. She'd provided a list of property owners stretching far beyond the lake. All but one area had private ownership.

The satellite view helped provide a more accurate point in her search. But with the limited zooming and blanket of trees and mountainous terrain, it had been difficult to pinpoint a house in the mass of green. What she did find was several narrow roads leading eastbound off Highway 23. The roads were visible enough through the sky view, but all else remained hidden. It was obvious to her that a road still seen through the app meant someone used it often enough to keep the forest undergrowth from reclaiming the property. Out here, she knew she could find a den of wolves. At least two wolves. Kelly confirmed Michael Winters was at his business office before she headed out into his hunting territory. At least this wilderness was once a hunter's dream. Likely, they never used the grounds again after her abduction and escape.

Kelly didn't doubt that their encounter with the wolf pack was only an opportune moment for the hunters. None of the girls could come up with a logical answer as to how someone had targeted them. It was simply a chance meeting that altered their lives.

Because the cell reception was spotty at best, Kelly had the forethought to bring printouts of the highway and the few roads that sprouted from it.

The first off-shoot road she took led to a scenic point. Judging by the litter of alcohol bottles, cigarette butts, and discarded condoms, it was easy to assume what happened on this dead-end road.

Kelly stepped out of the car and paced around the edge of the open space. She visually searched the adjoining woods, hoping to find any footpath leading somewhere else. But the growth was thick, showing no signs of anyone wandering through the forest.

The next turnoff was to a small camping area. Outfitted with a large gazebo, picnic tables and several metal fire rings gave her pause. It might make a reasonable ambush point. Travelers stopping on a long haul to cook up hot dogs and get some much-needed sleep before an early departure could make for good prey. The wolves could lie in wait for exhaustion to overcome the travelers. Then, with a swift pounce, the wolves snared their next victim.

Kelly hadn't thought about it until now. Did the wolf pack kill the men who were with the women they fixated their sights on? Did they kill the men right away and bury the bodies in the expanse of endless woods? Or did they keep them alive long enough for the man to witness his loving wife, girlfriend or daughter being senselessly brutalized by three men until her dying breath?

Although the three wolves could easily out-muscle a single man, especially if they threatened the woman with pain, Kelly was willing to bet they chose to kill him, because this pack was only formidable against innocent, unsuspecting girls.

Following Highway 23 for several miles, Kelly pulled onto the narrow shoulder. Though she hadn't seen a car in nearly half an hour, she didn't want to risk one suddenly coming around the bend, only to find a parked car in the middle of the road.

Kelly looked at the satellite image printout. By all accounts, she should have seen the turnoff nearly a mile ago. Turning the car around, she drove the mile back slowly. She watched the left side for gaps in the trees or any evidence of tire marks running off into the thicket.

With her mind fixed on one thing, the sports car that suddenly passed her on the left scared the crap out of her. It was almost distraction enough that she nearly missed the object of her search.

Hitting the brakes, Kelly checked the mirror to make sure no other cars were coming up behind her. She reversed while angling for the far edge of the shoulder. Throwing her car into park, she stepped out.

It was an odd thing. Tires marked the dirt just off the shoulder, and then suddenly stopped at the tree line. It was like someone frequently pulled into this spot and then backed up as if to reverse direction on the highway.

Kelly stepped to the edge, peered between a half dozen saplings, and found the continuation of tire tracks.

"What the shit? What kind of sense does this make?"

Then Kelly saw it. The wooded area dividing the tire path held metal tracks set into the ground. After studying the tracks and the saplings, she could see that the trunks of the trees were sitting in some kind of wooden box. Further inspecting the charade, Kelly saw that they weren't even real trees. The facsimiles were so well done that she wasn't even sure about their authenticity until she fingered several of the leaves and branches. It was a road-dividing device used either manually or by remote control that rotated the concealed box of fake saplings to allow entrance to the wolves' den.

The whole thing acts as a blind. A simple cover to keep any passersby from mistakenly going down that road, she thought.

Instantly, she found extreme joy, followed by outright terror. She knew the cabin was down this path, but she had to make sure.

Hitting the remote lock on the car, Kelly turned and followed the tire tracks. After nearly three-hundred yards down the path, she finally spotted the small slice of hell where her captors had held her unwillingly for five weeks.

Her breath quickened. The numbness and shaking started in her hands. The goddamn panic was quickly charging like a raging bull. She stepped off the path, sat against a large elm, pulled her knees to her chest, and wrapped her arms around her legs. With deliberate slow actions, she inhaled through her nose and exhaled out her mouth.

"It starts and ends in the mind. It starts and ends in the mind. No one here can harm you."

Again, Kelly managed to push it back, caging the beast before it left her immobile on the forest grounds.

When her heart found a steady rhythm, and the shaking subsided, she pushed herself up. She wanted to go back to the car and haul ass out of these godforsaken woods. But more importantly, she wanted a closer look at the damnation house.

No cars were out in front of the cabin, but she knew it didn't mean no one was there. One of the wolves could very well have been a hermit who never left the property. Maybe one of the other wolves brought supplies to him in exchange for using the property for sport hunting. Here he'd keep the new catch alive for weeks, slowly torturing the poor girl into an endless manic mental collapse. Kelly knew that was the stage found right before someone longed for death.

Circling the cabin with her eyes constantly switching around, Kelly found a dirt bike parked by the back door, perfectly designed to maneuver the surrounding rugged terrain. What she also found was a branch underfoot. To her ears, it was the thunder crack of a sudden storm. Holding still, she waited for the squawk of rusty hinges and the immediate appearance of a man in a wolf mask. She also prepped herself for a mad dash back through the woods to her car. No sound came from the cabin. She also didn't see any of the curtains pulled aside.

Kelly shook off her stealth mode, feeling more confident the cabin was vacant. Even though the back door was locked, someone hadn't completely pulled down the blind to the sill. No lights burned inside, but sun rays poured through the front windows, giving her a slight offering of what hid inside.

The furniture was an '80s thrift store find. Nothing built for comfort or an eye-pleasing necessity. Everything was a common-use space filler and nothing more.

Kelly saw it on the other side of the motorcycle. The slanted storm shelter doors were protruding from the ground a foot above the earth. It was her exit from purgatory all those years before.

Moving to the doors, she listened for any noise out of the ordinary. She still wasn't sure if anyone was home. More importantly, she listened for the pleading cries for help. It was very possible the pack had another victim in the cellar.

Pressing her ear to the narrow split between the doors, Kelly listened intently for any signs of movement. After a span of silent moments, she pressed her lips to the crack.

"Hello? Is someone down there? It's okay to answer if you are. I can help you. They held me here a long time ago. I can get you out."

Pressing her ear back against the door, she waited. Although it was only seconds, Kelly felt as if an entire day had ticked by. The anticipation of hearing movement, or more importantly, a weak cry for help, would give her the ultimate satisfaction that she could free the prey from the wolf trap.

She called through the crack again. No answer followed.

It's the girl you were following. Isn't it, you sick fuck? You're planning on her being your next toy.

She had already assumed the woman in the Lexus was a potential victim. Now she was certain the wolf was going to pounce soon. He was readying himself to switch from the stalking phase to the hunt, and finally the capture.

When Kelly stepped from the woods, she froze at the sight of a state trooper vehicle parked behind her car. She had no chance of melting back into the woods, because he looked up at the sound of a snapping branch. Through his sunglasses, he watched her. His expression was featureless, showing neither startlement nor apprehension.

Kelly wasn't entirely sure what to do. Was she supposed to go talk to him and explain why she parked on the side of the highway? Should she explain what she was doing in the woods? Or should she just get in her car and drive away?

The officer spared her the indecision. He pulled the door lever and stepped out. He tipped his wide-brimmed hat back with a forefinger as he walked toward her.

"I was beginning to think I was gonna need to have your car towed. I figured it was a breakdown, and the driver had someone come pick them up, maybe gonna come back later for it. Everything all right then?"

"Oh, yes, I suppose so. I'm sorry for parking here, but my stomach hasn't been doing well since I ate an egg salad sandwich. Maybe the mayo was bad. I knew it was coming only a minute before it did. I had barely got into the woods before I started throwing up."

"Hmm. Nothing's worse than seeing your lunch in reverse. You were in there for quite a bit."

"All I could do was kneel, throw up, wait, and throw up more. It finally passed. If it's okay, I'd like to get on my way."

"Where did you get the sandwich? Was it Rooster's in Bixby? I just want to make sure I don't make the same mistake."

Kelly thought this was a sly way for him to catch her in a lie. Rooster's could have been a hardware store for all she knew.

"No. I brought it with me in the cooler. I should have checked the expiration date on the mayo before making it."

He leaned a bit forward and peered into the backseat. Her red cooler was on the seat, holding several bottles of water.

"What's your name? Where are you heading?"

Kelly didn't like this. One of the wolves had worn a badge that glinted off the basement light, partially visible between the open weave of the burlap sack over her head.

Are you one of the wolves?

She was sure he had already run her license plate, receiving instant identification and place of residence. To lie now would be a foolish error. She needed to stay up front that everything was copacetic, that a mere upset stomach was the only reason for the brief delay in her travels.

"Kelly Lewis." Even though she knew there was no law requiring her to answer an officer where her destination would be, she said, "Heading over to Richmond. Planning a fun weekend with my old roommate. I've never been able to experience the city's nightlife. Jessie promised me a crazy couple of days. I really shouldn't, but I suppose life deserves its moments of fun."

He smiled at this, unaware of the façade of her story.

"Well then, take extra care. The wrong parts of Richmond can be nothing but a mess of trouble for a couple of young ladies. Don't trust any guys you come across."

He tipped his hat and turned.

"Thank you. And thank you for stopping. I'm feeling much better. Hopefully, the sickness has passed."

"I hope so. Have a good weekend, Ms. Lewis."

Kelly made her departure slowly, appearing as if she weren't in a panicked state to flee the area. When the deputy took to the highway, he offered a beep of the horn and was gone around the bend.

Kelly released an anxious breath and fell back in her seat.

"This goddamn stress is going to kill me," she said.

Reyna Mathers stepped out of the shower, and Michael Winters watched. Everything about her drove his lust to an unquenchable longing. Her youth, breathtaking beauty, intelligence, and personal desire to become something iconic in life would be crushed tonight. He would obliterate every ounce of her hope to see all of life's fulfillments flourish.

Reyna wiped her hand across the steam-covered mirror and flipped the vent switch on, triggering the motor to life beside Michael's ear. Through the vent slats he watched, and he waited. She didn't bother covering up with a towel or robe. She never did. Michael was all right about that.

Reyna was singing something softly at first, then the verses built up and her enthusiasm built with it. The hairbrush became the microphone as she unknowingly put on a show for one audience member.

"I should not be left to my own devices. They come with prices and vices. I end up in crisis. I wake up screaming from dreaming. One day, I'll watch as you're leaving. 'Cause you got tired of my scheming."

Michael opened an app, and hearing the lyrics, the app came back with:

Artist—Taylor Swift

Song—Anti-Hero

Released 2022 from the album *Midnights*.

Michael watched with a growing smile as she danced and sang.

No, sweetness, I'm the anti-hero. Mommy and Daddy aren't here to save your precious body.

After Reyna dressed, she stepped from the bathroom and immediately stopped. From the shadowed space, Michael watched her stare, perplexed by the extended attic ladder. Her eyes traveled up each rung. He thought this was the perfect horror movie moment.

Stepping to the bottom rung, she asked, "Mom? Dad? Kenny? Who's up there?"

The most dangerous man alive! He thought.

Reyna took each rung with caution. Her eyes never drifted from the hovering blackness. Michael read the tension in her body, the muscles gearing up to take flight the moment the situation became questionable.

"I swear, Kenny, if you jump out at me, I'm gonna sock you in the face. Don't go crying to Mom when you get broken teeth."

Reyna took one more rung and reached into the darkness, searching for the light switch.

Michael's hand shot from the shadows, seizing Reyna's wrist, and with ease pulled her from the relative safety of the hallway light and into the eager hold of the wolf.

Cassie had tried to braid her own hair.

"So, we're going for rat's nest style today?" Kelly asked.

"I'm pretty."

"The prettiest. Come here and let me fix that before school."

Cassie hopped like a bunny to the dining room table. She turned so Kelly could begin working the knots free.

"What a mess you made. How about next time you let me do it or let me show you how? Hopefully, we won't have to shave you bald," Kelly told her.

Cassie laughed at this. Kelly was pretty sure Cassie wouldn't care if she were bald or even had a mohawk. She was a kid who liked to have fun and cared very little about how the world perceived her. It seemed to Kelly like a perfect way to live.

Kelly's eyes switched up to the small TV on the kitchen counter. A breaking news story was unfolding.

Kelly hurriedly grabbed the remote and cranked up the volume.

"District Attorney Martin Mathers arrived home late last night to find a shocking discovery. His twenty-two-year-old daughter, Reyna, was missing. The family first thought Reyna was studying at a friend's house, but as the hour got late, they phoned her friend to find out she had never arrived. The family then reviewed the home security video, only to find an unrecognizable individual enter the home and leave an hour later with what appears to be Reyna's unconscious body."

"Holy shit. He got her," Kelly whispered.

Cassie turned with her mouth gaping.

"Bad word, Mommy!"

"It was. I'm sorry."

Kelly quickened her pace to untangle Cassie's hair. Kelly's fingers moved with repetitive motion to complete the fastest ponytail braid she had ever done.

"Okay. Go get your backpack. We need to go."

A school picture of Reyna popped up on the screen. Kelly vividly remembered the face she had seen exiting the gym. The wolf's next prey. It was absolutely the same girl.

After dropping Cassie off at school, Kelly called the restaurant. It was another sick day she needed, but now she was beginning to worry if Giselle would realize how they managed just fine without her. Would they start to think how unnecessary she was for the business and cut her loose? She shook off the paranoia for now. More important things needed her attention.

Retrieving her cell, Kelly rolled through her contacts, ready to call the one person who might have answers.

A thought intruded, and Kelly clicked off the power button. Leaning back in the driver's seat, she ran through possible scenarios where contacting Tilly might doom everything.

If I tell her I followed the wolf as he followed the girl who's now missing, a tornado of a mess and a dead girl will be the result.

Kelly knew that if the wolf caught a scent of the authorities on his trail, he'd kill the girl and dump her body somewhere in the vast wilderness. Reyna Mathers would become another missing girl statistic. Kelly couldn't take any action that would jeopardize the girl's life. She knew it was time to initiate the plan.

——— · · ✕ · · ———

Research and surveillance proved that Michael Winters was single, happily, to Kelly anyway, not a father. At least, not a father to a child he knows about.

A two-story home with five bedrooms, four bathrooms, and a four-car garage was probably modest by the wolf's standards. His money and power had given him leeway in life far too often, and Kelly decided it needed to end tonight.

From this week's previous shadow game she'd played with him, she knew he typically arrived home around nine o'clock. But then again, he'd just caught a moth in his web, and maybe he needed to feed tonight. Maybe he needed his new prize to feel the pain of his teeth tattooing across her body.

Kelly knew the girl wouldn't be at his home. Michael Winters was many things, but stupid wasn't one of them. The girl would be at the cabin, held at a place where authorities couldn't trace back to him or the others.

Kelly knew from experience that the pack held regular jobs. They'd left her alone for days until the weekend came around. It was during those gaps of time that the moment of escape became the most desperate and the most opportunistic.

Now, Friday night had come, and the pack would meet. Playtime was on the schedule, covering the next two days of unholy entertainment for them. Reyna would spend countless hours in terrifying abuse, and a pain that would eventually follow the nerves down to her very soul.

Not this time. Not again while I have breath in this body, Kelly thought, and stepped out of her car.

She'd parked over two blocks away. What she didn't need was one of Michael's adjacent neighbors catching her car on surveillance and turning it over to the police when the investigation into Mr. Winters' disappearance got underway.

Wearing black jeans, black sports shoes and a dark blue hoodie was the best she could do to blend into the night. She also had the frame of mind to grab a black cloth nose and mouth covering, a relic from the Covid pandemic. As she got closer to the house, Kelly pulled up the hood, melting further into the shadowed landscape.

Sliding onto the wolf's property, she crouched and slowly turned. From the edge of the hedges, she watched the neighbors' front porches and lit windows. The absence of voices and movement convinced her that her approach went unnoticed.

There was little doubt in Kelly's mind that Michael's house had a surplus of cameras. As she moved away from the street and closer to the house, she began spotting the dim red glow of night vision cameras at the corners of his home. His digital device would already have recorded her presence on the property. She expected it and knew that it didn't matter. Nothing could ever prove that she'd visited his home.

Two days before, on a previous scouting mission, she'd determined there was only one way into his home. Kelly never held any tech wizard aptitude, so bypassing any home alarm was a dead end. She was sure she wouldn't even be able to pick a deadbolt, much less hack anything. So, going through the garage was the only way.

Kelly had seen the action done several times in movies and television shows. By concealing herself beside the garage gave her a chance to slide inside before the door closed. It was a simple solution to gain entry by simply waiting for Michael to come home.

Kelly pushed her back deep into the hedges beside the foundation. There she waited with quaking nerves until headlights scarred a path through the heavy shadows of the long driveway. Her throat latched closed, refusing to take in more air.

Michael activated the garage door. As it rolled up on greased wheels, Kelly heard the distinct pulsing of her heart throughout her body with an emphatic rhythm of a marching band at a halftime show.

The Mercedes coasted inside, and Kelly felt the resistance of her body's willingness to move.

Now or never. Now or never. Now or never. Reyna will suffer a long, terrible death if you don't move your ass now! Go, dammit!

The voice won the fight as Kelly pushed herself from the hedge. The garage door reversed position, closing off her chance to right many wrongs in the world.

The smooth and painted concrete allowed Kelly to slide inside noiselessly as the engine died. The garage door made a soft seal and stopped. The pings and ticks of heated metal coming from the car were the only sounds inside the large garage space.

Kneeling at the rear bumper, Kelly waited with near-fractured nerves for something to happen. Briefly, she thought he'd spotted her intrusion in the mirror as she crawled inside, and now he was debating on how to proceed with this unexpected situation. Then the door opened, and the muscular wolf pushed himself from the vehicle. He began whistling as a jangle of keys slipped into his pocket. She heard him retrieve several items from the backseat, and then the car door shut.

The clack of his steps moving away gave Kelly the courage to move to a half stance. Spying over the trunk lid, Michael moved to the inside door and disappeared through it.

Kelly released a held breath. More than ever before, the edge of a full panic attack was on the horizon. Her mind pounded it down as much as possible. If it overcame her now, it meant certain death for Reyna and herself.

Cassie came to mind. The angel who saved her from a self-destructive lifestyle after returning home. Cassie the incredible. Cassie the brave. Cassie is a brilliant ray of sunlight in a world full of reaching shadows.

Kelly stood. The garage door opener light hadn't blinked off yet as she walked to the door. With slow hands, she grasped the door frame and pressed her ear to the door. She figured the first thing he was doing was using the bathroom, as most people do when getting home.

Gently, Kelly grasped the handle and rotated. She allowed the door only an inch gap to survey the interior. A massive, brightly lit kitchen most chefs would be envious of was all she could see. Michael was nowhere in her field of vision, and his absence worried her. Again, her mind went to the idea of this being a trap.

278

A toilet flushed, followed by the sound of a sink running. Behind her, the opener's light blinked out. Now, she had to work with only the kitchen light shining through the crack. She slid the backpack straps off her shoulders, grasped the top loop, and pulled it around the front. She worked the zipper open and reached inside. Her fingers moved across the nylon rope, a roll of duct tape, and found the device Kara had created. She pulled it free and then searched for the remote. With both instruments of control sitting on the single step in front of her, she quietly zipped the bag closed and strapped it across her back.

A shadow moved across the kitchen, momentarily canceling the light. Kelly quickly looked up. She geared her leg muscles to pounce. Michael had his back to her as he stood at the kitchen counter. His whistling switched to singing. It took a minute, but Kelly was sure it was a Taylor Swift song, but which one she couldn't tell. The oddity of one of her songs being in this killer's head further pushed this experience to another level of insanity.

She saw that Michael had made himself a mixed drink. Undoubtedly, loosening himself up for tonight's festivities. Kelly only hoped that a single drink would buzz his mind and slow his reflexes.

He carried his drink to the living room. A TV was turned on to a sports station. Kelly heard the announcer discussing the matchup between Cleveland and Cincinnati.

Kelly tested the hinges a bit more while pushing the door open wider. With the television volume so high, she didn't think he would hear the slight squawk of ungreased hinges. It didn't matter. The door rotated without a sound. Stepping inside, Kelly stayed to the right, keeping to the shadows of the hallway. She rotated the handle, pushed the garage door closed, and let the handle quietly spring back into place.

Kelly heard ice move around in his glass as he took another drink. Seeing he was still on the sofa, she followed the hallway to the back rooms. The doors were all open, allowing her to glimpse inside without being caught by the surprise of someone else being here. The bedrooms and bathrooms were strangely normal. She half expected to find medieval torture devices, sadistic artwork, or even an area of satanic ritual sacrifice.

When Kelly reached the bottom step that led upstairs, she instantly stopped when the television's volume went mute. A vibration came from the living room, telling her exactly why he'd killed the volume.

"Josh, my man. I'm gonna head out that way about ten o'clock. Right. You know it. She'll be all primed up. I'll see you when you get there."

The game commentary resumed.

Kelly was about to start up the stairs when a thought came to her. She had no better chance other than right now to drop the device over his head. She could easily crawl across the carpet to the back of the couch. From there, she could drop the device in place and have total control over him.

Michael accessed the photo file on his cell. The pictures he'd taken of Reyna Mathers earlier at the cabin were there, waiting for his viewing. He knew that keeping such evidence in his possession was considered idiotic. However, not only was it a burner cell, untraceable to him, but the encryption was unhackable, except maybe by only a few brilliant minds. Even if someone managed to bypass the security, there was a second firewall to access the photo files. If someone entered two incorrect codes, all the phone's downloads, photos and even the default software went through a virtual shredder, making the device nothing more than a paperweight.

The first photo was taken just after he'd shoved the girl onto the mattress. Face down with a burlap sack fixed over her head, Reyna struggled to get herself turned over to face her kidnapper. He'd taken the photo then, at the height of her confusion and terror. It was a shame he couldn't see her expression. It would have added to his delight. Ready to cycle through the other photos, Michael stopped himself. He wanted to get on the road and begin a thrilling weekend of torment.

He turned off the phone and slid it into his pocket. He aimed the remote and killed the TV. His house fell into an unearthly quiet, as if he were the world's last inhabitant. He pushed off the sofa and went to the kitchen. He fixed another highball and downed it in two large gulps. Standing at the counter, he took a deep breath, waiting for the pleasant burn to fade.

——— · ·)(· · ———

Kelly had just managed to work her way around the left side of the sofa as Michael rounded the right side. The area was thick with shadows, so her dark clothing easily blended.

She watched him make another drink, priming himself with liquid courage to handle the task he was getting ready to tackle. Standing at the counter, another drink quickly vanished. He looked up then, and stared into the dark of the living room, right at Kelly. His eyes unwavering, locked onto her near-panicked gaze.

"This is going to be fun."

Kelly felt the tension course throughout her body, seizing all her muscles in place.

Fuck! Please don't be talking to me. Please be one of the sadistic voices in your head, she thought.

"This life of mine, this freedom to do what I want, when I want, is only available to those who truly know what it's like to feel alive. I am unstoppable."

Kelly's muscles compressed into springs under tension. She had no idea if she could control the situation in a face-to-face attack, but now she had no choice but to find out.

"The bitch is waiting for you. Let's get this party started."

The statement gave Kelly pause. It didn't at all sound like he was directing the statements at her but commenting to himself.

Reyna. He's talking to himself about Reyna. Kelly thought and managed to get her muscles to relax a little.

Michael disappeared down the hallway, followed by the sound of urine in the toilet. Kelly hurriedly followed. Keeping her back against the wall, she waited, praying that he would turn right after exiting the bathroom. With Kara's device in one hand and the remote in the other, she mentally prepped herself for instant action.

Michael flushed the toilet. The sink ran and then he dried his hands. A microsecond before the light flickered out, his shadow fell across the hallway wall.

Stepping out of the bathroom, Michael turned right.

Kelly lifted the device high, accommodating his extra six-inch height over her. She moved her body with him. Her feet glided over the carpet. With her thumb poised on the button that would activate the tension spring, Kelly looped the device over his head. The wire, which interrupted his field of vision, caused him to duck in reflex, but Kelly had already gained control of the button and pressed it.

The whip of wire sounded as loose material instantly coiled inside the control box. Michael's reaction caused the loop to fall short of his neck. Instead, it hung up on his chin as it tightened. He grabbed at it, working his fingers between his skin and the braided wire. A choking groan escaped him as Kelly's panic now became his.

Kelly's taekwondo training came to her like an opportunistic flash. She side kicked the back of his knees, causing him to buckle. She then threw her weight against his back, forcing him face down and into a vulnerable position.

The wolf immediately rebelled. With an adrenaline surge of strength, he pushed himself onto all fours and began bucking like a rodeo horse.

The thrashing almost caused her to lose grip on the remote. With the situation nearly out of her control, her index finger found the button she needed. The screw gun motor began cranking, pulling Michael's chin to his chest as the wire forcefully tightened. The added pain sent another outburst from his body, causing Kelly to pitch forward and into the hall in front of him.

Michael grabbed at her. As the wire forced his head down, Michael's eyes rotated so far up that it seemed as if he were trying to see inside his own skull.

Kelly delivered a panicked kick, causing the cartilage of his nose to crunch under her heel. Michael took the blow like a champion boxer as his determination to overcome her in the fight held the pain at bay. The second kick achieved exactly what she had hoped it would. The rubber sole of her sneaker ran a brutal track down the side of his face, snagging the wire and forcing it over his chin and jaw. The snap of the loose wire pulled taut. Kelly back-pedaled as her finger squeezed the green T button.

The eagerness to seize her became a faded objective as continuing to live won over his actions. His fingers desperately dug at the skin of his neck, trying to work those digits under and get a grip on the device that was squeezing the life from him.

"Stop fighting and I'll ease it up. Keep fighting and you'll die right here," Kelly said with exhaustion.

Michael's face transitioned from crimson to a deep purple as the device blocked the blood flow. As he looked at Kelly in quiet suffering, she momentarily expected his bulging eyes to volcano from the sockets. Finally, he gave in. He thrust his arms out, showing surrender.

Kelly released the green button and briefly pressed the red, slightly reversing the gears to give Michael much needed breath. He drew in a stuttering gasp of air, followed by a coughing fit that shot a splatter of blood across the white carpet.

"If you make any action I don't like, or if you say anything that pisses me off, I'm going to activate the device until your head comes clean off. Understand?"

Michael nodded and subconsciously tried to get his fingers behind the wire. Kelly instantly pressed the green button, snugged the wire down even more.

"Keep your goddamn hands off the wire. If you follow my instructions, you might live through the night. Maybe."

In defeat, Michael moved his hands away. Kelly eased the wire again.

"What do you want from me? Take what you want and just go," he croaked.

Kelly pushed herself from the floor, sliding her back up the door frame. She wasn't going to take her eyes off him until she had him fully bound.

"It's quite a feeling, isn't it? The very moment you realize you've lost total control. The vulnerability, the unknown, and the dread that at any moment you might lose your life at the hands of another starts to work in your mind like a plague. You can move into a kneeling position, but that's it. Anything else, and the squeeze starts again."

Michael obeyed. Keeping his hands visible, he pushed himself onto his knees. He sat on his heels and watched Kelly with utter contempt.

"So, what is it? Do you want money? I can give you plenty. I have a nice stash here at the house. I can get you more if you give me accounts to transfer it to. Whatever you want, and then you can go."

Despite the situation, Kelly chuckled at his offer.

"Let's get a little more comfortable. We're going to move into the dining room. Any stupid idea about action against me that runs through your head had better stay there. One false move gets you dead. Understand?"

"I do. I'm more interested in finding out why you're here than to try to overcome you."

As he forced himself into a standing position, he wiped the back of his arm across the destroyed cartilage of his nose. A red trail went from mid-forearm to index finger. "I'm highly impressed with you. No one has ever gotten the drop on me like that. Not only that, but you got into my house far too easily."

Entering the dining room, Kelly said, "I'm a girl of exceptional talent. Pull the chair out and have a seat. Then, I want you to put your arms straight down. Remember that I'm in full control. Any wrong move puts you bowing at Satan's feet."

He snorted through his bloody nose and did as she commanded.

Shrugging the backpack off her shoulders, Kelly kept a tight grip on the remote. Her finger remained tense on the activation button, waiting for him to make a bad move. Removing the thick zip ties from the bag, she fixed one hand and then the other onto the chair's legs. There were cross supports connecting the legs together, so there was no way he could tip the chair over and slide free from his seat. As an added security measure, she also zipped his upper arms to the back support. Then she did his ankles, making sure to do it from the side so he wasn't able to kick out at her. When the chore was done, she took a relieved breath. Sitting across from him, she placed the remote on the table, keeping it within easy reach.

"There. That's so much better, don't you think? Now we can chat."

His eyebrows arched. He said, "Okay. But it must be a revealing conversation. I'm not good at small talk. Why don't we start with an introduction? I'm assuming you know me, at least a little, anyway. So, what's your name and what brings you by at this hour?"

"Wow, really? You're lost in confusion?"

Michael half-closed one eye as the other focused up and to the right, a telltale sign he was trying to access a buried memory. A spark of light came, and he studied Kelly for a moment.

"Ah, you're the chef. The one from Quintela's. Were our compliments not satisfactory enough? Seems strange to hold a simple grudge for several weeks."

"You are correct. I am the chef at that restaurant. However, we met long before that, nearly five years before, to be exact."

His eyes narrowed, desperately trying to place her.

"Fucking unbelievable. Nothing? Really? How about this? You're the one who gave me these souvenirs."

Kelly stood and lifted her hoodie and the shirt beneath. She felt no shame in exposing skin to this man. He had already seen all she had to offer. Michael's face went sickly pale as the blood retreated from his head. Kelly almost thought he would pass out just by viewing his own artwork. His eyes switched up to her face, and a moment of total clarity washed over him.

"Kelly Ray. It can't be. You're dead. You should be nothing more than bones on the forest ground."

"So sorry to disappoint you. That's what you get for underestimating me from day one," Kelly said and dropped her shirt. She sat down and leaned against the chair's back. "My last name isn't Ray anymore. You made me change it unofficially. There was no way I could step back into my old life with three twisted fucks possibly still looking for me. I had to keep my return to the world ultra-secret. Only my family and close friends know that I walked out of those woods. As far as the authorities know, I'm still a missing person."

"Those bites on your body were payback. You mutilated my hand on that first day. I had to teach you a lesson."

"Sure. That makes sense. Punish someone for defending their own life. One thing I'm curious about. Why did you put a sack over my head? I'm sure you do that to all the girls. Why?"

"Compliance. When a girl starts believing we're trying to conceal our identities, it gives her hope. She begins building faith that we're not planning on killing her and we'll release her someday. So, she holds back any resistance that might be there."

"Who are the other two wolves?"

"I don't know what you're talking about, bitch."

Kelly clicked her fingernails on the table and reached for the remote.

"Incorrect answer."

Kelly hit the button, causing Michael's face to go red instantly. His mouth bobbed open and closed as if he were trying to speak. She released the button and watched, giving him ample opportunity to consider his options whether to play along or not.

Michael's glassy eyes began fading just as his life faded from the body. He went face down onto the table's surface. Kelly knew it must have hurt like hell to reinjure his nose. His confined body began convulsing. She reversed the wire, allowing the oxygen to flow once again.

After another round of gasping and coughing, Michael sat up in the chair. Kelly had never seen a look so sinister. If he wasn't tethered to the chair, she was sure he would spring across the table and use his favorite tool to tear her into tiny pieces, bite after bite.

"Would you like to offer a different answer in round two? I've got all night." After a seething contempt washed over his features, Kelly said, "Suit yourself."

Before her finger fully pressed the button, Michael said, "Wait. Just wait a goddamn second! Let me catch my breath and get my bearings. We can talk. Just stop trying to kill me."

"I haven't even begun that stage. I'm just playing. You know, like you with all those girls over countless years. I know you have Reyna. I'm here to make sure with every bit of energy and will in my body that you won't do it to another innocent girl. When you see me get serious about killing you, you'll see me go to the kitchen and begin selecting utensils. I assure you those instruments will be amusing to me, painful to you, but more importantly, a way to get all the information I want. There are plenty of useless pieces of you I could cut away without actually killing you. The most useless thing of all would be that vile thing between your legs. Not a single soul on the planet would miss that abomination, except maybe you. Plus, I spotted a nice lighter on the hearth to cauterize any wounds. So, let that sink in. This is the last time I'll ask. Who are the other two wolves?"

Michael's eyes ran back and forth across the table as his mind tried grappling with the landslide of the situation.

Kelly pushed back, stood, and went to the kitchen. With horror-struck attention, Michael watched her begin going through the cabinets, searching for a specific object.

"Hold on! I said I need to catch my breath."

Kelly pulled a glass out of the cabinet, went to the refrigerator, and filled it with water.

"Untwist your panties. I'm just thirsty. I'm still listening."

"There's only one other wolf, as you call us."

"Bullshit. There's three of you."

"There were three of us. Vance died over two years ago from pancreatic cancer. It's only been the two of us since then."

"What, you couldn't find another degenerate to take his place? It seems like the easiest thing in the world to do. The world is full of wretched people like you. At least, people who want to be like you, with a little guidance."

"You're like me. Here you are after breaking into my home, torturing me for pleasure."

"There's a massive divide between us. In those aspects, we're on different sides of the Grand Canyon, Michael. I'm only working information out of you. I get no pleasure from it. Also, you're no innocent soul. You completely deserve what you're getting. You're a despicable demon. I'm an avenging angel."

He laughed at her statement, followed by a hoarse cough.

"Now, who's spewing bullshit? Can you honestly say you get no enjoyment from pressing that button and watching me choke to death? Of course you do. You're human. After all you went through—the humiliation, pain, fear, and despair of believing you wouldn't survive—you're now giving yourself what your heart and mind have longed for during the last five years. Tell me, have you had a single relationship since escaping the woods? Have you connected with anyone the way you would have if that day had never happened to you? I'll answer that for you. Of course you haven't. We stole that from you. We broke the trust in your heart, and that's why you can't move forward with another person. Can you honestly say you don't want to punish me for stripping away those possible experiences?"

"All right. You serve an interesting point. But I'm not here to debate with you. Who is the other wolf? Is he a cop?"

"Why do you ask?"

"There was a badge. I saw it several times through the material you had over my head."

Michael nodded. "Not a cop, though. That was Vance. He was a bank security guard in Richmond. At least until the cancer got so bad."

"So, who is the other?"

"His name is Josh Witt. He runs a general store in Calmun."

"Is he a large man?"

Michael rotated his lower lip out and said, "Large? No, he's average size."

Kelly hit the button, and the choking began again. After a minute without any air, she loosened the wire a little.

"Stop lying to me. Do you honestly think I don't remember? I remember every fucking bit of it. It replays every night in my dreams. The one with the badge was average size. The other one was heavy, maybe not so much fat, but muscle, as if he frequented a gym. I remember his weight very much, and the smell as if he'd just finished a workout. Lie to me again, and I will do the world a favor and exit you from it."

"Okay. Yes, Josh is a large man. He does bodybuilding sessions with troubled youth."

"How fucking noble of him." After a minute of staring him down, Kelly asked, "What was Vance's first name?"

"Vance was his first name. Vance Bannon."

"And he's dead, you say?"

"He is."

"I'll check on the truth of that later. You wouldn't mind if I used your bathroom, right? You can just hang out here. I'll be just a moment. If I hear any noise I don't like, your head is gonna pop off like a dandelion."

Kelly stood and disappeared down the hall. She relieved herself with the door open, all the while keeping her ears tuned for sounds of struggling. The ties were strong, and the dining room chairs were oak, so Michael's chance at breaking free was a small blip on the radar of possibility.

She knew she had to get on the move. There was no telling when the other wolf would head for the cabin. She had to get there before he did. She had to get Reyna free.

Standing in front of the mirror, Kelly cupped cool water and brought it to her face. It was a welcome relief, even if it was fleeting. She studied her reflection, marveling at how she had pushed herself through bouts of panic to fight through and overcome the monster in the other room.

Kelly, the vigilante of all things fucked up in the world. Baby girl, I'm gonna finish this nonsense tonight, and then I'm gonna come home better than I have ever been before. Momma's gonna be an all-new person, Cassie. You'll see.

Something went over in the other room. Seizing the remote from the sink, Kelly shot down the hallway. Stepping into the living room, she fully expected to find Michael unbound from his restraints, standing with a gun in hand, prepared to finish her off. But he wasn't there, or in the adjacent living room. As she ran to the table, she pressed the green button. Gurgling gasps of a closing airway came from the floor on the other side of the table. She stepped around, seeing Michael overturned sideways in his chair. She hit the red button, giving him air.

Michael shifted his eyes, capturing every expression she offered, and said, "It's Kelly Ray. The bitch is alive and is holding me hostage in my home."

Narrowing her focus, wondering what the hell he was talking about, Kelly found that Michael had accomplished the impossible. Next to his head was the cordless home phone. He had managed to knock it free from its cradle and somehow made a phone call.

Kelly stormed forward and stomped down on the receiver, canceling the connection.

Michael laughed. It was a deep-throated, devilish laugh that drove a knife into her final strand of patience. A laugh stating that the tables had turned.

"You're fucked now," he said.

Kelly leaned down, and with a trembling fury, she smashed the remote across his skull.

——— · · ✕ · · ———

Tap, tap, tap.

Michael's blood hitting the wood floor had an almost metronome rhythm to it.

Kelly leaned forward in the chair, watching with morbid fascination. Her mind tried making familiar images out of those clustered drops just as some see figures in clouds. She hadn't intended to hit him so hard. She meant only to hit him hard enough to render him unconscious. The onslaught of anger at that moment came from a place of bottled rage. The edge of the metal remote controller had dug deep, peeling open a long section of his scalp. It became a hang-up in the plan. She didn't want the blood evidence in her car, so she dumped him in the trunk of his Mercedes and used his vehicle for the drive to the middle of nowhere.

"Michael? Can you hear me? What's the keypad code for the basement door? I need you to answer, or I'm going to hurt you again."

"They're coming for you," he said as his head lulled left and then right while his body struggled to wake.

"They? I have a distinct feeling you lied to me again. They're both alive, right? What else have you lied about? Probably everything. It doesn't matter. You're all finished tonight. If they come, I'll destroy them, too."

Michael laughed in disbelief.

Kelly leaned forward and slapped Michael across the face. The act caused a splatter of blood to climb the wood-paneled wall.

"Look around, Michael. We've taken on a new setting."

He did look around then. Even with the wave of fuzziness, he recognized his playhouse.

His breath left him. It was the sound of defeat, of knowing there were no more secrets left to bargain with.

"How did you find it?"

"I spent five weeks here. Remember? After two days in the woods, probably going in circles for part of it, I arrived at the lake where you assaulted my friends and me, and then made me vanish."

Kelly hit him again. A quick jab to the face, catching half her knuckles on the bridge of his crooked and swollen nose.

His face pulled tight as he was unable to cradle the injury.

"Goddammit! Stop doing that."

"That one was impulse. I won't apologize for it though. You deserve much worse. You deserve a lifetime of agony for all the lives you've destroyed. What's the code to the basement?"

"There's nothing down there."

"Except Reyna Mathers. I know you took her. I know she's here. I followed you from the gym as you followed her. Yes, that was me whom you saw approach the man washing his car. I guess it wasn't so difficult to fool you."

Kelly twitched her finger on the remote.

"Shit. All right. It's 35184. Just stop choking me and hitting my nose."

Kelly stood. Just before heading to the steel basement door, she shot another fist into the center of his face. She couldn't help smiling as he screamed and whirled a tornado of foul words.

The entire cabin served its purpose as a haven for sadistic men. There was nothing cozy about it. The furniture was simple and cheap, probably purchased at a thrift store. There were animal heads mounted in every room. Deer, black bears, and bobcats offered a gruesome display for men who desired to kill anything beautiful. On the tabletops were smaller animals. A few ducks posed in flight, and several taxidermy foxes were positioned in a run. She didn't doubt they'd killed all these innocent creatures on the property.

Oh, how the wolves love to hunt all living things.

Kelly stopped next to the table beside the basement door. Another fox was on this table. Its fur had an unusual streak of a white lightning bolt going diagonally across its eye and down the muzzle. She recognized it from another life, a life of flight from these godforsaken woods. They had killed the adorable fox she watched from her bed of leaves on that second night. And now the festering fire of hate grew even more inside her heart, mounting to the brink of eruption. Nothing was sacred or off limits to these men. They killed out of want, not out of need.

She punched in the code, and the electronic lock buzzed, allowing her to turn the doorknob. Standing on the top step, she faced the staircase with frozen muscles. Like the scenes of a popular horror movie, floods of images came cycling back. Terror-stricken memories are best forgotten, but impossible to erase. Pushing herself forward, Kelly took the steps with quick action. She needed to get through it before another bout of panic reared its ugly head and paralyzed her.

The metal door at the bottom didn't require a code. Three deadbolt latches kept the wolves' new chew toy securely inside. The door rotated on quiet hinges. Kelly was prepared for two things. One, she would find a scared shitless young woman cowering in a corner like an abused animal, too terrified to make a stand. Or two, the girl had prepped herself for an offensive attack. Much like Kelly had done on several occasions, the girl could be ready to spring an ambush from the area beside the door or from the shadowed corner.

Kelly really didn't want her teeth knocked out, especially by someone she was trying so desperately hard to save. She inched the door open enough so that her voice would flow across the confined space.

"Reyna Mathers, my name is Kelly. I know right now it's hard to trust anyone, but I promise that I'm here to help. I've come to take you out of here and bring you home. I know what you're experiencing. I was once like you. Five years ago, three men held me captive for five weeks until I escaped. I'm going to come in. Please believe that I'm here in peace. Together, we can leave this place. There are many people who are looking for you."

Kelly pushed the door open wider. Holding her hands out, she wanted the girl to see that she had no intention of bringing harm. She glanced around the edge of the door, ready to move if Reyna suddenly slammed her weight against it, trying to knock Kelly down. The lights were on, always on. Never did they blink off, and that was one thing that had driven her mad during her stay.

"Just stop right there. Please."

Kelly did stop. She looked to her left, where the voice had come from. There were limited places to hide in the basement, and Reyna took the most enclosed area. The girl was under the steel-framed bed. Pressed tightly against the wall, Reyna studied Kelly with wide, suspicious eyes. Kelly didn't blame her. Kelly would have had the same mindset if the roles were reversed. Trust no one in these situations. Trust can get you killed.

Kelly made a slow pace to the center of the room. With momentum only matched by a sloth, she crossed her feet, let her knees do a relaxed buckle, and sat on the floor. Now resting in an Indian-style position, she made a conscientious effort to keep her hands visible at all times.

Kelly offered the most genuine smile her body allowed. It was a smile rarely seen. Its last appearance was years before when the nurse placed a cloth-wrapped baby girl in her arms.

"It's good to see you. Have they hurt you yet?"

Kelly instantly clenched her jaw, knowing that had been the wrong thing to say. Comforting words rarely found their way from her mouth. Her bluntness always overwhelmed sensitive people. It had been that way ever since she had walked out of these woods.

"I mean, are you okay? Are you hurt at all?"

"I don't know who they are. You're the only person I've seen. Can you please let me go?"

"I told you. I'm not keeping you here. I was once right where you are. I have one of them upstairs. He's tied up. I want to show you, but only if you want."

Kelly shifted her legs so she could lean forward. Her hand was out, praying the girl would seize the lifeline. Reyna did reach out. Their hands came together with the touch of hope that all could be right in the world again. With a little help, Kelly gently pulled her away from the bed and into her arms. Reyna didn't expect the embrace, and she didn't fight it. She welcomed the gesture just as the first of many tears spilled. Her body hitched as breath struggled between the sobs. Kelly took it all in. The heartbreak and relief they had suffered were theirs to share.

"After all this, when we're safe, I can always be there for you. If you're angry, scared or whatever, you can call me. No one will know what you're going through more than me," Kelly told her.

"Thank you. Thank you for finding me," Reyna said between breaths.

"I want you to come upstairs with me. I want you to see him. He's all tied up. He can't hurt you. Then you'll see that he's not a real monster, not really. He's just a man, only a man who likes doing terrible things to young women."

Reyna nodded against Kelly's shoulder. Guiding the girl toward the stairs, Kelly used the strength of her right arm to help keep the girl upright on wobbly legs. Mounting the steps was easier as Kelly figured the girl knew how close she was to freedom and going home.

Michael was still thankfully bound to the chair. His head hung forward, his chin resting on his chest. He appeared ready to black out as his eyes moved around in confusion.

"Good. You're still alive. Looks like that head wound doesn't want to stop gushing. Asshole, this is Reyna. Reyna, this is the asshole."

Reyna released Kelly as a crutch, then she moved like a lightning crack toward the chair. Kelly knew what was about to happen, and she felt no urge to stop it.

Reyna lashed out as only a traumatized girl could. She slapped, clawed, and pulled any parts of Michael she could grab. He had no choice but to take it, as his bound arms and legs could offer no defense. Reyna gripped a section of hair and pulled with nearly her entire weight. Michael expelled the most painful cry Kelly had ever heard. The cut across his scalp, caused by the edge of the remote bludgeoning, then tore further open by Reyna's attack. His skin stretched and then gave up resistance with a gruesome, wet sound.

"Okay, okay, okay," Kelly said as she grabbed Reyna's hand, forcing her to let go. "He deserves all that and more. If he's gonna die, it's gonna be slow. Let's just step back and take a breath."

Kelly was stunned by what Michael did next. He mentally broke. He started huffing with his breathing, and then the sobs came. He fully understood he'd lost control of his game and was likely never to regain the upper hand. She had defeated him in body and now fractured his mind. He'd become a helpless, pitiful man, admitting his only chance of survival was in the hands of a girl he'd long ago destroyed and another girl who was very nearly on that same path.

"Super glue?" Kelly asked.

"What?"

"If you have super glue here, it works well in place of stitches."

"Um, Christ. Let me think. Shit, I think you gave me a fucking concussion."

"My grief over the matter is very deep. It's probably a good idea not to fall asleep. Super glue?"

"Check the drawer next to the kitchen sink."

Kelly went to it while keeping her eye on Reyna and another possible outburst.

The drawer was a mess of odds and ends. It was one of those drawers every home in America had. A collection point for all small things lost and found.

Kelly raked her fingers through, churning the bottom items to the top. Something bit a fingertip, but shallow enough not to draw blood. She found a plastic squeeze bottle of fast-drying glue. She rotated the bottle, seeing the liquid inside moving freely and not yet a solid block.

Removing the cap, Kelly said, "Well, I'd say this is gonna sting a bit, but I don't give a fuck if it feels like lava. Reyna, I'm going to need your help. When I tell you, start pushing the wound closed."

Reyna stared as if Kelly had lost all sense and said, "Why are we helping him live?"

"Because he's a piece of shit rapist and murderer of young girls. Do you know what convicts around the country hate more than anything else? A piece of shit rapist and murderer of young girls or boys. His endless misery in prison will never end. To me, that makes it all worthwhile to save his pathetic life. Okay, push it together the best you can."

"What is this thing around his neck? Is it a shock collar or something?"

"It's a mechanical noose. Now push, push, push and hold it as long as you can."

Kelly drizzled the glue along the gash that was nearly six inches long thanks to Reyna's well-deserved tantrum.

Michael's breathing became a stutter, as if he'd just fallen through ice on a lake and suffered the shock of near-freezing water. He then moaned through clenched jaws.

Kelly said, "Toughen up, pussy. At least I'm not chewing on your body like a goddamn cannibal."

Reyna offered a puzzling look.

"Nothing. It doesn't matter. You need to hold it for as long as possible."

Kelly dropped the bottle and helped Reyna hold the gash closed.

"Crap. There's a lot of glue, and it's still bleeding. It's not drying fast enough. Keep holding it. I'll be right back."

Kelly returned to the drawer of clutter. At the back was a partial roll of duct tape. She figured it would be enough to get a couple of lengths across his scalp to help hold. She didn't waste time as she pulled a strip loose, slapped it across Michael's cheek and pulled it to the opposite side while keeping it taut. She did the same across the other side. Stepping back, Kelly couldn't contain the laughter as it rumbled from her. Reyna joined in as she released his scalp and stepped beside Kelly.

"It looks like, ah, shit, I don't know. What does it look like, Reyna?"

"Um. Well, looks like you got fucked up at a frat party and your roomies drunkenly had a good time at your expense."

Kelly shrugged and agreed that it was close enough. Then they both buckled over with laughter, much like longtime friends, now poking fun at the most ruthless man they'd ever encountered.

The tape pulled Michael's face up tight, giving him an unintentional shit-eating grin. His blond hair stood up in pointed tufts between the strands of tape. If it hadn't been for the seeping flow of blood down the outside of his right eye, it really would have looked like a frat prank. Kelly felt that not only did he deserve the pain from both the wound and the attempted medical treatment, but he deserved the humiliation just as much.

"Where are all the girls buried, Michael?" Kelly asked as the moment of fun took a permanent flight from here.

The laughter fell from Reyna's lips as she looked from Kelly to her captor.

"What are you talking about?" Reyna asked.

"This shitbag and his friends have been abducting girls for a long time. At least five years that I know of. How many have there been? Did it start with torturing and killing animals? Then you got a taste for it, but of course, you needed to evolve by honing your skills. So, you ramped it up to young girls. Then, maybe through some perverse website, you found a couple of local sadist fucks to play the game with you. I bet I'm right. How many so-called trophies have there been?"

Michael looked left and down.

Kelly pressed a forefinger into the head wound. Michael released a groan of pain and then a bout of anger.

"How many? Answer me, or I'm going to tear that gash open again. It'll make you piss yourself in front of two young women. The boogeyman wetting himself doesn't offer that macho I'm a scary guy vibe."

As Kelly reached out, Michael instinctively pulled back.

"All right. Just wait. I don't know. I can't give you an exact number."

Kelly pressed the wound.

"Shit. Forty-seven. All right? Are you happy now?"

Kelly stepped back. Luckily, a table was there to catch her fall. The shock worn on her face didn't compare to the magnitude of what was happening inside her mind.

"Is he saying he's killed forty-seven girls like us?" Reyna asked.

Michael shook his head. He said, "No. Forty-five. Two of them got away. At least for now."

Reyna went on the offensive again. Michael took only a brief beating before Kelly pulled her off.

"Where are they? Where did you put the bodies?" Kelly asked.

"Does it matter?"

"It matters. There are dozens of families out there that never received closure. Families who still believe their daughter will walk through the front door someday. You took it all away, and now you're going to give them what they need. So help me if you don't, I'll be delighted to push this button and pop your goddamn sick head off."

"Guess it doesn't matter anymore. We buried almost all of them at the bottom of a bluff five hundred yards due southeast."

"Nearly all?" Kelly asked.

"Yeah. Nearly. There were several girls I took before I bought this land."

"Where did you put them?"

"Weighed them down and pitched them over the side of my boat on a couple of different rivers. They're long gone, bones and all. Can you get me some aspirin from the bathroom? For some reason I have a wicked headache."

"That's a no-go on the aspirin. I like your pain. You've got so much more coming your way, because you're all over now."

A pair of headlights cut through the night. Piercing the front windows were high beams coming from a large vehicle. Kelly heard the grumble and knew it was a diesel engine.

With the strands of duct tape offering assistance, his smile grew. He said, "All over now? I think you spoke a little too soon, cupcake. Things are about to get very real."

Kelly had known fear. She had known the deepest level of frailty. She'd also experienced the hope of taking a permanent flight out of here. Right now, those moments came together again, shuffled into one agonizing sensation.

When the headlights winked out, Reyna said, "It's okay. I think it's the police! It looks like there are lights on the roof."

"That's correct. It's all right now because it is the police," Michael confirmed.

There's a laugh that villains do in old movies. It's the kind of laugh with a telling hint that the villain has suddenly taken the upper hand without the good guy being aware of it. It was the exact same laugh Michael delivered now.

"There's two of them," Reyna said, looking through the window, completely unaware that these men weren't here to save victimized women.

Kelly seized Reyna's arm, pulling the girl to the kitchen. Placing the device's remote on the counter, Kelly snatched two knives from the butcher's block and forced them into Reyna's hands.

"Listen to me closely. Those cops are his friends. They won't help us. They'll kill us if they get the chance. Go out the back door and into the woods and hide. If one of them sees you, I want you to stab him until you can't hold your arms up anymore. Do you understand?"

Reyna shook her head. "You want me to stab a cop?"

With both hands, Kelly pushed back the girl's black hair, curling it behind her ears, and then cradled each cheek as if talking to a child.

"They might be cops, but they're very bad men. They won't let you leave these woods alive. You have to do whatever it takes to survive. I can't lose you. It will kill me, too."

Reyna's head bobbed in Kelly's hands.

"That's good. Now go," Kelly said and pushed her out the back door.

It only took a split second before the forest night inhaled Reyna, drawing her deep into relative safety. Kelly's eyes were in panic mode as they switched across the living space. While scanning for some kind of weapon, her mind tried to figure out the best course of action to up her odds of survival.

Leaning in the rear corner behind the dining room table were three compound bows and an upright wooden box holding an assortment of arrows like a large quiver.

Kelly started for it, then stopped. With a quick change in direction, she went to the table beside Michael, picked up the lamp, and before he could utter another word, she drove the base into the side of his head. The blow did two things. It instantly took Michael out of the equation. It also canceled out the one light inside the cabin as the bulb's filament blew apart.

Kelly's logic was simple. Three on one was an impossibility. Two on one was a difficult challenge but gave her a better fighting chance. The endless property belonged to them. Judging by the dead animals cluttering the tables and walls, they were exceptional hunters.

Kelly's world now lay under a cloak of night. The half-moon offered little more than a candlelight to work with, especially inside the house. She tripped over an electrical cord, but stayed upright as she reached the corner. She selected the front bow leaning against the other two, and then gripped a fistful of arrows and pulled them from the wooden holder.

Gravel crunched as the men approached the house. The pacing was slow and steady, as they must have suspected she'd set a trap. Now, with the light out, they would be more cautious than ever.

Kelly quickly went back to the kitchen. The refrigerator nestled in the wall that divided both rooms held a good vantage point. With a sturdy wall and a metal box loaded with bullet-deflecting condiments, she had a chance. Arrows versus guns held no advantage, except maybe stealth. She could loose an arrow from a distance, and neither man would be able to pin-point the location of the shooter.

Now she felt completely stupid for trying to make a stand in a house with limited places of concealment. She realized the best place for a fight was outside, deep within the expanse of the woods.

Kelly reached for the back doorknob when the front door forcefully rotated open. Quickly, she retreated back to her shielded area, not wanting to catch a bullet in her spine as she fled. She nocked an arrow and readied for a fight.

Okay, Kelly, it's just like riding a bike, that is, if the bike were a pointed stick traveling at several hundreds of miles per hour. Easy peasy lemon squeezy.

Though it had been several years since she had last shot a bow with her father, there was confidence in her grip, making the sensation an almost natural feeling. She drew back the bow and easily held the position, waiting for an open shot. The only problem was that the latex gloves were making her hands sweat, and she worried the string would slide out of her fingered grip.

Kelly didn't want a kill shot. She wanted a shot to disable them. She thought that maiming one or both of them wasn't out of the question for men like these. She could never feel bad about that.

A flashlight clicked on. Kelly saw the light held in one hand and a gun in the other. The beam and barrel did a sweep across the front room and paused when the light revealed the unconscious and bloody man strapped to a chair.

"Michael? Holy Christ. Michael?"

"Let's leave Christ out of this," Kelly said and loosed the arrow.

Even with a marching band pounding of her heartbeat that caused her entire body to vibrate, the arrow nearly found its mark.

The arrow pierced a perfect hole between the radius and the ulna of the man's right arm near the wrist. A solid *thunk* followed as the arrow found a wooden wall to burrow into. The strobe light of the barrel flashed twice either in reflex from the damaged tendons or out of panic. The multiple concussions of the shots struck her temporarily blind and deaf. Working by touch, she maneuvered the bundle of arrows between her thighs, pulled one free and nocked it. With the halo of light fading from her vision, she pulled back the string to deliver another non-fatal shot.

A grizzly bear crashed through the door at her back just as she loosed an arrow. The jarring noise caused her aim to push high and to the right.

Kelly instinctively grabbed the bundle of arrows and spun. It wasn't a grizzly bear at all, but a mountain of a man whose suffocating weight she had endured time and again as the five-week assault had continued. In an arch, she swung the remaining arrows at the man. The broad tips skated a hard path across the left side of his face, taking skin and leaving behind rivulets of red.

Without even a groan of pain, he seized the front of her shirt with both monstrous hands, spun his bulk, and flung her like a sack of grain to the wall. Kelly hit with a velocity that nearly took the light from her eyes and, quite possibly, the life from her body. Something crackled on the right side of her rib cage. When the air came in, an invisible bull rammed its horns straight into her. She knew something had broken, bones most likely, but she didn't have a second to pull her focus from the fight. If she did, she would lose everything.

As the hulk barreled toward her, she saw an opportunity. Years of training flooded back. With a high back-spin kick, she introduced her heel to his temple. Propelling to the left, he stumbled, going down on both knees, but the back of the couch saved him from a complete sprawl across the floor.

Kelly glanced at the other man as she readied the bow for another shot. Her first shot had pinned his right arm to the door frame. He'd dropped the flashlight and now the beam spun along the floor, casting a horror show of light into darkness. Kelly saw why he'd released the flashlight. The arrow had forced the gun from his hand. Now he was trying to retrieve that lost weapon with his free left hand.

The gorilla was back on his feet. The cop at the door got his fingertips on the butt of the gun, trying to pull it closer. Kelly returned to attack mode, now understanding how dire the situation had flipped. Bringing the bow up and the string back, the black latex fingers of the gloves gave out. With the arrow half-cocked, the velocity behind the shot was only half of what it could have been, but it was enough. With the squeal of a stuck pig, the big man looked down in panicked disbelief. Much to Kelly's disappointment, the man hadn't lost the part of himself he adored so much. Instead, the metal tip bore deep into the fat and muscle of his inner thigh. The place Kelly knew held a major artery.

In the glow of the still-spinning flashlight, Kelly sprang forward, trying to dash through the back door. She needed to get into forest space before the cop pinned to the front wall got a full grip on the gun at his feet.

The mammoth man kicked out with his good leg and drove the dining room table in front of her, cutting off her escape. As Kelly began going over, he was able to fasten his giant hand to her shirt again. Pulling her from the tabletop toward him, his arrow-stung leg started giving out, causing a full-body collapse. Before he allowed himself to go down, he slung Kelly again with what momentum he had available.

The gun at the front of the cabin began a rapid fire. Before leaving the grip of the man, Kelly heard him grunt in pain. She prayed he now had an additional hole, this one caused by a bullet from friendly fire.

None of these thoughts mattered anymore as Kelly's body rose into space with a velocity unimaginable from a wounded and off-balanced man. Her tossed body struck the window horizontally, breaking through glass panes and the window dividers, making a harsh, involuntary exit from the cabin. Spears of fire rumbled through her side that had previously taken on damage. The pain was far more intense than anything else she'd endured. That is, until she hit the ground.

Kelly's blackout was brief enough that they didn't have time to assemble their injured army to stage a strong offensive. In fact, Kelly couldn't even see them through the shattered rear window. Like her, they were hurt and bleeding. It was quite possible they were attempting to close wounds before coming after her.

The terrain was anything but a soft landing. Jagged rocks had punched through skin in various places. A vicious road rash plagued her left side, while her right side felt a mimicking stun gun effect, electrifying to the point of paralysis with every breath taken. She knew fully well she needed to pin down her pain mentally, or the fight was already over. A shallow grave at the base of a bluff was in her near future if she didn't get back in the battle.

Kelly collected the scattered arrows and bow, and she pushed to her feet. The dark clothing she had chosen helped her become part of the night as she hobbled into the expanse of timber.

The gorilla charged out the back door, moving with a pained limp from the arrow jutting through his thigh and a freshly caught bullet in his back. With a storm of cursing, his knees buckled at the stairs. After a brutal fall, he did a thump-slam-slide down the wooden steps to the rocky bottom.

Kelly had the opportunity to pierce a final arrow into him and remove the man from the equation. The pale moonlight glinting off the badge on his chest signaled the perfect spot to place the point. Animals deserve mercy. Monsters deserve discipline in pain. Kelly had no intention of giving him an easy exit.

Like an intoxicated bear, the man clambered up, gripping the wobbly railing for support.

A howl of pain and possibly frustration came from inside the cabin. Kelly figured it was the other man breaking the aluminum arrow and freeing his arm from being pinned to the doorjamb. A second later, she discovered she was right. He stumbled to the exploded back windows and instantly started shooting into the wooded blackness.

"Stop the fucking firing, you dumb shit. I already got one bullet in me. If I get another one, I'm gonna twist your head until it comes off. Get your ass down here and help me."

"You're serious? I shot you?"

"Yeah, you shot me during your stupid tantrum."

Kelly now recognized the voice of the smaller man. It was the state trooper who had waited behind her car the day she discovered the cabin. It didn't surprise her. She had known one of them was a cop of some sort, but she hadn't expected both of them to be.

With cautious steps, Kelly melted deeper into the woods. She made sure to keep the men in view. As long as they stayed in place and the one kept waving his flashlight around, she could continue to control this moment in time.

Kelly thought of Reyna for the first time since the girl disappeared out the back door. She had no idea which way she went. She either pushed deeper into the woods or circled the house and quickly made for the highway to flag down help. Hell, she could have been only steps away from Kelly now, merged into the shadows, and as quiet as a mouse until the evident danger passed. The men weren't on Reyna's trail. They kept their focus on the bigger threat that had nearly incapacitated both of them in a matter of minutes.

The smaller man helped the other get his bearings. He then inspected the damage his bullet had done.

"Shit. I'm sorry. That bitch pinned my arm to the wall with a goddamn arrow. I was trying to shoot the bitch before she drilled a hole through my brain. Damn. That shot is bleeding a good bit. You're also losing blood fast from that arrow. We need to get some patches on these wounds and get you to the hospital."

The slim man began to turn, heading for the truck out front. The gorilla's massive hand seized him and held him in place.

"Get your ass back here. We don't leave this property until both of those girls are dead. If I bleed out before that happens, then you do whatever the hell you want to do. Are we clear?"

The slim man held up his arm, now sporting a leaking, bloody hole in his wrist. Holding back further protest, he nodded.

"Go inside and grab a bunch of shirts so we can wrap up these wounds until we finish this mess."

Kelly heard all this from her covered position. Part of her was relieved they were going to stand and fight. The other part of her felt disappointed because the pain throughout her body had intensified. She wasn't sure how much more abuse she could take before the will to exact justice simply wasn't there anymore.

After the man returned with a bundle of rags to help stem the flow of life from their bodies, the big man studied the line of trees.

Pointing, he said, "Head off to the left. I'm gonna do a search outside the house. She might have rounded her way to the front, trying to get to Michael's vehicle and haul ass out of here."

Clouds departed the area, and the half-moon glow dropped a blanket of ominous light across the property. Shadows shifted over the forest floor, and tree branches waved in the mild breeze. Kelly took a moment to enjoy the wind as it pushed off the summer humidity. She closed her eyes, and for a fleeting stitch in time, she could envision herself back at her house, sitting on the porch with a glass of wine and feeling a sense of normalcy.

To Kelly's right, the slim man vanished into a nest of trees. She lost sight of him where the forest canopy thickened and blocked the moon's rays. Even with a flashlight in hand, she heard him stumbling through the dense undergrowth.

Though both men sustained injuries, the big one was still far more formidable. Despite the freshly punched holes in his body, she knew he could easily squeeze her until the remaining unbroken ribs gave way and her organs became dartboards for those splintering bones.

With a careful sidestep, Kelly moved with him. His steps became her steps as she kept her eyes locked on him. He showed no signs of hearing the slight crackle of leaves as his flashlight beam swept across the house and surrounding space.

Her mind flicked through images of a movie she had seen so long ago. A Native American man stalked his prey through the wilderness as he blended with the environment. His arrow nocked, pointed down, but instantly at the ready to be lifted and drawn, followed by a quick but accurate sighting on the target before the arrow took flight. Kelly sought the courage and will to see this hunt come to an end in her favor, but the smallest factors can so easily manipulate the path of survival.

He disappeared around the front corner of the house. Kelly stayed in the thicket, keeping her cover. The beam of his light faded and then was gone.

Maneuvering the brush in near darkness became its own challenge as her every step tested the ground before fully committing. The slightest pressure on a fallen branch creates a distinguishable sound. She still had the advantage of having unknown whereabouts, and she'd be damned if she gave that up due to carelessness.

A croaked, near-panicked voice suddenly disrupted the night.

"Here! I'm in here, guys! Get me out of this fucking chair and get this goddamn thing off my throat!"

Kelly shifted her position in startled response. She'd forgotten about Michael. Now, the ever-changing outcome could slip through her fingers if they freed him.

She almost didn't hear it over her own crashing thoughts and Michael's bellowing for help.

The hulking shadow charged through the underbrush. It was a runaway train prepared to destroy anything on the tracks. Kelly had no time to decipher what it was. Instinctively, the bow rose, the string came back, and then the arrow soared toward whatever came to crush her down.

The aim, although desperately made, found soft tissue to bury into. The furious call of agonizing pain echoed across the thousands of acres of timber, overriding Michael's own pleads to be cut loose. Kelly instantly thought of a large animal unintentionally stepping on a spring trap.

The sounds of a creature's painful struggle erupted, voicing a longing to be released from the agony.

Kelly's vision fully adjusted to the night now, and she saw exactly what it was she put an arrow through. Moving closer, still silently enough to maintain concealment, she approached the beast. It stood nearly six and a half feet tall, built like a Kodiak with a temperament to match. The broadhead arrow had been a head shot, though not of the killing kind. Keeping well out of reach, Kelly surveyed the damage. The four-bladed razor tip had parted his lips and run a slicing track down the outside of his teeth and gums, and gruesomely made a path through the muscles connecting his upper and lower left jaw. To top things off, the tip sank firmly into a large oak, holding the big man there like a bug pinned to a corkboard.

Weakly, his hands worked at the arrow, attempting to twist it free of the tree. Then he tried to bend the aluminum. Because of the awkward positioning and his failing state of energy reserves, the effort held no reward. His multiple previous wounds had leaked enough blood that she no longer considered him much of a threat. In fact, she was willing to bet he now entered the last ten minutes of his life before the curtain closed on the final act.

He tried to speak. What came out was a jumble of vowels. Blood and saliva drooled from his lower lip and onto the forest floor. That was when he broke. Either from pain, frustration, shame or some other emotion, he began blubbering.

Kelly felt no pity. It was impossible to feel compassion for the slime of the earth, who preyed on innocent young girls to satisfy his own twisted fantasies.

The large cop's body began to sag as life ran from him. The arrow pinning his jaw to the tree still held him upright. She knew his fight was over.

Kelly decided she needed to find the other man before he cut Michael loose. She couldn't help it as she readied to part with the big man. A corny 80s action movie line popped into her head.

She patted his cheek and even managed a thick Schwarzenegger accent. She said, "Stick around. I'll be back."

Kelly stepped from the forest to the side of the house. The lights were still extinguished inside. The skinny man could have been watching her through the darkened window, ready to fire a shot through the head and end her retaliation. She pushed all morbid thoughts aside, keeping her focus where it should be. She walked around back, keeping her reflexes on edge for any sudden movement as she did with the big man.

Kelly knew the skinny man must have done a course correction when he heard both Michael and the big man begin screaming. What she didn't know was whether he was determined to hunt her down or ready to cut his losses and high-tail it the hell out of the woods to save his own skin. She hadn't heard an engine kick over, so she was certain he was still prowling these dark woods alongside her.

The sounds behind Kelly, sounds of a dying man, tapered off as she approached the rear of the cabin. She couldn't see the other cop's flashlight. She worried he had clicked it off as well, like the big man, and would also attempt an ambush in the blackness. She knew she couldn't fire another arrow unless an attack was obvious. Reyna was still out here somewhere, hiding. Kelly couldn't live with herself if she accidentally shot and killed the girl she'd come to save.

Ten yards from the back door, she could make out Michael's form inside, dimly lit by moonlight through the front window. He struggled with his bonds, desperately trying to break free to help his hateful troop recapture her.

Kelly moved off, sliding across the edge of the forest, ready to hunt the last one down before walking away from this madhouse for good.

It was a jack-in-the-box moment. Something sprung from the saplings at the base of an ancient oak. Kelly had no time for defense, but managed to pull herself back enough that the swinging thick branch didn't cave her head in. However, it did catch her right temple enough that the night suddenly became daytime, with an explosion of stars flooding her vision. Her brain signaled a possible relapse into unconsciousness as her legs gave out. She rapidly shook her head, trying to ward off the blackout.

A state-issued patrol boot came down on the two remaining arrows in her grip, bending the aluminum enough that there was no chance of them flying straight ever again. The skinny cop quickly stomped again, this time crippling the bones of her right hand.

Something much like a flair of angry hornet stings consumed her hand and forearm. She forgot her weapon as the destroyed fingers no longer had the power to hold it again. Kelly backpedaled to get out from underneath him. As she did, she was hit with a moment of brilliance. Her foot drove up and out. The action was so powerful it lifted his feet from the ground. He had crushed her hand, and in return she crushed his most priceless possession, the disgusting member he had so blatantly violated her with all those years ago.

There was no scream, just a hard release of air as he doubled over. The next kick caught him across the right jaw, pitching him back against the tree. His head offered a solid *thunk* as it rebounded off the tree trunk.

This was the moment he must have decided he couldn't overcome her with brute force and capture her alive, so the three of them could endlessly punish her for weeks or months until her body gave out. He no longer cared to keep her heart beating.

His undamaged left hand went for the gun on his patrolman's utility belt. As he fumbled with the snap, Kelly made the decision to run before the barrel cleared the holster and her ticket got punched.

With a desperate roll of her body, she gained enough momentum to get up onto her legs. Her depleted muscles caused her to almost go right back down. She managed five strides before the rocky terrain caused her ankle to roll.

The cop used the rough bark of the oak to pull himself up. His motivation to fight was exhausted. His chest pressed against the trunk as a labored breath worked from him. His face pressed to the bark as he watched Kelly give up her flight.

"I've got to hand it to you. I've never worked this hard to dispatch one of you bitches. You almost won. Almost. But someone must pay the piper."

With effort, he lifted his left arm. The gun wavered as he tried to center his aim.

The roar of gunfire blew through the woods hard enough that all sleeping creatures stirred from their slumber. Kelly knew she was dead. But the afterlife held as many curiosities as the real world. She knew there would be no pain because she'd been staring down the barrel when he fired. With one shot, he ushered her soul toward a far less beautiful place. It was a place away from Cassie, away from her three best friends, and away from a life she desperately and deservedly needed.

Blinding headlights illuminated the surrounding forest. The deep-throated rumble was not a gunshot at all, but the eagerness of a racing engine coming right at her. She knew it was Michael, finally free from his tethered bonds of the chair. He was racing to crush her into pulp on the rocky forest ground before the skinny man took away his last chance to get even from tonight's game of pain.

Looking over his shoulder, the skinny man studied the oncoming vehicle, deciphering who could be interrupting his grand finale. He realized his error in judgment far too late.

The grill of the truck collided with his body and then hammered into the tree trunk with the power of a locomotive facing a stalled car on the tracks. The crunching of metal as it wound around the oak struck Kelly deaf as her reeling mind grasped for comprehension.

The skinny man's upper body didn't move as his entire lower half, from his bottom ribs, disappeared somewhere between the tree and the ruined front end of the truck. The vibration rippled up the oak, causing only a slight tremor across the branches as the behemoth of a tree resisted severe damage.

Astonishingly, the skinny man was still alive. His body accepted shock before accepting death. He breathed and blinked several times. Then he released a violent cough, splattering blood and God knew what else of his internal mass across the oak's bark. His eyes rotated toward Kelly, who was still sprawled on the ground. There was something in his eyes, a quiet pleading, she thought. Maybe a longing to reverse the wheels of time and undo all the awful things accomplished during his lifetime. Maybe a silent begging for mercy. It didn't matter because his eyes didn't move ever again.

Jeremy M. Wright

The truck that had arrived carrying two sadistic men hissed as every type of fluid inside the engine leaked out. The door opened with a creak and a loud pop as the twisted hinges argued its use. Kelly couldn't see much as the lights still worked, keeping her blind. She propped up on her elbow, too exhausted to do anything else.

"Okay, Michael, you win. I'm done. Just remember that I could have killed you. I had the situation won, but you got the victory. So go fuck yourself."

He stepped up to her and kneeled. Reaching out, his hand smoothly cradled her face.

"Why didn't you ask for help? I would have been here in an instant if you had just asked."

Kelly knew that sweet, compassionate voice. Her tone was soft, as if speaking to a scared child. She shifted so that the light was no longer in Kelly's eyes. With beautiful blond hair, kind eyes and the glow flowing behind her, Kelly looked at the face of an angel.

Just then, Kelly released her frustration, anxiety, and fear. It melted away like ice cream on a blazing July day. Her body hitched. Kelly couldn't deny her tears and set them free. Tilly wrapped her arms around her, presenting an embrace that only honest love can offer.

"How badly are you hurt?" Tilly whispered in her ear.

"I feel nothing except you, here and now."

"Can you stand?"

"If this is all over, I can tap dance if you like."

Tilly began to reach for Kelly's right hand, but quickly cradled it instead.

"Oh, my God."

"There are likely a few broken digits, and maybe some ribs, but it won't sour my new mood. I don't know how it is you found me out here, but you're the best thing I've seen all week."

"Just all week? Here, give me your other hand."

Kelly did. With Tilly's help, she was able to get up, and leaning on her friend, managed to keep her knees from buckling.

"I've been tracking you since this whole thing started."

Heading toward the cabin, Kelly turned to look at her.

"Like tracking my phone? I hope you got a court order for that, or I might sue for invasion of privacy."

"My stalking you is the very least of your problems right now. Any ideas how to remedy this clusterfuck you created?"

"It's not like that at all. They created it. I was the remedy. Well, one is a splattered bug on the truck. Another is a pincushion hanging out over that way, likely bled out by now. He didn't have much life left before I came to hunt that dick over there. So that just leaves Michael. Oh, shit! There's a girl out here. Reyna!" Kelly suddenly remembered and began calling her name.

"Reyna Mathers? They're the ones who took her?"

Kelly stopped dead. Reyna stood on the back porch. Inside, a light was turned on. She faced the opening of the door. She didn't move, perhaps oblivious to Kelly's calls. Reyna trembled as if caught in a sudden winter embrace.

As Kelly and Tilly went up the back steps, they saw what Reyna held. Gripped in her right hand was the remote to the device. Kelly had left it on the kitchen counter as she prepped Reyna for a fight.

Kelly went to her gently, as if approaching a frightened puppy.

"Reyna? Are you all right?" Kelly asked.

"I fucked up. I mean, I think I really fucked up. What I did, I mean, I don't remember doing that," Reyna said and pointed with a shaking left hand.

Kelly stepped around her. The lamp beside the front window was on. In the light's glow sat Michael, still confined to the chair. Reyna had activated the device around his throat at its full strength. Surprisingly, the wire hadn't been able to cut through the skin but had instead squeezed until either the gear power or battery strength could give no more.

Michael's tongue and eyes bulged. He wore a mask of crimson, as all the blood had nowhere to go. His final moments of life had been pure terror as the soul of a demon wearing the face of a man had literally been squeezed from the body.

Justice had come full circle.

Kelly turned to Reyna. The lie came out easily. She wanted to spare Reyna a lifetime of bad dreams about killing another human. She said, "You didn't do that. I did that."

Confused, Reyna looked at her. "You did that? Why? Why did you? You had him tied to the chair."

"Listen to me. I did it because I was afraid his friends would cut him loose. I knew it was impossible for me to outmatch three men. So, I killed Michael. I had to."

Kelly worked the remote from Reyna's vice-like grip.

"Okay. Okay, I understand."

"What these men did to me so long ago is why I'm here. It's why I did these things. But I found you during all of this. I found you, and now you can go home. Your family needs you back, safe and sound."

"Yeah. They need me," Reyna said, dreamlike. Her knees buckled, but despite her fatigue, Kelly caught her. Slowly, they both went down to the wooden planks.

Kelly moved her hands to Reyna's cheeks. Although the pain still throbbed through her mangled hand, she gently wiped the girl's tears away.

Kelly said, "You've got a long and great life ahead of you. You're going to do incredible things. I want you to listen closely to me. All those things you're feeling now—the hate, confusion, and fear—need to be left out here. Don't take it with you. These men already took so much from you. So don't let them take anymore. All those feelings need to stay in these bad woods. Don't let them corrupt your life like they did mine. You're a piece of iron they broke themselves against. What happened out here saved so many girls from becoming victims. You're safe. I'm safe. And together we're virtually unbreakable. Do you understand?"

Reyna nodded.

Kelly took the young woman in her arms, never wanting to let go.

Tilly stepped out of the house. The device that had silenced Michael forever dangled in her hand. In Tilly's other hand was the remote that Kelly had dropped while catching Reyna's fall.

"We need to go," Tilly said.

Kelly told Reyna, "I need you to stay here. I need you to tell the authorities who you are and what happened out here. You must be the voice for all the girls who never made it home."

"You're leaving me here alone with—with—with dead men?" Reyna stuttered.

"It'll only be briefly. They will come quickly," Tilly said. She removed a phone from her back pocket and showed it to Kelly. "Is this Michael's phone? It was in this backpack. Is this your backpack?"

Kelly looked at the phone and bag on Tilly's shoulder and nodded.

"Good," Tilly said and disappeared back inside. She returned after several minutes, wiping her fingers across her shirt. "I had to push his tongue back inside so the facial recognition software would unlock his phone. Surprisingly, there are a couple of bars out here in bum-fuck nowhere. Not a great signal, but it'll do."

Tilly maneuvered through online sites, found what she needed and handed the phone to Reyna.

"It's all cued up. Just push the call button. Ask for FBI Special Agent Simon Stoll. They'll patch you through to his cell after you tell them who you are. Believe me, he'll leap out of bed and travel at the speed of light to get out here to you. You can trust him because I trust him implicitly. You'll have to send him a pin from Google Maps because even I don't know where the hell we are, and I'm standing right here."

Reyna nodded. As Kelly began to move away, Reyna took her arm and pulled her back. Their arms wrapped around each other for a final time.

"Thank you for finding me. You saved me. A long time from now when you think back on your life of all the good things you did, just remember that you saved someone."

Kelly smiled and said, "We saved each other." Turning to Tilly, she said, "I'll be right back. I have to make sure the gorilla has given up the ghost."

Tilly narrowed her eyes at the statement and watched Kelly disappear into the woods.

"Can I ask you something?"

"Sure," Tilly said.

"Who are you?"

Tilly smiled. "I'm nobody."

"How about her?" Reyna asked as she moved her head to where Kelly had slipped into the woods.

"That, my girl, is vengeance. When the cavalry gets here, you can tell them that. You can call her your savior or angel or whatever you like. I just ask that if she told you her name, you keep that to yourself. Don't lie to the FBI about anything that happened, but just please keep that one thing sacred. It'll be better for her if she does just as she told you to do. Leave it all out here. She doesn't need to suffer this burden anymore. She needs to free herself. You can help with that."

Reyna nodded. "I will. I swear it."

Kelly stepped out of the darkness, heading to the back porch. She paused and nodded to Tilly, confirming the third monster in the woods had drawn his last breath.

Kelly said, "When the authorities arrive, remember to tell them to search five-hundred yards due southeast. At the base of a bluff, like Michael said, they'll discover missing girls. Their families need closure."

Kelly and Tilly left Reyna to make a call and open a can of worms that would expose a group of serial killers operating for unknown years, totaling God only knows the actual body count of young women. Michael was born a great deceiver, so she couldn't count on his claim of forty-five women as his grand total.

Kelly knew the media frenzy would be extreme. She didn't care. She had played her part to the best of her abilities, and what happened from here was well beyond her control.

They walked up the slope of the gravel drive toward the highway in silence. Sliding into Tilly's SUV, they looked at each other and smiled.

"So that was the place they kept you?"

Kelly nodded. "It was. I think that cabin sits over the mouth of hell. Do you think Reyna will be all right?"

"She'll be on edge until Agent Stoll gets there. Then she'll be just fine. She's got a long road to travel to find mental stability again. But you know how to play and win that game."

"I do. I think after everything calms down and the media has found a new diabolical story to follow, I'd like to connect with Reyna. She needs someone to talk to and to help walk her through this. She's a strong girl, but she needs that connection. She'll need my help."

"You're definitely the one to guide her through it. So, I suppose I should get you to the hospital."

"I'm fine. What I need more than anything is to go home and see Cassie."

"I'm sure you haven't glanced in a mirror lately, but do you remember that corny horror movie we watched in junior high, *The Toxic Avenger*? Yeah. You look like that guy, minus the ballerina tutu."

"Well, I probably feel the same as getting dipped into toxic waste. I'll manage. There's nothing much the ER can do for broken ribs and fingers, other than tape them up."

Kelly looked at her right hand. Several of the fingers were limp and cocked in an unnatural way.

"The best thing about taking taekwondo lessons for years is that it builds your immunity to pain. You learn to channel that pain and transform it into something else."

Kelly pinched the end of her middle finger, the most grossly contorted one, and pulled it straight. There were dull crackles of joints and possibly splintered bones moving back into place.

Kelly groaned and repeated the action to the other fingers.

Following the dark highway at a steady clip, Tilly glanced over several times, cringing at each sound.

When Kelly finished, Tilly asked, "So, were you able to channel the pain somewhere else?"

"Fuck no! And I'm pretty sure I pissed myself a little."

Tilly couldn't help it. She fell against the door laughing, while trying to maintain control and keep them on the road.

It was infectious. Kelly forgot about the throbbing spikes rumbling throughout her body and joined her friend in a roll of stress-relieving laughter.

"How did you know about the other girls buried out there?" Tilly asked as they both settled down.

"It was one of the things I worked out of him during our interrogation session. I didn't expect this night to go ape-shit crazy like that. After I had Michael under control at his house, I used the bathroom. I came out to find him tipped over after knocking the house phone loose and managed to call his friends. He must have dialed with his nose or something. So, I took him out to the cabin I'd found with a little help from Skylar's property search. They must have got to Michael's house and realized I had fled and taken him with me. They probably tracked his phone. I wasn't smart enough to turn it off. I had too many other things on my mind."

"You know, the three of us would have come running if you'd just called. We'd do anything for you."

"I know. I really do. I was too scared to drag all of you this deep into it and risk one of you dying. I couldn't live with that."

"We probably would have survived, and you being the one who died. Did you ever think of that? We're three badass chicks to the core."

Kelly smiled and nodded.

"No doubt. How do you feel about that cop back there? I mean, what you did to him and all?"

"He was a multiple rapist and murderer and was about to punch the ticket of my best friend. I'm just sorry I can't revive him, so I could kick him in the balls and then squash him into that tree again."

"I kicked him in the balls after he stomped my hand. I've got to admit, it was very satisfying."

"I bet. Are you going to be okay, I mean, in the long run?"

Kelly thought it over before answering.

"Yeah. I've got you three, Cassie, and my family to help me through it. The nightmare of those men still being out there will probably fade soon. I can now have closure on that. Now the nightmares of this awful night will start. But I'm content with that. It all came to an end with good destroying evil. Those dreams I can live with."

After an hour, they left the Virginia wilderness behind and found the bright lights of Richmond. The city had a different feel at night, as people lurked along the dark streets. They rolled to a red light in the downtown district. A group of men across the street eyed their vehicle.

It doesn't matter anymore, Kelly thought as she stared back at them. *I'm no longer afraid of monsters.*

Tilly's SUV eventually found Kelly's house, and she parked in the driveway.

"I'm assuming your car is at or near Michael's house. Right?"

"About two blocks away. We can get it sometime tomorrow."

"Okay. I'm gonna pick you up at about noon and take you to the hospital. I don't want to argue with you about it. That's what we're doing. Then we'll stop and get your car."

"I'm not arguing. I'll tell the doctor that it was a car accident or a stumble down the stairs. But you are right. I need to have my ribs X-rayed. Maybe they can at least give me some good pain management drugs."

"I love you," Tilly said.

"I love you more. Thank you for what you did. Although I still might file charges against you for tracking my phone. Who knows? We'll see."

Tilly looked at the house and said, "Go on. Give her a hug for me."

Kelly stepped out and quietly closed the door. Going up the front porch, the security lights activated. She entered the code into the deadbolt, and the door unlocked. As Kelly stepped inside, the security alarm signaled with a soft chirp, giving her sixty seconds to disarm the unit. After entering the code and receiving a flashing green light in acknowledgment, Kelly went into the living room. Cassie's babysitter, Mara, was asleep on the couch. The TV glowed with a message. The streaming service wanted to know if she was still watching. Kelly hit NO and turned it off. She flicked on the stairs and hallway lights as she moved up to the bedrooms. Stopping at Cassie's door, she nudged it open a little farther.

She stood there, hovering in the doorway for countless minutes, watching her precious child wander the fields of endless dreams.

Cassie's blond curls slightly obscured her features. It didn't matter. Kelly knew every square inch of that wonderful face.

Cassie stirred a bit. Perhaps the glow of the hallway light tricked her mind into believing dawn had come early. Her eyes slowly worked open. Her small hand pushed the curls away from her face.

She saw her mother watching her and smiled.

Just like Tilly's laughter, Cassie's smile was infectious.